Short Stories of the Civil Rights Movement

An Anthology

Short Stories of the

EDITED BY **MARGARET EARLEY WHITT**

The University of Georgia Press ATHENS

JAMES BALDWIN

LERONE BENNETT JR.

ALMA JEAN BILLINGSLEA-BROWN

ROSELLEN BROWN

R. V. CASSILL

VAL COLEMAN

Civil Rights Movement

HENRY DUMAS

JUNIUS EDWARDS

ANTHONY GROOMS

JOANNE LEEDOM-ACKERMAN

LEE MARTIN

DIANE OLIVER

ZZ PACKER

NATALIE L. M. PETESCH

MIKE THELWELL

JAMES W. THOMPSON

JOHN UPDIKE

ALICE WALKER

EUDORA WELTY

JOAN WILLIAMS

Credits for the use of copyrighted material appear
on pages 341–43, which constitute an extension
of the copyright page.

© 2006 by the University of Georgia Press
Athens, Georgia 30602

Set in New Caledonia by Bookcomp, Inc.
Printed and bound by Maple-Vail
The paper in this book meets the guidelines for
permanence and durability of the Committee on
Production Guidelines for Book Longevity of the
Council on Library Resources.

Printed in the United States of America

10 09 08 07 06 C 5 4 3 2 1

10 09 08 07 06 P 5 4 3 2 1

Library of Congress Cataloging-in-Publication Data
Short stories of the civil rights movement : an anthology /
edited by Margaret Earley Whitt.

     p. cm.

  ISBN-13: 978-0-8203-2799-0 (alk. paper)

  ISBN-10: 0-8203-2799-9 (alk. paper)

  ISBN-13: 978-0-8203-2851-5 (pbk. : alk. paper)

  ISBN-10: 0-8203-2851-0 (pbk. : alk. paper)

    1. Short stories, American.   2. Civil rights movements—Fiction.
3. United States—Race relations—History—20th century—Fiction.
I. Whitt, Margaret Earley, 1946–
PS648.C53S58 2006
813'.0108358—dc22   2006012104

CONTENTS

ACKNOWLEDGMENTS

Before it appears on the shelf, every book requires the participation of many people. I am grateful for the ongoing support and encouragement of Nancy Grayson, associate director and editor in chief of the University of Georgia Press, who believed in the project when it was but an idea in e-mail correspondence. Others at the press who take their work seriously and with whom I feel fortunate to have worked include Jo Heslep, Jennifer Reichlin, and Jon Davies. Back at the University of Denver, I had help from Laura Opincariu, Amy Klein, and Joseph Labrecque in the Center for Teaching and Learning. Katie DuMont, Ronna Bloom, Helene Orr, and Carol Samson offered good advice on drafts of the introduction. I am also thankful to Joyce Kinkead, Jeanette Harris, and Lady Brown for guidance and instruction and good food along life's way, and to Sarah Gordon and Patsy Yaeger, whose scholarly work on the South continues to inspire me and deepen my own studies. M. E. Warlick listened as I repeatedly talked through the project, and my students read these stories with me in classes over the years and have shown me how these fictional offerings can help us all to feel more keenly the facts of this particular time and place. I am grateful, too, for support from Charley and Jessica Whitt, as well as Wintry and Paul Smith.

Special thanks to all of the writers who gave permission for their stories to be published in this anthology.

This volume is dedicated to the Pearls of Gerton and to my grandsons, Spencer and Axel Whitt, who have been born in a post–civil rights movement world. May the harsh lessons of those times be instructive messages for today.

INTRODUCTION

The time is 6:01 p.m. on April 4, 1968, in Memphis, Tennessee. A shot rings out at the Lorraine Motel outside room 306. At 7:05, Martin Luther King Jr. is pronounced dead.

I am a senior at a small, historically white, church-related liberal-arts college in North Carolina. On this same April night students have gathered in the campus science hall to listen to an invited guest—Robert Jones, the grand dragon of the Ku Klux Klan. As editor of the campus newspaper I am there to cover the story. Before Jones can begin, our class president rushes into the packed room.

"Mr. Jones," he says, "we have just gotten word that Martin Luther King has been assassinated. Do you have any comment?"

The room is profoundly quiet. Jones speaks. Two black students—the only ones present—rise and leave the room. The rest of us—now all white—simply sit.

Thirty years pass. It is the fall of 1998—reunion weekend. I return to the college's science hall to meet with my classmates. Our class president greets us with the reminder that the last time we assembled in this room was the night of King's assassination; then he reminds us of what Robert Jones said. Oddly, I remember Jones's words differently. So does the classmate sitting next to me. We each carry that moment with us, but we carry it variously. And then the thought occurs to me: That night in 1968 we had remained seated. Why had we stayed in the room that night? Why did we, on that of all nights, not leave with the black students? This question is the genesis of this book.

Looking back, I see how our passivity was the result of having known only a segregated world. Segregated public schools, churches, camps, libraries, entertainment centers, shopping areas, and neighborhoods molded me and most of my southern classmates. Though I finished high school in 1964, ten years after *Brown v. Board of Education of Topeka,* our public schools were segregated still. Even when civil rights activities were a large part of current events, I have no memory of any discussion at school or home with this focus. My first personal memory of civil rights events is the walk from Selma to Montgomery, Alabama, in March 1965. I joined the story there; and three years later, participating in an intensive independent study project on the Voting Rights Act of 1965, I came to understand that every ending, of course, has a beginning.

Since 1998, I have been visiting historically relevant sites, reading, listening, and talking in preparation for writing about and teaching the history and literature of the civil rights movement. And I have been trying to answer, too, the question of the lifelong friends with whom I came of age: Where *were* we during these times?

Because literature can help us "feel" history, I searched for ways to impress the urgency of those days on my students. Most had read Harper Lee's *To Kill a Mockingbird* in middle school, and they remembered, long after their reading, the rage they felt at the injustice of Tom's guilty verdict. I wondered if I could design a class focused primarily on the history of the movement that would also include some creative responses to these life-altering events.

I think of the feelings inspired by my recent visit to the Vietnam Memorial in Washington, D.C., with its fifty-eight thousand names of those who died or were reported missing in Vietnam, as similar to the effect that a creative response to a life-altering event can have. I stood next to a middle-aged man who was using a pencil and paper to rub one name off the wall as he wept. Here was an individual story. While the monument's massive size seemingly allowed me to distance myself emotionally from what it represents, its meaning became intensely personal once I observed someone at the wall who had found a personal connection, a special name inscribed among the thousands.

I wanted that moment for my students—the kind of experience that reading a good story can create for its reader. I wondered if in the impersonal yesterdays of history, I could find short stories with characters, perhaps the age of my students, who could bring the meaning of the civil rights movement alive. I know it would have made a difference to me if I had been able to read the pieces gathered here and, even more ideally, if I could have discussed them in a classroom. So I went in search of stories.

Those that I found focus on the civil rights movement from the mid-1950s, the time that it is most widely recognized as having started, and run through King's assassination in 1968, with a few in the last section that look back on the meaning of this period in history. The movement, however, has long taproots.

After the Civil War ended, the passage of the Thirteenth Amendment, abolishing slavery; the Fourteenth Amendment, expanding guarantees of federally protected citizenship rights; and the Fifteenth Amendment, barring restrictions on race and voter registration, opened the door for equality among all male citizens. During Reconstruction, black citizens were elected to public office and enjoyed a brief period celebrating their new rights. After Reconstruction, however, the birth of the Ku Klux Klan and the influence of the Democratic Party in the South resurrected and assured white dominance. The next half century was among the bloodiest in African American history, with lynchings common throughout the South.

During these years, many voices argued for civil rights. Booker T. Washington and W. E. B. Du Bois brought different perspectives to the table, the former more accommodating to white dominance than the latter. Marcus Garvey, with his Universal Negro Improvement Association, led the largest black organization in the country through which he promoted black economic development and celebrated Africa and racial pride. The National Association for the Advancement of Colored People (NAACP), founded in 1909, began fighting injustices in the courts one case at a time. Charles Houston, a Harvard-educated Howard faculty member, trained a generation of lawyers to fight Jim Crow through the NAACP's auspices. Houston and Thurgood Marshall traveled thousands of miles throughout the South meeting with small groups of people and listening to their grievances. A. Philip Randolph, head of the Brotherhood of Sleeping Car Porters, called for a march on Washington in 1941 to demand equal inclusion for blacks in the war effort. In 1942, on the campus of the University of Chicago, the Congress of Racial Equality (CORE) was established and became a pioneer in organized demonstrations.

Both World Wars, in their own ways, spurred the fight for civil rights at home. World War I was to have made the world safe for democracy and, it would seem, democracy safe for its citizens at home. But the African

American soldier returned to face the same denigrating circumstances he had left. In search of greater opportunities, thousands of black citizens departed the South for the northern cities in what became known as the "great migration." World War II was to fight fascism abroad. Having found more hospitable treatment overseas, black soldiers were frustrated to return to ongoing racial inequality at home. They had every reason to expect an end to second-class citizenship. In the twenty-year period from the 1930s to the 1950s, membership in the NAACP in the South grew from under 20,000 to over 150,000. Through these local branches of the NAACP, war veterans and others had an infrastructure through which they could meet and respond to local injustices.

These factors, then, led to three events directly responsible for starting the modern civil rights movement. First, on May 17, 1954, the Supreme Court case of *Brown v. Board of Education of Topeka* declared that separate was not equal and opened the doors for school integration, thus, overturning *Plessy v. Ferguson* (1896), which had approved segregation as legal and constitutional. Next, the country reacted to the lynching of Emmett Till, a fourteen-year-old Chicago youth visiting relatives in Money, Mississippi, who on August 24, 1955, went to Bryant's Grocery and Meat Market and allegedly made comments to a white woman, the owner's wife, Carolyn Bryant. Four days later, Till was abducted from his great uncle's home by Bryant's husband and his half brother and soon thereafter Till's bloated body was taken from the Tallahatchie River. A picture of his corpse, which ran in the September 15, 1955, *Jet* magazine, became the horrifying face of the consequences of racial hatred in America. The third event that contributed to the start of the movement was the beginning of the Montgomery, Alabama, bus boycott in December 1955. Launched by Rosa Parks's December 1 refusal to give up her seat on the bus, this 381-day boycott involved over fifty thousand people and catapulted Martin Luther King Jr. into the role of chief spokesperson for the nonviolent agenda of the movement. The time from 1954 until King's assassination in 1968 changed the course of American history and, in particular, the life of the southern United States. The Jim Crow environment was legally challenged, and ordinary citizens stood up to demand their rights.

Short Stories of the Civil Rights Movement is a collection of twenty-three stories, each focusing on a particular moment of the civil rights movement. The historical event in each story has a permanent effect on the characters, reshaping the way the characters view their environments. If the character lives, the event becomes a turning point, a vision for a better world.

The stories are grouped into sections that parallel the news headlines of the day: School Desegregation (1954 on), Sit-ins (1960 on), Marches and Demonstrations (1963 on), and Acts of Violence. In the last section, Retrospective, characters look back on their personal involvement with the movement, attempting to figure out what they missed, why they cannot move beyond those times, or what they need still to discover. Within each section, the stories are arranged in chronological order according to the events they recount. The collection includes twenty writers—eleven black and nine white. Ten stories were written during the 1960s, the others after the heyday of the movement had long passed.

In the first section of stories, writers confront the issue of desegregation, which came into being with the *Brown* ruling in the 1950s and which continues through to the present. Although the *Brown* decision occurred in 1954, not until the fall of 1957 did President Dwight Eisenhower face his greatest domestic challenge. To honor his oath of office to uphold the Constitution of the United States, he ordered a thousand troops of the 101st Airborne Division of the U.S. Army to escort nine black students into all-white Central High School in Little Rock, Arkansas. Central High School was not the first school to integrate; but with the presence of both a large white mob and the military, it remained the biggest story about a community's compliance with *Brown*. School integration throughout the South did not come swiftly; and even now, after the schools have been integrated, social activities lag behind. Not until May 2002, for example, did Taylor County High School in central Georgia vote to hold its first integrated prom. The stories selected here offer a way to look closely at individuals playing their small roles in the changing face of public education in the South.

The four stories about school desegregation remind us that each student represents a larger world. Though isolated in a new environment, each comes to the new school from a difficult situation. In some cases, parents have lost jobs or had their homes bombed and are concerned about whether sending their children into a hostile situation is the right thing. In other cases, the children are from families who worry about what the integrating children will mean for those left behind. One story is told from the perspective of a white student who, like her black peers, brings with her the concerns of parents and neighbors. Although the new law of the land states that "separate but equal" is no longer constitutional, the law has no way to account for the human responses to forced compliance.

Five stories are about sit-ins, a common form of civil rights protest. One of the first and most famous sit-ins occurred on February 1, 1960. In that case, four young male students at North Carolina A & T State University in Greensboro, North Carolina, walked into the downtown Woolworth's, sat at the counter, and ordered coffee. Their simple action launched a wave of similar incidents across the South. (Months earlier, in Nashville, Tennessee, James Lawson had been conducting workshops on the use of nonviolent tactics in anticipation of organized sit-ins.) Within weeks after February 1, students from historically black colleges and universities, along with many supportive white students, were sitting-in, asking for service at lunch counters that had traditionally refused to serve black citizens. Leaders of the sit-ins in various cities became leaders of the Student Nonviolent Coordinating Committee (SNCC), which was born in April 1960 at Shaw University in Raleigh, North Carolina.

The two stories in this collection that are set in Nashville involve characters who are part of the organized effort that developed out of Lawson's workshops. Another two stories focus on characters who have heard about sit-ins but who, like the four young men in Greensboro credited with starting the sit-in phase of the movement, act on their own. Without benefit or support from an organization, they come to understand their limits and find myriad ways in which individual courage, set apart from national organizations, has its own set of complicated concerns. While these four stories allow readers to see what can happen both inside and outside organized efforts, the final story in the group considers a different kind of sit-in, one that takes place in the segregated bathroom facilities of a small-town department store. This prizewinning story later appeared in Langston Hughes's anthology *The Best Short Stories by Black Writers, 1899–1967* and is the only story in Hughes's anthology about the civil rights movement.

The next section of stories concerns the protest marches and demonstrations that were mainstays of the movement. Many of the marches were direct reactions to some unjust event—a bombing, a killing, a beating; others were reactions to unfair employment procedures or responses to being denied voter-registration rights. Although no state in the South was immune from such demonstrations, perhaps attracting the most media attention were those that transpired in Alabama.

In 1963 people around the globe watched and listened for news of Birmingham: the fire-hosing of black citizens; the police attack dogs; the jailing of thousands of men, women, and children who participated in planned, peaceful demonstrations. A few weeks after the successful August 1963 march on Washington, where King delivered his "I Have a Dream" speech, Birmingham again erupted when a bomb exploded at the Sixteenth Street Baptist Church and killed four young girls who were attending Sunday school. Two years later, in March 1965, the last hurrah of the modern civil rights movement, marchers were turned back twice but finally succeeded the third time in walking from Selma to Montgomery, Alabama. An estimated thirty thousand people joined the final triumphant moment on Dexter Avenue in front of the steps of the state capitol to listen to speeches by leaders of the movement, who would be together here for the last time. Within hours a voting rights bill was on its way to becoming law in the corridors of the nation's capital.

Of the five stories that respond to marches and demonstrations, one focuses on the fire-hosing of black citizens in 1963 Birmingham, one on the march on Washington, one on a rally in Florida, one on the fifty-mile march from Selma to Montgomery, and one on Boston—after Selma. Each story complicates the history of the event. In Birmingham, the protagonist does not want to participate in the demonstration; instead, he desires to run away from confrontation. In Washington, a parable of gloom counters the hopeful message of King's "I Have a Dream" speech. In Florida, a woman's participation in a rally directs attention to the male hierarchical power within the movement. In Selma, the diary keeper parallels Viola Liuzzo, the Detroit mother who was murdered by Klansmen a few hours after the voting rights march ended because she had responded to Dr. King's "Bloody Sunday" call for people of conscience and faith to come to Selma. In Boston, a white husband is emotionally crippled when his wife returns from Selma, and he is forced to deal with her participation in the movement.

The next section captures the violence surrounding the movement. Killings and beatings were common techniques used to attempt to intimidate and discourage the movement's participants, who were often without recourse. In Jackson, Mississippi, in June 1963, NAACP activist Medgar Evers was assassinated walking from his car toward his front door, but his killer continued to roam free for over thirty years. During Freedom Summer 1964, while college students from around the country flooded Mississippi, volunteering their time in Freedom Schools for children and in voter-registration drives for adults, the FBI searched for three young men—James Chaney, Andrew Goodman, and Michael Schwerner—who were reported missing in June and whose bodies were not found until August. Only recently, in 2005 was eighty-year-old Edgar Ray Killen convicted of manslaughter for his role in their murder. That same Freedom Summer voter-registration drive culminated in the formation of the Mississippi Freedom Democratic Party (MFDP), which attempted to seat itself in Atlantic City, New Jersey, at the National Democratic Convention. Though unsuccessful in 1964, the MFDP paved the way for integrated representations from southern states in all subsequent presidential conventions.

Of the six stories that respond to acts of violence, one, told from the perspective of a white racist killer, specifically parallels the facts of the Evers's assassination. Another story recounts the beating to death of a black pastor, by law-enforcement officials, for trying to buy a ticket out of town on the white side of a bus station. The other four stories are set amid voter-registration activity. The violence in those stories runs the gamut from verbal emasculation to rape. Preventing black citizens from obtaining the right to vote in various pockets of the Deep South was clearly one way for whites to maintain power. These stories suggest just how strongly those in power resisted change.

The final three stories offer retrospectives on the movement, which was, by the time that Martin Luther King Jr. was assassinated in Memphis, Tennessee, in 1968, transforming into something different. No longer was the movement so much about integration as it was about racial pride. And correspondingly, no longer was King's message of nonviolence as effective in rallying the people. After passage of the Voting Rights Act in August 1965, a more militant face began to appear within the ranks of organized civil rights activity. The Black Power movement originated within SNCC in 1966 when Stokeley Carmichael became leader and banished whites from the membership. Established leaders within the NAACP, the Southern Christian Leadership Conference, and the National Urban League were concerned about the distrust of all whites that the new SNCC advocated.

Meanwhile, that same year on the other side of the country in Oakland, California, Huey Newton and Bobby Seale founded the Black Panther Party, a group inspired by the speeches of Malcolm X that advocated black self-defense. The party's vision was to serve the needs of oppressed people, and they pioneered free social-service programs, among them a free breakfast program and a testing program for sickle cell anemia. When Newton was arrested in 1967 and charged with the murder of an Oakland police officer, Eldridge Cleaver and Seale contacted Carmichael, who agreed to become the prime minister of the party.

While the Black Power movement provided a conclusion to the civil rights movement, in its reaction against racism, it also placed an emphasis on black cultural heritage. In the late 1960s and 1970s, as a result of the heightened black consciousness and racial pride that came with the movement, student activists requested black studies courses. In popular culture, Afro hairstyles and clothing inspired by African dress became fashionable. An aesthetic response to the Black Power movement also blossomed in the form of the Black Arts movement, which included a number of the writers represented in this collection, as well as many other artists.

Despite the many gains that had been made during the civil rights era, when King died, many American cities ignited in flames. It was a dark day, filled with overwhelming hopelessness for many. Vietnam, the assassination of Robert Kennedy, and the victory of Richard Nixon dominated headlines in the last years of the 1960s instead of gains in equal rights. With the shot that felled the civil rights movement's chief spokesman, Martin Luther King Jr., the heyday of the southern arm of the movement died.

The last three stories, then, provide a sense of closure to the era and to the collection, as characters look back on their of involvement with— or their guilt about noninvolvement in—the civil rights movement. All of these characters have feelings that are so intense and long lasting that they have difficulty moving forward in time. For them, these stories suggest, no subsequent period in their lives has been so rich and purposeful or so full of missed opportunity as the days of the movement.

The civil rights movement made massive gains in toppling the Jim Crow South. Participants boycotted stores and transportation systems, marched in the streets, registered to vote at their own peril, and went to prison. Some gave their lives. A few activists surfaced as leaders; but without the thousands of unnamed and unknown citizens, the movement could not have achieved its many successes. The stories in this collection offer us characters who give a voice to those unnamed, unknown citizens who changed the way we live today.

Short Stories of the Civil Rights Movement

School Desegregation

Brown v. Board of Education of Topeka (1954) was the name assigned to four cases bundled into one: *Brown* (from Kansas), *Briggs* (from South Carolina), *Davis* (from Virginia), and *Gebhart* (from Delaware). All of them were challenges to *Plessy v. Ferguson*'s 1896 claim that separate but equal was indeed constitutional. Though the cases involved numerous lawyers, the two whose names stand out are Thurgood Marshall, for the students in whose names the cases were argued, and John W. Davis, for the opposition. Marshall would go on to become the first black justice of the Supreme Court. At the time, however, Davis had argued over a hundred cases before the Supreme Court, more than any other lawyer in the nation's history, while Marshall had argued just over a dozen cases. When the case was first introduced, Fred Vinson was the chief justice of the Court, but after a rehearing of the case had been ordered, Vinson suddenly died in September 1953; Eisenhower then appointed Earl Warren as chief justice. Warren saw that a case so important that it would change the entire face of American public education would need to be unanimous, and he worked toward that end.

Brown was argued in two parts: the first ruled that segregation was not constitutional; the following year, the second determined the manner in which desegregation should take place: "With all deliberate speed" was the decision, but not the reality. School boards in the South realized that violence could be an effective deterrent to desegregation. While black children entered white schools in some communities with little to no problems, where violence did occur, television news crews, still in their early years of existence, were on the scene. This coverage of mob violence discouraged other communities from even trying to integrate their schools.

Perhaps the biggest story of the century in Little Rock, Arkansas, was the desegregation of Central High School. One of the most beautiful high schools in America, Central agreed to open its doors to a limited number of black students in the fall of 1957. Though more students and their parents had attended a meeting with the district superintendent in August, only nine students turned out on September 3, the first day of school. Governor Orval Faubus, having predicted the violence that would become reality, ordered the Arkansas State Guard to block the entry of the nine black students. On September 23, these students tried again and successfully entered a side door, but once inside the school, officials feared for their lives, and before noon they were escorted away in police cars from within the bowels of the school building. Finally, on September 25, with the help of President Eisenhower's calling out the 101st Airborne, the nine students were escorted through the front doors of the high school to start a year of schooling that would be like no other. Over a thousand troops bivouacked on the school's grounds; each student had an assigned trooper as an individual guard. According to Melba Pattillo Beals's *Warriors Don't Cry: A Searing Memoir of the Battle to Integrate Little Rock's Central High*, to date the only book to tell the story from the black students' perspective, no day really became better than another. These students turned into warriors on a battlefield.

In this section, four stories depict the experiences of black children in formerly white schools. In "See What Tomorrow Brings" (1968), set in an undisclosed southern town, the story's protagonist is one of four black students to enter Central High, with events and happenings inspired by the real Central in Little Rock. Focusing on the first day of school, the story is as much about the parents' concerns for their child as it is about his fear, isolation, and worry over what the next day will bring.

"First Day of School" (1966), set in Kentucky, and "Neighbors" (1966), set in Alabama, also shed light on the perspective of parents, a reminder that when children were the first to integrate a white school, their parents often had to endure death threats—by letter or by anonymous phone call. Houses were bombed; neighbors feared what might happen to them. Parents often lost their jobs. Besides all the normal stresses of going to school for the children—what to wear, where to walk, who will become a friend, how not to get lost in the building—the possibility of real danger haunted and often hounded them.

Set in northwest Mississippi, "Spring Is Now" (1968) tells its story through one white girl's view of the only black boy in her school. Racial stereotype meets individual person. All the ways that had been assigned to a race now have to be filtered, considered, and maybe dismissed when one representative of all that talk becomes human and real.

JAMES W. THOMPSON (ABBA ELETHEA)

See What Tomorrow Brings

James W. Thompson (1935–), a Detroit-born poet and editor of *Umbra* during
the late 1960s, was part of the Black Arts movement of the late 1960s and
1970s. He later changed his name to Abba Elethea and continued his work
as a columnist, dance critic, and poet-in-residence at Antioch University. His
work has been presented at international festivals in Africa, Europe, and the
United States, and he has published in such journals as *Quicksilver*, *Pegasus*,
the *Gallery*, *Sail Review*, *Negro History Bulletin*, and *Negro Digest*. "See What
Tomorrow Brings" appeared in the *Transatlantic Review* in the summer of 1968.

Laughter exploding in an extremely hollow room, that's how this day has
been. Its echoes will linger to haunt Muhdear, for days to come. I could
tell, immediately, when I came home that she had worried herself sick.
She flew from the kitchen like a startled sparrow, her hands perched nervously upon her hips—all set to raise the roof!

"Not going through this worry tomorrow," she commanded. "Soon . . .
school is out, you bring your butt home—just the way you leave here—in
that station wagon. You hear me?" She frowned. Before I could open my
mouth, she smiled. The little wrinkles about her eyes curved like tooled
icing on a chocolate cake. "Wasn't too bad, was it Honey. And tomorrow
will be easier. First of anything's always the worst to take. You get used
to it." Turning toward my father and sister, who were sitting in the living
room, she sighed: "Guess we can eat now." Muhdear went back to the
kitchen to re-heat the supper that had turned cold.

"Humphf," Ella Mae said, "you really showed out today—worrying
everybody. Like I always say, you don't think about nobody but yourself."
It's my sister's habit to accuse others of the crimes she's most guilty of
committing. "You knew just as well we'd be worried." I can't imagine Ella
worrying about anything, most of all me. "When those deputies come here
and said you was nowhere to be found, Muhdear almost died. She sent

daddy to hunt you up. The whole neighborhood was up in arms." I knew that there wasn't any way for me to explain my reason for having come home late and unescorted, at least not to Ella. My father, to my surprise, remained stony and silent. During supper he stared at me with granite eyes.

Muhdear had prepared my favorite meal: pork chops, smothered in onions, with fried corn and mashed potatoes. "Honey-boy," Muhdear winked at me, "guess what! I made new curtains for your room." She tapped her plate, intermittently, with her fork. "Know what," she said, "think maybe we can get that studio bed you been just raving to have." Muhdear looked at me, then she looked at my plate. I wasn't hungry. I tried to eat. Ella kept interrupting with questions. "Well, what's it gonna be like tomorrow," she wanted to know. I wouldn't dignify that question with an answer. There are so many tomorrows, and today had just been one of them.

When I discovered the sun, I had been dressed for over an hour. It inched across the sky, a flaming snail on a bleached rock. The sound of Muhdear fussing over her extra-special breakfast drifted from the kitchen along with the scent of cinnamon and strong coffee. It was a wonderful breakfast. (Muhdear makes the best cinnamon pancakes in the world, and these had banana bits in them.) It was an important morning. I was one of four Negroes entering Central High.[1] I was the only one whose parents weren't professionals. I didn't feel half as anxious as the rest of the family. The neighbors had discussed it with the relish of vultures pecking over a delicate dish. You would have thought that I was going to visit the Queen. As I sat looking out of the window, for a moment I wished that I had had their enthusiasm. I didn't feel at all shook; if anything, I felt numb. All I could think of was the time I sat on the front porch with Daddy (The yard lay damp with dew, and the sweetness of evening burst in wisteria and rose, jasmin and mint, mixed with the stinging scent of Dad's cigar and kerosene from the porch lamp—where moths dizzied themselves and the light. Daddy insists on using this lamp), talking about his job and my future. He looked at me. A deep sigh ended in a smile.

1. This Central High School is not intended to be the Central High of Little Rock, Arkansas, where nine black students integrated in the fall of 1957. However, much of the description of mob activity and fear among the black students evokes the violence that occurred at Little Rock's Central High.

He spoke softly, "Honey, sometimes . . . I look upon apples as they hang in trees and wish to have their ripe indifference. One day . . . *you'll* know the feeling."

Muhdear was standing on the porch with me when the two deputies came. She had been reminding me of how I should act. She repeated the same words over, and over, and over. I had ceased listening long ago. "Com'on, boyah," one of the deputies shouted. "Jesse," my mother called, "it's time!" My father stepped onto the porch. He stood, his thumbs tucked in his overalls, his fingers rolled in huge fists. His face, a tight, dark mask, was enlivened only by the brown eyes that darted from the deputies to our front walk (the walk that he had made with bright reddish-brown bricks). The way his head was cocked, the way he held his body, cheered and frightened me. Muhdear monkeyed with my collar again. And for what must have been the twentieth time, she smoothed my tie. "There'll be a pack out there," Muhdear began, "don't let them get your goat, honey. They're more afraid of you than you are of them." Her eyes squinted toward the guards and widened into mine. They hovered over me. Daddy pinched the back of my neck and thumped the back of my head with his fingers. Muhdear dried cool hands on her apron. She does this at the strangest times . . .

When news came that Archie, the rebel hereabouts, had been chased and shot by the Rensalar Boys, she rushed over to his house. I was right on her tail. The other neighbors were leaving when we got there. Muhdear still had on her apron. Mrs. Matthews and Muhdear sat in the front room. I lingered in the hall. She tried to console Mrs. Matthews, who was trying hard not to cry.

"Louise, they kilt my baby."

"Now, Lucille, don't talk about it any more."

"I gotta talk about it—I gotta make myself believe it. I knowed Archie were always on for devilment, only this time . . . You know, I tole him time and time again, 'Archie.' (Her voice cracked. She paused, and her hands armored her head; she looked across the room at Archie's picture on the mantelpiece, anchored in a sea of lace.) 'Archie,' I'd say, 'if you so hot on gettin' back at the world, you'll just have to rise above it.' You knowed Archie . . . never paid a mind to me. I think, maybe, he kinda thought

I was crazy. Oh, I know . . . some things I tole him sounded strange. Louise . . . it was *all* I knew." (The whole time she spoke, Muhdear dried cool hands in the folds of her apron.)

"Well, Lucille, if you just gotta talk about it . . ."

"You know them Rens'lar Boys. Archie worked for their father, sometime, at the gas station. They shot him! They were drunk . . . Wanted some fun . . . Seems they tole Archie they wanted a live coon to hunt, and he were it. They went and got their guns and hounds, play-acting, you know. It seems that when Archie conceived their seriousness, he started to run. Why he didn't just com'on home I'll never know. Instead, he lit out behind the gas station into those woods. They chased him . . . shot him down . . ." (She stopped. For a long while she seemed not to breathe. She rocked back and forth on that old red leather chair, her arms clasped across her stomach so tight I could see the veins in her arms from where I stood in the hall.)

"IN THE BACK . . . shot him . . . MY BABY." (She took a deep breath.)

"And they CUT him."

"Henry, you can go on the porch now."

Muhdear said this without looking in my direction. I knew better than to object, so I went out and sat under the window. I heard Mrs. Matthews ending, "They had no call to do that . . . no call." Then she cried bitterly, and I went back in to see what I could do. Muhdear hadn't moved. She wasn't even crying. In the folds of her apron, she dried cool hands, just as she had done this morning.

When we neared the school, the sun that I'd found so beautiful was crashing over the entrance of Central High. It fell in fake golden specks at the foot of the steaming crowd, casting acute shadows through the calm green trees. They hung like hothouse specimens adopted by a bleak season. (It seems that I read that somewhere.) School. The thought hit me. The chilled air bit the whites of those glaring eyes surrounding the station wagon. Every face that I looked into, as the car crawled, glistened. The din: "Two, four, six, eight, we don't wanna in-urr-grate," split the morning. Arms flailed the air with homemade signs. Bodies hunched. Jaws were thrust dangerously forward, cutting grotesque lines: carving one massive and miserably tortured crowdface. I sat in the back of the station wagon, my back pressed against the hot leather seat. A tomato splashed against the window on my left. I didn't flinch. I felt suddenly tired and tense. I looked out at them, and I could have killed them all and never have felt a thing.

The men, lurching about, were wearing washable work clothes. I spotted an occasional white shirt. And the women, the ones that I could see, wore cotton housedresses and light coats. They looked as though many lusty infants had suckled at their breasts far too long. The fat ones sagged like old sows. I wanted to laugh. They looked useless and extremely weary. Yet there they were, as my father says, their infernal female spirits stirring. They had come to nourish a dying tradition. It was from them that the men had gathered their will, succored their violence which is the bottom of their fear, and strangely, it was for the women that the men now raged in a barbaric marriage, to the accompaniment of flash-bulbs.

The car stopped. The pack writhed and screamed in a wild revival beat. "Two, four, six, eight, we don' wanna in-urr-grate." Little children were sewn in cardboards. NIGGERS NEVER. GOD SAVE US FROM NIGGERS. NO BLACKS IN OUR SCHOOLS. I didn't know whether I should feel angry or proud. Dad had said, way back during the summer after we'd made up following weeks of silence, that when this day came, I should feel proud. "The beautiful story that will become history," he'd said, "is all about you, honey, and you must hold to your dignity and not be daunted." I held. Their children stood, in their huge signs, blank and bewildered. I saw a few burrow between knees in fright when the voice of the rout rose threateningly. They were pummeled, squized, held high, knocked and shaken. I was locked behind glass and steel, waiting for their parents to calm down. Their pathetic little bodies reacted to the changing pressures with wails and tears. They were not soothed. The attention of their mothers and fathers was focused on me. The deputy had maneuvered the car so that it stood directly in front of the entrance, ringed on both sides by the Army and the State Police. When the door opened for me, the frenzy increased. The white-topped helmets of the troopers bobbed, sparkling in the sunlight, a striking contrast to the damp disheveled heads they fought to restrain. I wondered if their ears were ringing like mine. They were closer to the den.

Locked between the shoulders of the deputies, I began climbing the steps. I knew that in the minds of those two who were protecting me there was also the feeling that I was an invader. They had not made their feelings secret—I had been told during the drive. The patience of my fathers who had defied the singular death of time, who had traversed from chattel to changling was now concrete in me; I was the black challenger mounting the forbidden stairs; and all of the forces of their depressed and fantastic heritage were fermenting within me. It has yet to erupt! I felt as though I moved in a vacuum, my objective receding, my movement motionless. It was all Jules Verne.[2] The shrill screams of the pack behind me set my stomach on fire. My throat felt parched. I think that I swallowed constantly. "Say, yeh black bastard, we don' wancha here," fell on my ears— gnawed at the back of my brain. It seemed as though the sun cracked over me, a huge egg, depositing a hot yoke. I wished for a big mirror to turn upon the crowd, then a machine gun. And I wondered, what was it, other than stupidity, that was supposed to be so damned superior about these people. They're barbaric, I told myself. For some reason I stopped on the steps for a moment. One of the guards caught me by the arm. "Com'on now, Nigra," he drawled, "we gotta git you inside." I looked over the face of the building. The American flag fell over the heavily carved masonry of the peaked entrance. I smiled. Vines crept up the dark brick walls, mint-green on brown. The Army stood, legs spread, guns bayoneted held at their sides. I wanted suddenly to shout "TENCHUT." They were silent and unblinking. "Here, blackie," someone yelled. "Two, four, six, eight, we don' wanna in-urr-grate," the crowd chanted. I don't know what possessed me, but I spun around. Flash bulbs, popping, blinded me momentarily. My two heavy-set guards, puffing and sweating, and swearing, too, grabbed my arms. They drug me up the two remaining steps. I looked back once more before entering the building. A white man, very tall and very red, screamed to me. "That's right, black-boy, show'em what you're made of." I think that he would have said more, but he was swallowed

---

2. Born in France, prolific writer Jules Verne (1828–1905) was one of the founding fathers of science fiction. His novels, often in the form of extraordinary voyages, such as *Twenty Thousand Leagues under the Sea*, were widely popular during his lifetime and into the twentieth century.

by men with clubs, flying. I could not see him any longer. I wonder who he was?

Inside, I was greeted by six students. Four boys and two girls. They had come to wish me luck. Each class today was trying. I'm a senior, and the other three are juniors, so we don't have classes together. And we have a different lunch hour. A redhead tripped me in my history class. And now that I know who he is I have decided to fix him. I don't know what I'm going to do. I don't intend to let him get away without paying. Maybe they should not have chosen me for this; Daddy is not a professional, and he has taught me several different ways to skin a cat, and that redhead doesn't know it yet, but he's got a skinning coming. It will have to be quiet and very indirect, and something that he will not forget.

I knew that among the students I was very visible, and I knew, too, that no one really wanted to see me. Before the last bell I made for the side exit hoping to avoid the deputies. The black and white station wagon was there in front of the door. I was relieved when I saw that it was empty. I was on the sidewalk in seconds. The street looked as though it had been abandoned after a parade. Bits of string, cardboards, and cigarette butts littered the sidewalk. Dark pools of water stood in the gutter, morning's souvenirs, left by the fire hose that had been used to disperse the crowd. I walked along quickly, looking back, hoping that no one would spot me. When I reached my hideaway in the grove at the edge of town, I sat down. I was trembling, so I threw stones in the stream with all of my might. I heard my heart pounding, and I was shocked by the stinging taste of tears. I jumped up, and in an effort to relieve the tremors, I started singing. The road that leads to the grove looked wide and endless beneath the fading arc of trees. I bet my voice must have echoed into the mountain of the evening as I walked singing just as loud as I could, "Hurry down sunshine . . . See what tomorrow brings." And the sun died, bleeding across the sky.

R. V. CASSILL

The First Day of School

Born in Iowa, R. V. Cassill (1919–2002) wrote two dozen novels and seven collections of short stories. He taught at the universities of Iowa, Purdue, Columbia, Harvard, and Brown. He was also the recipient of grants from Fulbright, Rockefeller, and Guggenheim. "The First Day of School" appeared in the *Northwest Review* in 1958 and was reprinted in his 1966 collection, *The Happy Marriage*.

Thirteen bubbles floated in the milk. Their pearl transparent hemispheres gleamed like souvenirs of the summer days just past, rich with blue reflections of the sky and of shadowy greens. John Hawkins jabbed the bubble closest to him with his spoon, and it disappeared without a ripple. On the white surface there was no mark of where it had been.

"Stop tooling that oatmeal and eat it," his mother said. She glanced meaningfully at the clock on the varnished cupboard. She nodded a heavy, emphatic affirmation that now the clock was boss. Summer was over, when the gracious oncoming of morning light and the stir of early breezes promised that time was a luxury.

"Audrey's not even down yet," he said.

"Audrey'll be down."

"You think she's taking longer to dress because she wants to look nice today?"

"She likes to look *neat*."

"What I was thinking," he said slowly, "was that maybe she didn't feel like going today. Didn't feel *exactly* like it."

"Of course she'll go."

"I meant she might not want to go until tomorrow, maybe. Until we see what happens."

"Nothing's going to happen," his mother said.

"I know there isn't. But what if it did?" Again John swirled the tip of his spoon in the milk. It was like writing on a surface that would keep no mark.

"Eat and be quiet. Audrey's coming, so let's stop this here kind of talk."

He heard the tap of heels on the stairs, and his sister came down into the kitchen. She looked fresh and cool in her white dress. Her lids looked heavy. She must have slept all right—and for this John felt both envy and a faint resentment. He had not really slept since midnight. The heavy traffic in town, the long wail of horns as somebody raced in on the U.S. highway holding the horn button down, and the restless murmur, like the sound of a celebration down in the courthouse square, had kept him awake after that. Each time a car had passed their house his breath had gone tight and sluggish. It was better to stay awake and ready, he had told himself, than to be caught asleep.

"Daddy gone?" Audrey asked softly as she took her place across the table from her brother.

"He's been gone an hour," their mother answered. "*You* know what time he has to be at the mine."

"She means, did he go to work today?" John said. His voice had risen impatiently. He met his mother's stout gaze in a staring contest, trying to make her admit by at least some flicker of expression that today was different from any other day. "I thought he might be down at Reverend Specker's," John said. "Cal's father and Vonnie's and some of the others are going to be there to wait and see."

Maybe his mother smiled then. If so, the smile was so faint that he could not be sure. "You know your father isn't much of a hand for waiting," she said. "Eat. It's a quarter past eight."

As he spooned the warm oatmeal into his mouth he heard the rain crow calling again from the trees beyond the railroad embankment. He had heard it since the first light came before dawn, and he had thought, Maybe the bird knows it's going to rain, after all. He hoped it would. *They won't come out in the rain*, he had thought. Not so many of them, at least. He could wear a raincoat. A raincoat might help him feel more protected on the walk to school. It would be a sort of disguise, at least.

But since dawn the sun had lain across the green Kentucky trees and the roofs of town like a clean, hard fire. The sky was as clear as fresh-washed window glass. The rain crow was wrong about the weather. And still, John thought, its lamenting, repeated call must mean something.

His mother and Audrey were talking about the groceries she was to bring when she came home from school at lunch time. A five-pound bag of sugar, a fresh pineapple, a pound of butter. . . .

"Listen!" John said. Downtown the sound of a siren had begun. A volley of automobile horns broke around it as if they meant to drown it out. "*Listen* to them."

"It's only the National Guard, I expect," his mother said calmly. "They came in early this morning before light. And it may be some foolish kids honking at them, the way they would. Audrey, if Henry doesn't have a good-looking roast, why then let it go, and I'll walk out to Weaver's this afternoon and get one there. I wanted to have something a little bit special for our dinner tonight."

So . . . John thought . . . she wasn't asleep last night either. Someone had come stealthily to the house to bring his parents word about the National Guard. That meant they knew about the others who had come into town, too. Maybe all through the night there had been a swift passage of messengers through the neighborhood and a whispering of information that his mother meant to keep from him. Your folks told you, he reflected bitterly, that nothing is better than knowing. Knowing whatever there is in this world to be known. That was why you had to be one of the half dozen kids out of some nine hundred colored of school age who were going today to start classes at Joseph P. Gilmore High instead of Webster. Knowing and learning the truth were worth so much they said—and then left it to the hooting rain crow to tell you that things were worse than everybody had hoped.

Something had gone wrong, bad enough wrong so the National Guard had to be called out.

"It's eight twenty-five," his mother said. "Did you get that snap sewed on right, Audrey?" As her experienced fingers examined the shoulder of Audrey's dress they lingered a moment in an involuntary, sheltering caress. "It's all arranged," she told her children, "how you'll walk down to the Baptist Church and meet the others there. You know there'll be Reverend Chader, Reverend Smith, and Mr. Hall to go with you. It may be that the white ministers will go with you, or they may be waiting at school. We don't know. But now you be sure, don't you go farther than the Baptist Church alone." Carefully she lifted her hand clear of Audrey's shoulder. John thought, Why doesn't she hug her if that's what she wants to do?

He pushed away from the table and went out on the front porch. The dazzling sunlight lay shadowless on the street that swept down toward the Baptist Church at the edge of the colored section. The street seemed awfully long this morning, the way it had looked when he was little. A chicken was clucking contentedly behind their neighbor's house, feeling the warmth, settling itself into the sun-warmed dust. Lucky chicken.

He blinked at the sun's glare on the concrete steps leading down from the porch. He remembered something else from the time he was little. Once he had kicked Audrey's doll buggy down these same steps. He had done it out of meanness—for some silly reason he had been mad at her. But as soon as the buggy had started to bump down, he had understood how terrible it was not to be able to run after it and stop it. It had gathered speed at each step and when it hit the sidewalk it had spilled over. Audrey's doll had smashed into sharp little pieces on the sidewalk below. His mother had come out of the house to find him crying harder than Audrey. "Now you know that when something gets out of your hands it is in the Devil's hands," his mother had explained to him. Did she expect him to forget—now—that that was always the way things went to smash when they got out of hand? Again he heard the siren and the hooting, mocking horns from the center of town. Didn't his mother think *they* could get out of hand?

He closed his eyes and seemed to see something like a doll buggy bump down long steps like those at Joseph P. Gilmore High, and it seemed to him that it was not a doll that was riding down to be smashed.

He made up his mind then. He would go today, because he had said he would. Therefore he had to. But he wouldn't go unless Audrey stayed home. That was going to be his condition. His bargaining looked perfect. He would trade them one for one.

His mother and Audrey came together onto the porch. His mother said, "My stars, I forgot to give you the money for the groceries." She let the screen door bang as she went swiftly back into the house.

As soon as they were alone, he took Audrey's bare arm in his hand and pinched hard. "You gotta stay home," he whispered. "Don't you know there's thousands of people down there? Didn't you hear them coming in all night long? You slept, didn't you? All right. You can hear them now. Tell her you're sick. She won't expect you to go if you're sick. I'll knock you down, I'll smash you if you don't tell her that." He bared his teeth and twisted his nails into the skin of her arm. "Hear them horns," he hissed.

He forced her halfway to her knees with the strength of his fear and rage. They swayed there, locked for a minute. Her knee dropped to the porch floor. She lowered her eyes. He thought he had won.

But she was saying something and in spite of himself he listened to her almost whispered refusal. "Don't you know anything? Don't you know it's harder for them than us? Don't you know Daddy didn't go to the mine this morning? They laid him off on account of us. They told him not to come if we went to school."

Uncertainly he relaxed his grip. "How do you know all that?"

"I listen," she said. Her eyes lit with a sudden spark that seemed to come from their absolute brown depths. "But I don't let on all I know the way you do. I'm not a. . . ." Her last word sunk so low that he could not exactly hear it. But if his ear missed it, his understanding caught it. He knew she had said "coward."

He let her get up then. She was standing beside him, serene and prim when their mother came out on the porch again.

"Here, child," their mother said to Audrey, counting the dollar bills into her hand. "There's six, and I guess it will be all right if you have some left if you and Brother get yourselves a cone to lick on the way home."

John was not looking at his sister then. He was already turning to face the shadowless street, but he heard the unmistakable poised amusement of her voice when she said, "Ma, don't you know we're a little too old for that?"

"Yes, you are," their mother said. "Seems I had forgotten that."

They were too old to take each other's hand, either, as they went down the steps of their home and into the street. As they turned to the right, facing the sun, they heard the chattering of a tank's tread on the pavement by the school. A voice too distant to be understood bawled a military command. There were horns again and a crescendo of boos.

Behind them they heard their mother call something. It was lost in the general racket.

"What?" John called back to her. "What?"

She had followed them out as far as the sidewalk, but not past the gate. As they hesitated to listen, she put her hands to either side of her mouth and called to them the words she had so often used when she let them go away from home.

"Behave yourselves," she said.

DIANE OLIVER

Neighbors

Diane Oliver was a friend of the first black student to attend previously all-white
Harding High School in Charlotte, North Carolina, in 1957. That historical event
inspired her writing of this story. "Neighbors" first appeared in the *Sewanee
Review* in the spring of 1966. The story was reprinted in the O. Henry Award
anthology and Gloria Naylor's *Children of the Night: The Best Short Stories by
Black Writers, 1967 to the Present* (1995). Oliver died in a motorcycle wreck in
1966.

The bus turning the corner of Patterson and Talford Avenue was dull this
time of evening. Of the four passengers standing in the rear, she did not
recognize any of her friends. Most of the people tucked neatly in the
double seats were women, maids and cooks on their way from work or
secretaries who had worked late and were riding from the office building
at the mill. The cotton mill was out from town, near the house where she
worked. She noticed that a few men were riding too. They were obviously
just working men, except for one gentleman dressed very neatly in a dark
grey suit and carrying what she imagined was a push-button umbrella.

He looked to her as though he usually drove a car to work. She immediately decided that the car probably wouldn't start this morning so
he had to catch the bus to and from work. She was standing in the rear
of the bus, peering at the passengers, her arms barely reaching the overhead railing, trying not to wobble with every lurch. But every corner the
bus turned pushed her head toward a window. And her hair was coming
down too, wisps of black curls swung between her eyes. She looked at
the people around her. Some of them were white, but most of them were
her color. Looking at the passengers at least kept her from thinking of
tomorrow. But really she would be glad when it came, then everything
would be over.

She took a firmer grip on the green leather seat and wished she had on her glasses. The man with the umbrella was two people ahead of her on the other side of the bus, so she could see him between other people very clearly. She watched as he unfolded the evening newspaper, craning her neck to see what was on the front page. She stood, impatiently trying to read the headlines, when she realized he was staring up at her rather curiously. Biting her lips she turned her head and stared out the window until the downtown section was in sight.

She would have to wait until she was home to see if they were in the newspaper again. Sometimes she felt that if another person snapped a picture of them she would burst out screaming. Last Monday reporters were already inside the pre-school clinic when she took Tommy for his last polio shot. She didn't understand how anybody could be so heartless to a child. The flashbulb went off right when the needle went in and all the picture showed was Tommy's open mouth.

The bus pulling up to the curb jerked to a stop, startling her and confusing her thoughts. Clutching in her hand the paper bag that contained her uniform, she pushed her way toward the door. By standing in the back of the bus, she was one of the first people to step to the ground. Outside the bus, the evening air felt humid and uncomfortable and her dress kept sticking to her. She looked up and remembered that the weatherman had forecast rain. Just their luck—why, she wondered, would it have to rain on top of everything else?

As she walked along, the main street seemed unnaturally quiet but she decided her imagination was merely playing tricks. Besides, most of the stores had been closed since five o'clock.

She stopped to look at a reversible raincoat in Ivey's window, but although she had a full time job now, she couldn't keep her mind on clothes. She was about to continue walking when she heard a horn blowing. Looking around, half-scared but also curious, she saw a man beckoning to her in a grey car. He was nobody she knew but since a nicely dressed woman was with him in the front seat, she walked to the car.

"You're Jim Mitchell's girl, aren't you?" he questioned. "You Ellie or the other one?"

She nodded yes, wondering who he was and how much he had been drinking.

"Now honey," he said leaning over the woman, "you don't know me but your father does and you tell him that if anything happens to that boy of his tomorrow we're ready to set things straight." He looked her straight in the eye and she promised to take home the message.

Just as the man was about to step on the gas, the woman reached out and touched her arm. "You hurry up home, honey, it's about dark out here."

Before she could find out their names, the Chevrolet had disappeared around a corner. Ellie wished someone would magically appear and tell her everything that had happened since August. Then maybe she could figure out what was real and what she had been imagining for the past couple of days.

She walked past the main shopping district up to Tanner's where Saraline was standing in the window peeling oranges. Everything in the shop was painted orange and green and Ellie couldn't help thinking that poor Saraline looked out of place. She stopped to wave to her friend who pointed the knife to her watch and then to her boyfriend standing in the rear of the shop. Ellie nodded that she understood. She knew Sara wanted her to tell her grandfather that she had to work late again. Neither one of them could figure out why he didn't like Charlie. Saraline had finished high school three years ahead of her and it was time for her to be getting married. Ellie watched as her friend stopped peeling the orange long enough to cross her fingers. She nodded again but she was afraid all the crossed fingers in the world wouldn't stop the trouble tomorrow.

She stopped at the traffic light and spoke to a shrivelled woman hunched against the side of a building. Scuffing the bottom of her sneakers on the curb she waited for the woman to open her mouth and grin as she usually did. The kids used to bait her to talk, and since she didn't have but one tooth in her whole head they called her Doughnut Puncher. But the woman was still, the way everything else had been all week.

From where Ellie stood, across the street from the Sears and Roebuck parking lot, she could see their house, all of the houses on the single street white people called Welfare Row. Those newspaper men always made her angry. All of their articles showed how rough the people were on their street. And the reporters never said her family wasn't on welfare, the papers always said the family lived on that street. She paused to look across the street at a group of kids pouncing on one rubber ball. There were always white kids around their neighborhood mixed up in the games, but playing with them was almost an unwritten rule. When everybody started going to school, nobody played together any more.

She crossed at the corner ignoring the cars at the stop light and the closer she got to her street the more she realized that the newspaper was right. The houses were ugly, there were not even any trees, just patches of scraggly bushes and grasses. As she cut across the sticky asphalt pavement covered with cars she was conscious of the parking lot floodlights casting a strange glow on her street. She stared from habit at the house on the end of the block and except for the way the paint was peeling they all looked alike to her. Now at twilight the flaking grey paint had a luminous glow and as she walked down the dirt sidewalk she noticed Mr. Paul's pipe smoke added to the hazy atmosphere. Mr. Paul would be sitting in that same spot waiting until Saraline came home. Ellie slowed her pace to speak to the elderly man sitting on the porch.

"Evening, Mr. Paul," she said. Her voice sounded clear and out of place on the vacant street.

"Eh, who's that?" Mr. Paul leaned over the rail, "What you say, girl?"

"How are you?" she hollered louder. "Sara said she'd be late tonight, she has to work." She waited for the words to sink in.

His head had dropped and his eyes were facing his lap. She could see that he was disappointed. "Couldn't help it," he said finally. "Reckon they needed her again." Then as if he suddenly remembered he turned toward her.

"You people be ready down there? Still gonna let him go tomorrow?"

She looked at Mr. Paul between the missing rails on his porch, seeing how his rolled up trousers seemed to fit exactly in the vacant banister space.

"Last I heard this morning we're still letting him go," she said.

Mr. Paul had shifted his weight back to the chair. "Don't reckon they'll hurt him," he mumbled, scratching the side of his face. "Hope he don't mind being spit on though. Spitting ain't like cutting. They can spit on him and nobody'll ever know who did it," he said, ending his words with a quiet chuckle.

Ellie stood on the sidewalk grinding her heel in the dirt waiting for the old man to finish talking. She was glad somebody found something funny to laugh at. Finally he shut up.

"Goodbye, Mr. Paul," she waved. Her voice sounded loud to her own ears. But she knew the way her head ached intensified noises. She walked home faster, hoping they had some aspirin in the house and that those men would leave earlier tonight.

From the front of her house she could tell that the men were still there. The living room light shone behind the yellow shades, coming through brighter in the patched places. She thought about moving the geranium pot from the porch to catch the rain but changed her mind. She kicked a beer can under a car parked in the street and stopped to look at her reflection on the car door. The tiny flowers of her printed dress made her look as if she had a strange tropical disease. She spotted another can and kicked it out of the way of the car, thinking that one of these days some kid was going to fall and hurt himself. What she wanted to do she knew was kick the car out of the way. Both the station wagon and the Ford had been parked in front of her house all week, waiting. Everybody was just sitting around waiting.

Suddenly she laughed aloud. Reverend Davis' car was big and black and shiny just like, but no, the smile disappeared from her face, her mother didn't like for them to say things about other people's color. She looked around to see who else came, and saw Mr. Moore's old beat up blue car. Somebody had torn away half of his NAACP sign. Sometimes she really felt sorry for the man. No matter how hard he glued on his stickers somebody always yanked them off again.

Ellie didn't recognize the third car but it had an Alabama license plate. She turned around and looked up and down the street, hating to go inside. There were no lights on their street, but in the distance she could see the bright lights of the parking lot. Slowly she did an about face and climbed the steps.

She wondered when her mama was going to remember to get a yellow bulb for the porch. Although the lights hadn't been turned on, usually

June bugs and mosquitoes swarmed all around the porch. By the time she was inside the house she always felt like they were crawling in her hair. She pulled on the screen and saw that Mama finally had made Hezekiah patch up the holes. The globs of white adhesive tape scattered over the screen door looked just like misshapen butterflies.

She listened to her father's voice and could tell by the tone that the men were discussing something important again. She rattled the door once more but nobody came.

"Will somebody please let me in?" Her voice carried through the screen to the knot of men sitting in the corner.

"The door's open," her father yelled. "Come on in."

"The door is not open," she said evenly. "You know we stopped leaving it open." She was feeling tired again and her voice had fallen an octave lower.

"Yeah, I forgot, I forgot," he mumbled walking to the door.

She watched her father almost stumble across a chair to let her in. He was shorter than the light bulb and the light seemed to beam down on him, emphasizing the wrinkles around his eyes. She could tell from the way he pushed open the screen that he hadn't had much sleep either. She'd overheard him telling Mama that the people down at the shop seemed to be piling on the work harder just because of this thing. And he couldn't do anything or say anything to his boss because they probably wanted to fire him.

"Where's Mama?" she whispered. He nodded toward the back.

"Good evening, everybody," she said looking at the three men who had not looked up since she entered the room. One of the men half stood, but his attention was geared back to something another man was saying. They were sitting on the sofa in their shirt sleeves and there was a pitcher of ice water on the window sill.

"Your mother probably needs some help," her father said. She looked past him trying to figure out who the white man was sitting on the end. His face looked familiar and she tried to remember where she had seen him before. The men were paying no attention to her. She bent to see what they were studying and saw a large sheet of white drawing paper. She could see blocks and lines and the man sitting in the middle was marking a trail with the eraser edge of the pencil.

The quiet stillness of the room was making her head ache more. She pushed her way through the red embroidered curtains that led to the kitchen.

"I'm home, Mama," she said, standing in front of the back door facing the big yellow sun Hezekiah and Tommy had painted on the wall above the iron stove. Immediately she felt a warmth permeating her skin. "Where is everybody?" she asked, sitting at the table where her mother was peeling potatoes.

"Mrs. McAllister is keeping Helen and Teenie," her mother said. "Your brother is staying over with Harry tonight." With each name she uttered, a slice of potato peeling tumbled to the newspaper on the table. "Tommy's in the bedroom reading that Uncle Wiggily book."

Ellie looked up at her mother but her eyes were straight ahead. She knew that Tommy only read the Uncle Wiggily book by himself when he was unhappy. She got up and walked to the kitchen cabinet.

"The other knives dirty?" she asked.

"No," her mother said, "look in the next drawer."

Ellie pulled open the drawer, flicking scraps of white paint with her fingernail. She reached for the knife and at the same time a pile of envelopes caught her eye.

"Any more come today?" she asked, pulling out the knife and slipping the envelopes under the dish towels.

"Yes, seven more came today," her mother accentuated each word carefully. "Your father has them with him in the other room."

"Same thing?" she asked picking up a potato and wishing she could think of some way to change the subject.

The white people had been threatening them for the past three weeks. Some of the letters were aimed at the family, but most of them were directed to Tommy himself. About once a week in the same handwriting somebody wrote that he'd better not eat lunch at school because they were going to poison him.

They had been getting those letters ever since the school board made Tommy's name public. She sliced the potato and dropped the pieces in the pan of cold water. Out of all those people he had been the only one the board had accepted for transfer to the elementary school. The other children, the members said, didn't live in the district. As she cut the eyes out of another potato she thought about the first letter they had received and how her father just set fire to it in the ashtray. But then Mr. Bell said they'd better save the rest, in case anything happened, they might need the evidence for court.

She peeped up again at her mother, "Who's that white man in there with Daddy?"

"One of Lawyer Belk's friends," she answered. "He's pastor of the church that's always on television Sunday morning. Mr. Belk seems to think that having him around will do some good." Ellie saw that her voice was shaking just like her hand as she reached for the last potato. Both of them could hear Tommy in the next room mumbling to himself. She was afraid to look at her mother.

Suddenly Ellie was aware that her mother's hands were trembling violently. "He's so little," she whispered and suddenly the knife slipped out of her hands and she was crying and breathing at the same time.

Ellie didn't know what to do but after a few seconds she cleared away the peelings and put the knives in the sink. "Why don't you lie down?" she suggested. "I'll clean up and get Tommy in bed." Without saying anything her mother rose and walked to her bedroom.

Ellie wiped off the table and draped the dishcloth over the sink. She stood back and looked at the rusting pipes powdered with a whitish film. One of these days they would have to paint the place. She tiptoed past her mother who looked as if she had fallen asleep from exhaustion.

"Tommy," she called softly, "come on and get ready for bed."

Tommy sitting in the middle of the floor did not answer. He was sitting the way she imagined he would be, crosslegged, pulling his ear lobe as he turned the ragged pages of *Uncle Wiggily at the Zoo*.

"What you doing, Tommy?" she said, squatting on the floor beside him. He smiled and pointed at the picture of the ducks.

"School starts tomorrow," she said, turning a page with him. "Don't you think it's time to go to bed?"

"Oh Ellie, do I have to go now?" She looked down at the serious brown eyes and the closely cropped hair. For a minute she wondered if he questioned having to go to bed now or to school tomorrow.

"Well," she said, "aren't you about through with the book?" He shook his head. "Come on," she pulled him up, "you're a sleepy head." Still he shook his head.

"When Helen and Teenie coming home?"

"Tomorrow after you come home from school they'll be here."

She lifted him from the floor, thinking how small he looked to be facing all those people tomorrow.

"Look," he said, breaking away from her hand and pointing to a blue shirt and pair of cotton twill pants, "Mama got them for me to wear to-morrow."

While she ran water in the tub, she heard him crawl on top of the bed. He was quiet and she knew he was untying his sneakers.

"Put your shoes out," she called through the door, "and maybe Daddy will polish them."

"Is Daddy still in there with those men? Mama made me be quiet so I wouldn't bother them."

He padded into the bathroom with bare feet and crawled into the water. As she scrubbed him they played Ask Me A Question, their own version of Twenty Questions. She had just dried him and was about to have him step into his pajamas when he asked: "Are they gonna get me tomorrow?"

"Who's going to get you?" She looked into his eyes and began rubbing him furiously with the towel.

"I don't know," he answered. "Somebody I guess."

"Nobody's going to get you," she said, "who wants a little boy who gets bubblegum in his hair anyway—but us?" He grinned but as she hugged him thought how much he looked like his father. They walked to the bed to say his prayers and while they were kneeling she heard the first drops of rain. By the time she covered him up and tucked the spread off the floor the rain had changed to a steady downpour.

When Tommy had gone to bed her mother got up again and began ironing clothes in the kitchen. Something, she said, to keep her thoughts busy. While her mother folded and sorted the clothes Ellie drew up a chair from the kitchen table. They sat in the kitchen for a while listening to the voices of the men in the next room. Her mother's quiet speech broke the stillness in the room.

"I'd rather," she said, making sweeping motions with the iron, "that you stayed home from work tomorrow and went with your father to take Tommy. I don't think I'll be up to those people."

Ellie nodded, "I don't mind," she said, tracing circles on the oilcloth covered table.

"Your father's going," her mother continued. "Belk and Reverend Davis are too. I think that white man in there will probably go."

"They may not need me," Ellie answered.

"Tommy will," her mother said, folding the last dish towel and storing it in the cabinet.

"Mama, I think he's scared," the girl turned toward the woman. "He was so quiet while I was washing him."

"I know," she answered, sitting down heavily. "He's been that way all day." Her brown wavy hair glowed in the dim lighting of the kitchen. "I told him he wasn't going to school with Jakie and Bob any more but I said he was going to meet some other children just as nice."

Ellie saw that her mother was twisting her wedding band around and around on her finger.

"I've already told Mrs. Ingraham that I wouldn't be able to come out tomorrow." Ellie paused, "She didn't say very much. She didn't even say anything about his pictures in the newspaper. Mr. Ingraham said we were getting right crazy but even he didn't say anything else."

She stopped to look at the clock sitting near the sink. "It's almost time for the cruise cars to begin," she said. Her mother followed Ellie's eyes to the sink. The policemen circling their block every twenty minutes was supposed to make them feel safe, but hearing the cars come so regularly and that light flashing through the shade above her bed only made her nervous.

She stopped talking to push a wrinkle out of the shiny red cloth, dragging her finger along the table edges. "How long before those men going to leave?" she asked her mother. Just as she spoke she heard one of the men say something about getting some sleep. "I didn't mean to run them away," she said, smiling. Her mother half-smiled too. They listened for the sound of motors and tires and waited for her father to shut the front door.

In a few seconds her father's head pushed through the curtain. "Want me to turn down your bed now, Ellie?" She felt uncomfortable staring up at him, the whole family looked drained of all energy.

"That's all right," she answered. "I'll sleep in Helen and Teenie's bed tonight."

"How's Tommy?" he asked looking toward the bedroom. He came in and sat down at the table with them.

They were silent before he spoke. "I keep wondering if we should send him." He lit a match and watched the flame disappear into the ashtray, then he looked into his wife's eyes. "There's no telling what these fool white folks will do."

Her mother reached over and patted his hand. "We're doing what we have to do, I guess," she said. "Sometimes though I wish the others weren't so much older than him."

"But it seems so unfair," Ellie broke in, "sending him there all by himself like that. Everybody keeps asking me why the MacAdams didn't apply for their children."

"Eloise." Her father's voice sounded curt. "We aren't answering for the MacAdams, we're trying to do what's right for your brother. He's not old enough to have his own say so. You and the others could decide for yourselves, but we're the ones that have to do for him."

She didn't say anything but watched him pull a handful of envelopes out of his pocket and tuck them in the cabinet drawer. She knew that if anyone had told him in August that Tommy would be the only one going to Jefferson Davis[1] they would not have let him go.

"Those the new ones?" she asked. "What they say?"

"Let's not talk about the letters," her father said. "Let's go to bed."

Outside they heard the rain become heavier. Since early evening she had become accustomed to the sound. Now it blended in with the rest of the noises that had accumulated in the back of her mind since the whole thing began.

As her mother folded the ironing board they heard the quiet wheels of the police car. Ellie noticed that the clock said twelve-ten and she wondered why they were early. Her mother pulled the iron cord from the

---

1. Born in Kentucky, reared in Mississippi, elected the first and only president of the Confederacy at a convention in Montgomery, Alabama, and inaugurated in Richmond, Virginia, Jefferson Davis (1808–89) had far-reaching ties to the South. His name appears on elementary, middle, and high schools all over the South.

switch and they stood silently waiting for the police car to turn around and pass the house again, as if the car's passing were a final blessing for the night.

Suddenly she was aware of a noise that sounded as if everything had broken loose in her head at once, a loudness that almost shook the foundation of the house. At the same time the lights went out and instinctively her father knocked them to the floor. They could hear the tinkling of glass near the front of the house and Tommy began screaming.

"Tommy, get down," her father yelled.

She hoped he would remember to roll under the bed the way they had practiced. She was aware of objects falling and breaking as she lay perfectly still. Her breath was coming in jerks and then there was a second noise, a smaller explosion but still drowning out Tommy's cries.

"Stay still," her father commanded. "I'm going to check on Tommy. They may throw another one."

She watched him crawl across the floor, pushing a broken flower vase and an iron skillet out of his way. All of the sounds, Tommy's crying, the breaking glass, everything was echoing in her ears. She felt as if they had been crouching on the floor for hours but when she heard the police car door slam, the luminous hands of the clock said only twelve-fifteen.

She heard other cars drive up and pairs of heavy feet trample on the porch. "You folks all right in there?"

She could visualize the hands pulling open the door, because she knew the voice. Sergeant Kearns had been responsible for patrolling the house during the past three weeks. She heard him click the light switch in the living room but the darkness remained intense.

Her father deposited Tommy in his wife's lap and went to what was left of the door. In the next fifteen minutes policemen were everywhere. While she rummaged around underneath the cabinet for a candle, her mother tried to hush up Tommy. His cheek was cut where he had scratched himself on the springs of the bed. Her mother motioned for her to dampen a cloth and put some petroleum jelly on it to keep him quiet. She tried to put him to bed again but he would not go, even when she promised to stay with him for the rest of the night. And so she sat in the kitchen rocking the little boy back and forth on her lap.

Ellie wandered around the kitchen but the light from the single candle put an eerie glow on the walls making her nervous. She began picking up pans, stepping over pieces of broken crockery and glassware. She did not want to go into the living room yet, but if she listened closely, snatches of the policemen's conversation came through the curtain.

She heard one man say that the bomb landed near the edge of the yard, that was why it had only gotten the front porch. She knew from their talk that the living room window was shattered completely. Suddenly Ellie sat down. The picture of the living room window kept flashing in her mind and a wave of feeling invaded her body making her shake as if she had lost all muscular control. She slept on the couch, right under that window.

She looked at her mother to see if she too had realized, but her mother was looking down at Tommy and trying to get him to close his eyes. Ellie stood up and crept toward the living room trying to prepare herself for what she would see. Even that minute of determination could not make her control the horror that she felt. There were jagged holes all along the front of the house and the sofa was covered with glass and paint. She started to pick up the picture that had toppled from the book shelf, then she just stepped over the broken frame.

Outside her father was talking and, curious to see who else was with him, she walked across the splinters to the yard. She could see pieces of the geranium pot and the red blossoms turned face down. There were no lights in the other houses on the street. Across from their house she could see forms standing in the door and shadows being pushed back and forth. "I guess the MacAdams are glad they just didn't get involved." No one heard her speak, and no one came over to see if they could help; she knew why and did not really blame them. They were afraid their house could be next.

Most of the policemen had gone now and only one car was left to flash the revolving red light in the rain. She heard the tall skinny man tell her father they would be parked outside for the rest of the night. As she watched the reflection of the police cars returning to the station, feeling sick on her stomach, she wondered now why they bothered.

Ellie went back inside the house and closed the curtain behind her. There was nothing anyone could do now, not even to the house. Everything was scattered all over the floor and poor Tommy still would not go to sleep. She wondered what would happen when the news spread through their section of town, and at once remembered the man in the grey Chevrolet. It would serve them right if her father's friends got one of them.

Ellie pulled up an overturned chair and sat down across from her mother who was crooning to Tommy. What Mr. Paul said was right, white people just couldn't be trusted. Her family had expected anything but even though they had practiced ducking, they didn't really expect anybody to try tearing down the house. But the funny thing was the house belonged to one of them. Maybe it was a good thing her family were just renters.

Exhausted, Ellie put her head down on the table. She didn't know what they were going to do about tomorrow, in the day time they didn't need electricity. She was too tired to think any more about Tommy, yet she could not go to sleep. So, she sat at the table trying to sit still, but every few minutes she would involuntarily twitch. She tried to steady her hands, all the time listening to her mother's sing-songy voice and waiting for her father to come back inside the house.

She didn't know how long she lay hunched against the kitchen table, but when she looked up, her wrists bore the imprints of her hair. She unfolded her arms gingerly, feeling the blood rush to her fingertips. Her father sat in the chair opposite her, staring at the vacant space between them. She heard her mother creep away from the table, taking Tommy to his room.

Ellie looked out the window. The darkness was turning to grey and the hurt feeling was disappearing. As she sat there she could begin to look at the kitchen matter-of-factly. Although the hands of the clock were just a little past five-thirty, she knew somebody was going to have to start clearing up and cook breakfast.

She stood and tipped across the kitchen to her parents' bedroom. "Mama," she whispered, standing near the door of Tommy's room. At the sound of her voice, Tommy made a funny throaty noise in his sleep. Her mother motioned for her to go out and be quiet. Ellie knew then that Tommy had just fallen asleep. She crept back to the kitchen and began picking up the dishes that could be salvaged, being careful not to go into the living room.

She walked around her father, leaving the broken glass underneath the kitchen table. "You want some coffee?" she asked.

He nodded silently, in strange contrast she thought to the water faucet that turned with a loud gurgling noise. While she let the water run to get hot she measured out the instant coffee in one of the plastic cups. Next door she could hear people moving around in the Williams' kitchen, but they too seemed much quieter than usual.

"You reckon everybody knows by now?" she asked, stirring the coffee and putting the saucer in front of him.

"Everybody will know by the time the city paper comes out," he said. "Somebody was here last night from the *Observer*. Guess it'll make front page."

She leaned against the cabinet for support watching him trace endless circles in the brown liquid with the spoon. "Sergeant Kearns says they'll have almost the whole force out there tomorrow," he said.

"Today," she whispered.

Her father looked at the clock and then turned his head.

"When's your mother coming back in here?" he asked, finally picking up the cup and drinking the coffee.

"Tommy's just off to sleep," she answered. "I guess she'll be in here when he's asleep for good."

She looked out the window of the back door at the row of tall hedges that had separated their neighborhood from the white people for as long as she remembered. While she stood there she heard her mother walk into the room. To her ears the steps seemed much slower than usual. She heard her mother stop in front of her father's chair.

"Jim," she said, sounding very timid, "what we going to do?" Yet as Ellie turned toward her she noticed her mother's face was strangely calm as she looked down on her husband.

Ellie continued standing by the door, listening to them talk. Nobody asked the question to which they all wanted an answer.

"I keep thinking," her father said finally, "that the policemen will be with him all day. They couldn't hurt him inside the school building without getting some of their own kind."

"But he'll be in there all by himself," her mother said softly. "A hundred policemen can't be a little boy's only friends."

She watched her father wrap his calloused hands, still splotched with machine oil, around the salt shaker on the table.

"I keep trying," he said to her, "to tell myself that somebody's got to be the first one and then I just think how quiet he's been all week."

Ellie listened to the quiet voices that seemed to be a room apart from her. In the back of her mind she could hear phrases of a hymn her grandmother used to sing, something about trouble, her being born for trouble.

"Jim, I cannot let my baby go." Her mother's words, although quiet, were carefully pronounced.

"Maybe," her father answered, "it's not in our hands. Reverend Davis and I were talking day before yesterday how God tested the Israelites, maybe he's just trying us."

"God expects you to take care of your own," his wife interrupted. Ellie sensed a trace of bitterness in her mother's voice.

"Tommy's not going to understand why he can't go to school," her father replied. "He's going to wonder why, and how are we going to tell him we're afraid of them?" Her father's hand clutched the coffee cup. "He's going to be fighting them the rest of his life. He's got to start sometime."

"But he's not on their level. Tommy's too little to go around hating people. One of the others, they're bigger, they understand about things."

Ellie still leaning against the door saw that the sun covered part of the sky behind the hedges, and the light slipping through the kitchen window seemed to reflect the shiny red of the table cloth.

"He's our child," she heard her mother say. "Whatever we do, we're going to be the cause." Her father had pushed the cup away from him and sat with his hands covering part of his face. Outside Ellie could hear a horn blowing.

"God knows we tried but I guess there's just no use." Her father's voice forced her attention back to the two people sitting in front of her. "Maybe when things come back to normal, we'll try again."

He covered his wife's chunky fingers with the palm of his hand and her mother seemed to be enveloped in silence. The three of them remained quiet, each involved in his own thoughts, but related, Ellie knew, to the same thing. She was the first to break the silence.

"Mama," she called after a long pause, "do you want me to start setting the table for breakfast?"

Her mother nodded.

Ellie turned the clock so she could see it from the sink while she washed the dishes that had been scattered over the floor.

"You going to wake up Tommy or you want me to?"

"No," her mother said, still holding her father's hand, "let him sleep. When you wash your face, you go up the street and call Hezekiah. Tell him to keep up with the children after school, I want to do something to this house before they come home."

She stopped talking and looked around the kitchen, finally turning to her husband. "He's probably kicked the spread off by now," she said. Ellie watched her father, who without saying anything walked toward the bedroom.

She watched her mother lift herself from the chair and automatically push in the stuffing underneath the cracked plastic cover. Her face looked set, as it always did when she was trying hard to keep her composure.

"He'll need something hot when he wakes up. Hand me the oatmeal," she commanded, reaching on top of the icebox for matches to light the kitchen stove.

JOAN WILLIAMS

Spring Is Now

Joan Williams (1928–2004) grew up in Memphis, Tennessee, but lived most of
her adult life in the Northeast. Her writing centered on the southern landscape,
especially Mississippi. She wrote five novels, one collection of short stories, a
number of uncollected stories, a teleplay, and some nonfiction. "Spring Is Now"
was first published in the *Virginia Quarterly Review* in the fall of 1968.

Sandra heard first in Miss Loma's store about the Negroes. She was buying cornstarch for her mother when Mr. Mal Walker rushed in, leaving his
car at the gas pump, without filling it, to tell the news. His hair plastered
to his forehead, he was as breathless and hot as if he had been running.
"The school bus was loaded and the driver passed up some niggers in
De Soto," he said. "They threw rocks at the bus and a brick that broke
the driver's arm." That was all he knew about that. "But," he said, pausing
until everyone in the store was paying attention. "There's some registered
for your high school in Indian Hill."

At that moment Sandra found the cornstarch. The thought of going
to school with Negroes leapt at her as confusedly as the box's yellow-and-
blue design. Coming slowly around the bread rack, she saw Mal Walker,
rapidly swallowing a Dr Pepper he had taken from the cold-drink case.
She put the cornstarch on the counter. Miss Loma fitted a sack over the
box and said, "Is that all?"

Sandra nodded and signed the credit pad Miss Loma shoved along
the counter. In Miss Loma's pierced ears, small gold hoops shook as, turning back to Mal Walker, she said, "How many?"

"Three I heard." Almost smiling, he looked around and announced—
as if the store were full of people, though there was only an apologetic-
looking country woman, with a dime, waiting for the party line to clear—
"If your kids haven't eat with niggers yet, they will have by Friday. I thank
the Lord I live in Indian Hill. Mine will walk home to lunch. When it
comes to eating with them, I draw the line."

"Sandra, you want something else?" Miss Loma said.

"No ma'am." Sandra went out and slowly up the hill toward her house opposite, thinking how many times she had eaten with Minnie, who worked for her mother, and how often her mother had eaten in the kitchen, while Minnie ironed. Even Grandmomma had said she would sit down with Minnie. Minnie was like one of the family, though Sandra could not remember that her grandmother ever had. For one reason, she was always in the living room looking at television. There now, she was shelling butter beans and Sandra passed behind her chair, saying nothing, because Grandmomma was hard of hearing. In the kitchen, Sandra put down the cornstarch and said, "Mother, Mister Mal Walker says there's Negroes coming to our high school."

"Are you sure?" Her mother, Flo, was frying chicken and stood suddenly motionless, a long-handled fork outstretched over the skillet full of popping meat and grease. She and Sandra had similar pale faces and placid gray-green eyes, which they widened now, in worry. "I guess we knew it was coming," Flo said.

"Three, he thinks."

In bifocals, Grandmomma's eyes looked enormous. She stood in the doorway saying, "Three what?" Having seen Flo motionless, she sensed something had happened and hearing what, she threw her hands to her throat and said, "Oh, you don't mean to tell me." With the fork, Flo stuck chicken pieces, lifting them onto paper toweling. "Now, Momma," she said, "we knew it was coming." Then Grandmomma, resigned to one more thing she had not expected to live to see, let her hands fall to her sides. "I sure do hate to hear it," she said. "Are they girls and boys?"

"I don't know," Sandra said.

"I just hope to goodness it's girls," Grandmomma said, looking at Flo, who said again, "Now, Momma."

At sundown, when her father came from the fields, Sandra was watching television with Grandmomma. The pickup stopped, a door slammed, but the motor continued to run. From the window she saw her father, a sturdy, graying man; he was talking to Willson, a field hand, who backed the truck from the drive as her father came inside. "Daddy," she said, "there's Negroes going to our school."

He stood a moment looking tired from more than work. Then he said, "I guess it had to happen." He frowned and his eyebrows drew together across his forehead. "The schools that don't take them don't get government money. I knew you'd be with them at the university. But I'm sorry you had to start a year earlier."

Grandmomma, looking up from her program, said, "I just hope they're girls."

"Oh, Grandmomma," Sandra said with irritation and followed her father across the hall. "Why'd Willson take the truck, Daddy?"

Having bent over the bathroom basin to wash, he lifted his head. "That boy of his sick in Memphis can come home tonight. I loaned him the truck to go get him," he said, and his splashed face seemed weighted by the drops of water falling away.

"The one that's had all that trouble with his leg swelling?" Flo said. She brought the platter of chicken to the table.

"He's on crutches but will be all right," the father said.

"I declare, that boy's had a time," Grandmomma said, joining them at the table. "When Willson brings the truck, give him some of my grape jelly to carry to the boy."

They bent their heads and Sandra's father said his usual long blessing. Afterward they looked at one another across the centerpiece of zinnias, as if words were left unsaid. But no one said anything and they began to eat. Then the father said, "Guess what happened? Willson and some of his friends asked if I'd run for road supervisor."

"Why, Tate," Flo said. "What'd you say?"

"I said, 'When would I find the time?' " he said.

"It shows the way they're thinking," Flo said.

"How?" Sandra said.

"They know they can't run one of them yet, but they want a man elected they choose," she said. "Still, Tate, it's a compliment."

"I guess it is," he said.

"The time's just going to come," Grandmomma said.

"Of course, it is," he said.

At six-fifteen the next morning, Sandra from her bed heard a repeated knock rattling the side door. There were the smells of coffee and sausage, and Flo, summoned, pushed her chair from the table to answer the door. Air-conditioning so early made the house too cold and Sandra, reaching for her thin blanket, kept her eyes closed.

"Morning, how're you?" It was Johnson, the Negro who cleaned the Methodist church. He had come to get his pay from Flo, the church's treasurer.

"Pretty good, Johnson, how're you?" Flo said.

"Good but not pretty." He and Flo laughed, then were quiet while she wrote the check. Sandra heard him walk off down the gravel drive and it seemed a long time before she fell back to sleep. Then Flo shook her, saying, "Louise wants to drive the car pool today. You have to be at school at ten to register. Hurry, it's after nine."

"Why'd Johnson come so early?" she said.

"Breakfast was the only time he knew he could catch me home," Flo said.

Drinking orange juice, Sandra stood by the refrigerator and Grand-momma called from the living room, "Are you going to school all winter with your hair streaming down your back like that? I wish you'd get it cut today."

"I don't want it cut," Sandra said.

"Well, I wish you'd wear it pretty like this girl on television then. Look, with it held back behind a band like that."

Sandra came into the living room to look. "Her hair's in a pageboy; it's shorter than mine," she said.

"At least comb it," her mother called from the kitchen.

"I combed it!" Sandra said.

"Well you need to comb it again," her mother said. "And eat something."

"I'm not hungry in the mornings," Sandra said and went out into the heat and down the steep driveway to wait for her friend Louise. There was no high school in their town and they went twenty miles away to a larger place. "Cold," Sandra said, getting in Louise's car.

"Turn that valve and the air conditioner won't blow straight on you," Louise said. She pushed back hair that fell, like a mane, over her glasses. "You heard?"

"About the Negroes?"

"Yes. I heard there were thirteen."

"Thirteen! I heard three."

Louise laughed. "Maybe there's none and everybody's excited about nothing."

There had been a drought all summer in northwest Mississippi. They rode looking out at cotton fields nowhere near bloom, corn limp and brown, and soybeans stunted, flat to the ground. Between the fields were stretches of crumbly dirt, enormous and empty, where crops failed from the drought had been plowed under. Nearby, a pickup raced along a gravel road and as far as they could see, dust trailed it, one cloud rising above the flatland. Once, workmen along the road turned to them faces yellowed by dust, with dark holes for eyes, and Sandra thought of the worry that had been on her father's face all summer, as farmers waited for rain. And all summer, wherever they went, her mother had said, "You don't remember what it was like before everybody had air-conditioned cars. All this dust blew in the windows. Whew! I don't know how we stood it."

And, not remembering she had said it before, Grandmomma would say, "You don't remember either what it was like trying to sleep. Sometimes we'd move our mattresses out into the yard and sleep under the trees. We'd wring out towels and put them on the bed wet to cool the sheets." That she had lived then, though she did not remember it, seemed strange to Sandra.

At school, she found out only that some Negroes had already registered. None were there and the teachers would answer no other questions. Standing in long lines all morning, Sandra found she watched for the Negroes anyway. Other students said they had done the same. She thought the Negroes had been paid more attention by being absent than if they had been present. On the way home, Louise said, "If it weren't such a mystery, I don't think I'd think much about them. If there's a few, I just feel I'm not going to bother them and they're not going to bother me, if they're not smart-alecky."

"I know," Sandra said. "What's the difference, three or thirteen, with the rest of us white?" They stopped on the highway at the Mug'n Cone for hot dogs and root beer. Nearing home, Sandra began to dread questions she would be asked, particularly since she knew little more than when she left. At Miss Loma's, she got out to buy shampoo. The old men were gathered on the store porch playing dominoes, and she said only, "Afternoon," though her mother always said they would be glad for conversation. She thought of when her grandfather had been among them and entered the store.

Miss Loma had already heard the news from the Indian Hill school. She and a Memphis salesman were talking about a family nearby, in the Delta, who passed as white, though people steered clear of them, believing they had Negro blood. "I'll tell you how you can always tell a Negro," the salesman said. "By the blue moons on their nails. They can't hide those."

"I've heard," Miss Loma said, her earrings shaking, "they have black streaks at the ends of their spinal cords. Now, that's what men who've been with them in the army say. Of course, I don't know if it's true. I doubt it." She and the salesman could not decide whether she ought to stock up on straight-lined or dotted-lined primary tablets. With a practical finger, Miss Loma twirled the wire school-supply rack. The salesman pushed back a sporty straw hat with a fishing-fly ornament and said, "Wait till school starts and see what the teacher wants. One thing I hate to see is, somebody stuck with primary tablets they can't sell."

An amber container decided Sandra on a shampoo. She brought the bottle to the counter. "I've heard," she said, "they wear makeup on TV that'll make them look whiter."

"Of course they do," Miss Loma said.

Also, Sandra had heard that Negroes never kissed one another. They made love without preliminaries, like animals, or did nothing. But she was afraid to offer that information. Sometimes, even her mother and father did not seem to know she knew people made love.

Miss Loma said, "Honey, take that shampoo on home as a present. Happy birthday."

"How'd you know it was my birthday?"

"A bird told me."

"Grandmomma," Sandra said.

"You heard about the little nigger baby up in Memphis that's two parts animal?" the salesman said.

"No!" Miss Loma said.

"It's got a little dear face and bare feet," the salesman said, and when Sandra went out, he and Miss Loma were laughing.

In his dusty, green pickup, Sandra's father drew up to the gas pump. Willson's wife, along with another Negro woman, stepped from the truck's cab and went into a grocery across the road. "I see you got your nigger women with you today, Tate," said one of the old men playing dominoes.

Lifting the hose, Sandra's father stood putting in gas, laughing. "Yeah, I carried them with me today," he said. "Sandra, I got to go on back to the field. There's a dressed chicken on the front seat Ida sent. Take it on to your Momma." Sandra opened the truck's door, thinking how many people made remarks about her father letting Negroes ride up front with him. He always answered that if somebody asked him for a ride, he gave it to them; why should they sit out in the open truck bed covered with dust and hit by gravel? She heard him call into the store, "Four-ninety for gas, Loma," and holding the chicken, Sandra waved as he drove off.

Ida's husband had been a field hand for Sandra's father and now was too old to work. Sandra's father let the old couple stay on, rent free, in the cabin on his land. Ida raised chickens and brought one to Flo whenever she killed them. When Flo went to the bakery in Indian Hill, she brought Ida something sweet. Sandra came into the kitchen now and put the chicken on the sink. "That's a nice plump one," Flo said. "If we hadn't had chicken last night, I'd put it on to cook. I hope your daddy let Ida know how much we appreciate it."

"He says he always thanks her," Sandra said.

"But I don't know whether he thanks her enough," her mother said.

The kitchen smelled of cake baking and Sandra pretended not to notice. "Aren't you going to ask about the Negroes at school?" she said.

"Honey, I couldn't wait for you to come wandering in. I called around till I found out."

"I don't see why they got to register at a special time. Why couldn't they register when we did?" Sandra said.

"I don't understand it myself," Flo said.

"I don't understand why they have to be there at all," Grandmomma said, on her way to the bathroom during a commercial. "I declare, I don't."

"Oh Grandmomma," Sandra said.

"I guess they didn't want to take chances on trouble during registration," Flo said. "If the Negroes are just there when school starts, no one can say anything."

"There's plenty of things folks could say if they just would," Grandmomma called.

"I thought she was hard of hearing," Sandra said.

"Not all of the time," Flo said. When Grandmomma came back through the kitchen, Flo said, "We haven't had anything to say about what's happened so far. Everything else has just been shoved down our throats, Mother. I don't know why you think we'd have a chance to say anything now." Sandra, going out and down the hall, wondered why her mother bothered trying to explain to Grandmomma. "What are you going to do?" Flo called.

"Wash my hair," Sandra said.

"Well, for heaven's sake, roll it up as tight as you can and try to keep it curled."

"I wish you'd put it behind a band like that girl on television," Grandmomma called, and Sandra closed the bathroom door.

The candles flickered, then burned, as Flo hesitated in the doorway, smiling, before bringing the decorated cake in to supper. The family sang "Happy Birthday" to Sandra. Her father rolled in a portable television atop brass legs and she jumped up with a squeal. Her hair, waved and tied with a ribbon to please them, loosened and fell toward her shoulders. Now she could see programs without arguing with Grandmomma.

Flo's face was in wrinkles, anxious, as though she feared Ida had not been thanked enough for a chicken, and Sandra knew she was to like her grandmomma's present more than ordinarily. On pink tissue paper, in a tiny box, lay a heavy gold pin twisted like rope into a circle. "Why, Grandmomma!" Sandra said in surprise. Her exclamation was taken for admiration and everyone looked pleased. When she had gone into Grandmomma's room as a small child, to poke among her things, she had been shown the pin. Grandmomma's only heirloom, it had been her own mother's. "I've been afraid I wouldn't live till you were sixteen," Grandmomma said. "But I wanted to give you the pin when you were old enough to appreciate it."

"She never would give it even to me," Flo said.

"No, it was to be for my first grandchild," Grandmomma said. "I decided that when Momma died and left it to me. It was all in the world she had to leave and it's all I've got. But I want you to enjoy it now, instead of when I'm gone."

Had she made enough fuss over the pin? Sandra asked later. Flo said she had, but to thank her grandmother occasionally again. "Mother, it's not really the kind of pin anyone wears," Sandra said. The pin hung limply, lopsided, on her striped turtleneck jersey.

Flo said, "It is kind of heavy and antique. Maybe you'll like it when you're grown. Wear it a few times anyway."

The morning that school started, Sandra hung the pin on her coat lapel and forgot it. She walked into her class and there sat a Negro boy. His simply sitting there was disappointing; she felt like a child who had waited so long for Christmas that when it came, it had to be a letdown. He was to be the only Negro in school. The others had changed their minds, the students heard. But by then everyone had heard so many rumors, no one knew what to believe. The Negro was tall and light-skinned. Louise said the officials always tried to send light-skinned ones first. He was noticeably quiet and the girls, at lunch, found he had spoken in none of his classes. Everyone wondered if he was smart enough to be in the school. From her table Sandra saw him eating by a window with several other boys. Still, he seemed alone and she felt sorry for him.

In the car pool with her and Louise were two boys, Don and Mark. Don, the younger, was an athlete. Going home that afternoon, he said the Negro was not the type for football but was so tall, maybe he would be good at basketball. Sandra thought how little she knew about the Negro and how many questions she would be asked. He had worn a blue shirt, she remembered, and he was thin. Certainly, he was clean. Grandmomma would ask that. She did not even know the Negro's name until Don said, "He lives off this road."

"Who?" she said.

"The colored boy, Jack Lawrence," he said.

"We could ask him to be in the car pool," Louise said, laughing.

Mark, sandy-haired and serious, said, "You all better watch your talk. I had my interview at the university this summer and ate lunch in the cafeteria. There were lots of Negroes and all kinds of people. Indians. Not with feathers, from India. Exchange students."

Dust drifted like clouds over fields, and kudzu vine, taking over the countryside, filling ditches and climbing trees, was yellowed by it. Young pines, set out along the road banks, shone beneath a sun that was strong, even going down. Sandra looked out at tiny pink flowers just appearing on the cotton and tried to imagine going as far away, to a place as strange, as India. That Indians had come all the way to Mississippi to school made her think about people's lives in a way she never had. She entered the house saying, before Grandmomma could ask questions, "Grandmomma, you know they got Indians from India going to Ole Miss?"

Grandmomma looked up through the lower half of her glasses. "You don't mean to tell me," she said, and it took away some of her curiosity about the Negro too. At supper, Sandra gave all the information she could. The Negro boy was clean, looked nice, and his name was Jack Lawrence. All the information she could give in the next month was that he went his way and she went hers. Finally even Grandmomma stopped asking questions about him. He and Sandra had no reason to speak until one morning, she was working the combination to her locker when a voice, quite deep, said, "Sandra, you left this under your desk."

Her dark hair fell forward. In the moment that she pushed it back, something in the voice's deep tone made her think unaccountably how soft her own hair felt. Jack Lawrence held out the book she had forgotten, his face expressionless. It would have been much more natural for him to smile. She saw for the first time how carefully impersonal he was. Other students had mentioned that he never spoke, even to teachers, unless spoken to first. She smiled and said, "Lord, math. I'm bad enough without losing the book too. Thanks."

"Okay. I just happened to notice you left it." He started down the hall and Sandra joined him, as she would have anyone going the way she was. She held her books against her, as if hugging herself in anticipation, but of what, she did not know. She had a curiously excited feeling to be walking beside anyone so tall. No, she thought, not anyone, a boy. They talked about the afternoon's football game, then Jack Lawrence continued down the hall and Sandra turned into her class. There was certainly nothing to that, she thought. But Louise, leaning from her desk, whispered, "What were you talking about?"

"Football," Sandra said, shrugging. She thought of all the Negroes she had talked to in her life, of those she talked to every day, and wondered why it was strange to talk to Jack Lawrence. Her mother complained that at every meal, Sandra's father had to leave the table, answer the door, and talk to some Negro who worked for him. They would stand together a long time, like any two men, her father propping his foot on the truck's bumper, smoking and talking. Now she wondered what they talked about.

Jack Lawrence's eyes, when she looked into them, had been brown. Were the eyes of all Negroes? From now on, she would notice. On her way to the stadium that afternoon, she wondered if her gaiety was over the football game or the possibility of seeing—not the Negro, she thought, but Jack Lawrence? Louise went ahead of her up the steps and turned into the bleachers. "I have to sit higher," Sandra said, "or I can't see," adding, "Lon's up there." Louise was crazy about Lon, the basketball coach's son, and rising obediently, she followed Sandra to a seat below him. Lon was sitting with Jack Lawrence. Looking up, Sandra smiled but Jack Lawrence turned his eyes to the game and his lips made no movement at all. When she stood to cheer, to buy a Coke, popcorn, a hot dog, Sandra wondered if he watched her. After the game, he and Lon leapt from the bleachers and went out a back way. That night, she slept with a sense of disappointment.

At school, she always nodded and spoke to him and he spoke back: but they did not walk together again. Most often, he was alone. Even to football games, he did not bring a friend. There was a Thanksgiving dance in the gym, festooned with balloons and crepe paper, but he did not come. On Wednesday before the holiday, driving the car pool, Sandra had seen Jack Lawrence walking along a stretch of country road, hunched into his coat. The motor throbbed loudly in the cold country stillness as she stopped the car and said, "You want a ride?"

He stood, looking as if he did not want any favors, but with eyes almost sore-looking from the cold, then climbed into the back seat with Don and Mark. The countryside's stillness came again as Sandra stopped at the side road he mentioned. With coat collar turned up, untangling long legs, he got out. She was aware of the way her hair hung, of her grandmother's pin too old and heavy for her coat, of the skirt that did not cover her knees, which Grandmomma said was indecent. And she was aware of him, standing in the road against the melancholy winter sunset, looking down to say, "Thank you."

"You're welcome," she said, looking up.

That night she asked her father whether she should have given Jack Lawrence a ride. Her father said she was not to give a ride to Negroes when she was alone. "Not even to women?" she said.

"Oh well, to women," he said.

"Not even to Willson?" she said.

Her father seemed to look inward to himself a long time, then he answered, "No, not even to Willson."

Thanksgiving gave Sandra an excuse to start a conversation. She saw Jack Lawrence in the hall the first day afterward and said, "Did you have a nice holiday?"

"Yes," he said. "Did you?"

Sandra mentioned, briefly, things she had done. "Listen," she said. "We go your way every day, if you'd like a ride."

"Thanks," he said, "but most of the time I have one." He turned to his locker and put away his books and Sandra, going on down the hall, had the strangest feeling that he knew something she did not. She remained friendly, smiling when she saw him, though he made no attempt to talk. He only nodded and smiled when they met and she thought he seemed hesitant about doing that. She asked the boys in the car pool questions about him. Why hadn't he gone out for basketball, how were his grades, what did he talk about at lunch, did anybody know exactly where he lived, besides down that side road?—until one day, Louise said, "Sandra, you talk about that Negro so much, I think you like him."

"Yes, I like him. I mean, I don't dislike him, do you? What reason would we have."

"No, I don't dislike him," Louise said. "He's not at all smart-alecky."

In winter when they came home from school, it was dark. Flo said, "If you didn't have those boys in your car pool, I'd drive you girls back and forth myself. I don't know what Don and Mark could do if anything happened, but I feel better they're there." Sandra's parents, everyone, lived in fear of something happening. South of them, in the Delta, there was demonstrating, and Negroes tried to integrate restaurants and movies in several larger towns. Friends of Sandra's mother began carrying tear gas and pistols in their pocketbooks. Repeatedly, at the dinner table, in Miss Loma's, Sandra heard grown-ups say, "It's going to get worse before it gets any better. We won't see the end of this in our lifetime." Grandmomma always added, "I just hate to think what Sandra and her children will live to see."

One day after Christmas vacation, those in the car pool again saw Jack Lawrence walking along the road. "Should we stop?" Louise said. She was driving, with Don beside her.

"Of course. Would you just drive past him?" Sandra said. She was sitting in the back seat with Mark, and when Jack Lawrence climbed into the car, she was sitting between them. They spoke of the cold, of the snow that had fallen after Christmas, the deepest they could ever remember, and of how you came across patches of it, still, in unexpected places. Side roads were full of frozen ruts. Jack Lawrence said he hated to think of the mud when a thaw came. There could be one at any time. That was the way their weather was. In the midst of winter, you could suddenly have a stretch of bright, warm, almost spring days. There was a silence and Jack Lawrence, looking down at Sandra, said, "Did you lose that pin you always wear?"

"Oh Lord," Sandra said, her hand going quickly, flat, against her lapel.

"Sandra, your Grandmomma's pin!" Louise said, looking into the rearview mirror.

"Maybe it fell off in the car," Mark said. The three in back put their hands down the cracks around the seat. Sandra felt in her pockets, shook out her skirt. They held their feet up and looked under them. Don, turning, said, "Look up under the front seat."

Bending forward at the same instant, Sandra and Jack Lawrence knocked their heads together sharply. "Ow!" Mark cried out for them, while tears came to Sandra's eyes. They clutched their heads. Their faces were close, and though Sandra saw yellow, dancing dots, she thought, Of course Negroes kiss each other when they make love. She and Jack Lawrence fell back against the seat laughing, and seemed to laugh for miles, until she clutched her stomach in pain.

"Didn't it hurt? How can you laugh so?" Louise said.

"I got a hard head," Jack Lawrence said.

When he stood again in the road thanking them, his eyes, glancing into the car, held no message for Sandra. Tomorrow, he said silently, by ignoring her, they would smile and nod. That they had been for a time two people laughing together was enough. As they rode on, Sandra held tightly the pin he had found, remembering how she had looked at it one moment lying in his dark hand, with the lighter palm, and the next moment, she had touched the hand lightly, taking the pin. Opening her purse, she dropped the pin inside.

"Is the clasp broken?" Mark said.

"No, I guess I didn't have it fastened good," she said.

"Aren't you going to wear it anymore?" Louise said, looking back.

"No," she said.

"What will your grandmomma say?" Louise said.

"Nothing I can worry about," Sandra said.

Sit-ins

On February 1, 1960, in Greensboro, North Carolina, Ezell Blair Jr., David Richmond, Joseph McNeil, and Franklin McCain, students at North Carolina A & T University, walked from their campus to the downtown Woolworth's. After purchasing some items from a cashier, they walked over to the lunch counter, sat down, and ordered coffee. They were refused service, but they sat quietly until closing time. They were not arrested; there was no trouble. The next day they returned. Within days hundreds of students were participating in the sit-in at Greensboro, and within weeks, students in cities all over the South had launched their own sit-ins.

Students would often make a small purchase of school items or hygiene products before sitting at the counter. When the waitress (Woolworth counters were staffed by women) would say to the student, "We don't serve coloreds here," the response from the student could then truthfully be, "You just did at another checkout, so why can't you serve me here?" It was a question, of course, that flummoxed most waitresses.

For months in Nashville and throughout the South, James Lawson, a seminary student at Vanderbilt, had been conducting workshops on nonviolence for students who were interested in sit-in participation at dimestore lunch counters. The workshops often included sessions where students practiced sitting at a counter while others in the group played the role of agitators. First these agitators would call the demonstrator disparaging names; then they would push or shove the demonstrator. Sometimes things might get out of hand: for example, someone might slip off the stool, or the pushing might become a bit forceful. The real challenge, though, was the difficulty of nonviolence—striking back was not an option. In Nashville, John Lewis and Diane Nash were two students who went to the workshops and became leaders in the movement. After the Nashville sit-ins, they would go on to participate in many other civil rights events. David Halberstam's *The Children* tells the story of those Nashville students who began their activism with sit-ins and how their involvement in the movement affected the rest of their lives.

In the spring of 1960 as the sit-ins spread across the South and in major chains throughout America, most notably Woolworth's, stores and cities handled the students variously. Some chose to post signs: Closed or No Trespassing. Some removed the stools so that no one could sit down. When mobs arrived in the stores, often police were not present. Thugs would hold lighted cigarettes to the skin of the students, push them off their stools, and once down, hit them. When police arrived, they would arrest the students rather than the instigators of the violence.

On Easter in 1960 a meeting was held on the campus of Shaw University in Raleigh, North Carolina, to organize student leaders from across the South. Ella Baker, long-time activist with the NAACP and the Southern Christian Leadership Conference (SCLC), was the convener. Leaders of SCLC had encouraged Baker to advocate that the students form a youth branch of the SCLC; instead, Baker encouraged the students to form their own group, and the Student Nonviolent Coordinating Committee (SNCC) was soon born. Organizers planned for about ninety students to participate in the Shaw meeting; more than three times that many appeared. The time was ripe for student action.

Students brought new life to the movement. Sit-ins, one kind or another, lasted throughout the following decade, continuing in most places until an agreement was reached that a lunch counter or other establishment would be integrated. In Greensboro, where it all began, the resolution took almost seven months. In the course of these events, many protestors went to jail, and this very act, heretofore a disgrace, became a badge of honor, even if at great cost. In court, the judge might well literally turn his back on the lawyer who advocated for the demonstrators. When James Lawson advised students to continue their protests, he was expelled from Vanderbilt. As the civil rights movement continued, students would engage in many other types of demonstrations as well, but sit-ins were the activities on which their nonviolent learning process began.

The first two stories in this chapter, "Beginning of Violence" (1985) and "The Welcome Table" (1996), are set in Nashville in 1960. The protagonist of the first is a female student at Vanderbilt who happens to be in Woolworth's on the day of the first sit-in. The white girl from Vanderbilt interviews the black girl from Fisk about the sit-in for the *Nashville Tennessean*. The sit-in becomes the medium through which both girls' lives are altered. In the second story, the male high school protagonist is taken by his father to participate in Lawson's nonviolent workshops. Participating in this exercise and trying to fit in with the popular students as the new boy at school converge to create a world for him where not knowing what to say where and to whom creates trouble that ripples out of his control.

The female characters of "Food That Pleases, Food to Take Home" (1995), set in Virginia, and "Doris Is Coming" (2003), set in Appalachia, operate in small towns without the support of organizations. They are solitary individuals who have relationships with their ministers that both frustrate them and challenge them. They are also tired—tired of the fear they feel when they go into a diner, tired of being told to take the food and leave with it, tired of not being recognized as individuals but as representatives of a darker race. In both stories, all three of the characters find out that life is much more complicated than a decision to participate in a sit-in.

"Direct Action" (1963) is a different kind of sit-in, this one in a restroom in a small town in Missouri. When an integrated group occupies the white restroom and chooses not to leave, a growing line outside the door demands access. The waiting whites are told to use the other restroom; they gasp at the thought of using a "colored" facility. The direct action of the college students becomes the impetus for more students to enter active engagement.

In each of the stories in this section, characters begin to see their own personal power to change their lives. Sit-ins are only the beginning.

JOANNE LEEDOM-ACKERMAN

The Beginning of Violence

Joanne Leedom-Ackerman (1948–) is a novelist, short-story writer, and journalist. A former reporter for the *Christian Science Monitor*, she has won awards for her nonfiction and has published stories and essays in numerous books and magazines. She serves on the boards of Human Rights Watch, the International Crisis Group, and the International Center for Journalists, and on the Chairman's Advisory Council of the United States Institute of Peace. "The Beginning of Violence" is in her 1985 collection, *No Marble Angels*.

Nashville, 1960

The wind shot through you that day like fate or some might say like the will of God. No matter what you did, it got you. It weaseled under the buttons of your coat, pulled off your scarf. You couldn't fight against it though you could stay indoors, but once you came out, you had to face the wind and find your way.

It was the day before Valentine's, and snow was falling in thick wet flakes, had been since early morning and threatened to keep on all afternoon. As I said, it was not a day to be outside, but I was. I was downtown on the arcade doing last minute shopping for a sorority party that night. We'd been decorating all morning, but we'd run out of crepe paper and balloons; and Janie, the food chairman, was afraid she'd run out of paper plates and cups so I said I'd go downtown and pick up everything.

I went to Woolworth's. At the Grand Ole Opry counter I bought a red plastic guitar set inside a big red plastic heart for the centerpiece on the officer's table. I was an officer. I was treasurer of the Kappa Alpha Thetas at Vanderbilt University.

I didn't feel like turning right around and going back into the cold so I stopped at the lunch counter for coffee and a grilled cheese sandwich. I was sitting there eating and reading "When Lilacs Last in the Door-Yard Bloom'd" for English class when a blast of air swept across my back. When

I turned to see who was holding the door open, I saw dozens of Negroes coming into the store. They moved straight down the aisles then disappeared among the cheap jewelry and face powders and school supplies.

I turned back around and finished my sandwich and Whitman's poem. I was about to pay and leave when three Negroes sat down at the counter, one of them next to me. They all held brown paper bags with purchases they'd made. The girl beside me smiled, showing a curve of white teeth and asking more than most people thought she had a right to ask. I looked over my shoulder and saw thirty or forty more Negroes lining up to sit at the counter.

It took me a minute to understand what was happening. I'd grown up in Arkansas and Tennessee, and in nineteen years I'd never eaten beside a Negro. I'd never sat next to one on a bus or gone to the same bathroom. Things were changing in the South, but these were facts I'd lived with. Once in high school in Little Rock I'd signed a petition favoring integration, and that had almost gotten me thrown out of cheerleading. Some people thought anyone for the Negro was a Communist. I wasn't a Communist; I just thought the Negro should have a chance. And yet even feeling that way, I wasn't prepared to have the order of things put to question right where I was sitting.

The girl kept smiling. She had a soft mouth and big, dark eyes. Her hair was straightened, and she wore it like mine, in a pageboy with bangs. She was taller than me, and under her coat she looked strong. When she saw my poetry book on the counter, she reached into her pocket and took out a copy of the same book. I couldn't help but feel she'd just drawn her gun. I glanced away. My eyes fell on her hands; they were the color of dry soil, large and muscular and deeply lined like an old woman's.

I glanced at her friend next to her, but her friend's eyes were flat and hard, and her mouth looked set to tell me her mind. It was this girl who got me moving again. I'd been about to pay and leave when they'd sat down. My purse was open on the counter, and I went on counting out the change. I closed my wallet and purse; I gathered my bags, stood and left. The act of leaving wasn't a decision so much as a resumption of the way I was already going.

Not till I was outside in the blowing snow, moving towards the bus did I think about what I'd done, not till I was getting on the bus did I hear the words of the waitress: "I'm sorry, we don't serve coloreds here." All the way back to Vanderbilt, and as I walked on campus through what by now was a small scale blizzard, I kept thinking about those words. At the party that night, dancing under the crepe paper streamers we'd draped from the ceiling to make a tent, I could still hear the words and see the face of the girl.

The next morning I read about what had happened at Woolworth's on page ten of the *Nashville Tennessean*. Without knowing it, I'd been in the middle of Nashville's first sit-in. I decided to write my own version of what I'd seen, and I turned it into the college paper. The paper ran the story under the headline: "At the Counter: A Student's View." The editor asked me to write on what happened next though no one knew what was going to happen next, but the editor thought something would. He told me I should stress the Vanderbilt angle. I wasn't sure what the Vanderbilt angle was, but that's the way I got involved. Before the year was over, I'd witnessed more than a dozen sit-ins.

The next time I saw the girl was two weeks later. In between the snow had kept falling, making it one of the worst winters in Nashville's history. During those days on the front pages of the *Tennessean*, Jack Parr[1] was battling NBC over his contract with the Tonight Show while in Washington Lyndon Johnson[2] battled for national civil rights legislation. A hundred miles away in Chattanooga fighting had broken out after sit-ins there. The Nashville sit-ins had stepped up but were still reported on the inside pages. So far no arrests had been made.

All week rumors had been going around that the largest sit-in ever would take place downtown Saturday. I decided to go. Jeff, my boyfriend, tried to argue me out of it then said he'd go with me, but he got sick after a fraternity party Friday night, and so I went by myself. No one at the sorority house could believe I would go, but I did.

When I got there, thousands of people were already on the arcade, and policemen lined the streets. Just after noon the first demonstrators

---

1. Jack Paar (1918–2004) is credited with creating the late-night television talk show. He was the host of *The Tonight Show* from 1957 until 1962.

2. Lyndon Johnson (1908–73) was vice president of the United States in 1960 when the sit-ins began. Not until after Kennedy was assassinated and Johnson moved into the presidency did he become an active advocate for civil rights legislation. He closed one of his speeches with "and we shall overcome," giving new energy to the movement.

showed up, including the girl. She was wearing the same oversized brown coat; on her head she wore a white crocheted cap. She walked with her head down, bowed against the wind. She didn't look at anyone. Most of the protesters were students, and they were glancing around at the crowds on the sidewalk. But she stared straight ahead. She was so focused that she didn't even answer her friend who spoke to her as they entered McClellan's Variety Store.

I followed them inside. The lunch area was packed with people standing about waiting to see what would happen. The girl made her way through the crowd to a seat at the counter. One by one other students took stools under the faded pictures of salisbury steak, Irish stew, hamburger deluxe. A railing separated the eating area from the rest of the store, and the press stood behind it among hair nets and hair rollers; I took my place with the press.

A waitress approached the girl. "I'm sorry; we don't serve coloreds here," she said. "You'll have to leave."

"A cup of coffee, please," the girl answered.

"I'm sorry, we don't serve coloreds," the waitress repeated.

"A cup of coffee."

Half a dozen white teenagers stepped into the area and started catcalling. They picked out a white demonstrator sitting near the girl. "Nigger lover! Nigger lover!" they taunted. A man with a cigar began blowing smoke into the face of the girl and the other students. Several more teenagers moved in, bumping against the protesters, trying to knock them off their stools.

The students didn't react. The girl pulled her poetry book from her pocket and opened it on the counter. She was starting to read when suddenly she let out a cry. I looked and saw a teenager squash his lighted cigarette on her back. I couldn't tell if he'd actually burned her or only ruined her coat. She jerked around. She stared straight at the boy. She met his jeer with a question which again asked more than people were willing to have asked of them. Her look must have shaken him or touched something in him because he stepped away. His friends started lighting their cigarettes and pressing them out on the backs of other students, but the boy left the store. The exchange took only a moment, but in it I saw some possibility, some viewpoint I hadn't considered before.

Before I could think about exactly what this was, however, someone shoved a white protester from his stool and began hitting him in the ribs. The man blowing cigar smoke laid a fist into the back of a black student. Other teenagers began pulling at the hair of the girls sitting at the counter. None of the demonstrators raised a hand to defend himself. I saw in the faces of many, anger and a struggle not to fight back. But in the face of the girl I saw something else.

The police finally arrived, but only after the teenagers had run away. They told the protesters they had to leave because the store management had decided to mop the floor. When they refused, the police moved in, taking hold of the students one by one and escorting them into police vans waiting outside. The girl was arrested.

I followed the rest of the day's events, including the beatings of several Negroes late in the afternoon at Woolworth's where no police were around. Members of the press, including me, watched as a white teenager pulled a Negro protester from a chair and hit him again and again in the face spreading open his nose with a fist, bloodying both their skins with the same blood and as another white pushed a Negro student down a flight of stairs, sending his arms and legs clattering against the metal. None of the experienced press stepped in to stop what was happening; instead they stood recording the incidents so I did the same. Yet inside I was trembling as if someone had hit me, and I wanted to strike back. I didn't know what to do with the violence I suddenly felt. I left the store.

I decided to meet the girl. I told the newspaper editor I wanted to write a profile of a demonstrator, and he agreed. I found out her name was Cynthia Davis. She was a senior at Fisk University. When I called her, she at first refused to be interviewed, said there were better people than herself, but I convinced her she was the one I wanted to talk to. She agreed to meet me at a diner near Fisk after classes Friday.

Fisk is only a few miles from Vanderbilt, but like most everyone else, I'd never been in the neighborhood let alone seen the campus. The streets around it were quiet and lined with trees and houses. The campus itself was much smaller than Vanderbilt's and more run-down. It had one main walkway. On both sides of the walk were dorms and classrooms. I decided to go in just to look. I stayed only long enough to walk to the end of the path and back again, but in that time the world closed in around me. I

was the only white person, at least the only one I saw, and I felt everyone
staring at me.

When I reached the end of the walk, I read the sign in front of a huge
Victorian Gothic building. I tried to concentrate on the fact that this was
the first building of the university, the first in the country built to edu-
cate Negroes, but the truth is I was thinking only about myself and the
color of my skin for all at once my skin seemed alive as if it were plugged
in and glowing and separate from me. For a minute I couldn't feel myself under it. To be suddenly separate from your body is scary. Everyone
thinks you're your body because that's what they see only you know you're
not. I've heard of people coming back after dying, saying they've watched
themselves from outside, watched everyone else watching their bodies
while they knew that wasn't them only they couldn't make themselves
heard. I don't want to go on too much, but that's what I felt: a separation I
couldn't make my way across. The space between me and my skin was like
the space between me and the Negroes, and in it was a kind of panic and
darkness I wanted to strike out against. For the first time I understood
why separation was the beginning of violence.

I hurried back to the car I'd borrowed. I locked the doors and sat for
a moment. Finally I started the engine and drove to the diner a few blocks
away.

It was five o'clock, and only a handful of students were at the counter
and in the booths. When I came in, they glanced up, and again I felt my
skin starting to glow. Behind the counter the waitress stared at me. She
had a thick ridge of brown hair and dull eyes. She was wiping the stained
formica with a rag which she tossed in the sink behind her without taking
her eyes off me.

At first I didn't see Cynthia in any of the tall wooden booths. From the
front of the restaurant I could see only the person sitting at the edge of
the booth facing forward. But then on the hook of the last booth I spotted
the rough brown coat. When I approached, I expected her to recognize
me as the girl she'd sat beside in Woolworth's, but instead I realized she
too saw me only as the singular white person in the diner.

She was studying at the table. She wore a grey knit sweater and a
white crocheted cap on her head. I'd never seen her without her coat.
She was much thinner than I expected. Her shoulders were narrow and

her neck quite slender. Again I noticed her hands; they seemed dispro-
portionately large now.

"Cynthia Davis?" I asked.

She nodded.

I sat down and moved towards the wall. Immediately I was hidden
from view of the other people. "Thank you for meeting with me." She
didn't answer. I glanced at her books on the table, and tried to think of
what to say. "Do you study here often?"

She nodded again, watching me without speaking. She didn't seem
hostile, only reserved. I'd wanted to meet her to find out where she came
from and how she'd arrived at this point in her life. Yet as she stared
at me without recognition, I realized I'd also come here to have her meet
me and approve of me, and her failure to recognize my imperative made
me falter.

I set right into the interview. I asked about her family. She was third in
a family of six children from Fayette County, Tennessee. Her father was
a preacher, a small plot farmer and owner of a modest dry goods store.
Her mother worked the farm and raised the children. Cynthia would be
the first of her family to graduate from college. At Fisk on a scholarship,
she was an A-student, an English major, and she hoped to go on to law
school next year.

She answered my questions without self-consciousness, and because
she was at ease with herself, I began to feel more at ease. When I'd run
through all the facts I wanted to know, I set my pad and pencil down.
Leaning forward on the table, I fixed my eyes on the translucent lobes
of her ears which supported the weight of heavy metal hoops. I stared at
these as I tried to form the question I had come to pose. Finally I asked,
"Why don't you fight back? The other day, when that boy burned you,
why did you just sit there?"

"He was bigger than me," she answered.

I frowned.

"What would it have proved?"

"That he can't get away with what he did."

She smiled. "But he can. We both know that. Fighting him wouldn't
have changed anything."

"How does getting beaten up or burned change anything?"

"It doesn't." She picked up a napkin from the table. She was quiet for a moment; then she asked, "You ever taken a hound dog hunting?" I smiled, surprised by the question. "When a hound dog gets a scent, he won't let go. He doesn't care if it's raining or it's getting dark or it's time to go home to bed. You can beat him; you can pull his collar till you choke him, but if he's got the scent, he'll do everything he can to take it to the end. Our movement's like that hound dog. We got the scent, and no one can beat it out of us or burn it out of us. The only thing they can do is show their own meanness."

She began folding the napkin in her broad hands. Her expression was serious, yet the corners of her mouth turned up, almost smiling, as though she were extending tolerance not only to me but to herself. "We used to think the white man controlled our lives," she said, "only since we can't control the white man, we thought we had no control. But it doesn't matter what white people say we are; it doesn't matter what unjust laws say we have to do. We know who we are. First and foremost we are God's children, and no one can turn us into hateful, beaten-down human beings; no one has that power. Power—that's the scent. It comes from treating a man right. Once you understand that, it will change your life. Jesus Christ showed us how. Mahatma Gandhi showed the people of India they could do the same thing."

As she spoke, her curious smile remained as if she understood the difficulty of her point of view. She spoke deliberately. She wasn't carried away by her words but reasoned through to her conclusions with a logic as careful as any lawyer's. "The righteousness of our cause will win over the hearts of good men and women and eventually change a whole system," she insisted. She glanced down at the napkin which she'd shredded into a small mound of confetti. She swept the paper into the palm of her hand and dumped it in the ashtray.

"From what I've observed," I offered cautiously, "your friends aren't as free of the hate and anger as you. Perhaps you understand more."

Her shoulders straightened against the back of the booth; her face roused. "Don't try to separate us," she warned. "You can't choose among us. What I understand, we all understand."

"I don't think that's true. Your friend next to you, both times I saw her, she was angry. She wanted to strike back; I saw it in her face. You didn't. I understand what I saw in her; I don't understand what I saw in you."

"I'm angry. Anyone not angry is asleep. But we have to struggle with our own weaknesses as well as with society's."

"But if your movement depends on society having a conscience and that conscience stirring . . . well, frankly, I doubt how many good-hearted men and women you're going to find."

"Then that doubt is your weakness, isn't it?" she offered.

I looked up. She stared at me with a calm, penetrating gaze which struck at that separation I'd felt on campus, first from myself then from others. I didn't answer. Instead I began asking about her friends, again setting her apart from them. Again she held to the group, answering only in the plural. She emphasized she was committed to the *Christian* ethic of nonviolence for only as one was able to yield himself to God's goodness was he able to express his own and see goodness in others. Yet as we talked now, I felt uneasy for she'd seen something in me which I hadn't seen, yet which, when named, I knew: a doubt, a smallness of belief, a smallness of heart. I had wanted her to know me, but now I resented what she'd chosen to know. I found myself wanting to expose something in her.

We talked almost an hour as the diner started to fill with students. One by one the booths around us sounded with chatter. Cynthia was leaning closer to me so we could hear each other, her head propped between her ashen palms, her sweater pushed up above rough elbows. Finally as the interview wound down, circling around questions I'd already asked, the quick light in her eyes resumed a quieter glow and her half smile drew back into the reserved lines of a stranger's.

I wrote my article for the paper the next week. It brought me immediate attention. I didn't exactly glorify Cynthia Davis, but I set her up as an example of a generation of blacks with expectations to achieve beyond their parents and with a commitment to American ideals of equality. In writing it, I forgot for the moment my own discomfort over what she'd seen in me, and I wrote in an inflated prose that would touch the sentimental strain in a white, liberal audience. I also told the story of a girl's ambitions which would offend those of a different persuasion. In the article I mentioned only that Cynthia's family lived in Fayette County.

The next week a reporter for the *Nashville Tennessean* called me to ask if the *Tennessean* could run my story as a side piece with a larger article they were doing on inter-college contact in the civil rights movement. The reporter was particularly interested in the fact that I'd gone over to Fisk to have the interview. I agreed. It would be my first paid article. Because the audience of the *Tennessean* was statewide, the editor wanted to know exactly where Cynthia's family lived, and so I gave him the town's name just outside of Memphis, and he printed it.

I thought of calling Cynthia and telling her about the story, but I didn't. I suppose I was afraid she'd object. I was also in the middle of mid-terms. I finally did call her Sunday, the day the article appeared. I phoned that afternoon, but she wasn't in. I left a message for her to call me back and then forgot about her. For the next few days friends and people I hardly knew stopped to talk about the story. They didn't talk so much about what it said as the fact I'd had it published in the *Tennessean*. Finally on Wednesday when I hadn't heard from Cynthia, I called again, and this time a friend of hers got on the phone.

"Cynthia's not here," she said. The friend's voice was strained, but matter-of-fact. "Her father's store was bombed Sunday night. Her brother's in the hospital. I don't know when she'll be back." Her friend didn't say anything about the article. I didn't know if she or Cynthia had even seen the article. I couldn't be sure the bombing was a result of the article.

I didn't see Cynthia Davis again. I phoned her several times, but she was never there. Then school got busy. I was starting to write freelance for the *Tennessean*, and I quit calling. At one of the sit-ins that spring I saw her friend, whom I recognized from that first day at Woolworth's, and I went over to her. She answered my questions formally. She told me Cynthia had taken a leave from Fisk to help at home and in the store until her brother got out of the hospital. She told me nobody knew how long that would be or how her brother would adjust for among his injuries, his right hand had been blown off.

The Nashville sit-ins kept on through the spring. There were more arrests, more beatings of Negroes, negotiations with white business and political leaders, a cessation of arrests and sit-ins during negotiations, an economic boycott of downtown stores, a bombing of a black lawyer's home.[3] But finally on May 10, less than three months after the first sit-in, an agreement was announced. Six downtown lunch counters would

3. Z. Alexander Looby's home was bombed on April 19, 1960. During the demonstrations Looby (1899–1972) was one of the attorneys who provided money and legal services for those college students who were arrested and jailed. The bombing of his home was the impetus for the first major protest walk of the movement— over four thousand people, walking silently, to the steps of city hall for a talk with Nashville mayor Ben West (1911–74), who served from 1951 to 1963.

open on an "unbiased basis." The victory was the first of many to follow in Nashville. In the annals of southern history in the early 1960s, the Nashville movement was considered a nonviolent success story. Cynthia Davis was not among the names who moved onto prominence out of that movement. To my knowledge, she never returned to Fisk.

I've thought about Cynthia Davis from time to time since then. Once the following fall on the way back to school, I drove through Memphis with the intention of going to see her, but I lost courage. To be honest, I didn't want an answer. If there was an answer. I didn't want to be told that what happened was my fault. In some ways I was sure it was; and yet in others, no matter what anyone said, I wouldn't accept the blame. I didn't know what to do with it, and I didn't see how having it helped anyone.

I changed because of what happened in small, slow ways. By the spring of my junior year, I'd dropped out of my sorority. I became wary of my own ambition. I began to regard it as a subtle, unpredictable beast which, if I was not alert, would bite with sharp teeth.

When I think about what happened now, I account it to the wind. To what happens because of all that's happened before for reasons you don't understand because you're in the middle of them and because you don't understand yourself. I don't account it to fate or the will of God or any other cosmic design. I account it to my ignorance of design. And as I said, to the wind. I let the flow take me with it because I hadn't learned to face the wind, to pick up the scent but not be blown about. Because I didn't heed dark, unexposed places in myself, I fell inside one of them and perhaps took another with me.

LEE MARTIN

The Welcome Table

A product of rural Illinois, Lee Martin (1955–), professor of English at Ohio State University, has also taught at James Madison University and the University of North Texas. He is a novelist, short-story writer, and memoirist. His work has been nominated for both a Pulitzer and a National Book Award. "The Welcome Table" is in his 1996 collection, *The Least You Need to Know*, the recipient of the Mary McCarthy Prize in Short Fiction.

Three nights a week, when I was seventeen, my father took me downtown and made me shout "monkey," and "nigger," and "coon." He made me shout these things, he said, because he loved me. "Put your heart into it," he told me whenever my voice would falter. "Go on. Get with it. Give it everything you've got."

It was 1960, a touch-and-go time in Nashville. An activist named James Lawson[1] was organizing students from the black colleges, and because my father sold greeting cards to black-owned variety stores, he had gotten word of the lunch counter sit-ins that were about to get underway. He had decided to hook up with the integration movement because he couldn't resist the drama of it. "This is history," he said to me one night. "The world is going to change, Ed, and someday you'll be able to say you were part of it."

He had volunteered my services as well because he knew I was at an age when it would be difficult for me to stand up for right, and he wanted me to get a head start on being a man of conscience and principle.

Our job was to prepare the students for the abuse they were sure to get. So, on those nights, in classrooms at Fisk University, we stood over

1. During the fall of 1959, James Lawson (1928–), a divinity student at Vanderbilt, taught both black and white students how to organize sit-ins and other forms of direct action that would force America to confront the immorality of segregation. Later, he was a leader in the Freedom Rides of 1961. A student of Gandhi's nonviolent tactics, he saw the struggle in terms of his Christian faith.

the young men and women, and did our best to make their lives sad. My father was a handsome man with wavy hair and long, black eyelashes. He had a friendly smile and a winning way about him, but when he started his taunting, his face would go hard with loathing.

"Get the niggers," he would shout. "Let's get these monkeys out of here."

At his urging, I would join in. "Nigger," I would say, and my jaw and lips would tighten with the word.

We would pick at the students' hair. We would shove at them and pull them down to the floor.

When the workshop leader would call our demonstration to a halt, we would help the students up, and brush off their clothes, and laugh a bit, just to remind them that we were playacting. But always there would be heat in their eyes, because, of course, it was all different for them.

One of the students was a young man named Lester Bates. He had a reddish tint to his hair, and his hands were broad and long-fingered. One night, during a break, he clamped his hand around my wrist. I was holding a bottle of Coca-Cola, and he said to me, "Don't drop it. Hold on, boy. Keep a grip."

I could feel my hand going numb, my fingers tingling, and just when I was about to drop the bottle, Lester grabbed it. "This is going to get ugly," he said. "You know that, don't you? This whole town is going to explode." He took a drink from the bottle and handed it back to me. "Days like this make a body wonder what kind of stuff a man is made of."

He stood there, watching, and I did the only thing I could. I raised the bottle to my lips, and I drank.

I wanted to feel good about what we were doing—my father and I—but I hated him for bringing me into those classrooms. I hated him because he made my life uncomfortable. Some nights, on the way home, he would imagine a car was trailing us, and he would pull to the side of the street just to make sure we were safe. "There are limits," he said to me once, and he said it in a way that made it clear that he was one who knew those limits, and I was one who did not.

My father was Richard Thibodeaux, but it wasn't his real name. The previous spring, he had fled a scandal in New Hampshire. He had managed a cemetery there, and in the harsh winters, when the ground was so frozen graves were impossible to dig, the corpses were preserved in charnel houses until the spring thaw. Then, sometime in April, assembly-line burials began: the air shook with the raucous sound of heavy machinery digging the plots, the cranes hoisting concrete liner vaults from flatbed trucks. Sometimes, in the rush, the wrong bodies were put into the wrong graves, a fact that came out when one of the grave diggers spilled the news.

After that, we didn't stand a chance. It was a small town, and the rumors were vicious. We were cannibals, devil worshippers; we all had sex with corpses.

"How can we live here now?" my mother said one night to my father. "You've ruined us."

So we came south to Nashville. My mother, who had been there once to the Grand Ole Opry, chose it for its friendliness.

"Anywhere," said my father, "away from this snow and ice."

Any city, he must have been thinking, large enough to forget its dead.

Our first morning there, we left my mother in the motor court cabin we had rented, and went looking for a cemetery. "That mess in New Hampshire," my father said. "Let's put it behind us."

Nashville was brilliant with sunshine. My father put the top down on our Ford Fairlane 500, a '57 Skyliner with a retractable hardtop, and we drove past antebellum estates with guitarshaped swimming pools and manicured lawns landscaped with azalea bushes and dogwood trees. My father whistled a Frank Sinatra tune—"Young at Heart"—and for the first time since we had left New Hampshire, I believed in what we were doing.

"Don't think I'm a wicked person," my father said.

"I don't," I told him.

"People make mistakes, Ed." He lifted a hand and rubbed his eyes. "This must seem like a dream to you."

"It's something interesting," I said. "Something I might read about."

"That's you." He slapped me on the leg. "Steady Eddie. Just like your mother."

My mother was at a time in her life when her looks were leaving her, but instead of complaining, she had developed a habit of surrounding herself with beautiful things. In New Hampshire, she had learned how to do eggshell art. She would take an egg and poke a hole in each end with a pin she had saved from an old corsage. Then she would insert the pin and break the yolk, hold the egg to her mouth, and blow out the insides. She would soak each eggshell in bleach, dry it, and then spray it with clear acrylic paint.

The paint strengthened the shell, and my mother could then use cuticle scissors to cut away a section: an oval, or heart-shaped, or teardrop opening into the hollow egg. Inside the shells, she painted background scenery, and then with plaster of paris, she built platforms on which she could position miniature figures, some of them only a quarter of an inch tall, to create scenes she would then name: "Chateau against Snow-Covered Mountains," "Collie Waiting by Stone Wall," "Skier Sliding down Icy Slope." It was a precise and painstaking art, each motion calculated and sure. The shells were surprisingly strong, and she rarely broke one. If one did happen to shatter, she would throw it away and start again. "Why curse your mistakes?" she said to me once. "Why not look at them as new opportunities?"

My father had come to Nashville, hoping for a new start at life, and that day in the cemetery, beneath the boughs of a cedar tree, he found what he was looking for: the headstone of a child who had died at the age of two in 1920, the year of my father's birth.

"That's going to be my name now," he said. "Richard Thibodeaux. It's a good southern name, don't you think?"

"What about your old name?" I asked him. "What about my name?"

He said he would go to the County Clerk's office and get a copy of Richard Thibodeaux's birth certificate. Then he would pay a visit to the Social Security Administration and apply for a card under his new name. If anyone got curious about why, at his age, he was just then getting around to applying for a card, he would tell them his parents had been Baptist missionaries, that he had been born in Tennessee, but had gone with his parents to South America where he had spent nearly all his adult life carrying out their work.

"What about me?" I said. "What's my story?"

My father put his finger to his lips and thought a moment. "That's a snap," he finally said. "I met your mother, the fair and pious daughter of a coffee plantation owner, an American from New Orleans, married her, and nine months later, you were born. You were a delicate child, given to fevers and ailments of the lungs. Finally, we had no choice but to send you back to America, away from the tropics, to live with your aunt in Memphis." He put his arms around me and pressed me to him. "And now here we are, united again. You see how easy it is? I'll tell anyone who gets nosy we're starting a new life."

And that's what he did. Once he had the birth certificate and the social security card, the rest was a breeze. We rented a modest home, and my father became Richard Thibodeaux, region five sales representative for the Glorious Days Greeting Card Company. He finagled some school forms from a print shop he knew and concocted a set of records for me. He gave me a near-perfect attendance record at Memphis East High School, excellent marks in citizenship, better grades than I had ever been able to manage.

"There," he said. "Now, you're set. A completely new profile. *Alacazam*."

He wanted to make sure no one ever linked our name with what he had begun to call "that misery in New Hampshire."

"I lost my self-respect there," he said to me. "That's the worst thing that can happen to a man."

My mother's eyes sparkled when she learned our new last name. "Penny Thibodeaux," she said, and I knew, like me, she had fallen in love with the elegant sound of those three syllables.

In school, when teachers called me by my full name—*Edward Thibodeaux*—I answered "yes, sir," or "yes, ma'am." I developed a soft-spoken gentility and impeccable manners. The change of climate, my father said, had done us a world of good.

It was a sweet time for us there in Nashville. Saturday evenings, we drove downtown to the Ryman Auditorium and took in the Opry. My father's favorite singer was Hawkshaw Hawkins. He was tall and lean, and he wore his cowboy hat cocked back on his head. My mother preferred Jan Howard because she was graceful and had a sweet smile. After the show, we would cruise down Broadway, the top down on our Skyliner. We would drive by the music and record shops, and sometimes my mother would slide over next to my father, and I would lay my head back and close my eyes and let the night air rush over my face and give thanks for Nashville and the second chance we had hit upon there.

"The Athens of the South," my father said once. "Milk and honey. Folks here know style when they see it."

Each day at noon, whenever he was on his route, he would find a public rest room where he could change his shirt.

"You can tell a man by his clothes," he explained to me. "A tidy man lives a tidy life."

He wore suspenders, and linen suits, and wingtip shoes he polished and buffed each night before going to bed. He had monogrammed handkerchiefs and ties. He carried a new leather briefcase full of sample cards, and when he swept into stationery shops and drugstores, he doffed his Panama hat, and said to the ladies behind the counters, "It's a glorious day for Glorious Days."

The Glorious Days Greeting Card Company specialized in sensitivity cards: genteel messages to commemorate birthdays, anniversaries, weddings. Selling them, my father said, made him feel he was contributing to the general celebration of living. He had been occupied too long with the burying of the dead, with mourning and grief.

"A gloomy Gus is a grumpy Gus," he said one day. "But that's all behind me now. Nothing but blue skies. Isn't that right, Ed? Hey, from here on, we're walking the sunny side of the street."

I know my father didn't mean to make trouble for me, but of course, that was the way it all worked out. Some boys at school had seen the two of us going through the gates at Fisk University, and before long, the word was out that I was a "nigger lover."

One day, a boy named Dale Mink said a group was going downtown to stir up a ruckus. He was the center on our basketball team and an honor student. He had already won a scholarship to Vanderbilt. Even now, I don't think he was a thug; he was just caught up in the ugliness of those days. The way of life he had always known was changing, and he was afraid. "Those nigras think they can get away with this," he said to me. "You're either with us, or you're not."

The lunch counter sit-ins had been going on for over a week. Downtown, at Kress's, McClellans, Woolworth's, Walgreens, black students were occupying stools even though the ten-cent stores had chosen to close their counters rather than serve them.

My father came and went through these stores, selling Glorious Days greeting cards. Each evening, at dinner, he told us how the students sat there, studying for their classes. They were remarkable, he said—"as sober as judges"—the young men in dark suits with thin lapels and white shirts as bright as judgment day, the girls poised, as they unwound their head scarves and folded their duffle coats over the backs of their stools.

Sometimes, my father said, a waitress would call him back to the kitchen and set him up with a hamburger and a Coca-Cola, on account of she knew him as a man on the road who needed a hot lunch.

"You actually do that?" my mother said one night. "You sit there and eat while those poor kids do without?"

In those days, my father had a smugness about the new life he was inventing for us. He was so sure of the right direction we were taking, he had convinced himself that we deserved special liberties.

"I never thought," he told my mother. "Call me an idiot. Lord alive."

My mother was, by nature, a cheerful woman, and once we had left New Hampshire, she did her best to believe her life had been handed back to her. She worked part-time in an arts and crafts shop, and afternoons, when I came home from school, she asked me to help her with her eggshells. She sensed, better than my father, how brutal these times would become—how they would ruin people—and she was determined to maintain a certain beauty and delicacy in my life. She showed me how to transform a quail egg into a basket by cutting out the handle and adorning it with pearls and velvet ribbons. Together, we made eggs into cradles and lined them with lace.

This all seemed to me a terribly womanly thing to do, but slowly her optimism won me. When I watched her paint background scenes on the eggshells—amazed at how a few strokes could create trees, clouds, blades of grass—I fell in love with the way vast landscapes yielded to her slightest effort. When I was with her, I believed she could shrink anything that was difficult or immeasurable.

"Proportion," she told me. "That's the key. Making things fit."

Finally, she let me paint scenes of my own, and when I did, my fingers tingled with the delicacy of their motions. In New Hampshire, I had fallen into some trouble—vandalism, truancy, petty thievery—and I convinced myself that each gentle stroke I made was saving me from a life of violence and mayhem.

I rode downtown that day with Dale Mink. In Kress's, a gang of boys from the high school were prowling behind the students at the lunch counter. The boys' shirt collars were turned up, and their heel taps were clacking over the tile floor. Somewhere in the store, a radio was playing WSM. Later, I would learn that the station's call letters came from its original owner, The National Life and Accident Insurance Company, whose motto was "We Shield Millions." But I didn't know that then. I only knew I was in a place I didn't want to be. I was there because things were getting hot for me at school—"nigger lover"—and like most people, I wanted my life to be easy and sweet.

The radio went off, and one of the boys stepped forward, closer to the students, and said in a low, steady voice, "Get your coon asses off those stools."

The students refused to turn their heads or let their shoulders slump with shame. I noticed, then, that one of the students was Lester Bates. He closed the book he had been reading and put his hands on the edge of the counter. The girl next to him turned her head just a fraction of an inch, and I could see her lips move. "This is it," she said.

The high school boys were squawking now: *nigger* this and *nigger* that. Some of them were jostling the students. Dale Mink elbowed me in the side. I knew he was waiting for me to join in the jeering. If there is one thing I would want people to understand, all these years later, it would be this: I didn't want to be Dale Mink, only something like him.

So I shouted, "Nigger."

I had done it hundreds of times with my father at training sessions.

"Nigger," I shouted, and I convinced myself it was only a word, that I was only one voice swallowed up by the voice of the mob.

But then the gang surged forward, and I saw Dale Mink latch onto Lester Bates. Dale jerked him backward, onto the floor, and soon I heard the dull thuds of punches and kicks finding cheekbones and ribs.

I'm ashamed to think now of the fear I helped cause Lester Bates and those other young men and women. I have never been able to watch news films from those days, and until now, I have kept my part in them a secret.

When I got home that afternoon, my mother was waiting for me so we could finish an eggshell we had been working on that week. It was a dining room scene. We had lined the inside of the shell with wallpaper, and had built a table and four chairs from balsa wood. We had upholstered the chair seats with velvet ribbons and made a tablecloth from lace. My mother had brought home three miniature figures from the arts and crafts store: a man, a woman, and a young boy.

"Here's your father and me," she said. She put the miniature man and woman into adjacent chairs. Then she handed the miniature boy to me. "And here's you. Go on, Ed. Have a seat."

I didn't know where to put the boy who was supposed to be me. After the scene at Kress's, I didn't know where I belonged. I closed my hand around the figurine and felt it press into my palm.

"There was a fight at Kress's today," I said. "At the lunch counter. A bunch of boys from school went down there, and I went along. I said some things, and now I wish I hadn't."

My mother put her hand over my fist. "Don't let yourself get caught up in this," she said. "Listen to me. People have to live their lives the best they can. We've had too much trouble as it is."

"I can't forget it," I said. "How do you forget something terrible you've done?"

"You do whatever you have to do to get beyond it." My mother opened my fist and took the figurine and sat it in the chair whose back was turned to us. "There," she said. "It's cozy, isn't it? Inviting. Let's call this one, 'The Welcome Table.'"

"There's nothing on the table," I said. "We're not doing anything."

My mother thought a moment. "We're waiting."

"For what?"

"Who knows?" She snapped her fingers. "Hey, Buster Brown, get out of your shoe. The sky's the limit. For whatever's going to happen next."

Because my mother worked at the arts and crafts store, she had made some friends. One of them was a woman named Dix Gleason, and sometimes in the afternoons she would drop by for a visit. My mother was thrilled and worried on these occasions, happy for the company, but afraid her hospitality would fall short of Dix's approval. "You'd think she'd give a party notice," she said the first time Dix's car pulled up to our curb. "Heaven's sake. What do I have in the kitchen? Mercy, let's see. What can I whip up to suit Miss Dix?"

Dix Gleason was a loud woman who left lipstick stains on my mother's drinking glasses. She called me *Eddie* in a whiny voice like Topo Gigio, the mouse puppet on *The Ed Sullivan Show*, and she called my mother *Henny Penny*, a nickname I knew my mother despised.

"Like I was some hysterical old dame," she said to me once. "Honestly. The idea."

Some afternoons, Dix brought her husband, The Commodore.

Commodore Gleason was an accident reconstruction specialist for the highway patrol. He was intimate with the facts of crash and disaster. At accident scenes, he measured skid marks, gauged road conditions, interviewed survivors. He calculated the speed of travel, the angle of impact, reconstituted the moment of poor judgment or unfortunate circumstance.

"I can raise the dead," he boasted to us once after he had testified at a coroner's inquest. "I can bring them back to that moment where everything is A-okay. They're driving a Chevrolet down Route 45, just before eight p.m. The road is dry, visibility is fifteen miles, their speed is fifty-eight miles per hour."

If he could only leave them there, he said, happy and safe in their ignorance. But he knew too much. He knew that thirty miles up the road a Pontiac was streaking their way, that they would meet head-on at the top of a hill just before sunset.

"It's a burden to know as much as I do," he told us. "Take it from me: men are fools more often than not."

I was afraid of The Commodore. He had a way of making me feel nothing in my life would ever be safe.

Once, he came to my school and showed a blood-and-gore film about highway safety and traffic fatalities. He was snappy and regulation in his uniform: necktie firmly knotted, collar tips pointed, badge gleaming, trousers pressed, belt buckle polished. He told us about head-on crashes, decapitations, body bags.

"I know what you're thinking," he said. "You're thinking, this can't happen to me. That's what we all think. That's why we have to prepare ourselves for every hazard. Even you cool cats. Hell, you think you'll live forever."

One afternoon, my mother had sent me to the store for ice cream, and The Commodore had insisted we take his car. "You drive, sport," he said to me.

Before I could start the car, he jerked the keys from the ignition.

"Imagine the moment, Edward." He shook the keys in his hand as if they were dice. "That instant of horror when you know you're losing control. Your speed is too high, the road is too slick, the curve is too sharp. You're at that place you never dreamed you'd be. Brink of disaster, pal. One wrong move, and you cross over. Too late to get yourself back to safe ground. What do you do?"

"Don't panic," I said.

"And?"

"React."

He tossed me the keys. "Okay, Speedy Alkaseltzer. Let's see if you've got any pizz."

The afternoon my mother and I finished "The Welcome Table," our doorbell rang.

"Ding-dong," Dix Gleason shouted. "It's Dix and The Commodore."

The Commodore was off-duty. He was wearing a salt-and-pepper sports coat and a bolo tie with a silver horseshoe clasp. His black hair was shiny with tonic.

"Sport," he said to me. "I'd say you've been in some trouble."

"Trouble?" my mother said. "There's been no trouble here."

The Commodore pointed to my shirt pocket where a corner had been torn away in the melee at Kress's. "I don't imagine your mama sent you to school with your pocket like that. And that lip of yours. Looks a little fat to me. Like it got in the way of someone's fist."

"You might as well come clean," Dix said. She was wearing a lavender cowgirl dress with golden fringe along the bottom of the skirt. "You can't put anything past The Commodore."

A stray punch had clobbered me at Kress's, but I didn't want to admit any of this to The Commodore. Luckily, my mother came to my rescue. "Just a scuffle," she said. "You know boys."

"Tempers are on the boil," The Commodore said. "What with the nigras all up in the air. I hear there's been some nasty business downtown today."

My mother was always on edge whenever The Commodore was around, but on this afternoon, she looked close to coming apart. She bustled about, pulling out chairs for Dix and The Commodore at our dining table, going on and on about the eggshell we had just finished and what a funny thing it was that it was a miniature scene of people sitting around a dining table, and here we were sitting around a regular-sized table.

"Like a box inside a box," she said. "Or those hand-painted Russian dolls. Oh, you know the ones I mean. Take off the top half and there's a smaller doll inside. Five or six of them like that all the way down to the tiniest one—no bigger than the first joint of your pinky finger, Dix—and the funny thing is, even though the last one is so much smaller than the first one, their features are exactly the same."

The Commodore picked up "The Welcome Table" eggshell from its ornate stand, and held it with his thick fingers. "I bet there'd be something different," he said. "Something small, practically impossible to pick out. I bet I'd find it."

"Be careful with that," Dix said, and she said it with a hardness to her voice like a woman who had lived too long with a reckless man. "You bust that and Henny Penny might lose her head."

"It must take a world of patience." The Commodore set the eggshell back on its stand. "I'd say you'd have to have a ton of love to pay such close attention to things."

My mother ran her hand over our tablecloth. "Why, thank you, Commodore." A blush came into her face as if she were a young girl, unaccustomed to compliments. "That means a great deal, coming from someone with your keen eye."

It had been some time since my mother had been able to enjoy friends. In New Hampshire, when the truth of my father's mismanagement became public, she closed our blinds and refused to answer the telephone or the doorbell. Now, despite Dix's forwardness and The Commodore's suspicious nature, she was thankful for Nashville and the chance it had given her to be gracious and hospitable. When she came from our kitchen that afternoon, the serving tray held before her, the dessert cups filled with sherbet, the coffee cups chiming against their saucers, she might as well have been offering her soul to The Commodore and Dix, so desperate she was to have people admire her.

The Commodore had gone out on the porch to smoke a cigarette.

"Run, get The Commodore," my mother told me. "Tell him his sherbet's going to melt."

He was sitting on our porch glider, a cigarette hanging from his lip.

He was reading a Glorious Days greeting card my father had left there. "Listen to this, Edward. 'May your special day be filled with sunshine and love.' Now that is a beautiful sentiment." He folded the card and tapped its spine against his leg. "Your daddy's not like me, is he?"

"No, sir. I suppose he's not."

"What you have to decide," he told me, "is whether that's a good thing."

I wanted my father to be noble and full of goodness. "He's been helping the Negroes organize the lunch counter demonstrations," I said.

The Commodore took a long drag on his cigarette. "How about you? What do you make of that?"

I touched my finger to my sore lip. "It's caused me some grief."

"Understand, I don't have anything against the nigras." He flipped his cigarette butt out into our yard. "But people here are set in their ways. I'm only telling you this for your own good. Whatever happens with this integration mess, your daddy has to live here."

When The Commodore said that, something lurched and gave inside me. The life we had invented for ourselves cracked and began to come apart. For the first time, I could see the raw truth of my family: we were cowards. If things didn't work out for us here, as they hadn't in New Hampshire, we could go somewhere else. We could choose a new name. We could do it as many times as we needed to—move away from ourselves, like opening one of those Russian dolls and finding another one inside. I saw us shrinking with each move we made until we got down to the smallest people we could be, the ones that wouldn't open, the ones made from solid wood.

The Commodore laid the greeting card on the porch glider. "Edward, your daddy ought to take care. You be sure to tell him what I said."

We were eating sherbet when my father came home. We heard his car pull into the driveway, and my mother smiled and said to me, "How's that for luck? Your father's home early. Won't he be surprised to see we've got company?"

"Your husband?" Dix said. "My stars. We finally get to meet the mister."

My father came through the door and walked right up to the dining table and sat down across from The Commodore as if he had been expected. He kept his head bowed, and I could tell something was wrong. His hands were on the table, and his fingers were trembling, and the eggshell was wobbling on its stand. We all bowed our heads, as if we were asking a blessing, and for a long time, no one spoke.

Then my mother said, "Richard?" And she said it with the cautious tone I remembered from New Hampshire.

My father still wouldn't raise his head, and I'm not sure he even knew there were other people sitting at his table, people he didn't know, and wouldn't care for once he did. "I saw a boy killed today," he said, and his voice was barely a whisper. "That's all I want to say about it."

"Killed?" my mother said, and I think she knew, even then, that trouble had found us.

That's when The Commodore spoke. "An accident?"

Dix slapped his arm. "Mr. Thibodeaux said he doesn't want to say any more about it." When she said that, her voice steeled with warning, I could tell she had never gotten used to The Commodore's intimacy with accidents and deaths, hated him for it, no doubt, in ways she might not even have known.

But The Commodore wouldn't keep quiet. "I hope you weren't involved with it. That's all I'll say."

My father raised his face, and I could tell he was trying to hold himself together. His jaw was set, and his lips were tight, but his eyes were wet, and I could see he was crying.

"Probably some of that nigra mess," The Commodore said. "Is that it, pal?"

It was clear to me, then, that The Commodore hated something about my father, feared it, perhaps, and I decided it was the fact that my father was a careless man.

"If it is," The Commodore went on, "you asked for your trouble. Like those hotrodders who think the speed limit means everyone else but them. They don't see the danger. Buddy, you get out there on the wild side, something's bound to go wrong. Hell, you know it. I wouldn't think you'd have any call to cry over that."

"What's your name?" my father said to The Commodore. He turned to Dix. "Is this your husband?"

He wasn't crying now; his voice had that edge to it I recognized from the sit-in training sessions.

"His name's Commodore Gleason," Dix said. "We're friends of your wife. Dix and The Commodore."

"The Commodore's with the highway patrol," my mother said.

"He does accident reports," I told my father, hoping to explain The Commodore's interest in the boy's death, and somehow make my father feel better about all this.

"What do you do at an accident scene?" he asked The Commodore.

"I put it all together," The Commodore said. "Gather the facts, pal. Tell you how it happened."

"Talk to the survivors, do you?"

"That's right."

"Tell them you're sorry for their trouble?"

The Commodore gave a little laugh. "Say, what kind of a bastard do you think I am?"

"Do you mean it when you say it?" my father asked. "When you tell them you're sorry?"

"Listen, pal."

"Do you?

"I'm there to get at the facts." The Commodore slapped his palm down on the table, and the eggshell wobbled again, and my mother put her hand to her mouth. "I'm there to get at the truth, pal. It's my job to know things." The Commodore stood up and pointed his finger at my father. "Just like I know what you're up to with the nigras. It's people like you who'll ruin the South. Even your own boy knows that. He's been clubbing niggers downtown today."

It's funny how your life slows down during the moments you wish you could speed away from and leave behind you forever. I could see the smallest details: the way the gold fringe on Dix Gleason's dress turned silver in the sunlight slanting through our window, my mother wetting her finger and rubbing at a spot of sherbet that had stained her white tablecloth, the way one string of The Commodore's bolo tie was shorter than the other, my father's shoulders sagging as if all the life had left him.

"Is that true, Ed?" he said to me.

I remembered the way I had shouted "nigger" at Kress's, how I had pushed my way out of the mob once the fighting had started. I had run outside, and had started walking, wanting to get as far away from Kress's as I could. I had walked and walked, and then I had caught a city bus and come home, and now The Commodore had lied about me, and because I felt so guilty about my part in the trouble downtown, because I wanted all this between The Commodore and my father to stop before it went too far, and The Commodore found out all there was to know about us—that our name wasn't Thibodeaux, that my father had made mistakes in New Hampshire, that we had tried our best to bury these facts—I said, yes, it was true.

My father slumped down in his chair. "I'm sorry," he said. "Folks, I'm sorry for all of this."

And The Commodore said, "Damn straight you're sorry. I could have told you that from the get-go."

The boy who died that day was not a Negro as we all had first believed. It was, as I would find out later, Dale Mink. He had come from Kress's, jubilant, the way he was after a basketball victory. He must have been feeling pretty full of himself. He was seventeen years old, a basketball star on his way to Vanderbilt, and he had the juice of a fist fight jazzing around in his head. When he ran out into the street, and saw my father's car, he must have been dazzled by how quickly misfortune had found him.

It was, my father finally told us, something he had played over in his head time and time again after he had told his story to the police: the street had been wet with rain, and the police vans had pulled up to Kress's. The officers were gathering up the black college students, arresting them for disorderly conduct, and the white boys who had attacked them were spilling out into the street. They were raising their arms and shaking their fists. My father glanced into his rearview mirror and noticed the way the skin was starting to wrinkle around his eyes. When he finally looked back to the street, there was Dale Mink, and it was too late for my father to stop.

My mother and I didn't know any of this when Dix and The Commodore left our house.

"He knows about you now," my mother said to my father. "He'll tell it over and over. And then where will we be?"

"Were you there?" my father asked me. "At Kress's?"

"I went with a boy from school. I didn't hit anyone. I said some things. That's all."

"You said things? Provoked those poor students? What did you say?"

I let my face go wooden, the way Lester Bates had when he had gripped the lunch counter, and the taunting had begun, "Things you taught me," I said.

My father lifted his hand, and with his finger, he brushed a piece of lint from his eyelashes. I wanted to think that he was an unlucky man— "Trouble knows my name," he had said in New Hampshire—but I could see he was actually a man of vanity. I knew that was a dangerous thing to be in the world. It meant forgetting others and concentrating only on yourself, and, when that was the case, all kinds of lunatic things could happen.

"I'm hungry," my father said. "I swear, Penny. I'm starved."

We were sitting at our dining table, and outside the light was fading. The eggshell was still upright in its stand, and what I remembered was how, when my father had first sat down, we had all bowed our heads and stared at it. I like to believe now that each of us, even The Commodore, was thinking, what a lovely scene. "Inviting," my mother had said earlier. The people around the miniature table seemed cozy and content. We must have looked at them with a desperate yearning. They were so small. They were so far away from us and everything that was about to happen in our home.

ANTHONY GROOMS

Food That Pleases, Food to Take Home

Born in Charlottesville, Virginia, Anthony Grooms (1955–) is a poet, short-story writer, playwright, and novelist. A recipient of several Fulbrights, he is a professor of English at Kennesaw State University near Atlanta, Georgia. "Food That Pleases, Food to Take Home" is in his 1995 collection, *Trouble No More*, winner of the Lillian Smith Award.

Annie McPhee wasn't sure about what Mary Taliferro was telling her. Mary said that colored people in Louisa should stand up for their rights. They were doing it in the cities. Mary said that Channel Six from Richmond had shown pictures of Negroes sitting in at lunch counters. She laughed that "colored people" were becoming "Negroes." Walter Cronkite[1] had shown pictures from Albany and Birmingham. Negroes were on the move.

On the church lawn one bright Sunday, Mary caught hold of Annie's arm and whispered, "What choo think of Reverend Green's sermon?" She knew Annie had eyes for Reverend Green.

"It was nice," Annie said. She pushed the pillbox back onto her head and patted her flip curl.

"But don't you think he was right about doing something?"

"'Course he right," Annie said with a smack of her lips, "but ain't nobody gone do nothing." Then she saw a glint in Mary's eye. "What you gone do and where?"

"We could march."

"Who gone march?" Mary held her hat against the wind that rustled through the fallen oak leaves.

"We could organize a march downtown. We could march down Main Street and tell them white folks that we want our rights."

1. Walter Cronkite (1916–) was the *CBS Evening News* anchor from 1962 to 1981. Except for a few years in the mid-1960s, his newscast was the ratings leader.

"And that'll be the end of it, girl. Who gone march with you? Everybody around here is scared to march."

Mary pulled on Annie's elbow and guided her away from the folks gathering in front of the clapboard church to the pebbly space next to the cemetery. "I know what you thinking, girl. But I'm too tired of it to be scared. I wish something *would* happen around here and I figure we just the ones to start it."

"*You* the one." Annie put on her dark glasses. "Tell me who I look like?"

"Hummph." Mary turned up her lips for a second. "I don't know, girl. Elizabeth Taylor?"[2]

"Nurrrh, child. You know I don't look like no 'Lizabeth Taylor. Somebody else. Somebody even more famous than that."

"Richard Burton."[3]

"I'm gone kill you. Do I look like a man?" Annie gave Mary one more chance: she stepped back, her heel sinking into the soft hill of a grave, and put her hands on her hips. The wind folded her dress against her thighs. "Look at the hair and the glasses."

Mary frowned as she examined Annie and finally she gave up.

"Jackie Kennedy![4] Don't I look just like Jackie Kennedy?"

"Yeah, with the sunglasses, I guess you do," Mary said. "Anybody would, even me, if I had them sunglasses on."

"It'll take more than a pair of sunglasses . . ."

"But for real," Mary continued and started toward the parking lot, "we could start something. We could make the news if we did something in Louisa. I can just see myself sittin' up there on Walter Cronkite."

"Sittin' in the Louisa jail be more like it. Them white folks don't want no trouble."

2. In a six-decade career in the movie industry, Elizabeth Taylor (1932–) has been on the cover of *Life* eleven times (a record) and has won two Academy of Motion Pictures Awards for Best Actress. In the 1960s, she and Richard Burton met and fell in love during the making of *Cleopatra*. They quickly divorced their spouses and married each other.

3. During the 1960s, Richard Burton (1925–84) was often mentioned in connection with Elizabeth Taylor, and his career became entwined with hers. A Welshman, he is considered by many as one of the greatest actors who ever lived.

4. Jacqueline Kennedy (1929–94), the wife of President John F. Kennedy, was among the most attractive first ladies in the history of the country, and because of television, everybody knew it. And everybody saw her, again and again, on the day her husband was assassinated and fell into her lap. They saw, too, her pillbox hat and her young son saluting the president on the day of his funeral procession. She was widely loved and admired by the people.

"It don't matter what *they* want. Just like Reverend Green said, it matter what's right."

"Then how come *he* ain't doing it?"

"I bet he will if somebody started it. You know he's a preacher and he just can't run out and start no stuff." Mary placed her palms on the hood of the used Fairlane she had bought in Richmond with a down payment she had saved from factory work. She leaned up on her toes as Reverend Green was known to do and deepened her voice. "The Lord helps them that helps themselves. Amen. Say, the Lord provides!"

Annie swatted at her and giggled. "Somebody gone hear you."

"The Lord will part the Red Sea of injustice and send down the manna of equal rights."

"Bill Green don't sound like that." Annie folded her arms.

"Since when you call him 'Bill'?"

"Since when I want to."

Mary's round cheeks dimpled and her teeth contrasted with her purplish black face. "Just think how *Bill* Green would like it if we did something."

"How do you know what *Reverend* Green would like?" Annie whispered pointedly.

"I just bet he would."

They dressed to kill. They put on Sunday suits, high heels, and pillboxes. Mary wore her good wig. They put on lipstick and rouge and false eyelashes and drove to town in Mary's Fairlane. They had decided to sit in at May's Drugstore. They parked at the far end of the one-stoplight street, deserted in the cool midmorning. People were at work in the factory, or in the fields, or at the schools. The few people they passed stared at them, but no one knew them.

"Don't you just hate it?" Mary said, seeming to bolster her anger as they walked down toward the store. "If you go in there, the minute you step in the door, ole lady May will break her neck running over to you— 'Can I he'p you'—you know, in that syrupy sweet way. She won't let you look around for a second."

" 'Fraid you gone steal something." Annie looked straight ahead down the street of wooden and brick shops. The perspective was broken by the courthouse square and the little brick jailhouse beside it. Annie forced herself to match Mary's determined stride lest her legs tremble so badly she fell.

"Or just *touch* something. And a white person—they can put their hands on anything they want. Pick up stuff and put it back. Like they own everything."

"Lord, you know we better not touch nothing unless we ready to pay for it. Better have the money in your hand." Annie's voice trailed and stopped abruptly when she caught a glimpse of the sheriff's car parked behind the courthouse. What would Bill Green think if she got arrested? she wondered. She thought about the stories she had heard from her uncles, her mother's younger brothers, about spending time in the jailhouse for speeding or drinking. They told about the sheetless cots, the stench of the pee pot, but said that the sheriff's wife's biscuits were good. Annie did not want to try the sheriff's wife's biscuits. She did not want to be dragged out of May's by the sheriff, to be touched by his big hands with the hairy knuckles she had once seen up close when he had come to give a talk at her high school. The thought of being close to him, his chewed cigar and the big leather lump of holster and gun sent shivers through her. But Bill Green had said they should stand up. Bill Green had said that God would send the manna of justice if they would only stand up.

Mary grimaced and balled up her fists as if to force her anger to a boiling point. "White people make me sick. Every last one of them. Sick. What I'd really like to do is to take ole lady May by her scrawny little neck and choke her."

Annie tried to laugh, but her voice was too jittery. "We're suppose to be *peace* demonstrators."

"I'd like to kick a piece of her butt."

"I don't like her either," Annie said, thinking what Reverend Green might say, "but let's do this the right way. Let's just go in and ask to be served and . . ." Annie stopped under May's green awning.

"And when she don't?" Mary whispered. "What then?"

Except for the awning, May's was a flat-faced, white clapboard building with a flat roof and a stepped crest. Only one of its double doors opened to admit customers. A bell jingled when they entered. Annie stood with Mary by the door, her eyes adjusting to the dimness, and breathed in a mixture of smells dominated by dust and wood polish. To her right was the cashier's stand with a display of pocket combs, and crowded on long narrow shelves in the middle of the store were goods: bolts of cloth, children's dolls, sewing kits, toiletries, firecrackers, shotgun shells, fashion magazines, and among everything, *The Central*, the town's weekly newspaper. In the back, the RX sign hung from the ceiling above the druggist's counter, hidden behind the clutter of inventory. Along the left wall was a linoleum-topped lunch counter with five backless stools anchored in front of it. It was junked with jars of pickles, loaves of sandwich bread, buns and cake plates bearing doughnuts and pies. The spigots of a broken soda fountain were partially hidden in the clutter. Behind the counter was a grand mirror with ornate framing. It was placarded with menus and handwritten signs announcing "specials." The mirror was grease-spattered on one side from a small electric grill that sat on a shelf. On the other side, two huge coolers stood bubbling lemonade and orangeade. A broken neon sign above the mirror announced, "FOOD THAT PLEASES, FOOD TO TAKE HOME." High above were shelves on which rested plastic wreaths of cemetery flowers.

"She must be in the back," Mary whispered, "else she would've said something by now." Mary stepped quietly to the lunch counter and shot Annie an impatient frown. The scents of bath soaps and powders had attracted Annie as she passed the display, but she dared not touch them. "Maybe we should just buy something."

"What for? You scared?"

Annie straightened. "Do I look scared?"

"Like you gone pass a watermelon. Just do like I do. She gone be scareder than us."

The storage room door behind the lunch counter was open. A low voice came from the room, and suddenly they heard a long moan, as if someone, or some animal, were grieving.

"Jesus," whispered Annie. She pulled on Mary's elbow.

Mary pushed closer to the counter, took a deep breath, and pulled herself up onto the first stool. She sat for a moment, her eyes as excited as a child's on a fairground ride. "You ever sit on one of these?" She caught herself for being too loud. She put on a serious face, her lips folded under so as not to look too big, placed her feet on the shiny circular footrest, and adjusted her skirt.

Annie looked over her shoulder, expecting to see Mrs. May's stick-like figure marching hurriedly toward them, but all was still except for the putt-putting of the ceiling fans.

Mary beckoned to Annie to sit on the stool beside her, and gingerly as a child testing hot bathwater, Annie sat. She pulled herself up on the stool, forgetting to smooth her skirt as Mary had done. She sat ready to jump down at any moment; when the moan came again, she jumped.

"Be there in a minute," drawled a woman from the storage room. It was not Mrs. May's voice, which was thin and whiny. A heavy woman, dressed in a blue calico shift with a lace collar safety-pinned at the neck, stepped from the storage room. Her gray curls were pulled back. Her face looked soft, and her eyes were large and round. When she saw the girls, the woman looked confused for a moment, then she looked frightened and wrung her hands. "May I help ya?" she asked.

Annie looked at Mary, and Mary at Annie. They had never seen this woman before. After a moment, Mary drew a breath and said, "We would like to order." The woman pointed to the menu and stood back as if ready to retreat into the storage room. The moan came again from the room.

"We don't want no takeout," Mary said, growing bolder. "We want to eat at the counter like white folks. We want you to write it down on your little pad and bring us silverware wrapped in a napkin."

"But . . ." the woman said, and then she blanched. "But . . ."

The moan came again, loudly. She returned to the storage room.

When the woman came back she was shaking. "I . . . I can't serve colored."

"Why can't choo?" Mary said. She tried to sound sophisticated. "You have the food. You have the stove. All we want is a hamburger and some fries." She pointed to the orangeade. "And some of that orange drink."

The woman came slowly to Annie. Nervously, she put her hand out to the edge of the counter like she wanted to touch Annie. "I don't want trouble, miss," she said. "I'm just helping out my sister-in-law, Ella May. She's very sick, you know. She's got a gall bladder. I'm not even from here. I'm from West Virginia. I don't want any trouble."

"Yes, ma'am," Annie said, then cleared her throat, took a deep breath, and fought to control her jittery voice. "We just want our rights."

"Listen," the woman said, "I will give you some food if you'll just take it on home." Then she added in a whisper, "Mr. May will be back from the hospital soon and . . . please . . ."

"No," Mary said firmly, crisping her endings the way their English teacher Miss Bullock had told them was proper. "We done come all the way from Washington, D.C. We are part of President Johnson's civil rights committee.[5] And we gone report you to the Doctor Martin Luther King."

The woman stepped back from the counter. She bumped against the ice cream box. She seemed not to believe Mary but was too afraid to say otherwise. "Mr. May will return soon," she said, too uncertain to be threatening. She strained to see out the front door. Annie knew she was looking to see if somebody white was out there, and spun in a sudden fright. Two black boys were brushing hayseed from their hair in front of the window.

"If it were up to me . . ." the woman said. "If it were up to me, I would be glad to serve you. I don't mind colored. Honest. I'm from West Virginia."

"It *is* up to you," Mary said, a crooked, dimpled smile on her face. "Who else is here? How come you don't want us Negroes to have our rights?"

"Please," the woman said, clasping her hands together, "I don't want to have to call the police. Don't make me call nobody." She strained again to see the street.

The moan came again. No one moved. They let the moan and the putt-putt of the fans bathe them. Annie felt the moan in the pit of her stomach. She held onto the seat of the stool. Maybe Mrs. May was dead, she thought, and someone was crying. They shouldn't be causing this trouble if Mrs. May was dead. "Well, maybe we should come back when Mrs. May is here," Annie said vacantly, all the time moving a little ways down the counter, focused on the crack in the doorway to the storage room. She could only see a bare light bulb and switch cord and cans on the shelves.

"I'm not taking a step until I get served," Mary said. "I don't care if Miss May—if the owner—ain't here. You in charge and I want my rights."

The woman put her hand out to Annie. "What if I made you a nice sandwich and you can take it with you? I'll let you have it free of charge."

"Ain't that some mess?" Mary said, putting her hands on her hips.

5. Johnson did not become president until November 22, 1963, so the time of the story must be over three years after the sit-in movement began in Greensboro, North Carolina, on February 1, 1960.

"You even *give* us food, but you don't want us to sit and eat it like people. You rather see us go out back and eat it like a dog. I know how you white people is. I done seen it. You have your damn dog eat at the table with you, but you won't let a colored person. Do I look like a dog to you?"

"I don't own a dog," the woman said. She no longer wrung her hands but gripped one inside the other. "I don't own this place. I'm just helping my sister-in-law like I told you. And besides, it is the law. Like I told you, I got nothing against you. Not in the least. But what would Mrs. May or Mr. May say if they walked in here and I was letting you eat? They wouldn't like it."

"I don't care what they like. The customer is always right."

The moan came again, this time discernible as a word: "Maaahhma."

"What's that?" Mary asked, her eyes wide.

"It's nothing to you," the woman said.

Annie saw a movement, a shadow, behind the door. It was a slow, awkward swaying. The door squeaked and moved slightly. Annie looked first at Mary and then at the woman.

"I'll tell you what *is* my business," Mary said. "This here piece of pie is. And I got a good mind to help myself to it right now." She reached out for the lid of the pie plate.

"Don't let me have to call somebody."

"Call who you like. I ain't scared. I'll go to jail if I have to."

"Don't be ugly," the woman said and waved her hand. She might have been snatching a fly out of orbit. "Just take it and go."

The moan came again, deep and pathetic. It reminded Annie of the mourning doves that she could hear from her bedroom window just after sunrise, only it was not so melodic as doves.

"Go!" the woman shouted. "You're upsetting him."

The shadow swayed again, and the door, squeaking, was pulled open farther. Annie moved closer to the door, directly in front of it, separated from it only by the counter gate. She knew there was someone there, some "him" the woman had said, but something monstrously sorrowful and she couldn't imagine what it was.

Mary hopped down from the stool. "I told you I wanted it here." She jabbed her finger on the countertop. "Why don't you admit it? You just like every white person I ever seen. Just as prejudice' as the day is long."

"I'm not!" the woman said. "You don't understand the position I'm in . . ."

"Maaaaahhhmmaaa."

"I'm coming." The woman made a step toward the door, then she turned back to Mary. "I'm not prejudice'." Her face was contorted. The moan came again, with a resonating bass. "Baby," the woman said to the figure behind the door, and then to Mary, "eat here, then. Eat all you want. I don't care."

Mary stood stiffly, smiled. There was a small silence. "Serve me," she demanded.

"Serve your goddamn self," the older woman said, her voice rising to a screech.

Annie heard the argument, and glanced now and again at Mary and the woman, but now the door was slowly swinging open, and she could see the thick fingers of a man holding onto the edge of it. He was a big man. Big and fat like the sheriff. Annie looked at the woman. She felt her lips part. The moan, almost a groan, vibrated in her chest. The man was like an animal, a hurt animal, calling for his mother, Annie thought. Now she was afraid in a different way. She remembered what her father had told her about hurt animals, how they turned on people who tried to help them, how their mothers attacked ferociously to save them.

"Serve yourself." The woman had turned toward Mary. Her entire body trembled, her hands, now unclasped, fanned the air. She pushed a loaf of sandwich bread across the counter toward Mary. She slapped a package of hamburger buns, causing it to sail and hit Mary on the shoulder. She threw Dixie cups, plastic forks and paper napkins. Mary ducked below the countertop. "Serve yourself," the woman screamed. "Eat all the goddamn food you want."

"Maaahhma."

Stepping cautiously as if walking up to a lame wild dog, Annie slipped through the counter gate. The door pulled all the way open and the man stood there. Annie's heart skipped a beat; she reached back for the counter so she wouldn't fall. First she saw his barrel chest, bulging out in odd places under a pinned-together plaid flannel shirt; then his thick neck, stiffly twisted so that one ear nearly lay against his hulking shoulder. His lips were thick and flat. One side of his face was higher than the other, like a clay face misshapen by a child's hand. His eyebrows were thick ridges that ran together at the top of his wide flat nose.

"Maaaaahhmmaaa."

"He's just a baby," the woman came to the door and took the man's hand. She pulled him into the open, behind the counter, and rubbed the back of his hand furiously. His presence seemed to calm her. She glanced toward Mary and then to Annie. "It's the new place." She smiled as if inviting a stranger to look at an infant, then shot a look at Mary. "He's not used to being over here." She patted the hand and the big man smiled deep dimples. She pinched his cheeks. "Just a baby."

"What's wrong with him?" Annie asked, recovering from the sight of him.

The mother sighed. "Just born thatta way, child. Just born like that." She looked back at Mary who was straightening her clothes and wig. "Maybe we'll all sit and have a piece of pie."

The man smiled at Annie, and Annie managed to smile back. She reached behind her for the counter gate.

"Don't worry," the woman said. "He is as gentle as a fly. He likes to be around people." She changed to baby talk. "Don't you, Willie?" Then she held out the man's hand to Annie. "Here. Pat the back of his hand. That's what he likes."

Annie looked at his face, drool in the corners of his mouth. He had gray eyes that swam lazily in their sockets. Now she looked at the offered hand. It was the whitest hand she had ever seen, with thick, hairy knuckles and nubbed nails.

"Go on and pat him," the woman said. "He's just a boy—your age. Go on, he likes it."

She had never touched a white boy. She reached out for the hand hesitantly. The woman encouraged. Annie wanted to look at Mary, to see what she thought, but she could not break her focus on the man's hand. She saw her hand, so obviously brown, move into her focus, and then move closer and closer to the pale hand until her fingertips touched it.

"Go ahead and give him a pat."

The man's hand was soft and damp, unlike any hand Annie had ever touched. She lifted her hand and patted the big hand twice, and then twice again. The man moaned, not any word but like a dog enjoying a belly rub.

"See," the woman said. She looked at Mary. "See. We are just people like you are. We don't want to hurt nobody. Not a soul." She took back the man's hand and smiled at Annie. "Tell you what. I'll cut us all a piece of pie."

"Can we have it at the counter?" Mary glared at the woman, her lips poked out.

The woman sighed loudly. "Won't you understand?"

"Then eat it by yo'self."

The woman turned to Annie and touched her hand, "Won't *you* understand?"

Annie hesitated. The doorbell jingled and Mr. May came in. He was wiping under his straw fedora with a handkerchief. "I'll be glad if that old witch did die," he was saying as he made his way to the back.

Mary spun around and pretended to be interested in the bath soaps. "You being he'ped?" he asked gruffly as he approached her.

"Yes, suh," Mary said.

The woman was trying to push the man back into the storage room. Mr. May stopped and put his hands on his hips. "Damn, Sally, what is he doing out in the store? He's liable to scare somebody to death . . . and what! . . . in the hell is that gal doing *behind* the counter?"

"It's all right." The woman turned and waved Annie through the counter gate. "She was just helping me with him."

"Look at this place? What the hell happened here? Goddamnit, can't you control that freak?"

"It's all right," the woman said from inside the room where she was pushing the man. "Y'all run along now."

"That wasn't fair," Mary said as they walked back to the Fairlane. "How come that stupid gorilla had to be there? How come *she* had to be there in the first place? Ole lady May the one I wanted to be there. I could have said something if it hada been her." Annie said nothing. They passed the monument to the Confederate dead, standing in the courthouse yard.

"I don't know," Annie said. She was beginning to tremble on the inside. The world seemed complex and uncertain. She remembered touching the man, her brown hand against his white one. He was like a baby, soft and damp, and yet something about him, not just his size and his twisted face, frightened her. But she had been charmed by him for a moment, charmed by his softness and his dimples. She remembered the look on the woman's face when she had patted the man's hand. She thought the woman had loved her for a moment.

"We never gone get our rights." Mary clenched her teeth. "Especially with you around pattin' that goddamn monster on the hand."

"What was wrong with that?" Annie said. She knew there was nothing wrong with it. He couldn't help the way he was born.

"If you don't know . . . !" Mary reached out quickly and pinched Annie on the arm just above the elbow. She squeezed her nails into the pinch and twisted it before she let go. "Some civil rights marcher you is. Bill Green will be 'shame' to know you."

Annie whimpered and put her hand over the pinched spot. "No!" she blurted, "I *want* my rights."

"Shit." Mary took Annie by the elbow and led her to the car. "I know you was tryin' . . . I know . . . it's just that we won't ever get nothing, nothing—unless we, we . . . uggghhh!"—she grimaced—"*kill* them, or something."

They reached the car and got in, then Annie began to cry. Mary touched her hand to comfort her, but Annie pushed her away. Mary sped the car out of town on a road that cut through fields turning brown in the hot autumn sun. Annie put her head on the dash. Things were very complicated, far more complicated than she had ever thought.

MIKE THELWELL

Direct Action

Former SNCC field secretary Ekwueme Michael Thelwell (1939–) is a professor
of black studies in the W. E. B. Du Bois Department of Afro-American Studies
at the University of Massachusetts. A scholar, activist, and author, Thelwell
was born in Jamaica. During the days of the civil rights movement, he was
active in voter-registration drives in the South and served as the director of
the Washington office of the Mississippi Freedom Democratic Party. "Direct
Action" appeared in *Prize Stories 1963* and in Langston Hughes's *The Best Short
Stories by Black Writers* (1967).

We were all sitting around the front room the night it started. The front
room of the pad was pretty kooky. See, five guys lived there. It was a
reconstructed basement and the landlord didn't care what we did, just so
he got his rent.

Well, the five guys who lived there were pretty weird, at least so it
was rumored about the campus. We didn't care too much. Lee was on a
sign kick, and if he thought of anything that appeared profound or cool—
and the words were synonymous with him—wham! we had another sign.
See, he'd write a sign and put it up. Not only that; he was klepto about
signs. He just couldn't resist lifting them, so the pad always looked like the
basement of the Police Traffic Department with all the DANGER NO
STANDING signs he had in the john, and over his bed he had a sign that
read WE RESERVE THE RIGHT TO DENY SERVICE TO ANYONE.
Man, he'd bring in those silly freshman girls who'd think the whole place
was "so-o-o bohemian," and that sign would really crack them up.

Anyway, I was telling you about the front room. Lee had put up an
immense sign he'd written: IF YOU DON'T DIG KIKES, DAGOS, NIG-
GERS, HENRY MILLER, AND J. C., YOU AIN'T WELCOME! Across
from that he had another of his prize acquisitions; something in flaming red letters issued a solemn WARNING TO SHOPLIFTERS. You've
probably seen them in department stores.

Then there was the kid in art school, Lisa, who was the house artist and mascot. Man, that kid was mixed up. She was variously in love with everyone in the pad. First she was going with Dick—that's my brother. Then she found that he was a "father surrogate"; then it was Lee, but it seems he had been "only an intellectual status symbol." Later it was Doug "the innocent." After Doug it was Art—that's our other roomie— but he had only been an expression of her "urge to self-destruction." So now that left only me. The chick was starting to project that soulful look, but hell, man, there was only one symbol left and I wasn't too eager to be "symbolized." They should ban all psychology books, at least for freshman girls.

Anyway, I was telling you about the room. When Lisa was "in love" with Dick she was in her surrealist period. She used to bring these huge, blatantly Freudian canvases, which she hung on the walls until the room looked, as Doug said, like "the pigmented expression of a demented psyche." Then Lisa started to down Dick because of his lack of critical sensitivity and creativity. She kept this up, and soon we were all bugging Dick. He didn't say too much, but one day when he was alone in the pad, he got some tins of black, green, yellow, and red house paint, stripped the room, and started making like Jackson Pollock.[1] The walls, the windows, and dig this, even the damn floor was nothing but one whole mess of different-colored paint. Man, we couldn't go in the front room for four days; when it dried, Dick brought home an instructor from art school to "appraise some original works."

I was sorry for the instructor. He was a short, paunchy little guy with a bald patch, and misty eyes behind some of the thickest lenses you ever saw. At first he thought Dick was joking, he just stood there fidgeting and blinking his watery little eyes. He gave a weak giggle and muttered something that sounded like, "Great . . . uh . . . sense of humor. Hee."

But Dick was giving him this hurt-creative-spirit come-on real big. His face was all pained, and he really looked stricken and intense.

"But, sir, surely you can see some promise, some little merit?"

"Well, uh, one must consider, uh, the limitations of your medium, uh . . . hee."

1. Jackson Pollock (1912–56) was the leading talent of the abstract expressionist art movement, famous for his "drip and splash" method of painting, which consisted of splattering paint onto a canvas on the floor.

"Limitations of medium, yes, but surely there must be some merit?"

"Well, you must realize—"

"Yes, but not even *some* spark of promise, some faint, tiny spark of promise?" Dick was really looking distraught now. The art teacher was visibly unhappy and looked at me appealingly, but I gave him a don't-destroy-this-poor-sensitive-spirit look. He mopped his face and tried again.

"Abstractionism is a very advanced genre—"

"Yes, yes, advanced," Dick said, cutting him off impatiently, "but not even the faintest glimmer of merit?" He was really emoting now, and then he started sobbing hysterically and split the scene. I gave the poor instructor a cold how-could-you-be-so-cruel look, and he began to stutter. "I had n-no idea, n-no idea. Oh, dear, so strange . . . Do you suppose he is all right? How d-do you explain . . . Oh, dear."

"Sir," I said, "I neither suppose nor explain. All I know is that my brother is very high-strung and you have probably induced a severe trauma. If you have nothing further to say, would you . . . ?" and I opened the door suggestively. He looked at the messed-up walls in bewilderment and shook his head. He took off his misty glasses, wiped them, looked at the wall, bleated something about "all insane," and scurried out. He probably heard us laughing.

Man, these white liberals are really tolerant. If Dick and I were white, the cat probably would have known right off that we were kidding. But apparently he was so anxious not to hurt our feelings that he gave a serious response to any old crap we said, Man, these people either kill you with intolerance or they turn around and overdo the tolerance bit. However, as Max Schulman[2] says, "I digress."

The cats in our pad were kind of integrated, but we never thought of it that way. We really dug each other, so we hung around together. As Lee would say, "We related to each other in a meaningful way." (That's another thing about Lee. He was always "establishing relationships." Man, if he made a broad or even asked her the time, it was always, "Oh, I established a relationship today.") Like, if you were a cat who was hung up on this race bit, you could get awfully queered up around the pad. The place was about as mixed up as Brooklyn. The only difference, as far as I could see,

2. Max Schulman (1919–88) was a prolific American novelist and playwright; comedy for television was one of his specialties.

was that we could all swear in different languages. Lee's folks had come from Milan, Dick and I were Negro, and Art, with his flaming red head and green Viking eyes, was Jewish.

The only cat who had adjustment problems was Doug. He was from sturdy Anglo-Saxon Protestant stock; his folks still had the Mayflower ticket stub and a lot of bread. When he was a freshman in the dorm, some of the cats put him down because he was shy and you could see that he was well off. And those s.o.b.'s would have been so helpful if the cat had been "culturally deprived" and needed handouts. Man, people are such bastards. It's kind of a gas, you know. Doug probably could have traced his family back to Thor, and yet he had thin, almost Semitic features, dark brown hair, and deep eyes with a dark rabbinical sadness to them.

Anyway, we guys used to really swing in the pad; seems like we spent most of the time laughing. But don't get the idea that we were just kick-crazy or something out of Kerouac,[3] beat-type stuff. All of us were doing okay in school—grades and that jazz. Take Art, for instance: most people thought that because he had a beard and was always playing the guitar and singing, and ready to party, he was just a campus beatnik-in-residence. They didn't know that he was an instructor and was working on his doctorate in anthropology. Actually, we were really more organized than we looked.

Anyway, this thing I'm telling you about happened the summer when this sit-in bit broke out all over. Since Pearl Springs was a Midwestern college town, there was no segregation of any kind around—at least, I didn't see any. But everyone was going out to picket Woolworth's every weekend. At first we went, but since there was this crowd out each week and nobody was crossing the line anyway, we kind of lost interest. (Actually, they had more people than they needed.)

So we were all sitting around and jiving each other, when I mentioned that a guy we called "The Crusader" had said he was coming over later.

"Oh, no," Dick groaned; "that cat bugs me. Every time he sees me in

3. Jack Kerouac (1922–69) wrote the now classic *On the Road* (1957), the book that launched a new social and literary movement, centered in the artists' communities of San Francisco and New York City, one that operated outside the rules of the establishment. He was the leading light of the beat generation, a term that he coined.

the cafeteria or the union he makes a point of coming over to talk, and he never has anything to say. Hell, every time I talk to the guy I feel as if he really isn't seeing me, just a cause—a minority group."

"Yeah, I know," Art added. "Once at a party I was telling some broad that I was Jewish and he heard. You know, he just had to steer me into a corner to tell me how sympathetic he was to the 'Jewish cause' and 'Jewish problems.' The guy isn't vicious, only misguided."

Then Lee said, "So the guy is misguided, but, hell, he's going to come in here preaching all this brotherly love and Universal Brotherhood. And who wants to be a brother to bums like you?"

That started it.

Dick was reading the paper, but he looked up. "Hey, those Israelis in Tel Aviv are really getting progressive."

"Yeah, them Israelis don't mess around. What they do now?" Art asked. He was a real gung-ho Zionist,[4] and had even spent a summer in a kibbutz in Israel.

"Oh," said Dick, "they just opened a big hydroelectric plant."

Art waded in deeper. "So what?"

"Nothing, only they ain't got no water, so they call it The Adolf Eichmann[5] Memorial Project."

Everybody cracked up. Art said something about "niggers and flies."

"Niggers and kikes," I chimed in. "I don't like them, either, but they got rights . . . in their place."

"Rights! They got too many rights already. After all, this is a free country, and soon a real American like me won't even have breathing room," cracked Lee.

"Hey, Mike," someone shouted, "you always saying some of your best friends are dagos, but would you like your sister to marry one?"

"Hell no, she better marryink der gute Chewish boy," I replied.

"And for niggers, I should of lynched you all when I had the chance . . ." Art was saying when The Crusader entered. This was the

---

4. Zionists are people who support the return of the Jewish people to their homeland and the resumption of Jewish sovereignty in Israel.

5. Adolf Eichmann (1906–62) was chief of the Jewish Office of the Gestapo. It was his job to round up Jews and send them to concentration camps, which usually meant to their deaths.

cat who organized the pickets—or at least he used to like to think he did. A real sincere crusading-type white cat. He looked with distaste at Lee's sign about kikes and niggers.

"Well, fellas, all ready for the picket on Saturday?"

"Somebody tell him," said Lee.

"Well, you see," I ventured, "we ain't going."

"Ain't going!" The Crusader howled. "But why? Don't you think—"

"Of course not. We are all dedicated practitioners of non-think. Besides, all our Negrahs are happy. Ain't yuh happy, Mike?" Art drawled.

"Yeah, but I don' like all these immigran's, kikes, dagos, an' such. Like, I thinks—"

"And Ah purely hates niggers: they stink so," Lee announced.

The Crusader didn't get the message. "Look guys, I know you're joking, but . . . I know you guys are awful close—hell, you room together—but you persist in using all these derogatory racial epithets. I should think that you of all people . . . I really don't think it's funny."

"Man," said Dick, "is this cat for real?"

I knew just what he meant: I can't stomach these crusading liberal types, either, who just have to prove their democracy.

"Okay, can it, guys. I think we ought to explain to this gentleman what we mean," Art said. "Look, I don't think I have to prove anything to anyone in this room. We're all in favor of the demonstrations. In fact, nearly half the community is, so we don't think we need to parade our views. Besides, you have enough people as it is. So we're supporting the students in the South, but why not go across the state line into Missouri and really do something? That's where direct action is needed."

"Oho, the same old excuse for doing nothing," The Crusader sneered.

I could see that Lee over in his corner was getting mad. Suddenly he said, "So you accuse us of doing nothing? Well, we'll show you what we mean by direct action. We mean action calculated to pressure people, to disrupt economic and social functions and patterns, to pressure them into doing something to improve racial relations."

"Very fine, Comrade Revolutionary, and just what do you propose to do, besides staying home and lecturing active people like me?" The Crusader's tone dripped sarcasm.

Lee completely lost control. "What do we propose to do?" he shouted.

"We'll go across the state line and in two weeks we'll integrate some in-stitution! That'll show you what direct action means."

"Okay, okay, just make sure you do it," said The Crusader as he left.

Man, next day it was all over campus that we had promised to in-tegrate everything from the State of Georgia to the White House main bedroom—you know how rumors are. We were in a fix. Every time Lee blew his top we were always in a jam. Now we had to put up or shut up.

The pressure was mounting after about a week. We were all sitting around one day when Doug proclaimed to Lee, "We shall disrupt their social functions, we shall disrupt their human functions—You utter nut, what the hell are you going to do?"

Lee was real quiet, like he hadn't heard; then he jumped up. "Hu-man functions! Doug—genius. I love you!" Then he split the scene, real excited-like.

About an hour later Lee came back still excited, and mysterious. "Look," he said, "we're cool. I have it all worked out. You know that big department store in Deershead? Well, they have segregated sanitary fa-cilities."

Dick interrupted, "So? This is a Christian country. You expect men and women to use the same facilities?"

"Oh, shut up, you know what I mean. Anyway, we're going to integrate them. All you guys have to do is get ten girls and five other guys and I'll do the rest."

"Oh, isn't our genius smart," I snarled. "If you think that hot as it is, I'm going to picket among those hillbillies, you're out of your cotton-chopping little mind."

"Who's going to picket?" Lee said. "Credit me with more finesse than that. I said direct action, didn't I? Well, that's what I meant. All you guys have to do is sit in the white johns and use all the seats. I'll do the rest."

"And the girls?" I asked.

"They do the same over in the women's rest rooms. Oh, is this plan a riot!" The cat cracked up and wouldn't say any more. Nobody liked it much. Lee was so damn wild at times. See, he was a real slick cat. I mean, if he had ten months with a headshrinker he'd probably end up Presi-dent. But, man, most of the jams we got into were because the cat *hadn't* seen a headshrinker. Anyway, we didn't have any alternative, so we went along.

The morning we were ready to leave, Lee disappeared. Just when everyone was getting real mad, he showed, dragging two guys with him. One was The Crusader and the other cat turned out to be a photographer from the school paper. So we drove to Deershead, a hick town over in Missouri. All the way, Lee was real confident. He kept gloating to The Crusader that he was going to show him how to operate.

When we arrived at the "target," as Lee called it, he told everyone to go in and proceed with stage one. All this means is that we went and sat in the white johns. The girls did the same. Lee disappeared again. We all sat and waited. Soon he showed up grinning all over and said:

"Very good. Now I shall join you and wait for our little scheme to develop." He told The Crusader and the photographer to wait in the store for our plan to take effect. Man, we sat in that place for about an hour. It was real hot, even in there. The guys started to get restless and finally threatened to leave if Lee didn't clue us in on the plan—if he had one.

Just as he decided to tell us, two guys came into the john real quick. We heard one of them say, "Goddamn, the place is full." They waited around for a while, and more guys kept coming in. All of a sudden the place was filled with guys. They seemed real impatient, and one of them said, "Can't you fellas hurry up? There's quite a line out here."

"Wonder why everyone has such urgent business?" drawled Lee. "Must be an epidemic."

"Must be something we ate," the guy said. His voice sounded strange and tense. "Hurry up, fellas, will you?"

I peeped through the crack in the door and saw the guys outside all sweating and red in the face. One cat was doubled up, holding his middle and grimacing. I heard Lee say in a tone of real concern, "I tell you what, men, looks like we'll be here for some time. Why don't you just go down to the other rest room?"

"What!" someone shouted. "You mean the nigger john?"

Then Lee said ever so sweetly, "Oh, well . . . there's always the floor." And he started laughing softly.

The guys got real mad. Someone tried my door, but it was locked. I heard one guy mutter, "The hell with this," and he split. For a minute there was silence; then we heard something like everyone rushing for the door.

Lee said, "C'mon, let's follow them." So we all slipped out.

Man, that joint was in an uproar. There was a crowd of whites milling around the door of both colored johns. The Crusader was standing around looking bewildered. Lee went over to the photographer and told him to get some pictures. After that, we got the girls and split the scene.

In the car coming back, Lee was crowing all over the place about what a genius he was. "See," he said, "I got the idea from Doug when he was saying all that bit about 'human functions.' That was the key: all I had to do then was figure out some way to create a crisis. So what do I do? Merely find a good strong colorless laxative and introduce it into the drinking water at the white coolers—a cinch with the old-fashioned open coolers they got here. Dig? That's what I was doing while you guys were sitting in."

Just then The Crusader bleeped, "Hey—would you stop at the next service station?"

The guy did look kinda pale at that. I thought, "And this cat always peddling his brotherhood and dragging his white man's burden behind him all the time." Oh, well, I guess I might have used the cooler, too.

Well, there was quite a furor over the whole deal. The school newspaper ran the shots and a long funny story, and the local press picked it up. Deershead was the laughingstock of the whole state. The management of the store was threatening to sue Lee and all that jazz, but it was too late to prove any "willful mischief or malice aforethought," or whatever it is they usually prove in these matters. The Negro kids in Deershead got hep and started a regular picket of the store. Man, I hear some of those signs were riots: LET US SIT DOWN TOGETHER, and stuff like that. The store held out a couple of months, but finally they took down the signs over the johns. Guess they wanted to forget.

That's the true story as it happened. You'll hear all kinds of garbled versions up on campus, but that's the true story of the "sitting" as it happened. Oh, yeah, one other thing: the Deershead branch of the NAACP wanted to erect a little statue of either me or Dick sitting on the john, the first Negro to be so integrated in Deershead. You know how they dig this first Negro bit. We had to decline. Always were shy and retiring.

ZZ PACKER

Doris Is Coming

Born in Chicago, reared in Atlanta, and currently living in San Francisco, ZZ
Packer (1973–) is Jones Lecturer at Stanford. She has published stories in the
New Yorker and *Harper's,* and her work has been selected for inclusion in *The
Best American Short Stories.* "Doris Is Coming" appeared in her 2003 collection,
Drinking Coffee Elsewhere, a Best Collection nominee for the Pen Faulkner
Award for Fiction.

Doris Yates stood in the empty sanctuary and wondered if the world
would really end in a matter of hours. It was New Year's Eve, 1961, and
beyond the pebbled amber church windows the world seemed normal
enough; the bushy teaberry and arum pressed their drupes against the
windowpanes as if begging to be let in, the speeding Buicks and Fords
on Montgomery Road sounded like an ocean. Farther out in the world
other Negro youths sneaked out of their homes and schoolrooms to sit
stoically at the Woolworth's while whites poured catsup on them. King
and Kennedy were transmitted onto the television screens of Stutz's Fine
Appliances and Televisions. Whenever she went there, Doris would sit
with old Stutz while he smoked and complained: "No news of Lithuania!"
he'd say with a disgust one would have expected to settle into resignation
since there never was—and never would be—any news about Lithuania.
Just as she thought that the world might end that very night, sunlight
illumined the windows, clear as shellac, bright as if trying to wake her.
She remembered the bottle of furniture oil at her feet and the rag in her
hand and began to polish the pulpit.

Cleaning the church was her mother's job, but that day, the day the
world would end, it was hers. Her mother cleaned house for the Bermans,
the one Jewish family in Hurstbourne Estates. Doris's father picked up
her mother just outside the neighborhood because the Bermans' neighbors had complained that the muffler of Edgar Yates's old Hupmobile

made too much noise. This meant Doris's mother Bernice had to walk nearly a mile to meet Doris's father, and was too tired to clean the church besides.

"They sure can cut a penny seventy-two ways," Doris's father would say whenever the Bermans were mentioned. It was his belief that all Jews were frugal to a fault, but Doris's mother would correct him. "It's not the men that's like that, it's the women." Once, when this exchange was playing out, Doris had said, "Can't be all that stingy. It was a Jew man who gave Dr. King all that money." She waited, not knowing whether she would get swatted for talking. Bernice and Edgar Yates were firm believers that their seven children should be seen, not heard. Doris was lucky that time; all her mother did was make a sound not unlike the steamy *psst* of the iron she was wielding and say, "Proves my point. It's not the men, it's the women."

Nevertheless, the furniture polish she stroked onto the pulpit was donated by Mrs. Berman and the rag she held had once been little Danny Berman's shirt. As Doris wiped down the pulpit, she thought of the Jewish boys from up North getting on that bus in Anniston, taking a beating with the rest of the Negro students.[1] She'd seen it all with her family on TV, from the store window of Stutz's. It was important, historic, she felt, but underneath the obvious importance there had been something noble and dangerous about it all. She'd called the NAACP once, to see how old one had to be to join a sit-in, but when she couldn't get through and the operator asked if she'd like to try again, her suspicions were confirmed that all those Movement organizations were monitored. Once she'd even asked Reverend Sykes if she could go to a march, just one, but the answer had been no, that Saints didn't go to marches. Then he quoted the scripture that says, "One cannot be of two masters, serving God and mammon both."

She could hear the main church door open and felt a rush of cold air, the jangle of keys being laid upon wood. The service wouldn't begin for another two hours or so, and she felt cheated that her quiet time was being disturbed. At first she thought it was her mother, then, for a brief

1. As the Freedom Riders were leaving Anniston, Alabama, on May 14, 1961, the bus was firebombed. Several people were injured, one critically.

moment, Reverend Sykes. When Sister Bertha Watkins appeared at the far end of the aisle, she tried to hide her disappointment.

Sister Bertha unbuttoned her coat, inhaling grandly, the way she did before she began her long testimonies. "Well, are you ready?"

"Almost, ma'am. I'm doing the dusting and polishing before sweep and mop."

"No," Sister Bertha smiled. "Not 'Are you finished?' *Are you ready?* For the Rapture?"[2]

According to the Pentecostal Assemblies of the World, an organization comprising the Kentucky-Tennessee-Ohio tristate area, the countdown to the end of the world began in 1948. That year marked the founding of Israel as a nation, and the countdown to the arrival of the Second Coming of Christ. A preacher from Tennessee had put the first Rapture at '55, seven years after Israeli nationhood, and when the Rapture had not occurred, the Pentecostal Assemblies of the World recalculated, slating the Second Coming for the last day of 1961.

On New Year's Eve, after she'd cleaned the church, Doris took her seat at her usual pew with the other girls her age. Girls who spent much of the service wondering whether Reverend Sykes conked his hair or if it was naturally wavy like that; why he hadn't found a wife yet and which of them would make likely candidates. They passed around notes that got torn up and stuffed into an innocent Bible; they repressed their laughter so that it would sound like a cough.

The service began like most, with testimonies, though tonight there were more people than usual. Doris listened to Brother Dorchester testify that he'd heard birds chirping about the end of the world. Sister Betty Forrester stood and said, "May the Lord take me tonight, because I *sho* don't want to go to work tomorrow!"

When Reverend Sykes rose, everyone gave a great shout, but he sent them a serious look, placing his folded hands on the podium.

"Bear with me, Saints. It's New Year's Eve, and while the world out there jukes around, I want to talk about another holiday. I want to talk about Thanksgiving. Now, y'all may be thinking, 'Why is Reverend Frank-

2. The Rapture, in some Christian theologies, is defined as the time when the church will be united with Christ at his second coming.

lin Sykes talking about Thanksgiving? Don't he know he a few months too late? Don't he know he a little behind? Don't he know that our Lord and Christ and Savior Jesus is coming tonight? Don't he know *anything?*' "

"Yes y' do," a Sister in the back of the church piped up.

Reverend Sykes smiled. He could look thirty or forty or fifty, depending on how he smiled and for whom. "Like I've told y'all before, I'm just a country boy. And in the country when *Daddy* wanted to get some meat on the table by *Christmas*, he knew how to get it. You see, 'fore Thanksgiving came *around*, we'd go out and catch us a turkey. Now you can train a horse to bite on the bit. Train the ox to go the straight *and narrow* way. But Saints! You can*not* train *no turkeys*! Even the chickens will come when you feed them, and in time, lay their eggs in the nest. All the other birds—the *gooses* and the *sparrows* and the *chickadees*—will go *south* when the winter comes. And the Lord shows them the way to go north in the spring."

"Amen," a few women called out. Doris also said, "Amen," though a bit late, wondering where he was heading with it all.

"When the raaaain comes pouring *down*—they won't try to run and hide. No, Saints! They don't heed the Lord's call like the other animals. All the turkey wants to do is follow all the *other* turkeys! They get so *tangled up* in one another, that they will *push* the weak ones on the bottom, but guess what? *All* the turkeys gonna drown! That's right. Don't be a gaggle of turkeys, Saints! Because when the *raaain* comes—!" He walked back to the pulpit and closed his Bible as if that was all he needed to say.

"Preach it, Brother!"

People were up on their feet, shouting, for they now knew the turkeys were all the sinners of the world and the rain was the Rapture that would surely occur that night. They danced and shouted in the aisles like never before. Doris stood as well, looking to see if her mother had arrived, when she spotted a white lady, standing, her hands swaying in time with everyone else's. She definitely wasn't one of the white Pentecostal women who occasionally visited colored churches. This lady had auburn hair, in deep waves that grazed her shoulders like a forties film star's, whereas saved white women were forbidden to cut their waist-length hair, the straggly ends like dripping seaweed. Those women wore ruffles and brooches from the turn of the century, but this lady was dressed in a smart, expensive-looking suit. Then it hit Doris—the white lady wasn't a lady at all, but a girl. Olivia Berman, Mrs. Berman's daughter. Beside Olivia was Doris's mother, who, despite the commotion, was completely silent. Why was Olivia Berman, a Jewish girl, here?

Everyone else was so caught up that no one noticed that Doris's mother wasn't, but Doris could not concentrate. If Jesus had come at that very second she would have been left behind because she wasn't thinking of Him.

It was nearly one o'clock in the morning and 1962 when they quit their shouting and settled into prayer. Jesus hadn't come, and the children—up past their bedtimes—began to grumble and yawn. When the last hymn had been sung, the last prayer spoken, and the last "Amen" said, Doris found herself outside, buoyed by the night air, scrambling to find the rest of her family. It wasn't hard with a white girl around. The rest of the congregation swirled around them, looking at them but saying nothing. There was no ignoring Olivia: her whiteness, her strangely erect posture, her red hair, the abrupt way she had of tossing her head like a horse resisting a rein.

Outside, everything was extremely as it had been. Jesus had not arrived, but Doris wished He had, if only to keep everyone speculating why Doris and her mother had brought a white girl to church.

"You remember Olivia," her mother said after the service. "She'll be going to Central." Her voice was changed, all the music gone out of it and replaced with the strange, overenunciated syllables she used talking to white folks or imitating them. Bernice Yates usually bade each and every Saint a good night, but that night she looked only at Doris and Olivia.

Before Doris could remember to be polite, she said, "Why are you going to public school? What happened?"

Her mother shot her a look. "Nothing *happened.*"

"It's okay, Bernice," Olivia said, lightly touching Doris's mother's shoulder.

Doris cringed. Not even her father called Doris's mother by her first name. Only Mrs. Berman—who paid her mother a paycheck— could call her Bernice.

If Olivia caught the ice in Doris's eyes, she didn't let on. "You see,

Doris, I got kicked out. I'm in need of some saving myself, that's why I came here tonight."

Doris's mother laughed, high and irregular. "Miss Olivia loves to kid around."

"I changed my name, Bernice. Livia. Not O-livia. And I'm not kidding around. I came to find out all about Christian salvation."

Doris watched as her mother looked at Olivia. It was hard to tell whether Olivia was making fun of them. Though Saints were gladdened when anyone became interested in the Holiness Church, this was too much. Jews were Jews, and that was that.

Doris remembered how she'd always thought of how lucky the Jews were: Reverend Sykes had said that whether or not they believed in Jesus, they wouldn't go to hell like other nonbelievers, because they were Chosen. That would mean heaven would be stocked with nobody but Pentecostals and Jews. Doris thought how strange it would be, getting whisked away to heaven only to find things much the way they were when she used to help her mother clean at the Bermans': Mrs. Berman with her pincurls whorled about her head like frosting on a cake, little Al and Danny Berman playing the violin, eyes rolling to the ceiling at Stravinsky's beautiful, boring music. She remembered when Al and Danny quit the scherzo they'd been practicing and started up "Take Me Out to the Ball Game," sawing on their expensive violins as if they were country fiddles. Mr. Berman had let out a primitive yell, thudding something to the ground, the only time Doris had seen him mad.

Olivia Berman offered to drive them home. Doris's mother said that with her daughters Etta Josephine and Doris now there, the car would be too full, and implored Miss Olivia to go ahead home. Doris's mother insisted that no, it was not too far for them to walk. That they'd been doing it for years.

She was the only Negro student in the class, the only Negro in all her classes. And though Mr. Fott, her Honors History teacher, rarely called on her, she was fine with it. She was relieved that he graded fairly, though sometimes he'd comment on her essays with a dark, runic hand: *Do you mean Leo XIII believed the state must remain sub-ord. to the interests of the indiv. composing it? Despite his antipathy of laissez-faire policies?* At least he didn't speak to her the way Mrs. Prendergast always did, slowly, loudly, as if Doris were deaf.

On the first day Olivia came to Mr. Fott's class, she wore earrings like tiny chandeliers and a pillbox hat, like Jackie Kennedy,[3] though no one wore hats to school. She entered minutes after the bell had rung, and though Mr. Fott made efforts to flag her down, chide her for tardiness, introduce her to the class, she rushed straight to where Doris was seated and cried, "*Doris!*" Doris made no move to get up, but Olivia descended upon her in an embrace, then turned to the class in mock sheepishness, as if she could not help her display of emotion. "Doris and I haven't seen each other in *forever*."

That, of course, was a lie; they'd just seen each other three days ago. But before that night at church, Doris hadn't seen Olivia in years. For the longest time Doris could have sworn she'd heard her mother saying something about Olivia going to a girls' boarding school. But that turned out not to be true: two or three years ago, at supper, when Etta Josephine had asked about her, Doris's mother had said, "You know what? I don't know where they keep that girl? But you know how white folks is. Got family living on the other side of the planet. Hop on one a them airplanes like they going to the corner store." Then she lowered her voice to a gossipy whisper. "But you know what? Now that you mention it, I do believe she's in the sanatorium." Doris hadn't believed it at the time, and had gradually forgotten about her.

"Miss . . ." Fott glanced down at his roll book. " . . . Berman, is it?"

"Why, yes. It is."

"Miss Berman, please be seated. For the record, miss, this class starts on time."

"Who does that Mr. Fott think he is, Doris? I mean, what's his problem?"

Outside school only a few of the yellow buses had pulled into the lot. Doris had been waiting for hers when Olivia—Livia—had spotted her. Livia stared, mutely insistent that Doris answer.

---

3. The wife of President John F. Kennedy, Jacqueline Kennedy (1929–94) often held sway in matters of style. She was widely known for bringing the pillbox hat into high fashion. Made from felt or straw, the pillbox was dome or egg shaped.

"He thinks he's the teacher, Livia," Doris finally said, "a man to be respected." She hugged her coat tight around her, praying for her bus to pull into its space and save her. She wished her old friend Helen was around so that she wouldn't be such a target for Livia, but now that Helen was in all-colored classes and Doris was in white ones, she rarely saw Helen. "All those white folks make me nervous," Helen had once said when she'd walked Doris to English. It hadn't occurred to Doris to *be* nervous, but now she was more annoyed than nervous; annoyed that this girl would use her mother's first name, annoyed that this girl would come to her church, her school. "Your mother never talks about you," Doris said, suddenly angry. "And where've you been all these years? Where'd you come from anyway?"

Livia took a cigarette from a silver case that looked as thin as a card, then lit it. She inhaled, nostrils dilating, eyes rolling in ecstasy. "I came from walking to and fro upon the earth. And up and down on it." She looked askance at Doris, as if to see whether Doris recognized that she was quoting from the Book of Job: Satan's answer to God's question, *Whence comest thou?*

"Don't use Bible verses that way," Doris said, then added, "and don't talk to me in class." She immediately regretted the words: her mother would slap her if she found out Doris had insulted the daughter of her only employer.

Livia looked at her, surprised. "Don't talk to you? I was doing you a favor. I mean, who *does* talk to you, Doris? Who? Name one person."

"I don't need anyone to talk to. Especially not white people. I talk to my family. I talk to the pastor."

"Reverend Sykes," Livia said thoughtfully, as though it were the title of a poem. She exhaled, and the smoke mazed ghostly around her face, then lifted like a veil above her pillbox hat. "Yes, Reverend Sykes. I don't think Reverend Sykes lets you do the things you want."

"Love not the world, neither the things that are in the world," Doris said. But the retort sounded hollow: she could not help but remember how Reverend Sykes had disapproved of her going to sit-ins, and wondered what Livia knew about Reverend Sykes besides what she'd seen that night at church. And why had Livia come to church at all? Doris decided that she said things purely to shock, said things so that people like Doris's mother could say nothing in return while Livia sat back in smug satisfaction, observing what she'd wrought.

Doris's bus had arrived, and though she tried to think of the worst thing she could say to Livia before parting, all she could manage was, "And I hate your hat."

When she got home it was dark. The boys were running about the house and Etta Josephine had not come back from her job shucking walnuts. But she knew her father must be home; she could hear him hammering away. Her father was trying to build a third bedroom where their back porch had been, but the partition made from blankets never kept out the draft. She turned on the kitchen stove to warm the house and start dinner, wondering why her father had picked winter, of all times, to tear down two major walls of the house. The *pock, pock* sound of nails being hammered into place had somehow grown spooky, as though some force were chipping its way into the house and would eventually take them all whether they invited it in or not.

She dialed the living room radio to its highest volume so she could hear it in the kitchen, over her father's pounding and sawing. She'd finished mixing the meal and egg yolk for the cornbread and had begun frying chicken when the white radio announcer delivered news about the Albany Movement in Georgia;[4] how the colored leaders of that area had petitioned for sewage, paved roads, and a moratorium on the stoning of Negro ministers' houses. It was suspected that the colored citizens of Albany would protest once again if their grievances weren't met, the announcer said. Then the announcer finished on a note of his own that made Doris so mad she forgot to pay attention to what she was doing and burned her hand on the skillet. *When*, he implored, *will the tumult end?*

Doris had excused herself after dinner, saying she needed to gather leaves for her biology-class leaf collection. And though she knew she was headed

---

4. The Albany Movement, in and out of the news from 1961 until 1965, was formed as an umbrella organization to coordinate the differences in leadership styles between the youthful SNCC, which operated from a grassroots position, and the NAACP and SCLC, which operated by working through the established older black leaders of the community.

to Stutz's, she hadn't exactly told a lie. She *did* need to collect leaves for Mrs. Prendergast's class, though they weren't due until the end of spring.

"Dorrie!" Mr. Stutz said when she entered his store that night. "It's Dori-ka!" He took a break from smoking his cigarette to cough, loud and insistent.

She'd supposed that Dori-ka was some Lithuanian diminutive, but she'd never asked him. She liked that she had another name, in some other language, and didn't want to ruin the mystery of it by finding out what it meant.

"Hello, Mr. Stutz. How's your wife and family?"

Stutz made a face and waved his hand. "Want, want, want. They all want. I tell them, in Lithuania, you are freezing. Here, in America, your brain is frying!"

He laughed at his own joke, though Doris didn't know what was so funny. She didn't always understand him, but she liked his accent. And he seemed lonely. Sometimes, when he stood among his televisions and appliances, he looked like the only person in a graveyard, so she tried to laugh when he laughed.

"Game show is not on, Dorrie. But come. Take chair."

She sat on the stool next to him, and for a while they did not speak. They watched *Marshal Dillon*, Stutz smoking his cigarette peacefully. Then they sat through *The Lloyd Bridges Show*, and when it was over, Stutz said, "Ah. He should not try that show. He was better in *Sea Hunt*."

Doris had not been able to enjoy either of the programs: she could not forget the radio broadcast she'd heard earlier, how the announcer seemed to loathe the colored people of Albany when all they'd wanted was to march for decent sewage disposal without being stoned for it. She thought of what Livia had said about Reverend Sykes not letting her do what she wanted, then looked at Mr. Stutz and announced, "I'm going to go to a sit-in."

He looked at her, puzzled. "Oho! First I am thinking, She is already *sitting*, she is already *in* store." He shook his head then raised a single finger. "You mean like TV."

"Yes," she said. "But they're not just on TV. They do it for real."

"I know that they are *real*," he said, as if she'd insulted his intelligence. "But I think: Good maybe for others. Not so good for Dorrie."

She leapt from the stool on which she'd been sitting. "What do you mean 'not so good'? You think I should just walk around and not care that I have to use a separate everything! That my father shouldn't be able to vote!"

"Dorrie *not yell at Stutz!*"

She sighed her apology, and after a few deep breaths, he seemed to accept it.

"I not say it *baaad*," he said, trying to reconcile. "But Dori-ka is *nice girl—*"

How could Stutz not understand? She was about to object, but he placed a stern hand on her arm to keep her from interrupting him.

"Nice girl. I like Dori-ka. I don't want people to put *Senf* and catsup all over Dori-ka like they do on TV."

Whenever he and Doris had watched news footage of the sit-ins in Greensboro, they'd seen whites as young as the Negro students squirting mustard and catsup all over the protesters.[5] It had amazed her that the students could sit so still, taking it, occasionally wiping themselves off, but never shouting or hitting.

"And Dori-ka," he said, "I am businessman. I think of things from business perspective. If you do what they say called 'integrate,' what will everyone here do?" He waved his hand beyond the window, to where Amos Henry cut meat in his butcher shop, where Mozelle Gordon ran the little store that sold sundries. And there, also in his gesture, was Thomasina Edison, who did everyone's hair, her hot comb heating in its little pod, waiting to do its Saturday-night miracles. "All these business," Stutz said, "all of them Negroid. All," he said, placing his hand on his heart, "but Stutz."

"Now, when someone need hairs cut, they go over *there*. When they need meat cut in half, they go over *there*." He pointed out the window as though outside lay the seven wonders of the world. "When you 'integrate,' I predict, everyone will go to white, none to black. Why? Because white America will build big palace. They will say, 'Why go to Negroid store? Little-bitty tchotchke store? We have everything here!'" Then, with a flourish of his hand, he said, "No more Negroid store. Poof. All gone."

---

5. As the sit-ins continued, mobs often gathered behind the students to torment them in various ways, such as holding lighted cigarettes to their skin or using condiments as weapons. The more-violent protesters were likely to be in Jackson, Mississippi, or Nashville, Tennessee.

She didn't think that would happen. Couldn't imagine anything like it. But even though Stutz didn't really understand, she felt something like affection for him. When the *Red Skelton Show* theme music began playing, she knew it was time to leave. She stood in front of him, and though both made as if to hug each other, they didn't.

A week later, after Wednesday-night Bible study, Doris decided to ask for a meeting with Reverend Sykes. Her mother would take at least half an hour to make her rounds, hugging and God-blessing everyone in sight, and her brothers could spend all night outside playing stickball in their winter coats.

"Of course, Doris," Reverend Sykes said when she asked to speak with him. "It's been a while since we had one of our talks." He gathered his Bible notes from the pulpit and led her to his office: a hymn-book closet that had been only half cleared of books. He gestured for her to take the seat opposite his and made a little laugh. "Remember when you read some book about digestion, then asked why stomach acid didn't kill Jonah when he was in the belly of the whale?" He smiled, remembering.

It was true. Doris used to want to know why it was fair for David to have Bathsheba's husband killed, just because he wanted to marry her himself; why Jacob got to have Esau's birthright, when Esau's only fault—as far as Doris could see—was that he was hairy.

"This isn't a question," Doris said, "though it involves a Bible story. It's more of a theory."

Reverend Sykes made a mock-impressed face at the word "theory."

"Well, I was thinking about how Jesus turned two fish and five loaves of bread into enough to feed five thousand people, showing how when you feed a physical hunger, folks are more receptive to hearing a message that'll then feed their spiritual hunger."

"Amen," Reverend Sykes said, nodding. "Couldn't a said it better myself. A spiritual hunger that needs to be fed by the Word of God."

"But Reverend Sykes," Doris said, "what if a thousand had to eat their bread and fish in the valley, while the rest got to eat theirs up on the hill? That's what's happening now. We colored have to eat our fish and bread in the valley. The white folks get to eat theirs up on the hill."

He rubbed his eyes with his fingertips. "Well, it seems like you've got a decision to make, Doris. Do you wanna starve, but keep your house with a hilltop view? Or do you wanna live in the valley with a full belly? Hmm? And what's so wrong with the valley, Doris? The Lord says, 'Consider the lilies of the field, how they toil not, neither do they spin . ..' "

"But Reverend Sykes," she said, voice quavering, "what if the valley is flooded? And why should you have to choose?" She was already near tears, and if she continued in this vein, whatever she said would surely start her crying.

"Doris," he said. He reached across the desk and placed her hands in his, holding them solemnly. "This is about those marches and sit-ins, isn't it? Now I know there's *Dr. King* out there," he said, making the name sound like a fad, "calling himself *preaching*. But do you want to be with all those girls and boys who'd go to jail in a second? Not even caring how much their mamas and daddies have to pay to get 'em out. Do you want that?"

The answer seemed to be no, but it got caught in her throat, like a hummingbird. She finally said, "They're only asking to be treated equal with white folks. Like how God would treat them. That's why the other churches support the sit-ins."

Reverend Sykes let go of her hands and kicked his feet up on the desk. "And these *other* churches. I suppose they're Baptist and A.M.E.? Now, them folks think you can sin on Saturday night and sing hungover with the choir Sunday morning. Did you see that mother of that unsaved family that came in on New Year's? That woman! Coming to church in a red dress, of all things."

Doris hadn't noticed any such woman, she'd been so surprised to see Olivia in the pews. But she looked hard at the Reverend and said, "Yes. I remember. The night the Lord was supposed to come."

"Today," Livia said, "you'll be sick." This was the Tuesday after Doris had spoken with Reverend Sykes. After Mr. Fott's class, Livia took Doris by the crook of her elbow, steering her away from third-period French.

Livia played hooky all the time, and though Doris knew this was what Livia had in mind, knew it was wrong, there was something thrilling about riding in a car with someone besides her parents, going someplace she knew would not be church.

"I can't," Doris said, though she knew she would.

"Alice is already waiting in the car." Alice, another girl in History class, spoke to Livia because speaking to Livia always got you noticed. Alice had begun to dress like Livia, one time even wearing a pillbox hat to class.

Livia drove a turquoise-and-white Mercury Park Lane, a far cry from Doris's father's Hupmobile. They saw *Splendor in the Grass* at the Vogue, Livia sitting in the colored balcony with Doris. Finally Alice came up, too. It was the second movie Doris had seen since her family had joined the church. The first had been a French movie she saw for extra credit, the one time she'd gone against the church's teachings without confessing what she'd done.

They drove from St. Matthews to Germantown, covering the city. When they got to Newburg, Alice let out a long sigh. "I bought my dress for the Winter Dance," she said, turning to Livia. "It's a long satin sheath with roses on either side of the straps. The straps are that minty green color everyone's wearing, but the rest is one long flesh-colored sheath. Mama would die if she saw it, but what's bought is bought."

"Flesh colored?" Doris said.

"I know! Scandalous!"

"You mean, the color of your flesh?" Doris said.

"Well, who else's would it be?" Alice looked to Livia as if searching for a sane opinion.

"You mean *your* flesh color. And Livia's and Mr. Fott's. Not mine."

Alice stared at Doris. "For the love of heaven, it's just a word."

Livia said, "But why use the word if it's not accurate? It's simply not the color of everyone's flesh."

"Well, how should I say it? What should I say when describing it? Say, 'Oh, I bought a dress the color of everybody else's skin except Doris's'?"

"I'm not the only one."

"I could say it was a flesh-colored dress and everyone would know what I was talking about. Everyone would know exactly what I was talking about."

"I'm sure they would, Alice," Livia said. She laughed, high and free. "*Everyone* would."

Alice pinched her fingers together, as though holding a grain of salt. "It's those little things, Doris. Why do your people concentrate on all those little, itty-bitty things?"

Why should she care about what Alice said? That phrase. "Your people." Livia had kicked Alice out of the car right there on Newburg Road, where cabs didn't come and buses were scarce. It was a hard thing to do—kick someone out of a car—and Livia had had to open the passenger side door, drag Alice out against her will, tug and tug until Alice, unwilling to make too much of a scene, finally stayed put on the sidewalk. Her face scrunched up mean and hateful, as if she was too proud to cry, though obviously she wanted to. Livia looked disappointed that Doris wouldn't help kick Alice out, but Doris hopped into the front seat where Alice had sat just the same.

"That's better, now, isn't it," Livia had said, as if she'd done it all for Doris, but Doris didn't speak to her the whole way home. Alice had annoyed her, offended her, but she didn't see any sense in doing anything about it. Acknowledging too much just made it hurt worse. Livia's self-satisfaction and self-righteousness felt just as bad as Alice's thoughtlessness. When Livia drove Doris to the West End part of town where Doris lived, she seemed to delight in seeing so many Negro faces.

During supper, Doris hardly said anything, and no one seemed to notice. Charleroy and Edgar talked excitedly about stickball, about grade-school gossip, about their teacher's bosom until, finally, their mother told them to hush.

It was the family's habit to walk after supper, a leisurely stroll that made them feel wealthy. Once they got to Stutz's Fine Appliances, they'd stop and survey the fifteen or so TVs on display as if they were finicky purchasers looking for the exact one that would suit their needs. In the beginning, Doris's mother would make noises of approval or disapproval of the various models, and her father would crane his neck to examine the side finish and sturdiness of the cabinets. They had all played along when they'd started going to Stutz's so long ago, though they all knew that they didn't have the money and wouldn't for a long time. As far as Doris knew, she had been the only one to actually go inside and talk to the old man.

They stood outside of Stutz's swaddled in coats and watched Lucy and Ethel and Fred beg Ricky to let them on his show. Lucy, ridiculous in a ballerina costume, Ethel in a cha-cha dress, and pudgy Fred in the same dress but wearing a Shirley Temple wig.

Old man Stutz came outside, hobbling. "Hello, friends. Hello, Dorrie."

They looked at Doris, and a chill went through her as if she didn't have a coat on at all. Never before when she and her family visited at night had Stutz been there, only his son, the one he called Lazybones, who never made an effort to go out and greet window shoppers.

"Hello, Mr. Stutz. Mr. Stutz, this is my family." She went through the introductions, and her parents fell silent. The boys pinched each other and tried not to laugh.

"All the answers," Stutz said, wagging and pointing to Doris with a little too much exuberance. "She knows all the answers to all the game shows! You want to buy?" He gestured extravagantly at the television they'd been watching.

Her mother laughed as she had at Livia. Nervous, uncertain. "Well, mister, we'd like to. We're working on it."

"Work on it, work on it!" Stutz said, smiling broadly and bobbing his head.

When they left to walk back home her mother said, "That little Russian man sure is funny-looking."

"Woman, you always got to talk 'bout how someone look," her father said. "Someone nose always too big or too little. Or they teeth missing. Or they breath stank."

"Can't help it if he's funny-looking."

"Lord made him that way. He Russian."

"Rich as he is, he can do something to his face. Keep it from being so funny-looking."

"He's Lithuanian," Doris said, "not Russian."

And little Edgar, popping her on the thigh, said, "Who asked you?"

A few weeks after the car ride and movie, Livia did not show up for class. Doris assumed she was playing hooky, but then two days passed, then three; still no Livia. Finally she went to Livia's homeroom teacher to check whether Livia had been in school at all. She'd been marked present that day, and though Doris looked for her, she couldn't find her. She was not in Fott's class, hadn't stopped by to lean up against Doris's locker and dole out pithy bon mots.

As soon as the last bell rang, Doris searched the front of the school, and when she did not find Livia there, she walked to the student parking lot. There, the white kids stared at her the way department store clerks stared at her family when they went to try on clothes. They stared, then looked away as if they hadn't seen anything at all.

Doris ran toward the gym, remembering how the smokers always hovered near it. Doris was out of breath, but Livia didn't seem to notice or care. She stood there and smiled as though awaiting introductions at a cocktail party.

"Doris," she said.

"Where've you been?" She wanted Livia to say, *To and fro upon the earth and walking up and down on it*. That was always Livia's answer. *Say it*, Doris willed. *Say it*. She'd missed those lines from Job, missed Livia more than she thought she would. *Say it*.

"I've been around," Livia said. She sounded drunk. "Around and around."

"*Around*? What about school? What about—" She caught herself before she could say, *What about me?*

"I hate to say it, Doris, but my time here is limited."

Doris thought death, sickness. Livia going insane like Natalie Wood in *Splendor in the Grass*; she imagined Livia laid up with satin sheets like Greta Garbo in *Camille*, the movie she'd seen for extra credit for French class.

"*No*," Livia said, reading her mind. "Nothing serious. I'm going to school up North. I can't stand it down here anymore. You shouldn't either."

She didn't know what Livia could mean by that: Where would she go? What choice did she have? And had she known things to be any other way? Only rich folks like the Bermans could afford to go wherever they wanted.

"My mother said you were in the sanatorium," Doris said. "Was that where you were before? Is that where you're going?" She checked Livia's face for some crumb of emotion.

Livia smiled brightly, as if Doris never ceased to amaze her, then drew Doris up in a hug. "Oh, Doris," she said. "Don't you know that the real crazy people are the ones who do the same thing over and over again? Expecting a different result every time?"

On the school bus all the Negro kids talked like a party, relieved to be going home. When they spoke to her, it was either a question about Holy Rollers or a question about what whites did in class, how they acted and how they treated her.

"Do they throw things at you?" one boy asked.

"Naw," a girl answered in her stead. "She'd beat 'em up like Joe Louis."

She got off right before Stutz's. None of the televisions were on window display. Without the televisions, the windows were dustier than she'd remembered. It seemed as though someone had stolen them all, but there was no broken glass. She cleared the film of dust off the window and peered in. In the rear of the dark store, televisions sat mutely on the floor like obedient children. Someone was moving around inside. The figure took a large box down from the counter and set it on the floor. He remained hunched over it for a long time, heaving, as if to gather strength for the next one. When the figure finally stood, she saw that it was old man Stutz himself.

She tapped on the window, saw him frown, then, recognizing her, smile with all his wrinkles. He invited her in with a grand sweep of his arm, like a baseball player winding up to pitch. "Come in, come in," he said, though the glass was so thick she could only see him mouthing the words. She threw her hands up. "How? The door is locked?" He frowned. Then, understanding, unlocked the door.

"Mr. Stutz." She started to take off her coat, out of habit, but the store was so cold she kept it on. "How are you?"

He wiped his forehead with his handkerchief, folded it in fourths, then eighths, then put it in his pocket. He rubbed his huge eyelids. "Oh, not so good, Dorrie. Moving out. Almost two weeks now, you haven't heard?"

She tried to remember the last time she'd seen him. Perhaps a month ago. "No. I guess I haven't been by in a while."

"This is the problem. You see it? This is the very problem. People

come by. They watch. Laugh at Lucy. Ha ha ha, look at Lucy, love Lucy."
He made a crazy face, though whether it was supposed to be Lucy or
Ricky, Doris could not tell. Then Stutz's face went from crazy to somber.
"The people, they love Lucy, they go home. No one buys. No sales, no
money. No money, no Stutz." He threw up his hands like a magician making himself disappear. "No Stutz," he said again. He ambled over to the
nearest chair, brought out a second one for Doris. She sat, watching him
settle into his. He coughed for a long time, then brought out his handkerchief and pressed it against his lips. "And other things," he said, "but
I don't want to offend."

Her skin prickled. "What other things?"

"The neighborhood."

"They're good people."

"Yes," Stutz said sadly, his eyes wise and sclerotic, "Good people."
He swept his hand toward the barren store window. "This neighborhood.
Good people, yes, but what's-their-name, right here on Fourth Street.
Chickens in the yard. Scratch, scratch scratch. Cockadoodledoo. Lithuania in America. And those boys, playing baseball in the middle of the
street. Do cars want to stop and buy from Stutz if they will get a crack on
their windshield? I don't think so." Stutz shook his head in a slow, ancient
way. "Good people. Yes. But."

It was true. Sister Forrester still kept chickens in her yard, and her
brothers' friend Juny Monroe got every boy a mile around to play stickball in the street. The games lasted for hours. She could understand how,
surrounded by televisions all day, one would be able to see that the rest
of the world was different from Fourth Street, prettier, more certain, full
of laughter and dresses and men who wore hats not only when they went
to church but when they went to work in offices and banks too.

Old Stutz seemed to see something in Doris's eye and said, "Aha!
But as they say, there is a silver lining. A smart girl you are, Dorrie. You
go learn, come back, make better. You see. I planned it all out for you.
Just do."

"It's not that easy."

He waved his hand. "Easy? Easy? I come from Lithuania. I leave my
wife and my Lazybones son behind. I work. I send money. They come.
Now my wife watches television and points. She wants a fur. Okey, dokey.

I say, 'I go to the wood and catch you a fur.' She says, No no no no, and slams all the doors."

She wanted to say, *But you're white*. She wanted to say, *In another generation, your Lazybones son will change his name from "Stutz" to "Stuart" or "Star" and the rest of America will have forgotten where you came from*. But she couldn't say it. He coughed and this time unfolded the handkerchief and spat into it, so instead she said, "And I suppose you had to walk to school, twenty miles, uphill, in the snow."

His face brightened, surprised. "Aha! I see you are familiar with Lith-uania!"

She walked from Stutz's and up along Fourth Street. When she got to Claremont, the street where she lived, she kept going, past Walnut and Chestnut and all the other streets named after trees. She hit the little business district, which was still lit for New Year's, the big incandescent bulbs on wires like buds growing from vines, entwining the trees and lighting the shop facades. When she walked farther, she felt, for the first time, some purpose other than solitude motivating her. She rushed, and did not know why, until she found it. Clovee's Five and Dime. As soon as she saw it, she knew what she was doing.

It was warm inside, and she made her way to the soda fountain, even warmer from the grill's heat. A white man stood at the ice cream machine and whirred a shake. Two white men sat at the counter and talked in low, serious tones, occasionally sucking up clots of shake through a straw.

There was one waitress, hip propped against the side of the counter, wiping the countertop with a rag that had seen cleaner days. Without looking up she said, "Sorry. We don't serve colored people."

"Good," Doris said. "I don't eat them." She remembered Helen telling her that this was the line someone had used during a sit-in, and Doris was glad to have a chance to use it.

The waitress frowned, confused, but when she finally got it, she laughed. "Seriously, though," the waitress said, turning solemn, "I can't serve you."

The two men talking looked over at her and shook their heads. They began talking again, occasionally looking over at Doris to see if she'd left.

"What if I stay?"

The waitress looked to the man making the shake, eyes pleading for help. "I don't know. I don't know. I just don't make the rules and I feel sorry for you, but I don't make 'em."

The man walked over with a shake and gave it to the waitress, who bent the straw toward herself and began to drink it. "Look," the man said to Doris, "I wouldn't sit here. I wouldn't do that."

"You wouldn't?"

"I wouldn't if I were you."

She sat. Shaking, she brought out her World History book. She'd made a book cover for it with a paper bag, and she was glad she'd done it because she was sweating so much it would have slipped from her hands otherwise. She set it on the counter, opened it, as if she did this every day at this very shop, and tried to read about the Hapsburgs, but couldn't.

It occurred to her that other students who did sit-ins were all smarter than she; they'd banded together, and had surely told others of their whereabouts, whereas she had foolishly come to Clovee's all by herself. She stared at her book and didn't dare look up, but from the corner of her eye she noticed when the two white men who'd been talking got up and left.

The man at the ice cream machine made himself some coffee and beckoned the waitress to him. When he whispered something to her, she swatted him with the rag, laughing.

Once Doris felt the numbness settle in her, she felt she could do it. She tried at the Hapsburgs again.

The waitress said, "Student? High school?"

"Yes, ma'am. Central."

"My daughter's over at Iroquois."

"We played them last Friday." Doris didn't know what the scores were, didn't care, but had heard about the game over the intercom.

"Well." The waitress started wiping the counter again, going over the same spots.

When Doris closed her book, about to leave, she said, "I just want you to know I'm leaving now. Not because you're making me or because I feel intimidated or anything. I just have to get home now."

The waitress looked at her.

"Next time I'll want some food, all right?"

"We can't do that, but here's half my shake. You can have it. I'm done."

The shake she handed over had a lipstick ring around the straw, and a little spittle. Doris knew she wouldn't drink it, but she took it anyway. "Thanks, ma'am."

Outside Clovee's Five and Dime, the world was cold around her, moving toward dark, but not dark yet, as if the darkness were being adjusted with a volume dial. Whoever was adjusting the dial was doing it slowly, consistently, with infinite patience. She walked back home and knew it would be too late for dinner, and the boys would be screaming and her father wanting his daily beer, and her mother worried sick. She knew that she should hurry, but she couldn't. She had to stop and look. The sky had just turned her favorite shade of barely lit blue, the kind that came to windows when you couldn't get back to sleep but couldn't quite pry yourself awake.

Marches and Demonstrations

The impetus for the marches that took place during the days of the civil rights movement was a deep sense of injustice. African Americans were tired of being ignored, mistreated, discriminated against, denied the right to vote, or refused employment in certain businesses. Patience was not paying off. But a large number of people walking peaceably, often singing, presented a powerful image that the television camera could take to the American public to garner sympathy and support. Possibly hundreds of marches and other types of demonstrations occurred during the heyday of the movement.

One such demonstration occurred in 1951 when sixteen-year-old Barbara Johns, a student at a black school in Prince Edward County, Virginia, called for a school strike and led 450 students out the door. Johns's school lacked a number of amenities compared to the local all-white high school—no gymnasium, no lockers, no cafeteria—and the school, built for 180 students, housed more than twice that many. Extra students were put in temporary plywood shelters covered with tarpaper and heated with potbellied stoves. The students planned to strike until a new school was built. Because of threats, Johns was sent by her family to live with her uncle in Montgomery, Alabama. That uncle was Vernon Johns, the activist minister of the Dexter Avenue Baptist Church. His church would become the first assignment for a young Martin Luther King Jr. in 1954.

Another demonstration occurred in April 1960 after the house of attorney Alexander Looby was bombed. Looby had defended the students who had been arrested in the Nashville sit-in movement. To protest the bombing, students began a march to city hall. Thousands joined the marchers in the silent walk—just the sound of their shoes clicking against the pavement, remembers C. T. Vivian, who was there that day. Once the protestors arrived at city hall, they met with Mayor Ben West, who admitted, when asked, that he couldn't say it was right to discriminate against a man based solely on the color of his skin. After that meeting, lunch counters in Nashville were soon integrated.

Such pictures of peaceful demonstrations changed in Birmingham in the spring of 1963 when Commissioner of Public Safety Eugene "Bull" Connor called out the police dogs and the fire hoses and aimed both at demonstrating children and adults. The force of the water from the fire hoses could take the bark off trees and knock people to the ground and roll them. The police dogs ripped the pants off grown men. Pictures of this bedlam went round the world. As the adults were arrested, children took their places. Before a resolution could be reached, over twenty-five hundred had gone to prison, some as young as six years old. The first story in this section, "Negro Progress" (1994), captures the activity of that spring in Birmingham. Through the eyes of a young man who hates to admit his own fear, his own insecurity about what is happening around him, he is forced to come face-to-face with the qualities that scare him and that will ultimately save him.

Shortly after the events in Birmingham, on August 28 of the same year, 250,000 people marched on Washington and gathered to hear speeches from at least a half dozen leaders of the movement. As history has borne out, the other speeches of that day have faded from memory in the face of Martin Luther King Jr.'s "I Have a Dream," arguably the most triumphant moment of oratory in all of the twentieth century. The second story in this section, "The Marchers" (1979), recalls that day, employing the call-and-response pattern that often accompanied King's speeches. In this parable, however, hope cannot triumph, even when it appears everywhere around.

"Moonshot" (1989), the third story in this section, spotlights a female civil rights veteran who is in charge of a mass rally in Cocoa Beach, Florida. Her role in the preparation of the event hints at the hierarchical structure between workers and the sponsoring organization's executives. The story also shows the differences in the roles that men and women played in the movement. The civil rights movement was a learning arena for women, who also were beginning to claim their own rights and places in the world; figuring out their working relationships with men was yet another challenge.

One of the most important marches in the movement was the fifty-mile walk from Selma to Montgomery in March 1965. The events leading up to this walk began in February in Marion, Alabama, when black citizens marched to the Perry County Courthouse to protest being barred from voting and state troopers beat them with clubs. When the troopers attacked his mother and grandfather, Jimmie Lee Jackson moved forward to protect them, and the troopers shot him in the stomach. He was taken to the hospital in Selma but died a few days later on February 26. Black leaders in the community were tired; they had had enough of the kind of violence that accompanied what was supposed to be their right as American citizens to vote. Someone proposed a march from Selma to Montgomery, taking Jackson's coffin with them and placing the body at the feet of Governor George Wallace. On March 7, 1965, six hundred people gathered to begin the walk. The leaders were John Lewis and Hosea Williams. As they crossed the Edmund Pettus Bridge, the demonstrators were met by state troopers. Chaos broke loose as the troopers threw tear gas and rode their horses into the melee, swinging clubs at both men and women. Over fifty people went to the hospital. The day became known as "Bloody Sunday." Television cameras interrupted the major networks that Sunday night, and people all over America saw what was happening in Selma.

Two days later, Martin Luther King Jr. and Ralph Abernathy of the SCLC led a second walk but were permitted only to kneel and pray on the Edmund Pettus Bridge before returning to the church that was their headquarters. The young leaders from the SNCC, Lewis and Williams, referred to this effort as "Turnaround Tuesday." On television, King asked for help, and people from all over the country began to arrive in Selma. By March 21 the courts granted legal permission. The marchers would be protected by federal intervention. "Selma" (1972) recreates in a diary format what Viola Liuzzo might have thought as she spent time in Selma, participating in the walk. Liuzzo was killed the evening of March 25 while shuttling marchers from Montgomery to Selma. As she was returning from Selma to pick up a second load, Klansmen pulled beside her car and shot her as she drove. She died instantly. In the story, Angelina, the fictional Liuzzo, records her last diary entry on what will be the last day of her life.

The last story in the section, "Marching through Boston" (1966), also alludes to the death of Viola Liuzzo and the march from Selma to Montgomery. In it, a woman, who has answered King's call and flown to Selma from Boston to participate, hears of the death of Viola Liuzzo, a mother of four, as she is returning home. The woman also happens to be a mother of four. Unlike "Selma," however, which focuses on the event itself and on a woman who died in its midst, this story focuses on the response of an anguished husband who can only contemplate all manner of what-ifs. The marches and demonstrations are real to him, but they matter in a way removed from those people who would directly benefit, for within hours of the conclusion of the walk to the steps of the capitol in Montgomery, President Johnson's administration began work on the Voting Rights Act. The initiative became law in the summer of 1965.

ANTHONY GROOMS

Negro Progress

Born in Charlottesville, Virginia, Anthony Grooms (1955–) is a poet, short-story writer, playwright, and novelist. A recipient of several Fulbrights, he is a professor of English at Kennesaw State University near Atlanta, Georgia. "Negro Progress," first published in *Callaloo* in the fall of 1994, is in his 1995 collection, *Trouble No More*, winner of the Lillian Smith Award.

The water hunted the boy. It chipped bark from the oaks as he darted behind the trees.[1] It caught him in the back. His lanky legs buckled. Then, as if the fireman who directed the hose were playing a game, the boy's legs were cut from under him, and he was rolled over and over in the mud.

From the distance of half a block, Carlton Wilkes watched the white ropes of water as they played against the black trunks and lime-green leaves of the trees. In the sunlight, the streams sparkled, occasionally crisscrossed or made lazy S's.

He had been on his way to his Uncle Booker's building when he first saw the children. They were wearing school clothes. He remembered that somebody in King's organization had called for a children's crusade, placing teenagers and children as young as six on the front lines of the city's civil rights demonstrations. Even when the first fire truck skidded to a stop across the street from the park and the firemen unwound their hoses and screwed them into the hydrants, he paid little attention. Uncle Booker had quite literally ordered him downtown. "It's only your damn future that's at stake," he had said. Uncle Booker had a way of exaggerating, but when it came to business, his feet were flat on the ground. There was little Negro business that went on in the city that Uncle Booker didn't have a hand in.

1. The setting is Kelly Ingram Park in Birmingham, Alabama, in the spring of 1963. In response to the peaceful protests of black children, Theophilus Eugene "Bull" Connor (1897–1973), commissioner of Public Safety, ordered the Birmingham Fire Department to hose the protestors. The force of the water was so powerful that it stripped bark off the trees and knocked to the ground any person caught in its path.

Then a child's squeal, the squeal and the whoosh-and-scour of the water, made him look up at the sometimes taut, sometimes lazy ropes the firemen directed. At first, the children taunted the firemen. They danced about, darting under the arcing streams and through the mist of the pressurized water. Then the boy was tripped and rolled with such force that Carlton thought he must have been hurt. He told himself to move, to run to the boy, but this meant passing the fire trucks. Then he saw the paddy wagons and the handsome German shepherds. His legs went rubbery.

His legs seemed barely strong enough to push in the clutch as he drove to Salena's house. He and Salena Parrish had been engaged for six months but had not set a date for the wedding. She was a nurse at the city hospital, one of the first Negro nurses there. When she opened the door he saw in her expression how harried he looked.

"What happened to you?" she asked, her gray eyes growing wide for a second.

The sight of her made his heart rush. Her light skin blushed in response to his breathlessness. He stumbled across the threshold, stammering. Not until she had taken him by the shoulders did he manage to speak.

"They . . . they are *hosing* children—shooting them down like . . . like the Boston massacre."

For a moment she looked horrified, then seemed to understand him and relaxed a little. "You mean *spraying* them with water?" She tightened the belt on her robe and turned on the radio. "Just *hosing* them with water?"

There was no news on the radio. She led him to the sofa, spoke soothingly to him, and brought him a drink. It was cheap whiskey, but it calmed him. She took his hand and asked him to tell her what had happened.

"Let me get another drink." He went to the decanter in the dining room. The decanter was made of gaudy cut glass. He poured a finger, swallowed it, and poured another. The trembling stopped; he felt a little more like himself. "Doesn't your old man ever buy good liquor?"

"You know it's only for display."

He talked a moment about what he had seen, but when he got to the part about rescuing the boy, he stopped.

"Then what did you do?" She leaned toward him.

He sipped the whiskey. "I came here."

"What happened to the boy?"

"I don't know."

"Well," she said and sat back on the sofa. "Probably nothing. The radio hasn't said a thing."

The trembling came back. He paced. "I just don't know. I have a sick feeling. I can't explain it. It feels like . . . like my whole insides want to come out." He stopped while she took the curler out of her bangs. "It feels like something bad is going to happen, and if I stay here—I mean if *we*—stay here we are going to be trapped in it."

"Well, there *is* a civil rights protest."

He took a breath. "Don't be sarcastic."

"I don't mean to be sarcastic. I'm just pointing out to you that something *is* happening. You don't realize it because you don't see it every day. And, well, you have options those people don't have. Money gives you options."

"What is that supposed to mean?"

"Just an observation." Then she added quickly, "Not of you—not so much of you, sweetheart—but of my patients. You feel you may get trapped. You can afford to go to New York or California. But most of them can't. At least not in the way I'm talking about."

"What's the difference in New York?" He closed his eyes. "I wish I could really get away from here. From this city. From the whole damn country." He sat on the sofa and took her hand. "I'm serious. Why don't we get married and go overseas? We could go to Amsterdam or Paris. I hear things aren't so bad over there."

"Paris? Oh sure, *mon cher*. And just what are we going to do in *Paris*? We don't have that kind of money."

"I'll sell Dad's part of the business to Uncle Booker. He buys up everything sooner or later anyway."

"He *is* a businessman."

Carlton remembered his meeting with his uncle. "And I'm not?"

He did not go right away to meet his uncle. Salena decided to go to the hospital and asked him to make lunch for her father. Her father, Mr.

Parrish, was a wiry, olive man with patchy gray fuzz on his head. He seemed agitated when he came in from his store and found Carlton in the kitchen warming up string beans and leftover turkey. "Where's Salena, Mr. Wilkes? She done got called in?"

"She went in before they called her."

"Volunteered her time? She know better'n that."

"I believe she felt they would call her anyway with the riot going on downtown."

"Riot?" He went to the washroom just off the kitchen. "I ain't hear tell of no riot. Heard they spraying them children. But spraying ain't a riot."

"No, sir. I guess not." Carlton watched Mr. Parrish's angular hips as he bent over the basin. "Anyway, Salena asked me to warm up some dinner for you." He poured the limp, sweet-smelling beans onto the plate with the turkey and candied yams. His stomach growled a little, but he decided not to eat until the old man invited him.

Mr. Parrish put the paper napkin to his collar and began his lunch. "You not in business today?"

"I had an appointment down with Uncle Booker, but . . . the disturbance was in the way."

"That's what I knew. They talk about hurtin' the white man, but they hurtin' the colored, too." Mr. Parrish sawed on his turkey. "Shuttlesworth and Walker![2] Call themselves preachers. Preachers ain't got no business in politics, if you ask me. Marchin' in the street ain't never got nobody into heaven." He motioned with the fork to a chair. "Help yourself, Carlton."

"I'm not very hungry."

"Can't work if you don't eat. That's what my daddy always told me. He was a farming man. Worked me sunup 'til midnight. I ain't lying. He was born a slave, you know. Had that slave working mentality. Nothing wrong with a work mentality. Two things I swore when I was a boy. One: I would get ahead any way I could—but ain't but one way—hard work. After my daddy died, Momma moved us over here to live with her brother who

2. Fred Shuttlesworth (1922–) is a civil rights activist who was minister of the Bethel Baptist Church in Birmingham. Although he moved to Cincinnati in 1961, he returned to Birmingham to call on Martin Luther King Jr. and the SCLC to join him in the launch of Project C[onfrontation], a multifaceted plan that included sit-ins, boycotts, and marches. After about five hundred adults were put in prison, children joined the demonstration, and about two thousand of them went to jail. Wyatt Tee Walker (1929–) was the executive director of the SCLC at the time and participated on the leadership team in Birmingham during Project C.

worked at the furnace. That when I saw how to make it: business. Momma opened the little dry goods store—just a handful of inventory—and I carried it on. My brother, Tom, he went back to farming—still farming—don't own a thing. Ain't got no pension. No nothing."

Carlton wiped sweat from his forehead back into his hair. He was wishing for a drink and the smell of the turkey was making him hungry. "What was the second thing?"

"I'll get to it." Mr. Parrish chewed. "Farming. That's what. Never gone lift another hoe in my life—unless it is to sell it. That's what your average Negro don't understand. He go out, break his back, whether it's farmin' or minin' or smeltin'—and ain't got a red cent to show for it. You got to be the middleman. The middleman or the owner. It's still hard work, but you got something in the end. Something you can sell if nothing else." He drank water. "Take yourself. You still young. You and Salena both. Well, she doing the best she can for a woman, but nursing—first colored girl or not—that's not what I want for her. She needs to settle in and raise the children and take care of the house. It's nice she got a skill and all to lean back on, in case something happens to you." He winked. "That's one thing that worries me so much about this going on. Interferes with business. White and colored, too."

"Mr. Parrish, did you *see* what was going on downtown?"

"I heard they was spraying children. Children ought to be in school, not the street—how do they ever expect to get a job out in the street? I wouldn't hire nay one of 'em—and what do they expect a white man to say if they have this on their record . . . ?"

"They were not spraying them. They were *hosing* them."

"What's the difference, Carlton?" Mr. Parrish stopped sawing the turkey with his fork. "What's the difference for us? It ain't fixin' to do nothin' but hurt us, one way or the other. Colored people too impatient. They want something and don't know what they gettin'. Now you tell me what sense it make for me to want to go all the way downtown and sit in at a white lunch counter to eat a hamburger, when my friend Harvey Brown got a rib shack not three blocks from here. And in your own business, Carlton, what good it gone be if they let us live up in Mountain Brook?[3] You can't sell no houses in Mountain Brook, and ain't no white ever gone buy a

---

3. In 1963, Mountain Brook was an affluent, all-white residential suburb of Birmingham.

house in Titusville.[4] People talkin' about gettin' their freedom. Freedom ain't worth a dime if you ain't got a dime." He punched the table with his finger. "Every dollar they spend with the white man is a dollar they ain't spent with us." He pushed back from the table and folded his arms. "We got to think this thing through. This marching business liable to drive every colored man in the city out of business."

The two men sat quietly for a moment as if considering this proclamation. Then Carlton shifted and cleared his throat. "Mr. Parrish, Salena and I have been talking. We figure if things don't get better we might go away."

The old man didn't look up. "Where to? Up North? Colored got the same trouble up North, only difference is they don't know it."

"We were thinking about Europe, maybe Paris."

"Paris, France?" Mr. Parrish looked at Carlton with incredulity. "You don't mean Paris, Kentucky? You mean Paris that in France? What the *hell* you going to do in Paris, France? You speak French? You got any family in France?" He sighed. "Son, white man own Paris just like he own Birmingham. Ain't a place in the world you can go—unlessen it's Red China—that the white man don't own. You can even go back to Africa, and you still got to deal with the white man. So you might as well save yo'self some running and deal with him right here."

Uncle Booker kept him waiting. From the window in the outer office he could see the park. It showed no evidence of the disturbance. The intercom buzzed.

"Mr. Wilkes," the secretary called to him. "He will see you now." Just before she opened the door for him, she whispered in a matronly way, "Straighten your tie."

Uncle Booker looked at his watch and shook his head.

"I was here on time, Uncle Booker. But there was a riot."

"You let that foolishness stop you?"

"It was more than just a little foolishness." Carlton walked quickly to the window. "Didn't you see it from here?"

"I saw it. But I didn't let it get in the way of what I had to do." Uncle

---

4. In 1963, Titusville was an all-black neighborhood within a few miles of downtown Birmingham.

Booker packed and lit his pipe. "Have a seat, son. Believe it or not, I was young once, so I know how it is to get excited about things that don't mean a difference to you one way or the other."

"But . . ."

"I know. I know." Booker waved him silent with a chubby hand. "You're concerned about your rights—about Negro progress—I'm for all that, too. Lord, I'd be a fool not to be. And believe me, sure as the sun comes up every morning, it's coming. Maybe these schoolchildren have started something. Maybe not. Maybe we'll be singing their praises or maybe we'll be burying them. Or maybe both." He puffed and swiveled in his chair. "And you got a part in this progress too."

Carlton's stomach churned. He couldn't see himself marching.

Booker put his pipe in the pipe rest. "This will sound awful hard, but it's the truth. For someone like you, educated up North and in a white school—and got a little money behind you—the only Negro progress is to make as much money as you can. Now, before you say anything stupid, let me remind you that for three generations, even before the end of slavery, the Wilkes family has been in one business or the other. We may not have gotten our rights from the white man, and damn it, I know we didn't get his respect, but we got what we wanted because we had money."

Carlton had heard it before. Uncle Booker recounted the Wilkes businesses, from the small farm and produce store his first free ancestor had, to the white-only barbershops Carlton's grandfather had owned, to the real estate company that Carlton's father had owned, and to Booker's own insurance company. Carlton studied the short, chubby man. It was hard to believe that he was related to him.

"Now, I have a deal for you," Booker continued. "It should make you and your lady very happy—and rich. There is a man, a Northerner—and I may add, a white man—who is proposing to build some stores in various places around the city. Mountain Brook will be the first one. These are what they call *convenience* stores. They'd sell sundries and quick items. This man needs a partner—an investor. Someone who knows the area, but yet isn't exactly one of the local Okies, if you catch my drift."

After a moment, Carlton spoke. "That would take a lot of money."

"You've got it. You'll need to sell off some of those slum houses your daddy left you, and it would be tight for a few years. But you're young, and you've got your young lady to fall back on. She's Parrish's only child, and you'll have what he leaves her. But the best part," he puffed on the pipe, "the very best part will be if this civil rights thing goes through, then you'll own property in Mountain Brook and black and white alike will already be buying from you."

Uncle Booker leaned back in his swivel chair and laid his intertwined fingers across his stomach. He seemed to have been caught in a daydream. Carlton went to the window again and looked out over the park. He remembered how he felt when he had seen the dogs, and turned quickly to Uncle Booker. "I don't know about going into business with a white man. People around here wouldn't like that. It could cause trouble." The mention of "trouble" was strategic. Trouble would be bad for business.

Uncle Booker leaned forward. "Nobody will know who owns what." He leaned back in the chair and frowned. "What's the matter with you, Carlton?"

"It's just that Salena and I had been thinking of leaving Birmingham. You know, going to someplace where we could get a good start."

"Like where?"

"Like Paris."

Uncle Booker's face was still for a moment, then he laughed. "How romantic!" He leaned forward and put his thick hands on the desktop. "Son, what do you see when you look out that window at Birmingham? Filthy smokestacks? A shabby little downtown? For certain it is not Paris. What I see is a town that black people helped to build. I see opportunity on every street corner. *Your* opportunity. You can't be afraid to claim it."

Carlton looked out the window again. In the distance he saw the columns of white smoke rising from the steel furnaces in Hueytown. Hueytown was home to the KKK. In another direction, he saw the rooftops of Titusville. Only last week bombs had been tossed into houses in Titusville. Then there was the park just in front of him. He returned to his seat. How could he make Uncle Booker understand? "Everything is changing here."

"Change can be good."

"It's just that . . . I'm afraid."

Uncle Booker leaned back again. He put the pipe in his mouth. "Of course, there is some risk. If you want to make money, you've got to take risks."

"It's not the business, Uncle Booker. I'm afraid. Afraid of what's happening here."

"Afraid?" Uncle Booker frowned and rocked forward abruptly. "Afraid? Afraid to make money?"

Carlton had started home after his talk with Uncle Booker, but the sight of the park stopped him. Close up, he could see the scars the water had left on the tree trunks and where it had stripped the leaves from shrubs. Here and there were puddles in the grass. He stood at the place where the boy had fallen. The grass was thin, and the ground had been churned up by running feet. It smelled fresh.

Remembering again what he had witnessed, he felt himself begin to shake. He looked at his hand. On the outside he was perfectly still, but on the inside everything trembled. He knew it was fear, but what did he have to fear?

Uncle Booker was right. He had nothing to lose if he played it smart. Money gave him options. He could invest and become very rich. The boycotts wouldn't hurt him. Or he could go to Europe. He couldn't live like a king in Europe, but he could live well for a long time.

He looked up from his hands and saw a police car circling the block. In the back, heads against the window, were two dogs.

No one had answered at Salena's, and he had started back to his car when he saw the men gathering on a neighbor's porch. Mr. Shannon, the neighbor, waved. He was carrying a hunting rifle. Several of the half dozen or so men carried guns. The three shots of good bourbon he had had on the way over kept Carlton's stomach still.

Mr. Shannon, a tall, brown man with a wide mouth, beckoned to him. "It's about to come on."

Carlton straightened his tie. "What's that, Mr. Shannon?"

"Walter Cronkite."[5]

Mrs. Shannon opened the window from the inside and pushed the

5. Walter Cronkite (1916–) was the *CBS Evening News* anchor from 1962 to 1981.

television to face the men. Walter Cronkite appeared inside the oval screen and spoke about Birmingham. Then pictures of the hosing came up. Carlton saw the lanky silhouettes of the children, dancing about in the white mist. A jet smacked a child and tossed her down.

"God," one of the men said.

The whole newscast was about Birmingham. No one made a sound. Even when the governor made a defiant speech no one said a thing, though Carlton could see Mr. Shannon's forearms tighten. When the newscast ended, the men looked at each other, their jaws set in anger and their fists twisted around the barrels of the guns.

"The Klan will be out tonight," one of them said.

"I'd like to see them," another said.

Mr. Shannon relaxed a little. "I don't reckon so. I reckon they're at home watching it like we are. But we'd better be on guard anyway."

"Any hooded bastard come sneaking around this neighborhood, I get me a piece of 'm," a man said.

"All you do is give Pooler a piece of mortuary business."

"Now, gentlemen," Mr. Shannon said, "we got a higher cause than to talk like that." He turned to Carlton. "Mr. Wilkes, won't you join us on watch tonight? Ever since the bombings started, we sit on different porches to see if we can't discourage whoever is doing it."

They looked like an unlikely militia—schoolteachers, millworkers, and brickmasons, fidgeting with their shotguns and hunting rifles. Someone dropped a shell and it rolled and stopped at Carlton's feet. His hand trembled as he picked it up and held it out to its owner. He worried that they would think he was afraid.

"How about it, Mr. Wilkes?" Mr. Shannon asked.

Carlton cleared his throat. "No. Not tonight."

"When?" Mr. Shannon looked directly at him but spoke softly. "Comes a time when enough's enough, and you got to do what you got to do. I say when the fire department that I pay my taxes to go and hose little colored girls, then the time's come."

"Amen," someone said.

"Shannon's the next Martin Luther King," another man said and provoked laughter from the group.

Carlton's throat was dry. "I was there this morning, Mr. Shannon. I saw it." The men grunted sympathetically. "What you saw on television, I saw face-to-face."

"Then you know what I'm talking about." Mr. Shannon held out his gun to Carlton. "I got another gun in the house. Besides, we'll take turns carrying the guns."

"No. I . . . I wouldn't know how to use a gun."

"Just carry it like you know how," someone chimed in.

Carlton backed down the stairs. "I'm sorry, gentlemen, I have an appointment—across town, and I . . . ."

"He's G. W. Parrish's son-in-law," one of them said. "He's too worried about business to be free."

"No call for that," Mr. Shannon said. "If the man's got business to do, then he's got business to do. He said he would join us another night."

"May not be another night."

One of the men made a joke. "One Wilkes'll rent you a house; the other one will insure it; Parrish'll sell you your stock; and Pooler will put you under, but nay one of 'em will fight for you." A stiff laugh came from the man who said it, a big, buck-toothed man Carlton knew as a brickmason. The other men only stared at Carlton, challenging him. He fumbled for an answer but realized it was no good. He couldn't stay with them now, even if he wanted to, but to run would make him a coward or, worse, a traitor.

Then a little girl, about five, a fragile, wide-eyed child with two erect plaits, came to the screen door. "Daddy," she called in a soft, quavering voice, "Daddy, are we going to get bombed tonight?"

Mr. Shannon opened the door, took his daughter into one arm, and wedged the rifle in the crook of the other. "No, honey, we ain't gonna get bombed."

Carlton drove aimlessly until after sunset. The police were setting up checkpoints, so he drove back to Titusville and waited around the corner for Salena to get home from her shift. Soon after midnight, he saw her park her car in the driveway, nod to the men on Shannon's porch, and go quickly up the stairs. He caught up to her just before she shut the door.

"You scared me," she said. "God, Carlton, you've been drinking."

"I've been thinking."

"Come in before you wake up the neighborhood. And for God's sake, don't wake up Papa."

Carlton sat on the couch while Salena put away her things. She came back wearing her uniform and no shoes. "Listen. Maybe you should go. Daddy will have a fit if we keep him up on a work night."

A little dizzy from the drinking, Carlton stood. "I just wanted to say . . ." She pulled the pins out of her nurse's hat. In the dim overhead light her features were sullen. "I wish we could listen to music," he said.

"Papa'll . . ."

"I know what he'd do, but—don't you feel like you're between a rock and a hard place?"

She seemed to think for a moment. "No. What do you mean? I feel very lucky, altogether. Very lucky."

"You want to be more than just lucky. Never mind. I . . ."

He put his palm to his head and sighed. "I'm an ass."

She said nothing, but took his elbow and pushed him back to the sofa. "What's on your mind?"

It took him a moment to prevent his voice from cracking. "I want to get away. I'm scared this thing is going to backfire."

She folded her hands around his. "We had a fairly quiet night at the hospital. Mostly white. They were scared, too. Scared of the 'race riot.' One old woman said it was Armageddon. But when I saw those pictures of the children on the TV, I was *proud*. I don't know what will happen to them. I don't think it'll be good, but at least they aren't letting the white people get away with it—I mean, they are at least standing up for something." She took off her hat. Her hair fell down on her neck and she pulled it back and set it with the bobby pin.

"You weren't scared?" he whispered.

"A little. Who wouldn't be? But you've got to go on with your work."

"What about Paris?"

She sighed. "I guess I could be a nurse in Paris. The question is, what are *you* going to do?"

He took a flask from his jacket.

"Don't. It's too late. You've got to work tomorrow, don't you?"

Hearing Mr. Parrish on the stairs, Carlton put the flask away.

"Let me see if I can't send him back to bed." Salena went to the foot of the stairs and called to her father, telling him nothing was the matter. The old man complained about his interrupted sleep and kept coming down. Reluctantly, Carlton started toward the door.

"Mr. Wilkes," Mr. Parrish blurted. "What brings you around at this hour?" He was wearing a dingy sleeveless undershirt and trousers. "Something wrong downtown?"

"Everything is fine, Papa."

"Them children up to something?"

Salena tried to turn her father around at the foot of the stairs, but he brushed past her, eclipsed Carlton on the way to the door, and looked out of the sidelight. "Shannon and his crew still sittin' up. Waiting for the Ku Klux Klan!" He faced Carlton. His age showed in the bags and spots under his eyes. "Tell you one thing, the Klan ain't waitin' for them. They in bed gettin' their rest so they can put in a full day. Klan gone strike, he go 'head and strike and then go home and get a full night. Ain't that right, Mr. Wilkes?" His bare feet scuffed against the scatter rugs as he limped into the dining room. "Mr. Wilkes," he said with a certain sarcasm, "won't you join me in a taste?"

"Oh, Papa!" Salena protested.

Carlton stepped between her and her father and pulled the flask from his jacket. "I owe you one, Mr. Parrish."

"I suppose you do." Mr. Parrish took a shot glass from the sideboard and held it for Carlton to fill.

"Papa," Salena said, "Carlton was just leaving."

Motioning to the sofa, Mr. Parrish invited Carlton to sit. "I'm sure he got more gumption than to come into a man's house in the middle of the night, wake him up and then *leave*. Besides, this Paris thing got me so I can't sleep." He sat. "Carlton, I'm a country man and I didn't have the privilege of the education that yo' daddy give you. But I do my share of readin' and I read about these colored fellows that run off to Paris cause they can't be free in this country. But you take a look at what they do, and they all singers and horn players. That's their *work*. I understand that some of them make good money at it, too." He sipped the liquor. "Now you see what I'm gettin' at? I don't hear you or Salena singin' or playing no horn. Lord, the girl's momma couldn't even get her to sing in the church choir. So tell me what you gone do in Paris? You just be livin' off what yo' daddy left you—givin' it all away to another bunch of white men. Now, I know things are supposed to be better overseas, but let me tell you this. No matter how bad it gets, and it done already been a hell of a lot worse than it is now, there is no place like your home." Finishing his drink, he started back up the stairs, then stopped and looked plainly at Carlton and shook his head. "You know, Carlton, Salena my only child."

The old man went up into the darkness, and Carlton turned to Salena. "I could look into getting passports tomorrow."

Salena threw her head back and sighed. "Carlton . . . I love you, but really . . . it's a silly idea."

The sun was above the rooftops when Mr. Shannon rapped on the window of Carlton's Lincoln. "I just wanted to see if you were all right, Mr. Wilkes."

Carlton's head was cloudy, and his neck ached from having slept on the armrest. He mumbled a greeting to Mr. Shannon and felt in his pocket for the keys. "Excuse me, I must have fallen asleep . . ."

"Don't worry about it." Mr. Shannon winked. "I remember when my wife and I were courting—besides, it's good to be young. Why don't you come in and have a cup of coffee and some eggs? Put something solid in your stomach."

Carlton tried to beg off the invitation, but Mr. Shannon insisted, and he found himself brushing the wrinkles out of his suit and running his tongue over his stale teeth.

Inside Mrs. Shannon, her hair in rollers, was scrambling eggs. She was a tall, dark woman with genteel features. Two girls sat at the kitchen table, one the little girl Carlton had seen the day before and the other an adolescent who seemed much perturbed by his appearance.

"I'll just have coffee."

"Oh, no, you won't," said Mrs. Shannon as she scooped grits and soft scrambled eggs onto a plate with sausage patties, toast and jam. The food smelled good and Carlton was hungry; he fidgeted to prevent himself from eating until all were seated and Mr. Shannon had said the grace. The older girl, Gloria, pretended to ignore him. She ate the sausages with her fingers, pinky up. Mrs. Shannon firmly told her to use a fork, and slowly, fastidiously wiping grease from her fingers onto a paper napkin, Gloria conformed. The little girl hardly ate for staring at him. He winked at her, trying to solicit a smile, and asked her name. She turned away, but prodded by her parents she told him, "Bonita."

"That's a pretty name. Spanish, isn't it?"

"I believe so," Mrs. Shannon said. "We took it from her grandmother"

Mrs. Shannon asked about the wedding plans. "Salena tells me nothing, you know. Not that it's my business, but a neighbor would like to know."

"We haven't set them yet," Carlton said. "Maybe soon. We've been thinking about going to Europe."

"That would be a nice honeymoon." Mrs. Shannon looked impressed. "I swear, Salena doesn't tell me a thing."

"She hasn't exactly agreed yet," Carlton confessed.

"It is expensive," Mrs. Shannon said slowly. For a moment it seemed to Carlton that she would give him a sympathetic pat on the hand. "You'd better travel while you are young. Once you have your children you'll be settled for a long time."

"I did get to travel over in the Pacific during the war, or 'the conflict'—whatever they called it. Korea." Mr. Shannon piped in between bites of egg and toast. He stopped chewing and looked at Carlton. "What you think about all this mess that Shuttlesworth and King stirred up, Mr. Wilkes? You think it gonna come to something?"

This was not the conversation Carlton wanted. He wanted to ignore Mr. Shannon and to turn back to Bonita with her erect braids and tiny, square, egg-covered teeth.

"We don't need to talk about that at the table," Mrs. Shannon said. And then more softly, "It upsets the children."

"Some children are out there in jail."

Mrs. Shannon scooted back from the table, asked if Carlton wanted a second helping, and barely waiting for him to clear his mouth to reply, she put another spoonful of grits on his plate.

"Some children are in jail," Mr. Shannon repeated. "I can't say that I'm not scared for them, but there comes a time when you got to—"

"Got to do nothing." Mrs. Shannon banged the pot on the stove. "None of mine are going down there to be killed by Bull Connor."[6]

"I'm not scared of Bull Connor," the older girl said.

6. For over twenty years, Theophilus Eugene "Bull" Connor (1897–1973) was commissioner of Public Safety for Birmingham. He was an outspoken segregationist, who patrolled the city streets in a white armored tank.

"You'd better be," her mother replied. She took a breath. "We're going to upset Bonita, so just let it rest,"

"It won't rest." Mr. Shannon took his plate to the sink. "Mr. Wilkes, I'm going downtown. I think a lot of us will be marching."

Mrs. Shannon cut a look at him. "You'd better be marching on to work, instead of jail. We don't have any money to get you out."

"Then I'll just stay." He went to the door. "Are you coming, Mr. Wilkes?"

Slowly, Carlton sat back from the table. He nodded toward Mrs. Shannon and stood. He felt a tremble in his knee. Gloria popped up and ran toward her father. "Can I go with you?" she asked.

The park was crowded with people of all ages. Carlton recognized no one, but Mr. Shannon, a schoolteacher, greeted many of the people, both adults and children. Policemen and firemen were gathering on three sides of them. Yet there was quiet festivity, as people greeted friends or sang hymns. Someone was singing *Gonna lay down my burden, down by the riverside* . . . Someone else led a small group in prayer.

A bullhorn crackled, and the crowd began to shift. Carlton's mind tripped over itself as he tried to fathom everything. He couldn't understand the instructions coming from the demonstration leaders. The bullhorn seemed to be circling the park. He thought it might be coming from Bull Connor's armored car, yet he couldn't see the car. He looked for Mr. Shannon and saw the top of his curly head several yards away. He tried to follow, but the crowd pressed against him and Mr. Shannon moved even further away. It occurred to him that the people were dressed nicely, in clean dungarees and sundresses, and that the firemen were preparing to hose them as they had done to the children the day before.

Behind the fire trucks and paddy wagons he saw Uncle Booker's insurance building. He thought that if he could make it past the trucks, he might be able to take refuge in the building. What Mr. Parrish had said was evident now. How much business would the store owners along Fourth Avenue do if there were rioting in the park? They had mortgages to pay and families to feed.

The demonstrators, singing and chanting, lined up at the park's edge. Carlton was close enough to see the face of one of the firemen. He was a square-jawed young man, covered with freckles. He held the hose against his body with one arm and gripped the throat of the nozzle with his hand.

Suddenly Bull Connor's armored car rolled down the street between the crowd and the firemen. At the window sat heavy-jowled Bull Connor himself. He wiped his glasses with a white hankie and spoke into a microphone which was amplified by a speaker on the roof of the car. The demonstrators did not disband, and the car moved on. A line of helmeted policemen and their dogs moved in, cutting off Carlton's retreat to Uncle Booker's building.

The young fireman adjusted the nozzle. It seemed to have been pointed directly at Carlton, but there was some confusion. The fireman was looking back at the pumper and yelling instructions. The men at the pumper had taken out their wrenches and were tampering with the hydrant intakes. The young fireman took aim again and braced himself. Carlton saw him push down the nozzle lever.

There was still an escape route, Carlton thought, if he could get to the back of the crowd and then slip behind the fire trucks. He began to push through the crowd. Things were getting too crazy. Somebody was bound to get hurt. Negro progress was supposed to be good for Negroes; he was a Negro, but this was not good for him. He would go to Europe. He pushed faster through the crowd, not caring whom he shoved or stepped on. If Salena didn't want to go, he would go without her. Someone grabbed his shoulder. He pulled away and was grabbed again. It was Mr. Shannon. "Hold on a minute, Mr. Wilkes. We are marching on City Hall."

Carlton was still for a moment. Mr. Shannon's hand felt like a vise on his shoulder. Then he shivered, and Mr. Shannon took away his hand.

"I'm sorry," Mr. Shannon said and looked away. Carlton flushed with embarrassment. Mr. Shannon spoke again, in a steady low voice. "Won't you please walk with me, Mr. Wilkes? If you won't, I'm not sure that I can."

For awhile, Carlton could not answer, and the two men stood while the crowd pushed around them. "Mr. Shannon," Carlton's voice quavered, "I'm afraid." The confession was accompanied with a great relief, but relief made him no less afraid.

"I'm afraid, too." Mr. Shannon hooked his arm in Carlton's and slowly the two got in step with the crowd. "But I feel I don't have much choice about being here. I've got my children to think about, for one thing. You're young, Mr. Wilkes. You don't have children yet, but someday you will. When you have children, then you will know that you have to make a choice to face your fears. I don't know what will happen today. We may be knocked in the head, maybe worse. Just keep thinking about the children. Think about all the children."

"All the children?"

"The children who were arrested."

Carlton tried to imagine the faces of the children. He imagined groups of children, their faces blurred by distance. He saw them as silhouettes or as flashes of color dashing in and out of the arcs of water. He saw the form of the boy who had been knocked down by the water. But he could not see the children as individuals, as people he knew. Because his father had money, he had been sent away to a boarding school in the North. Except for business, he had had only a little contact with these people, much less with their children. It had been a business errand to the hospital that had brought him and Salena together.

"Salena," he thought out loud. He had no children, but he had a future with Salena. He tried to imagine having children with Salena. How would they look? Her eyes? His nose? Her mouth and hair? Try as he might, he couldn't imagine the child's face.

Two by two, the demonstrators began to file across the street toward a gap between the police cars and the fire trucks. Secure on Mr. Shannon's arm, Carlton fell into step. They made it to where the park lawn and the pavement met before the line stopped. The demonstration leaders argued with the policemen. Again, Carlton saw the young, freckled fireman, now dragging the dead weight of his limp hose around and aiming it at the marchers. There was a murmur, and people began to kneel. Kneeling! Carlton thought. Kneeling like lambs to be slaughtered. He tried to pull away.

"Kneel and pray," someone said. "Kneel and pray."

Mr. Shannon held him tightly. "They say pray that the water won't come on, Mr. Wilkes."

Carlton shook his head.

"They are praying that the water won't come on."

They had gone crazy. It was one thing to get hosed when you were on your feet and able to run, but it was suicide to kneel down. Mr. Shannon pulled on him, his knees buckled and he landed squarely on the edge of the sidewalk.

The water didn't come.[7]

"Oh, God. Oh, God."

People sang and prayed. Carlton dared not move. It was as if the collective will of the crowd had frozen the hydrants. If he could only stay here now. Stay. If he didn't move. If he didn't shiver. If he were as still as ice, then the water wouldn't come. Time would hold still. He caught his breath. His ears began to ring. But nothing, nothing moved. Except now, a cold molecule of sweat was slowly pushing through a pore at the base of his scalp, and swelling into a quivering bead. He must not move! "Oh, God, oh, God." He imagined the boy, rolled in the streets by the jets of white water, and the dogs—oh God, the dogs. Why was he a Negro and so scared?

The eyes of the young fireman were round, and the hose had slipped from under his arm. He was backing away from the crowd, looking over his shoulder to his colleagues for support.

Carlton saw the fireman stepping back. It confused him. His concentration slipped and he began to note his surroundings. He was kneeling in a crowd, being held by a man he barely knew, while the firemen backed away and tampered with the hydrants. He had stepped out of his life into something stranger than life. He had a comfortable home which sat on a hill above Titusville. He had a fianceé who was one of the first colored nurses at the white hospital. He had a business to run and a Lincoln Continental.

Yet he was compelled to stay where he was, on his knees, in front of Bull Connor's firemen. For if he moved, if one hair sprung up from the pomade that held it close to his skull, then the water would come on. The bead of sweat trembled and began to roll in a meandering, ticklish path over his temple and across his cheek. That wasn't his fault! He couldn't help that. He hadn't done anything to cause it to fall.

Now other beads began to roll. He felt each one individually as it

7. On one day during the demonstrations, May 5, Connor ordered the hoses to be turned on, but the firemen refused to do so. The demonstrators were on their knees. The day has been referred to as "Miracle Sunday."

prickled across his skin. Each one was a cold prod inciting his body to revolt, to shiver, to stand up and run. But if he dared, then it would be the end of him. He would be rolled in the streets, chased and bitten by the dogs. He would be no better than the others.

"Courage, Mr. Wilkes. Courage." Mr. Shannon loosened his grip, and Carlton screamed and jerked away.

"Kneel, mister," someone said, but Carlton continued stumbling through the kneeling people, stepping on them, picking a route to the rear of the park.

Then there was a whoosh. Carlton turned to see the young fireman brace himself as the hose kicked and foamed and shot water. At first the stream scoured the asphalt and sprayed up a milky, prismatic mist; then the fireman gained control of it and directed it at the kneeling demonstrators.

The jets bowled the demonstrators over and knocked them down as they tried to rise. White arcs came from every direction, and Carlton realized that he was surrounded. He pushed people aside as he ran instinctively toward Uncle Booker's building. He made it to the curb just as a column of water came at him. Diving behind a parked car, he escaped the direct force. He edged along the side of the car and peeped around the fender to see in which direction the hose was pointed.

Just inside the park, he saw a young woman in a white dress. She was bent over and stumbling as she tried to dodge the jets of water. Carlton wiped his eyes to get a better look. His heart skipped a beat. Was it Salena? He wiped his eyes again. The young woman turned in his direction, and he saw that without a doubt it was Salena. Now she had stopped running and was trying to help a heavyset man out of the mud.

Carlton ducked behind the car again. His head was spinning and the water in his eyes had broken the world into fragments. He had a clear shot to Uncle Booker's building. If he tried to reach Salena the hoses would surely catch him. He tried to convince himself that she would be all right. She was strong, stronger than himself. Maybe she was too strong for him. Maybe he couldn't imagine children with her because they had no future together. She was claiming her future, here at the park. His future was in Europe.

He tried to imagine Salena's face. He held it in his mind for a moment, but it seemed the water in his eyes was also in his head. Every time he got the image of her to stand still, it was washed away by rivulets of water. Maybe he didn't love her. If he loved her, then he would be able to see her clearly. He would be able to run to her.

He looked for her again in the crowd and in a moment found her. The white uniform was now gray with mud. She had lost her shoes. She seemed dazed, no longer crouched and running but standing and limping, an easy target. Then he saw a jet of water coming toward her. "Salena!" He stood. The scene kept spinning around him. First Uncle Booker's building, then Salena, then the fire trucks. "Run," he heard someone scream at him. "Run, run, run!" It was himself screaming. He ran. He wasn't sure in what direction. The water punched his ribs and knocked out his breath. It slammed him to the asphalt, shoved his hips against the pavement and beat on his back. He lay and caught his breath as the runoff trickled and fizzed around him. Slowly he stood and made a clumsy step toward Salena.

HENRY DUMAS

The Marchers

Henry Dumas (1934–68) grew up in Arkansas and Harlem. He served in the
U.S. Air Force, as well as attended City College in New York and then Rutgers.
A writer of poetry and fiction, he was active in the Black Power movement.
At age thirty-three, he was mistakenly killed by a New York City transit
police officer. His stories were published posthumously through the efforts of
Eugene Redmond, his friend and creative collaborator from Southern Illinois
University, where Dumas went to teach in 1967. "The Marchers" appeared in
his posthumous 1979 collection, *Rope of Wind*, and in his collection *Goodbye,
Sweetwater* (1988).

In the dome the prisoner, alone in the silence of centuries, waited . . .

And all the people gathered together and began a trek across the land.
From every corner of the land they came. Crossing the great rivers and
mountains, they came on foot, in cars, buses, wagons, and some came IN
THE SPIRIT FROM OUT OF THE PAST . . .

Their leaders stopped them at every crossroad and made speeches,
reassuring them that to march against the white-domed city was sanc-
tioned by God Himself. And the people believed. They went forth in
processions, chanting, singing, and praying. Sometimes they laughed and
shouted.

All the leaders were men of learning. They were men who believed
that a law existed higher than the law of men. They believed that Justice
was that law. They were men who believed that Freedom existed when
men exercised restraint in doing that which they had the power to do,
and courage in doing that which they had never done. In speaking to the
people about these ideas, the leaders always spoke of Equality.

And the people believed. They marched gladly. Never in the history
of the nation had so many people who felt oppressed gathered in a great
multitude to express their grievances.

In the dome the prisoner waited . . . shackled to inertia by a great chain of years . . .

And the marchers grew in numbers. Work ceased. Factories puffed no smoke. The highways thronged. The past moved forward. And the great white dome in the great stone city became a hub to the troubled mind of a great nation traveling in a circle . . .

In the dome the silence was stirred by the sound of legions of feet marching. The rumble sifted through the years. The prisoner heard . . . and waited . . .

Then the marchers descended upon the city. And when the sun was high in the midday, they gathered together and built a great platform. Their leaders came and stood upon it and made speeches, and the people cheered and roared.

In the dome, where webs floated in the semidarkness like legions of ghost clouds, where echoes from the outside sifted in the dome, the prisoner . . . stood up.

Outside the dome the marchers listened to their leaders:

TODAY IS THE DAY!

And the people cheered.

TODAY IS THE DAY WE WILL SET OUR SOULS FREE!

And the people roared.

TODAY—and the leader pointed to the dome shining in the noon sun like a giant pearl half-buried in the sands of the sea—TODAY WE WILL OPEN THE GREAT DOOR OF THIS NATION AND BRING OUT THE PAST!

And the people cheered.

NO ONE CAN STOP US NOW! NO ONE! WE HAVE SERVED IN THIS LAND FOR CENTURIES. WE HAVE SLAVED FOR THOSE WHO OPPRESS US. WE HAVE BEEN CHILDREN TO THEM! BUT TODAY WE SHOW THEM THAT WE ARE MEN!

And the people cheered.

IF THE DOME-MAKERS SEND THEIR GUARDS, THEIR SOLDIERS, AND THEIR DOGS UPON US, WE WILL NOT FEAR . . . NO. FOR WE MARCH IN PEACE. WE MARCH IN THE NAME OF *HIM* WHO SENT US, AND WE ARE NOT AFRAID . . .

And the people knelt down and prayed.

JUSTICE WILL PREVAIL! FREEDOM WILL BE OURS! EQUALITY SHALL NOT BE TRODDEN DOWN!

Then another leader stood forth. He was very great amongst the people.

NOW . . . NOW IS THE TIME. TODAY . . . FREEDOM CAN WAIT NO LONGER. WE HAVE ACCEPTED TOKENS OF FREE-DOM TOO LONG.

And the people cheered.

OUR FATHERS WERE BROUGHT HERE IN BONDAGE. AND WE HAVE FELT THE SAME YOKE LIKE BEASTS IN THE FIELDS. BUT WE WILL WAIT NO LONGER. WE HAVE LIVED IN A TOMB FOR YEARS, AND WHILE WE SUFFERED WE SANG OUR SONGS AND FOUGHT AMONGST OURSELVES BECAUSE WE HAD HOPE. GOD GAVE US THAT MUCH STRENGTH TO GO ON. AND WITH THAT HOPE WE SURVIVED, FOR WITHOUT A VISION, WITHOUT FAITH, A PEOPLE WILL PERISH . . . LET US GIVE THANKS UNTO THE LORD . . .

And the people roared.

THE SUNSHINE OF A NEW DAY AND A NEW FRONTIER IS UPON US. RAISE YOUR HANDS, MY PEOPLE, AND STRIKE . . .

"Freedom Freedom Freedom!" echoed the people.

WE WILL REVIVE THE DEAD AND CONVICT THE LIVING!

"Justice! Equality!"

LISTEN, MY PEOPLE, AND REMEMBER THIS . . . FOR WHEN YOU TREK BACK TO YOUR CITIES AND TOWNS, THE PRESSURES OF LIVING MIGHT MAKE YOU FORGET.

REMEMBER THIS: YOU HAVE SERVED IN THE FIELDS. YOU HAVE SERVED IN THE KITCHENS, IN THE WAREHOUSES AND THE FACTORIES. YOU HAVE SHED YOUR PRECIOUS BLOOD FOR THIS NATION, AND ALL THE TIME YOU COULD NOT EVEN ENTER THE FRONT DOOR OF THE HOUSE LIKE A MAN . . . BUT TODAY, WE WILL KNOCK ON THE DOOR AND WITH THE ARM OF THE GREAT SPIRIT, WE WILL OPEN THE DOOR. WE WILL ENTER. WE WILL SIT DOWN AT THE FEAST TABLE, AND WE WILL REST AND NOURISH OURSELVES.

"Justice! Equality! Freedom!"

OUR BACKS AND OUR SWEAT HAVE BUILT THIS HOUSE.

"Yes, it's true!" roared the people.

THEN I FOR ONE THINK IT ALTOGETHER FITTING AND PROPER THAT WE LIVE IN THE HOUSE WE HELPED TO BUILD, NOT AS CHILDREN, NOT AS SERVANTS, NOT AS MAIDS, NOT AS COOKS, NOT AS BUTLERS, SHOESHINE BOYS, AND FLUNKIES! BUT MEN! THIS HOUSE IS OURS!

And the people applauded.

In the dome the words stung the prisoner. He stirred himself and took a step. But the weight of his chains shook him . . . and he fell.

Outside, the cheers grew louder. The dome trembled. Specks of dust leaped up from centuries of rest and wandered like souls in limbo. Suddenly a passion seized the prisoner.

From the ground he came up slowly, as if he were a lost seed in a sunless cave, a seed that had sprouted into a pale limp stalk trying to suck a bit of precious sunlight into its impoverished leaves.

Riotous cheers heated the day. The sun stood high and hot. Soldiers came. Dissenters and extremists—organized sometimes and sometimes not—jeered at the leaders and threw stones at many of the marchers. More soldiers came. The police rode around in patrol wagons. People fainted. And the great city seethed while its troubles flashed around the world.

A ray of light shot through a sudden crack in the dome. The beam stabbed the prisoner, and he fell back, groaning and moaning as if he had been struck by a great hammer.

"I remember," he wept, "I remember."

Then the doors came crashing open. The people rushed in. And they trod upon the sentiments, the truths, the lies, the myths, and the legends of the past in a frenzied rush to lay hold of Freedom. They cheered their leaders, and their leaders watched the movements of the soldiers and dissenters constantly. And no one knew who was to make the right move.

They lifted the prisoner, as if he were a flag, and carried him out of the dome, rejoicing as if a great battle had been won.

And when they carried him into the bright light of the noon sun, he felt a great pain in his eyes. He blinked, shook his head, moaned . . . for the intense light immediately blinded him.

And the people shouted, "Freedom, Justice, Equality!"

They put the prisoner on the platform and all the leaders gathered around for a ceremony. A hush descended like dust on a windless plain.

Shackled in his chains, the prisoner opened his mouth to speak.

"My eyes," he murmured. "If I could see . . . *see* this Freedom . . ."

The leaders all stood forth around him and hailed the people.

TODAY! TODAY! TODAY IS HISTORY!

"A drink, please," whispered the prisoner. "The heat . . . a drink . . ."

WE HAVE SET HIM FREE! GLORY TO GOD! THE LORD IS WITH US! LET US MARCH AS SOLDIERS OF THE GREAT SPIRIT! WE CAN SEE THE SPIRIT MOVING AMONGST US! WE CAN SEE! PRAISE GOD! OUR FREEDOM IS OUR SIGHT!

And the people cheered. The leader wrapped his arm around the prisoner, and the chains clanked and pinched the leader's arm.

LOOK! echoed the leader, OUR SOUL LIVES!

THAT WHICH WE THOUGHT WAS DEAD IS ALIVE! THAT WHICH WE THOUGHT WAS LOST HAS SURVIVED! And he raised his hand for silence. THE GREAT SPIRIT IS MOVING MIGHTILY AMONGST US. CAN YOU FEEL HIM?

The prisoner trembled. His lips hung open. "I want to see," he said. "Please, these chains . . . I want to walk . . . for I . . . remember . . . I remember when I had no chains . . ."

WE MARCH FOR OUR FREEDOM, boomed a leader. WE MARCH THAT OUR CHILDREN WILL NOT HAVE TO MARCH!

And the people roared like never before.

ALL OF US MUST BE FREE BEFORE ONE OF US IS FREE!

And the people applauded.

SO ENJOY YOUR FREEDOM! GIVE THANKS UNTO GOD, FOR WE HAVE WALKED BY FAITH, AND FAITH HAS GIVEN US LIGHT! WE HAVE PROVEN THAT WE CAN MARCH IN PEACE AND NOT IN VIOLENCE. FOR WHO AMONGST US TODAY DOES NOT KNOW THAT THE SPIRIT IS STRONGER THAN THE SWORD?

And the people sang and danced around the platform until all the leaders came down and joined them.

Beneath the sky the prisoner stood . . . alone . . . trembling, as if he were only a thin line of summer heat wavering in the noonday sun. His chains clanked and choked him.

Suddenly . . . as the people roared in a wild song of joy and freedom, the prisoner stared into the darkness of his sight, and except for the intense heat and the pain, he would have thought he was back in the dome . . .

Then the platform creaked, broke in splinters, and tumbled to the ground. The people laughed merrily and followed their leaders up the streets of the city. Today was a great day. Freedom had come to them . . . at least for a while . . . and the marching of their feet was their song of freedom . . .

The prisoner fell to the ground. The wreckage of the mob buried him, and the weight was like all the centuries linked together around his neck. The pounding of the marchers shook his flesh, and the heat of the day burned his thoughts away.

The sun beat down upon the great white dome. The sun beat down upon his head. And the dome was as white as ever before, and the prisoner was as black as night.

ALMA JEAN BILLINGSLEA-BROWN

Moonshot

Alma Jean Billingslea-Brown (1946–) is an associate professor of English at
Spelman College in Atlanta, Georgia, where she teaches courses on literature,
writing, and the African diaspora. She has also been a staff member of Martin
Luther King Jr.'s Southern Christian Leadership Conference. "Moonshot"
appeared in a 1989 collection of stories by writers living in Texas called *Out of
Dallas*, published by the University of North Texas Press.

Dusk sifted onto the squat, wood-framed houses and chinaberry trees,
attempting a truce between the burnt-orange sun and the coming sul-
try night. The girl stepped softly in her cushioned thong sandals, vaguely
aware that she did not know exactly how to get back to the church, but
confident that in such a tiny town she could not get lost. In one of the
trees not much taller than she, a nest of insects made her pause. She
thought what she heard was bees. But when she stopped and looked
closely, she saw a swarm of shiny, brownish-black roaches that were at
least two inches in length. And they did not buzz, but crackled as their
crisp, hard bodies intermingled with each other. There were hundreds of
them, some involved in the nest intertwining and others darting quickly
out the branches and down the trunk onto the sidewalk. One or two
crawled near her, so she raised her feet in the too-new sandals and was
quickly reminded of the soreness between her toes. Ordinarily roaches
frightened her, but not these. They lived outside. They were not scam-
pering inside kitchen cabinets or climbing stupidly up a wall, and they
were big and husky and they crackled when they moved. She stood a few
moments longer and thought about how she would remember this town.
Cocoa Beach, Florida. There they had roaches that nest in trees and walk
the streets.

  She had been able to do that for every one of the small towns she'd
worked in. There had always been something to make each one differ-

ent. In the county seat for Greene County, Alabama, the stop signs stood only five feet high, probably for pedestrians, she had concluded. Surely no thinking county commission would approve posting signs so low for drivers. She had been pulled over her first night for running three of them. When she thought of that little town in Alabama, she thought of Wilkins. Wilkins Knotts. One of the kindest human beings she'd ever known. When she first met Wilkins, she immediately relegated him to the rank of friend. He was too short, stocky and kind-faced for anything else.

The recollection of their friendship, while she was still standing near the nest of roaches, brought to her mind the soft summer evening when they sat and first talked on the porch steps of the Freedom House.

"Where you from, Wilkins?"

"Eutaw."

"Utah? Wow. You're the first person I've ever met from Utah. That's really something. What's it like out there? Do y'all ride a lot of horses and stuff? What in the world do people do in Utah?"

"The same things they do everywhere. Wake up, eat, work, make love, go to sleep."

"But there aren't many black people out there, are there?"

"Sure there are. About as many as anywhere else."

"That's funny. I always thought states like Utah, Wyoming . . ."

"States? Eutaw's not a state. It's in Greene County. Greene County, Alabama."

Two years later, long after Wilkins, disillusioned, neurotic and slightly alcoholic, had left for Chicago, she was assigned to Eutaw, Greene County, Alabama, and worked day and night to help elect Vachael Knotts, one of Wilkins' distant uncles, to the county commission. All through the long, sweaty mornings and afternoons, trudging from one little farm to another drinking too-sweet iced tea and lemonade, talking to one family after another to make the necessary connections, she thought of Wilkins and Chicago. It baffled her that whenever she mentioned his name, he was just matter-of-factly acknowledged as one of so-and-so's children or distant kin to Mr. Knotts who was running for county commissioner.

The Knotts family easily comprised a fourth of the population. They were, for the most part, well-to-do, highly respected farmers. She couldn't

understand why Wilkins had ever left. But so many things had been beyond her understanding since she had come south. So she worked hard,
ate well, slept little, and did all she knew to help Mr. Knotts' campaign.
For Wilkins partly.

The evening before the march in Cocoa Beach had been set as the date
for the mass rally. She had showered earlier and hoping to keep cool, decided to go braless under the cotton print sundress. She had concluded
also, when she slipped on her sandals, that she would have to walk from
the one-story pink stucco motel rather than take a taxi. The executive staff
had come in that afternoon, so all the rented cars had been claimed by
more important people. And with just twelve dollars of her per diem left,
she had considered a taxi extravagant. Again, she had been annoyed by the
caste system—executive staff and field staff. Field staff were project di-
rectors and workers like herself who were responsible for initial grassroots
organizing. They were sent deep south, to Georgia, Alabama, Mississippi,
sometimes Florida, with rented cars, gas credit cards, fifteen dollars a
day per diem money, and a contact list of local ministers to do whatever
was needed: run voter registration drives, organize political campaigns,
prepare for marches and demonstrations, rally a protest against a moon
shot—the reason for her being in Cocoa Beach.

She was still standing, intrigued by roaches nesting in trees when she
felt soft arms around her waist and moist lips on her neck. Skeeter.

"Hey, little sister. On your way to the church?"

"Yeah," she said untangling herself.

"Why you walking? They take all the cars?"

"They always do, don't they?"

"No." He jingled keys in his pocket. "I still got mine. But they took the
credit card. You got some gas money, we can take off after the meeting."

She turned to face him and asked earnestly, "Take off where? And
what for?"

"There's a nice club over in Orlando called the Laicos—that's social
spelled backwards. Jamming little place. You'd like it. Good band, cheap
drinks, and dynamite smoke. I was over there last night."

"No thanks." She drew the "no" out long. "I'm tired. I've been working, you know. Besides, we got the march tomorrow."

Masking his disappointment and squinting his eyes as he was prone to do when he tried to be serious, Skeeter became business-like. "You get the portable toilets?"

"Yeah, but only one. They doubled the price."

"What about the flat-bed trucks?"

"Yeah, I was able to get two of them. They should be over to the church by now. José was supposed to get some local entertainment since the Freedom Singers[1] couldn't make it."

Skeeter was silent for a moment. "Sleeping by yourself tonight?"

"I have that intention. Yes."

"Girl, you'd better give it up. Ain't healthy to keep locked too long. You too young. It's going to dry up on you."

"Sounds like a personal problem to me—mine."

"C'mon, why don't you give me some? We been working so well on everything else, think of what we could do between the sheets. We can go over to Orlando . . ."

"Forget it, Skeeter," she interrupted deftly.

"Damn, you hard. What is it? Lined with gold?"

"Platinum. Besides, it's mine. And sounds to me like you're begging."

"You got that right. Have to. Can't take it from you. And I don't ever intend to buy any. Begging is about all I can do."

"You shouldn't have to," she said hoisting her purse onto her shoulder. "There's enough free stuff around."

"Yeah there is. But not quality. And that's what I'm after these days. A little quality."

"Well, keep looking. Elsewhere." She turned to start walking. "C'mon, we'd better get on over to the church. What time is it anyway?"

"Time for you to give me a little bit." He grabbed her hand. "But you cold, girl. Hard and cold. I guess that's why I like you."

"I know. I know," she said pulling her hand away gently.

They walked a few steps in silence. Skeeter started for her hand again, but put his arm around her shoulder instead. "You're still in love, I see."

She looked down at her feet. "Yeah, I guess so," she said hoarsely.

---

1. The Freedom Singers formed in Albany, Georgia, in 1962. They often traveled, giving concerts to raise money for the civil rights movement. Their appearance at the Newport Folk Festival in 1963 elevated their fame. Founders of the group included Cordell Reagon and Bernice Johnson.

The church filled quickly. The young men and girls, with red roses in the lapels of shiny black polyester suits and on the shoulders of long black polyester dresses, marched in single file down the middle aisle. A matronly, middle-aged woman dressed in the same colors marched behind them. They arranged themselves in a semi-circle and the church grew quiet. The director blew her pitch pipe and the basses and baritones broke the silence in a deep, professional tone that belied both their age and training.

> *When Israel was in Egypt land*

The sopranos, altos and tenors responded.

> *Let my people go*

The basses and baritones again,

> *Oppressed so hard*
> *They could not stand*

The response again,

> *Let my people go*

The voice parts blended together for the chorus.

> *Go down—Moses—*
> *Way down in Egypt land*

A single baritone finished the first stanza.

> *Tell old—Pharaoh—*
> *To let my people go.*

The music, as it had countless times before, quivered her insides and made her head hot. She blinked her eyes dry and shifted on the pew.

While the Dunbar A Cappella choir marched out again in single file, an elderly lady in a white uniform and white gloves came over to her and whispered,

"You Carolyn Bankston?"

"Yes ma'am."

"Someone's looking for you out back."

"Must be the trucks," she whispered to Skeeter. "Catch you later."

When she walked back through the church kitchen, she saw him. He was fixing a plate from the mounds of fried chicken, potato salad, string beans, and corn bread squares. After he got a napkin and fork, he turned and raised his head. He looked good. The khaki suit had obviously been tailored and hung loose on his lean frame. He had lost weight and shaved his moustache.

"Well, you're looking prosperous, C. J. Every inch the competent Administrative Assistant to the President."

He gave her that embarrassed smile that she had never understood and put his plate down. "C'mere, baby."

She walked into his arms and rested her face in the space between his chin and shoulder. He pressed her to him. "You still sweet?"

"Sometimes."

"Damn, you feel good."

He rubbed his palms around her buttocks and pressed her closer. She felt him grow hard and brought her arms up to his chest to push him away. Gently.

"We're in church, you know."

"Can't help that. The Lord knows how much I missed my baby."

"I missed you, too," she admitted.

He held his chest back and brought his arms back up around her waist. "I see you're going braless now."

"Today, I did. God, it's hot in Florida."

"See? I told you," he said with growing irritation. "You're getting too free about yourself already. Next you'll be taking off your damn panties to keep cool. And I don't like that."

"Hey. Listen. They're my panties," she said half seriously.

He smiled. "Yeah, but what's in them belongs to me. Remember?"

"Naw, I don't remember all that. But I do remember agreeing to let things be for awhile. What're you doing here anyway?"

"Looking for love."

"C'mon, seriously. Did you come down for the march?"

"Naw, not really. I came to see about you and how you're doing."

She lowered her head slightly, then looked up into his eyes. "I'm doing O.K. Still struggling. Fighting sin."

"I know you are." He brought his hand up and cupped one of her breasts.

"C'mon, C. J. Cut it out. Somebody might come through here.

"Let 'em come. All they'll see is a man in love."

"With himself and what he wants."

"Look," he said softly, brushing her cheeks, nose, and eyes with his lips. "I have to leave tonight for Chicago. Why don't you come with me? That's why I really came down. We can stay at the Palmer House again, you can go shopping and. . . ."

"Shopping? I got twelve dollars to my name."

"I got money. And flight checks too. C'mon and go with me. You're finished here. The march is tomorrow and they can handle it without you, I guess. Heard you been raising hell down here. Organizing your butt off. Saw the leaflets too. You did a nice job."

"Thanks," she said and then hesitated. "But give me a raincheck on Chicago, O.K.? I really need to be here for tomorrow."

He let his hands drop from her waist and stood back a few inches. "It's hard for you to give in and be just a woman, isn't it?"

"No," she said slowly. "It's hard for me to forget and forgive—some things."

"Aw, come on. Not that again. I told you before you came down here not to come. All you had to do was wait. But no—you had to do it your way. You had to be up front too. You wouldn't listen."

"Listen to what?" she asked annoyed. "All that rhetoric about marching two steps behind? And wait? Wait for what? For all black folk to be free so you could move into some meaningful, but lucrative social action program and me start a baby farm?"

"Plenty of women have done it. But you didn't want to be a wife really. You wanted to get married, but you didn't want to become a wife. At least not the kind I needed."

"Maybe so," she said quietly. "You're probably right about that. Because to me wife means equal, partner. And that's not what it means to you at all."

"Hey." He raised the palms of his hands before her. "Let's not argue. You made your point. You're doing what you want to do, right? And if it gets too rough, you can always go back to your little middle-class family in Ohio and pick up all the missing pieces. But I can't. I can't do that. I didn't come south, Carolyn. I was born here. And you never understood the difference."

"And you never understood that I can't just settle for anything. That I cannot handle the 'first lady' bit, especially with a string of strong seconds behind me."

She lay naked under the sheets and listened to the shower running. When he came out, beads of water sparkled in his hair. He took two towels from the rack, wrapped one around his waist and walked over to the bed, using the second to dry his head and face. He looked over at her. She stared at the design on the spread. He sat down and bent his head over to finish the drying.

"We used to shower together. Remember?"

"I know," she said. "But you have a plane to catch and I have a few more hours. Besides, I'm tired. Maybe I'll sleep a little before I get up."

He lay down beside her, crossed his arms under his head and stared at the ceiling. "You're changing, Carolyn."

"So are you."

"But we still got something, at least for right now. If things keep going the way they are, though, I don't know how long it'll last."

"For you?"

"For both of us." He paused. "See, I know what I want and pretty much where I'm going. But you're not so sure anymore, are you?"

"About what I *don't* want, I am."

"Well, tell me about it. Talk to me."

"The first thing is that I don't want to be locked up somewhere playing wife and maybe mother while you're out . . ." She didn't have the words exactly.

"Out doing what? Screwing around?" he offered.

"Yeah. That's part of it. But mostly while you're out working. Not on a job, but changing things. Making things happen. I've had a taste of it, C. J. We did it in Greene County. We got the whole county commission and the sheriff elected. And I helped make it work. I couldn't sit in an apartment or go to class everyday if a chance like that came again. I'd have to go. Whether you were there or not."

"So if we straightened things out and got married tomorrow, you'd still want to stay?"

"With the movement? Yeah. I would."

"It wouldn't work then. At least not for me. I need an anchor. And I don't need to have to worry about my woman five or six hundred miles away working with whoremongers like Skeeter, who'd give his right arm to screw you, just once, so he could come back and tell me about it."

"Do you actually think I'd let something like that happen?"

"You're a woman."

She was quiet again. Then she began to remember how in Greene County she had gotten rumors about him and a couple of the women on the Chicago staff. They had not seen each other in nearly three months and the gossip distracted her. But she was so wrapped up in the campaign and so tired most of the time, she had never considered how she was affected. Yeah, he was probably right, she reasoned. She could weaken. He had.

"Well, I guess we're stuck then," she said finally.

"No. We don't have to be," he said, propping himself up against the headboard. "We don't have to have a plan, you know. If what we got going is worth anything, we can hang onto it as long as we're together. Like now."

"So? What do we do?"

"We go to the airport. If you decide to come with me, O.K. If you don't, that's O.K. too. I'll leave a flight check just in case you decide to come later." He waited a moment and then said softly, "I'm trying to work with you, baby. The best I know how."

"And after Chicago, what?"

"I don't know about after. But right now, there's a good chance you'd see Wilkins. I ran into him last week. Wilkins has finished seminary and been ordained. Got a nice little church over on the South Side. But other than that, Wilkins, Chicago, and the Palmer House, I can't promise much more—just another week together."

She stared into space and lay motionless for a while longer, arranging the image in her mind—kind-faced Wilkins, black robe, and pulpit. Then she looked over into C. J.'s eyes and he smiled. With an uncharacteristic suddenness, she swished back the sheets, stood up and clicked her tongue.

"O.K. You got it, buster."

While she showered, he packed her bags.

NATALIE L. M. PETESCH

Selma

Natalie L. M. Petesch (1924–) is the author of five novels and six short-story collections, all critically acclaimed. Reared in Detroit, she now lives in Pittsburgh. She is a recipient of the Pittsburgh Cultural Trust's Award for Creative Achievement by an Outstanding Established Artist. "Selma" was first published in the *South Dakota Review* in the summer of 1972 and was included in her 1974 collection, *After the First Death There Is No Other*, winner of the Iowa School of Letters Award for Short Fiction.

For Viola Liuzzo

March 8, 1965

I[1] asked myself, suppose a brick should enter through my window, as it did the car of my father many years before? Transfixed by love, by pain, I should be unable to speak to my dear ones. For fear of this, I have begun to write these things down, though in a jumble. It is a way of being with them always.

I came after I saw them on television, beating people on the Edmund Pettus Bridge.[2] This was not bearable to me. I said, Why are they striking

1. The first-person Angelina character in this story is based on Viola Liuzzo (1925–65), to whom the story is dedicated. Liuzzo left her home in Michigan, as well as her four children, to participate in the march. She was killed by Klansmen while she was shuttling marchers to Selma from Montgomery. She had delivered the first carload and was en route back to Montgomery to pick up others when Klansmen pulled beside her on Highway 80 and shot her as she drove. She died instantly. A monument on Highway 80 commemorates the place where she expired.
2. Edmund Pettus Bridge crosses over the Alabama River, connecting Selma, Alabama, and Montgomery via Highway 80. The beating of the people is a reference to March 7, 1965, "Bloody Sunday," when John Lewis (1940–) and Hosea Williams (1926–2000) attempted the first march to Montgomery in response to the shooting of Jimmie Lee Jackson (1938–65) in Marion, Alabama, on February 18; Jackson died on February 26 in Selma. Jackson had futilely attempted to save the life of relatives in a night march in Marion.

those innocent people praying to their God? And Nicola said: "Because God has not *answered* their prayers." I thought about this a long time; then I went to pack my bag. Because the way that God answers is mysterious. In me, He answered.

I kissed my children. Hardest of all was it to leave Francesca. She is only four, but suffers already when others are in pain. How does she recognize suffering so as to experience it? I do not know. Perhaps she absorbs it from the wind, from the radioactive air. Perhaps from my eyes. . . . But she is concerned with good and evil. She asks, Why must *you* go? Why not the mother of Carmella? I could not explain this. Why indeed? I put on my green cloth coat. I like its color, though it is old—the color of winter grass. I gathered together a toothbrush, a blanket, several pictures of the children. Should I take a camera? I decided against. If I shall have time to take pictures, what need of me to go?

Nicola drove me to the train station, where Cynthia, Bob, and Charles were already waiting. They had called me earlier, they were going, too. After much discussion it was decided that Charles would drive for me to Alabama our blue car, as Nicola wants me to have "safe transportation" when I arrive. I think that it is because of the Michigan license plate he does not wish me to drive it. But after? He does not expect that I shall remain quiet in Selma? That Charles will be there to drive the car for me? But Nicola tries to think of everything. It is strange that he has not yet thought of a way to make me happy. Perhaps this one thing is impossible. Perhaps it is merely one's fate—whether one has been happy or not.

From the moment we entered the train a strange peace descended on me. I have been for hours in the lounge, leaving Cynthia and Bob to themselves. I am sorry to be alone, yet I feel "purified" that I shall do this thing and others—friends, relatives, children, even loved ones from the past—shall not see me. But this is a corrupt thought: I become proud. What virtue can come of an action which already admires itself?

Therefore is it that I have been sitting alone. I wished to read from my missal, but I am ashamed to be seen reading my prayerbook like a priest. Yet it happens sometimes that the greatest desire for God is in a public place. They should make these books to be inconspicuous, so that we can, without false pride or immodesty, open and read.

Montgomery
March 9

A long tiring trip. Was it necessary to waste so many hours? I should not have listened to Nicola, but should have taken the plane. But Nicola says that a mother of small children should not take risks; then he gives me the statistics concerning air crashes, how many are fatal, etc., etc. But it is because he himself cannot breathe in high altitudes; as he fears for himself, so he fears for me also.

I am staying with a teacher from the Loveless Elementary School— Mrs. Criss. She is a very brave woman. She has been a teacher for many years. She says school teachers have not been active enough. She says she was on the bridge Sunday when they gave the order for the troopers to go forward.[3] Some of Sheriff Clark's men[4] had made holes in their clubs and put metal rods inside. She says it was very bad. I saw it also on television; but it is different when she tells me about it. She tells of the awful silence when, as the marchers kneeled in the dust, the posse-men put on their gas masks. I begin to tremble when she tells me this. I begin to wish myself there, humbling myself with the others, in the dust. I begin to feel a thirst for virtue.

We have many veterans from other struggles here: from SCLC,[5] from SNCC,[6] from The Mississippi Summer (last year).[7] There are those who claim we are already betrayed, that there are "black racists" rising up who hate the white man as bitterly as ever the Klan hated "niggers." I do not believe this. But even if it were true? Every religion has its Betrayer: the belief that all men are brothers is not a philosophy, it is a religion. Can

3. More than five hundred marchers had crossed the Edmund Pettus Bridge when state troopers on horseback attacked the marchers with clubs and tear gas. More than fifty people sustained injuries; no one was killed.

4. Sheriff James G. Clark, of Dallas County, Alabama, did all he could to prevent black citizens from registering to vote. Of those who could have registered in Dallas County, somewhere between 1 and 2 percent of them had. He was present on "Bloody Sunday."

5. The Southern Christian Leadership Conference was formed in 1957; Martin Luther King Jr. served as its president until his death in 1968.

6. The Student Nonviolent Coordinating Committee was an organization of young people formed in April 1960 that grew out of the sit-in movement. Both SCLC and SNCC were present in the protest in Selma.

7. During the Mississippi Freedom Summer 1964, college students from all over the country came to Mississippi to work in Freedom Schools and in voter-registration drives.

there be a religion without those who pervert it?—the Christ without anti-Christ?

There were four ambulances from the Medical Committee for Human Rights. The doctors and nurses were not, at first, allowed to pick up the eighty-four people who were lying on the highway, on the bridge, among the bushes—wounded. At last, leaving a trail of blood on the highway 80,[8] they rushed the injured persons to the Good Samaritan Hospital.[9] This is a hospital for the black people of Selma, established last year by the Edmundite Fathers. Those hurt very bad were the children and old people. They could not move quickly enough away from the clubs. The tear gas sickened them. They were torn by barbed wire. In the crash of horses and whips Mrs. Criss lost her blanket roll. She regretted this very much, she says, because a blanket can save your life. One young man (from Arkansas), she says, was being beaten with a bully club; but he shielded his head with his blanket. That saved his life.

It forces me to think: by what threads we are saved. A bullet flies, a boat overturns, a clot of blood forms. Our doctor once said that he became a physician in order to overcome death, that he felt himself to be a failure. Of course. It is as if a man were to become an astronomer to overcome space.

This young man, Mrs. Criss said, was nearly blinded by tear gas shot into his face. She said she saw the face of the man who did it, that it was done deliberately.

Afterwards, they threw tear gas into the First Baptist Church.[10] They went inside and threw one of our people through a church window. . . . They stood in the streets, fighting with the children, throwing big bricks at them. They tried to run down our people with horses.

Martin Luther has scheduled a second march for Tuesday. That is today. I have debated whether I should carry a blanket. I will wear a long skirt. It is good to have cloth on the ground where one kneels; otherwise the skin may break on the sharp stones. I have seen them with the

8. Highway 80 is the connecting road between Montgomery and Selma. Today it is a divided highway, but in 1965 it was divided for only part of the route.
9. Good Samaritan Hospital was also the place that treated Jimmie Lee Jackson. The Edmundite Missions, historically, have focused on the needs of the poor in the Deep South.
10. First Baptist was the headquarters for SNCC volunteers during the preparation for the march.

blood streaming from the broken skin. And I do not wish my blood to be seen.

March 9

It is so beautiful here, it hurts me to look at it. I sometimes think: at this moment someone is dying. It is not believable.

The earth here is constantly alive; the tiny insects like jewels fly everywhere around you. And trees like ships. If we could have such trees to look at now and then, the winters would not seem so hard. Even poverty would not be so ugly. For instance: outside Mrs. Criss' house there is a tree in blossom (I do not know its name). The house itself is all flaking shingles but the fernlike leaves flutter with hundreds of blossoms like pink and yellow butterflies. It makes me feel as if I have begun another life, in Naples perhaps.

But I am so ignorant I do not know whether such trees grow in Naples. When I think of my ignorance, I become ashamed, speechless. When I am in the cafeteria with the students, the *other*(!) students, they talk and talk. I listen attentively. I do not interrupt. Though they are young, they are wise, much wiser than myself at their age. Only after I have left them, I run to the book: *lapidary, existentialist, dominion.* I look them all up. Hypocrite that I am, I am ashamed to reveal my ignorance. I said to a student once as we stood near the Art Museum, and the summer sun sank, making lights on the ground: "Look at these beautiful polished stones," and he asked, smiling: "Since when have you become a lapidary?" I was frightened. I thought I had done something wrong. I threw away the stones. He picked them up and taught me: *quartz, obsidian, tourmaline, gneiss.* How is it some people, though young enough to be my children, already know everything? After all, it is I who am the lapidary one.

I have wasted my life. Ignorance was my crime. . . .

Because of the court order, there is much confusion about whether we will march. People say that because so many have come Martin Luther will be forced to march. I do not like this way of deciding. We must march, some say because of an "absolute principle." However, I do not know, really, what that principle is. So if the others march, I also will march.

Mrs. Paul Douglas is very dedicated; she says we must march. She looks very beautiful in her white gloves and pearls and small lavender-colored hat. She has the face of a saint. I would not mind one day to look like her.

About a thousand people have been waiting by Brown's Chapel.[11] At last Martin Luther has made up his mind. . . . He made a beautiful speech: "I have made my choice," he said. "I would rather die on the highways of Alabama than make a butchery of my conscience." We are relieved to get started. The waiting brings out our fear. . . .

This was very strange. As soon as we reached to the other side of the bridge Martin Luther stopped. Major Cloud[12] ordered us to stand where we were. Had we quickened ourselves to this great action only to stand submissively before the Blue Helmets? The sun was blinding. I looked upward, beyond the phalanx of troopers to where rows of telephones were standing like crucifixes on a hillside. We knelt on the stones: I was glad I had thought to wear my heavy skirt. I saw many priests and nuns. (The people of Selma say they are not real priests and nuns, but Communists in disguise.) Rev. Abernathy prayed over us all. He said: "We come to present our bodies as a living sacrifice."

There was one priest who did not uncover his head as we prayed. I wondered why. I thought St. Paul had made some rule about this. Then it occurred to me that he was not a priest but a rabbi. Here are all churches made one church. At such times we have a Vision of what the world may one day be. We are ready to die for each other. As Rev. Abnernathy[13] said: "We don't have much to offer, but we do have our bodies and we lay them on the altar today."

I wonder how my children are. Sylvia will take care of them. She is old enough. But it is a responsibility. And Nicola is not well enough. There are many things I should have told Sylvia. Though it is true she knows many things better than I. Mother and daughter in the same school!

Between radio news and writing letters home I have been trying to

11. Brown Chapel AME, on the same street as First Baptist Church, was the headquarters for the leaders of the SCLC during the preparation for the march.

12. Major John Cloud was the man who apprised the marchers that theirs was an "unlawful march" and would not be allowed to continue.

13. Ralph Abernathy (1926–90), who became Martin Luther King Jr.'s best friend during the days of the Montgomery bus boycott, was often by his side during the events of the civil rights movement. The quoted words from Abernathy and King are their actual words at the bridge on the second effort to walk to Montgomery.

do my schoolwork. It is difficult to study at my age. Most of the students in this sociology class, for instance, are young enough to be my children. Yet it is only in the mirror that I am thirty-nine; I blush like a child when Teacher smiles at me: "Angelina has the right answer!"

Reading the *Negro Revolt* when you are in the middle of the revolution seems, as my fellow-students say, "academic." I like better to be reading my *Walden*. If we are ready to live as Thoreau . . . but we are not: we must, always, carry our blanket. Lord, give me courage to carry, not a blanket but a cross.

King said at the church: "When Negroes and whites can stand on Highway 80 and have a mass meeting, things aren't that bad."

Mrs. Criss came in from church. I did not have the radio on. I was lying in the darkness, my rosary round my neck. It helps me when I worry about my children, what accident may befall them in my absence. I press the crucifix to my bosom. Sometimes it seems I can feel a heart, a pulse, beating against my palm. She told me about Reverend Reeb's murder.[14] (She called it murder, although there is a chance that he will live.) As I listened the cross in my hand seemed to burn; I cried out in pain.

We knelt and prayed together, though she is a Baptist. I remembered how Mrs. Chaney who is also a Baptist said: "I don't quite know how my boy wound up joining the Catholic Church, but we all worship the same God. . . ." Thus Mary was a Jew, and Christ? A Christ-ian.

Mrs. Criss recited the Lord's Prayer. I leaned on her shoulder. We mingled our tears.

He had left his church in Washington, D.C., so that he could give himself up to the meek and the poor. He had been working with the American Friends Committee in Roxbury.

Four or five men outside the Silver Moon attacked them (the ministers), calling, "Hey nigger!" Mrs. Criss says that his friends escaped, but that James Reeb's skull was split open. No one helped him. People from behind the window of the Silver Moon gathered to watch. There was no help anywhere. There was no Samaritan to succor him.

Reverend Reeb has four children. Who will care for them?

14. James Reeb (1927–65), a Unitarian minister and father of four, left the Silver Moon restaurant with two other ministers, where they were met by a white mob brandishing clubs. Someone smashed his head. He died on March 11, 1965.

We do not ask ourselves these questions before we come. If we did, our hand would shake, our mouth would go dry, our foot would slip.

March 10

He is still in a coma. His wife has flown to the hospital at Birmingham.

We have been standing in a vigil, waiting and praying. The rain never ceases. Hundreds of priests and nuns, with umbrellas and newspapers, black and white, we cling together so as to shield one another from the downpour. The rain falls like bullets on our tired bodies.

A clothesline keeps us walled off into a kind of compound here in Sylvan Street.[15] In defiance, with ecstasy in their voices, the children are singing: "A Clothesline is a Berlin Wall." We also sing, *We Shall Overcome*, but at times it seems to me we lack spirit.

Some are covering themselves with canvas. I must admit it is a blessing to be sheltered from the rain. We need blankets, for the nights are harrowing, and the ground is cold.

March 11

Mrs. Criss and I were standing together, leaning against the rope staring into the headlights of the police cars when suddenly, like a low thunder, the people all around us began to moan with grief. We knew at once that he had died.

March 15

Some say a senseless death. Four children orphaned. If his death is senseless, then no life is meaningful. For we all die, and who of us could say as the priest enters to anoint us, feet and head: It was well done. I hold fast to the belief that when the blow descended and he felt the agony of it throughout his soul, he prayed: "Now Lord, let thy faithful servant depart."

But perhaps he experienced only a longing to see his children.

15. Sylvan Street was the location of the headquarters churches. The street name has since been changed to Martin Luther King Street.

Other people have died. But his death obsesses me. I yearn to ask him: Why—? Others have died, but they left mourning parents; his death leaves mourning children.

They held a memorial service at AME this afternoon. I asked permission to attend. As there were to be hundreds of nuns and clergymen from all over the United States, I felt my presence "unnecessary." But I asked a priest here who said: "We are all *necessary*." So I went.

Martin Luther King spoke last. I have never seen so many different priests, ministers, rabbis. It was as if they had been gathered up from all lands, speaking all tongues. Greek Orthodox and Fundamentalist and Hebrew and Baptist and Catholic and Methodist, white and black, we sang *We Shall Overcome* together. A rabbi sang the "Kaddish." I had never heard it before. I think I would have liked such singing at my grave.

But I am in awe of his widow. Would I have had the courage, to say as she did that the cause of equality was so important that if her husband had to die for it, she accepted his death. . . .

There is to be a memorial march to the courthouse around sundown.

We started out from Brown's Chapel, arms locked. The Alabama sun was beginning to fade into twilight. With the darkness came the night-birds, the whirring of insects, the singing of katydids, the chanting of tree frogs. They are there in the daytime too, but it is as if when the night comes, we hear these things.

Three abreast, we walked. When the front line had reached the green courthouse, we stopped. Then Martin Luther spoke to us, standing on the steps as on a hillside.

Afterwards Mrs. Criss and I walked home together. It was very hot. I took off my shoes and carried them. I had cut myself on Sylvan Street, which is unpaved. In her home Mrs. Criss set me down by the kitchen table; she knelt and washed my foot; a stone had pierced it. She crossed it twice over with white tape and bound it carefully. I did not protest. It was good to be comforted. I felt very weary. I wished it were over.

Awoke in terror during the night, and wish to write this down before the image fades.

I dreamed that I lay on a table, like Gorki's father. Around my feet my children played. They did not know I was dead. Nor did I. I rose from the table. I beckoned to them. My face was white. Though I wept, no tears ran down my cheeks. I lifted my hand to my mouth. I was toothless and could not speak. My children, seeing me, my moving mouth, speechless, my tearless eyes, my white face, shrieked in terror. Nicola appeared and touched his fingertips to the wound which Mrs. Criss had bound: the blood spurted out. Then I lay quietly, accepting what had been wrought. My children picked up their toys and left. I was alone. Though I loved them, it hurt me that they would not stay by my body, but preferred their toys.

As I write this, the first birds of morning are beginning to come from the trees like a gradual increase of light. First chirping, then with a clear call.

March 16

Voter registration keeps me too busy to write. There are 29,500 people in Selma, about equally divided, black and white. Only one per cent of the people on the voting polls are Negro.

In Detroit ten thousand people, led by Mayor Cavanagh and Governor Romney[16] marched in protest against brutalities here.

March 20

Busy as we can be, preparing for the Long March. I am to be in charge of the oatmeal "detail" at breakfasts and (once we are at St. Jude's[17]) will be part of the transportation committee, shuttling the footsore and heavy-laden from Montgomery to Selma.

March 21

There were about three thousand of us. It was a clear morning. The air smelled like freshly baked bread. Dry, crisp, as though to feed our hunger. We were not noisy. Perhaps we were a little afraid. The women just outside the Chapel, as we turned on Alabama Street frightened me most.

16. Jerome Cavanagh (1928–79) served Detroit as mayor from 1962 to 1970. George W. Romney (1907–95) served Michigan as governor from 1963 to 1969.
17. St. Jude's Hospital, located on the edge of Montgomery, hosted the marchers on March 24, the last night of the walk. It was the first integrated hospital in the Southeast.

Why do they hate me so much? Their faces as they yelled at us were ugly with rage. They insult the nuns. Do they believe their own stories of birth control pills and black and white "orgies"? Or is it that, like children at vindictive play, they do not understand what they are saying? A Jewish boy once told me that as a small boy at the Bishop School he played a game in which one child was set in the center of a circle while the others chanted:

> Here comes a Jew
> All dressed in blue
> At the door he bends his knee
> But no matter what you say
> No matter what you do
> A Jew, Jew, Jew are *you*!

He said that they would scream the last line, pointing their fingers at the child kneeling in the school yard. Did they understand that their game was filled with their father's hate? I cannot believe it. Only children, chanting hateful tunes whose story was lost long ago.

Toward the noon hour the sun became very hot. We were very thirsty. The line was led by Martin Luther, with Rabbi Heschel[18] and Dr. Ralph Bunche.[19] But my favorite among the clergy is this Reverend Dom Orsini. He reminds me of Papa; he has the same eyebrows, though of course Papa did not have this black patch over the eye, about which there is something at once noble and pathetic. It is that a man with a dark eye-patch becomes more vulnerable: we know a single grain of dust from the highway could cripple his greatest work.

There is in fact a blind man among us. He is from Atlanta. I do not know his name.

When we walked past the Selma Arms Company, the women screamed "White niggers!" They were well-dressed, grey-haired ladies with hats and white gloves. I think they had just come from church.

---

18. Abraham Joshua Heschel (1907–72) had escaped Nazi Germany and felt compelled to participate in Selma.

19. Ralph Bunche (1904–71) won the Nobel Peace Prize in 1950, in part for his extensive negotiating of the armistice agreements between Israel and the Arab states. As an educator at Howard and Harvard, where he earned his PhD, Bunche's work with the United Nations was extensive, especially in dealing with Africa. He was a tireless spokesman on the subject of racial prejudice being without any scientific basis in biology or anthropology.

We had no trouble at the Edmund Pettus Bridge this time.

Only that a woman with a little boy no bigger than my little Francesca hurled filthy words at the Sisters. I sang as loudly as I could to drown out their words. Never before have I sung so—insistently. One of them (the Sisters) turned and smiled at me. It made me ashamed. Who was I to protect her from the foul words? She is protected by her innocence. But I sang in pain and anger, because having lived in sin, I know well the meaning of their words.

We sang Freedom songs, then rested, saving our breath for the march, for the gaps in our ranks that sometimes force us to run to catch up. We camped near Trickem Fork.[20] It is cold, very cold. Temperature below freezing, I think. There are only two tents, with kerosene heaters. We had spaghetti for supper—*not* Italian style. I am still on oatmeal detail. Breakfast will be at 7:00. Am too weary to write more. Feel as if I'd been stomped to death. . . .

Perhaps there will be a letter in Montgomery when we arrive Thursday. A note from my children would help me remember, perhaps, why I am here—cooking oatmeal in new garbage cans.

Someone pointed out Reverend Jarvis to me. He is from Detroit. Perhaps I will speak to him tomorrow. But tonight—.

March 22

Three hundred people to feed this morning—most of them cold and humbled with fatigue. Few of us slept well, in spite of the protection of the National Guard. The kerosene heaters did not work well, or perhaps they let them go out, perhaps it was safer in the tents without them. But everyone agrees it was cold. They find my oatmeal delicious. I say to them I wish I could fix some *lasagna* which my husband well likes. They laugh. There are teachers, ex-soldiers, psychologists. One of these analyzes aloud our "reasons" for being here. He does not say why *he* has chosen this place to be.

This morning, our numbers seem diminished. I try to remember who it is that has gone. Doubtless they left because according to the court order our number must be kept to three hundred (there is only a two-

20. Trickem Fork is located within twelve miles of Selma on Highway 80. It was the camping site for the first night en route to Montgomery.

lane highway from Trickem Fork.) But why did they permit themselves to be sent away? I do not know. Perhaps a weakening of their will, of their physical force. One priest has been sent to the hospital. They say he became terrified during the night, that he was weeping like a child. What torment for men. . . . We too are afraid. We see it in each other's eyes, but we pretend it is not there. Or we joke. On the longer marches it is always hard to sing. It is better to have some silent symbol, a voluntary burden to carry—a flag, or a child on one's back.

We passed a dirty, peeling, splintering shack, set up from the raw earth on stumps of bricks. Five rickety steps. Windows like a warehouse. Somebody said: "There's Rolen School. My grandson go to school there." I looked at the shack. What could my Sylvia, in spite of her natural gifts, have learned at such a school? At the sight of this shameful poverty I made the sign of the Cross as though I had passed a wreck on the highway. Father Sherrill Smith (he is from Texas) saw me do so, and gave me such a look. But I meant no irreverence.

Martin Luther told us: "You will be the people that will light a new chapter in the history of our nation."

But we were not thinking of history, only of the heat, which was like an inferno. From the blacktop highway the flames were licking our feet. They were burned, blistered, swollen so as to be impossible to put our shoes on again. We wanted only to bathe them in cool water.

During the last few miles (we made sixteen today) the wound of my foot reopened. There was blood in the shoe. I took off both shoes and carried them. A young black man walking by my side offered to carry them for me, but I only shook my head, too tired to thank him. I was ashamed to show the blood.

March 23

The rain was a blessing. I felt I could not have walked else. But I wished very much to keep off the burning highway. I tried whenever I could to sink my feet in the wet clay-like earth. The damp smell everywhere was like a *benedicite*. In the rain we were united. We lifted our faces to the heavens. Again we sang songs. We were cleansed by the water, which came upon us in great pounding rushes of rain, like the pounding with leaves at the ancient baths. Just as we passed the Big Swamp, the skies opened upon us their heaviest downpour. Birds which in the slanted rain-light resembled doves or peewits flew up from the swamps to the trees. On the trees the Spanish moss hung like the wet tangled hair of a woman. It was beautiful. There is something mysterious about the way that the host and the parasite together make a beautiful tree. The National Guardsmen would not look at us as we passed. They were angry, perhaps, to be out in the rain.

We are a strange-looking procession. We must look like fools to the people watching us. A blind man, a one-footed man (he too is from Michigan), a one-eyed priest, and nuns in plastic coats, like sailors. I have a strange habit: to look down at people's feet. There I see worn sneakers, always with the small toe boring through on either foot, and heavy boots, Wellingtons, and those they call "roughouts" and sandals, and leather oxfords, and some few like myself, wearing bare feet.

There is a saying I heard once: I complained that I had no shoes till I saw a man who had no feet.

Not far ahead of me I see the left leg and crutches of one of our marchers. His name is James Letherer.[21] The tough teen-agers never tire of taunting him. Perhaps they are shamed by him: having both shoes and feet, they do not walk. They mock him as he marches: "Left . . . Left . . . Left. . . ." But he ignores them. He has endured worse things.

Above us, suddenly, a plane. In spite of myself I feel a flutter of fear, for it would be easy for some psychopath to destroy us from off the face of the earth. But it is only leaflets, a message from the United Klans. They say Martin Luther is a Communist.

We did eleven miles today. Everything is wet, and it is difficult to cook anything. Still, I prefer it. My foot swells desperately. Impossible to write. The pencil smears on the paper. Also, I had nothing on which to write except my knee. A curly-headed boy with a beard (I do not know his name but he is one of those carrying a child like an amulet about his neck) said to me laughing: "You can use my back." So I made pretense of writing on his back. Somebody said: "She is a gentle yoke. . . ." But I thought the clergymen did not like this levity concerning the yoke of Our Lord, so I stopped writing.

21. James Letherer came to Selma from Michigan. He reported that he only wished he could do more to help the black citizens of Selma get the vote.

March 24

I am weary unto death. Sixteen miles to go today.

More people are coming every hour, it seems. We left our camp this morning at seven, after oatmeal and coffee. (Mrs. Criss had some peanut butter sandwiches which she shared with those around her.) Now leading us is the one-legged man (who, they tell me, is from Saginaw, Michigan), the Reverend Young from Atlanta,[22] and someone from SNCC. There are many American flags. It rains a little from time to time and our clothes are never really dry. A strange odor pervades the air, as of ripening melons, or love. My face has become nearly black from the sun. When I touch it, it is so dry from the heat that it wrinkles as if I had lived a whole lifetime on this march, and had become old in four days. If Nicola were to see me he would say, you must cover your head—protect yourself. But I cannot protect myself against anything anymore. I feel only a deep need to sleep.

Fourteen more miles to go tomorrow. As we crossed into Montgomery, suddenly there were many hundreds to join us. The clouds parted and as from a fountainhead, water descended. Then almost at once the sun came. We sang *We Shall Overcome*.

The new people who have joined us seem very fresh, very rested, very white. All of us from the first day are as burned as if we had been walking in the desert.

Many famous people, including Harry Belafonte,[23] singing on coffin crates built into a temporary stage.

March 25

We waited around St. Jude's this a.m. for what seemed hours. Something detained Martin Luther. We sat quietly waiting in the mud. The more energetic ones, the younger people, wandered about, looking at the "delegations" from Hawaii, from Denver, New York, Los Angeles. . . . Many

---

22. Andrew Young (1932–), one of the leaders of the march, was with King the day he died. He went on to become ambassador to the United Nations during Jimmy Carter's presidency and, later, mayor of Atlanta.

23. In the 1960s Harry Belafonte (1927–) was a popular singer, actor, and political figure. Along with Joan Baez (1941–), he entertained the marchers at St. Jude's the night before the gathering on the steps of the capitol in Montgomery.

are wearing UAW chef-type hats; others—more striking yet—are wearing yarmulkes, as a symbol of the solidarity between Negro and Jew.

Finally we started. Martin Luther's wife was with him this time. I had never seen her before. The people in front wore orange vests. Somebody played Yankee Doodle Dandy.

It was strange and wonderful to see so many barefooted priests. Because they were barefooted, I put on my shoes. It was not seemly for me to appear to imitate these saintly ones. It was well that I did so. The crush of thousands as we walked down Oak Street to Dexter[24] was a kind of ecstasy. We tried to hold onto each other—six abreast (women and children on the inside) but the momentum was often too great. Our lines broke, reformed. We panted, we ran to fill the gap in our ranks. People ran to give us things to drink, as we were thirsting. Cold drinks, soda bottles passed from hand to hand, black and white. People cried to us from the porches: "Freedom!" But it was restrained, as though it were a Passion Play. People ran to shake hands with one another. Somebody ran to me and took my hand as though to kiss it. He called my name: "Angelina!" he said; but it sounded like a question. He stood, smiling strangely, like a man filled with love or hate or both at once. Then he bowed, and raising up his camera slowly, like a weapon, took my picture.

One girl spat upon the ground as I passed: "Go to hell, nigger lover," she said.

I had placed a handkerchief at the bottom of my shoe, to ease the wound. At a stop street I paused to fold it; the handkerchief fell from my hand and was kicked away in the crowds. But it was not much farther. So we hobbled on. . . .

3:00 p.m. It is finished. We have made "the Selma-Montgomery March." I am sitting on Dexter Avenue with about twenty thousand people. Speeches are being made, but we barely listen. Most of us are resting. We still have work to do when the speeches are over. King is saying: "They told us we wouldn't get here. And there are those who said we would get here over dead bodies. . . . Segregation is on its death bed in Alabama . . . and Wallace will make the funeral. . . ."

24. At the foot of Dexter Avenue is the stately capitol. One block away on Dexter is Martin Luther King Jr.'s first church, Dexter Avenue Baptist—today, Dexter Avenue King Memorial Baptist Church.

There is much yet to be done. We can't stop here to eat. Nearly all shops and restaurants are closed. Those that are open show their unveiled hostility. Even getting back to St. Jude's where many have parked their cars, will be for some people, a formidable hike. In a few hours it will be dark, and we are, all of us, exhausted. We have arrived at our destination in a fever, an exultation, but also with despair. The despair comes from the feeling of not knowing why, exactly, we have consummated this particular act. It is a momentary terror, our *eli, eli*.

JOHN UPDIKE

Marching through Boston

Born in Pennsylvania, John Updike (1932–) is a prolific writer of poetry, essays, novels, and short stories and is well known for his four Rabbit novels about Harry Angstrom. His work has been frequently reprinted in *The Best American Short Stories* (ten times) and in the O. Henry Award anthologies (twelve times). He has also appeared on the cover of *Time* magazine twice. "Marching through Boston" first appeared in the *New Yorker* on January 22, 1966, and was reprinted in the O. Henry *Prize Stories 1967.*

The civil-rights movement had a salubrious effect on Joan Maple. A suburban mother of four, she would return late at night from a non-violence class in Roxbury with rosy cheeks and shining eyes, eager to describe, while sipping Benedictine, her indoctrination. "This huge man in overalls—"

"A Negro?" her husband asked.

"Of course. This huge man, with a *very* refined vocabulary, told us if we march anywhere, especially in the South, to let the Negro men march on the outside, because it's important for their self-esteem to be able to protect us. He told us about a New York fashion designer who went down to Selma and said she could take care of herself. Furthermore, she flirted with the state troopers. They finally told her to go home."

"I thought you were supposed to love the troopers," Richard said.

"Only abstractly. Not on your own. You mustn't do *any*thing within the movement as an individual. By flirting, she gave the trooper an opportunity to feel contempt."

"She blocked his transference, as it were."

"Don't laugh. It's all very psychological. The man told us, those who want to march, to face our ego-gratificational motives no matter how irrelevant they are and then put them behind us. Once you're in a march, you have no identity. It's elegant. It's beautiful."

He had never known her like this. It seemed to Richard that her posture was improving, her figure filling out, her skin growing lustrous, her very hair gaining body and sheen. Though he had resigned himself, through twelve years of marriage, to a rhythm of apathy and renewal, he distrusted this raw burst of beauty.

The night she returned from Alabama,[1] it was three o'clock in the morning. He woke and heard the front door close behind her. He had been dreaming of a parallelogram in the sky that was also somehow a meteor, and the darkened house seemed quadrisected by the four sleeping children he had, with more than paternal tenderness, put to bed. He had caught himself speaking to them of Mommy as a distant departed spirit, gone to live, invisible, in the newspapers and the television set. The little girl, Bean, had burst into tears. Now the ghost closed the door and walked up the stairs, and came into his bedroom, and fell on the bed.

He switched on the light and saw her sunburned face, her blistered feet. Her ballet slippers were caked with orange mud. She had lived for three days on Coke and dried apricots; at one stretch she had not gone to the bathroom for sixteen hours. The Montgomery airport had been a madhouse—nuns, social workers, divinity students fighting for space on the northbound planes. They had been in the air when they heard about Mrs. Liuzzo.[2]

He accused her: "It could have been you."

She said, "I was always in a group." But she added guiltily, "How were the children?"

"Fine. Bean cried because she thought you were inside the television set."

"Did you see me?"

"Your parents called long-distance to say they thought they did. I didn't. All I saw was Abernathy and King and their henchmen saying, 'Thass right. Say it, man. Thass sayin' it.'"

"Aren't you mean? It was very moving, except that we were all so tired. These teen-age Negro girls kept fainting; a psychiatrist explained to me that they were having psychotic breaks."

"What psychiatrist?"

---

1. Joan Maple has just returned to Boston from participating in the 1965 walk from Selma to Montgomery. She has left her four children at home with her angst-driven husband.
2. Viola Liuzzo (1925–65) was a Michigan mother of four who was killed by Klansmen as she was shuttling marchers back to Selma from Montgomery at the close of the event.

"Actually, there were three of them, and they were studying to be psychiatrists in Philadelphia. They kind of took me in tow."

"I bet they did. Please come to bed. I'm very tired from being a mother."

She visited the four corners of the upstairs to inspect each sleeping child and, returning, undressed in the dark. She removed underwear she had worn for seventy hours and stood there shining; to the sleepy man in the bed it seemed a visitation, and he felt as people of old must have felt when greeted by an angel—adoring yet resentful, at this flamboyant proof of a level above theirs.

She spoke on the radio; she addressed local groups. In garages and supermarkets he heard himself being pointed out as her husband. She helped organize meetings at which dapper young Negroes ridiculed and abused the applauding suburban audience. Richard marvelled at Joan's public composure. Her shyness stayed with her, but it had become a kind of weapon, as if the doctrine of non-violence had given it point. Her voice, as she phoned evasive local real-estate agents in the campaign for fair housing, grew curiously firm and rather obstinately melodious—a note her husband had not heard in her voice before. He grew jealous and irritable. He found himself insisting, at parties, on the constitutional case for states' rights, on the misfortunes of African independence, on the history of the Reconstruction from the South's point of view. Yet she had little trouble persuading him to march with her in Boston.

He promised, though he could not quite grasp the object of the march. All mass movements, of masses or of ideas supposedly embodied in masses, felt unreal to him. Whereas his wife, an Amherst professor's daughter, lived by abstractions; her blood returned to her heart enriched by the passage through some capillarious good cause. He was struck, and subtly wounded, by the ardor with which she rewarded his promise; under his hands her body felt baroque and her skin smooth as night.

The march was in April. Richard awoke that morning with a fever. He had taken something foreign into himself and his body was making resistance. Joan offered to go alone; as if something fundamental to his dignity, to their marriage, were at stake, he refused the offer. The day, dawning cloudy, had been forecast as sunny, and he wore a summer suit that enclosed his hot skin in a slipping, weightless unreality. At a highway drugstore they bought some pills designed to detonate inside him through a twelve-hour period. They parked near her aunt's house in Louisburg Square and took a taxi toward the headwaters of the march, a playground in Roxbury. The Irish driver's impassive back radiated disapproval. The cab was turned aside by a policeman; the Maples got out and walked down a broad brown boulevard lined with barbershops, shoe-repair nooks, pizzerias, and friendliness associations. On stoops and stairways male Negroes loitered, blinking and muttering toward one another as if a vast, decrepit conspiracy had assigned them their positions and then collapsed.

"Lovely architecture," Joan said, pointing toward a curving side street, a neo-Georgian arc suspended in the large urban sadness.

Though she pretended to know where she was, Richard doubted that they were going the right way. But then he saw ahead of them, scattered like the anomalous objects with which Dali punctuates his perspectives, receding black groups of white clergymen. In the distance, the hot lights of police cars wheeled within a twinkling mob. As they drew nearer, colored girls made into giantesses by bouffant hairdos materialized beside them. One wore cerise stretch pants and the golden sandals of a heavenly cupbearer, and held pressed against her ear a transistor radio tuned to WMEX. On this thin stream of music they all together poured into a playground surrounded by a link fence.

A loose crowd of thousands swarmed on the crushed grass. Bobbing placards advertised churches, brotherhoods, schools, towns. Popsicle venders lent an unexpected touch of carnival. Suddenly at home, Richard bought a bag of peanuts and looked around—as if this were the playground of his childhood—for friends.

But it was Joan who found some. "My God," she said. "There's my old analyst." At the fringe of some Unitarians stood a plump, doughy man with the troubled squint of a baker who has looked into too many ovens. Joan turned to go the other way.

"Don't suppress," Richard told her. "Let's go and be friendly and normal."

"It's too embarrassing."

"But it's been years since you went. You're cured."

"You don't understand. You're never cured. You just stop going."

"O.K., come *this* way. I think I see my Harvard section man in Plato to Dante."

But, even while arguing against it, she had been drifting them toward her psychiatrist, and now they were caught in the pull of his gaze. He scowled and came toward them, flat-footedly. Richard had never met him and, shaking hands, felt himself as a putrid heap of anecdotes, of detailed lusts and abuses. "I think I need a doctor," he madly blurted.

The other man produced, like a stiletto from his sleeve, a nimble smile. "How so?" Each word seemed precious.

"I have a fever."

"Ah." The psychiatrist turned sympathetically to Joan, and his face issued a clear commiseration: *So he is still punishing you*.

Joan said loyally, "He really does. I saw the thermometer."

"Would you like a peanut?" Richard asked. The offer felt so symbolic, so transparent, that he was shocked when the other man took one, cracked it harshly, and substantially chewed.

Joan asked, "Are you with anybody? I feel a need for group security."

"Come meet my sister." The command sounded strange to Richard; "sister" seemed a piece of psychological slang, a euphemism.

But again things were simpler than they seemed. His sister was plainly from the same batter. Rubicund and yeasty, she seemed to have been enlarged by the exercise of good will and wore a saucer-sized SCLC[3] button in the lapel of a coarse green suit. Richard coveted the suit; it looked warm. The day was continuing overcast and chilly. Something odd, perhaps the successive explosions of the antihistamine pill, was happening inside him, making him feel queerly elongated; the illusion crossed his mind that he was destined to seduce this woman. She beamed and said, "My daughter Trudy and her *best* friend, Carol."

They were girls of sixteen or so, one size smaller in their bones than women. Trudy had the family pastry texture and a darting frown. Carol was homely, fragile, and touching; her upper teeth were a gray blur of braces and her arms were protectively folded across her skimpy bosom. Over a white blouse she wore only a thin blue sweater, unbuttoned. Richard told her, "You're freezing."

3. The Southern Christian Leadership Conference was founded in 1957 with the help of Martin Luther King Jr., who served as its president until his death in 1968.

"I'm freezing," she said, and a small love was established between them on the basis of this demure repetition. She added, "I came along because I'm writing a term paper."

Trudy said, "She's doing a history of the labor unions," and laughed unpleasantly.

The girl shivered. "I thought they might be the same. Didn't the unions use to march?" Her voice, moistened by the obtrusion of her braces, had a sprayey faintness in the raw gray air.

The psychiatrist's sister said, "The *way* they *make* these poor children *study* nowadays! The *books* they have them *read!* Their *English* teacher *assigned* them *Tropic of Cancer*! I picked it *up* and read *one page*, and Trudy reassured me, 'It's all *right*, Mother, the teacher says he's a Tran-scen*dent*alist!' "

It felt to Richard less likely that he would seduce her. His sense of reality was expanding in the nest of warmth these people provided. He offered to buy them all Popsicles. His consciousness ventured outward and tasted the joy of so many Negro presences, the luxury of immersion in the polished shadows of their skin. He drifted happily through the crosshatch of their oblique, sardonic hooting and blurred voices, searching for the Popsicle vender. The girls and Trudy's mother had said they would take one; the psychiatrist and Joan had refused. The crowd was formed of jiggling fragments. Richard waved at the rector of a church whose nursery school his children had attended; winked at a folk singer he had seen on television and who looked lost and wan in three dimensions; assumed a stony face in passing a long-haired youth guarded by police and draped in a signboard proclaiming MARTIN LUTHER KING A TOOL OF THE COMMUNISTS; and tapped a tall bald man on the shoulder. "Remember me? Dick Maple, Plato to Dante, B-plus."

The section man turned, bespectacled and pale. It was shocking; he had aged.

The march was slow to start. Trucks and police cars appeared and disappeared at the playground gate. Officious young seminarians tried to organize the crowd into lines. Unintelligible announcements crackled within the loudspeakers. Martin Luther King was a dim religious rumor on the playground plain—now here, now there, now absent, now present. The sun showed as a kind of sore spot burning through the clouds. Carol nibbled her Popsicle and shivered. Richard and Joan argued whether to march under the Danvers banner with the psychiatrist or with the Unitarians. In the end it did not matter; King invisibly established himself at their head, a distant truck loaded with singing women lurched forward, a far corner of the crowd began to croon, "Which side are you on, boy?," and the marching began.

On Columbus Avenue they were shuffled into lines ten abreast. The Maples were separated. Joan turned up between her psychiatrist and a massive, doleful African wearing tribal scars, sneakers, and a Harvard Athletic Association sweatshirt. Richard found himself in the line ahead, with Carol beside him. Someone behind him, a forward-looking liberal, stepped on his heel, giving the knit of his loafer such a wrench that he had to walk the three miles through Boston with a floppy shoe and a slight limp. He had been born in West Virginia and did not understand Boston. In ten years he had grown familiar with some of its districts, but was still surprised by the quick curving manner in which these districts interlocked. For a few blocks they marched between cheering tenements from whose topmost windows hung banners that proclaimed END DE FACTO SEGREGATION and RETIRE MRS. HICKS. Then the march turned left, and Richard was passing Symphony Hall, within whose rectangular vault he had often dreamed his way along the deep-grassed meadows of Brahms and up the agate cliffs of Strauss. At this corner, from the Stygian subway kiosk, he had emerged with Joan—Orpheus and Eurydice—when both were students; in this restaurant, a decade later, he and she, on three drinks apiece, had decided not to get a divorce that week. The new Prudential Tower, taller and somehow fainter than any other building, haunted each twist of their march, before their faces like a mirage, at their backs like a memory. A leggy nervous colored girl wearing the orange fireman's jacket of the Security Unit shepherded their section of the line, clapping her hands, shouting freedom-song lyrics for a few bars. These songs struggled through the miles of the march, overlapping and eclipsing one another in a kind of embarrassment. "Which side are you on, boy, which side are you on . . . like a tree-ee planted by the wah-ha-ter, we shall not be moved . . . this little light of mine, gonna shine on Boston, Mass., this little light of mine . . ." The day continued cool and without shadows. Newspapers that he had folded inside his coat for warmth slipped and slid. Carol beside him plucked at her little sweater, gathering it at her bosom but unable, as if under a spell, to button it. In the line behind him, Joan, secure between her id and superego, stepped along, swinging her arms, throwing her ballet slippers alternately outward in a confident splaying stride. " . . . let 'er shine, let 'er shine . . ."

Incredibly, they were traversing a cloverleaf, an elevated concrete arabesque devoid of cars. Their massed footsteps whispered; the city yawned beneath them. The march had no beginning and no end that Richard could see. Within him, the fever had become a small glassy scratching on the walls of the pit hollowed by the detonating pills. A piece of newspaper spilled down his legs and blew into the air. Impalpably medicated, ideally motivated, he felt, strolling along the curve of the cloverleaf, gathered within an irresistible ascent. He asked Carol, "Where are we going?"

"The newspapers said the Common."

"Do you feel faint?"

Her gray braces shyly modified her smile. "Hungry."

"Have a peanut." A few still remained in his pocket.

"Thank you." She took one. "You don't have to be paternal."

"I want to be." He felt strangely exalted and excited, as if destined to give birth. He wanted to share this sensation with Carol, but instead he asked her, "In your study of the labor movement, have you learned much about the Molly Maguires?"[4]

"No. Were they goons or finks?"

"I think they were either coal miners or gangsters."

"Oh. I haven't studied about anything earlier than Gompers."[5]

"Sounds good." Suppressing the urge to tell her he loved her, he turned to look at Joan. She was beautiful, like a poster, with far-seeing blue eyes and red lips parted in song.

Now they walked beneath office buildings where like mounted butterflies secretaries and dental technicians were pressed against the glass.

---

4. The Molly Maguires, a secret organization of Irish-Americans in the coal-mining district of eastern Pennsylvania, fought against the injustices of mine owners. The organization reached its peak of activism in the late nineteenth century. The name comes from a woman who led an antiestablishment movement in Ireland in the 1840s.

5. Samuel Gompers (1850–1924) was one of the founders of the American Federation of Labor, as well as its first president, a position he held until his death. The organization grew from a few struggling labor unions to become the dominant labor movement in the country.

In Copley Square, stony shoppers waited forever to cross the street. Along Boylston, there was Irish muttering; he shielded Carol with his body. The desultory singing grew defiant. The Public Garden was beginning to bloom. Statues of worthies—Channing, Kosciusko, Cass, Phillips—were trundled by beneath the blurring trees; Richard's dry heart cracked like a book being opened. The march turned left down Charles and began to press against itself, to link arms, to fumble for love. He lost sight of Joan in the crush. Then they were treading on grass, on the Common, and the first drops of rain, sharp as needles, pricked their faces and hands.

"Did we have to stay to hear every damn speech?" Richard asked. They were at last heading home; he felt too sick to drive and huddled, in his soaked, slippery suit, toward the heater. The windshield wiper seemed to be squeaking *free-dom, free-dom.*

"I wanted to hear King."

"You heard him in Alabama."

"I was too tired to listen."

"Did you listen this time? Didn't it seem corny and forced?"

"Somewhat. But does it matter?" Her white profile was serene; she passed a trailer truck on the right, and her window was spattered as if with applause.

"And that Abernathy.[6] God, if he's John the Baptist, I'm Herod the Great. 'Onteel de Frenchman go back t'France, onteel de Ahrishman go back t'Ahrland, onteel de Mexican he go back tuh—'"

"Stop it."

"Don't get me wrong. I didn't mind them sounding like demagogues; what I minded was that god-awful boring phony imitation of a revival meeting. 'Thass right, yossuh. Yoh-*suh!*'"

"Your throat sounds sore. Shouldn't you stop using it?"

"*How* could you crucify me that way? *How* could you make this miserable sick husband stand in the icy rain for hours listening to boring stupid speeches that you'd heard before anyway?"

"I didn't think the speeches were that great. But I think it was impor-

---

6. Ralph Abernathy (1926–90) was King's best friend since the days of the Montgomery bus boycott and a constant presence by King's side.

tant that they were given and that people listened. You were there as a witness, Richard."

"Ah witnessed. Ah believes. Yos-suh."

"You're a very sick man."

"I know, I *know* I am. That's why I wanted to leave. Even your pasty psychiatrist left. He looked like a dunked doughnut."

"He left because of the girls."

"I loved Carol. She respected me, despite the color of my skin."

"You didn't have to go."

"Yes I did. You somehow turned it into a point of honor. It was a sexual vindication."

"How you go on."

"'Onteel de East German goes on back t'East Germany, onteel de Luxembourgian hies hisself back to Luxembourg—'"

"Please stop it."

But he found he could not stop, and even after they reached home and she put him to bed, the children watching in alarm, his voice continued its slurred plaint. "Ah'ze all raht, missy, jes' a tech o' double pneu-*mon*ia, don't you fret none, we'll get the cotton in."

"You're embarrassing the children."

"Shecks, doan min' me, chilluns. Ef Ah could jes' res' hyah foh a spell in de shade o' de watuhmelon patch, res' dese ol' bones . . . Lawzy, dat do feel good!"

"Daddy has a tiny cold," Joan explained.

"Will he die?" Bean asked, and burst into tears.

"Now, effen," he said, "bah some un*foh*-choonut chayunce, mah spir-rut should pass owen, bureh me bah de levee, so mebbe Ah kin heeah de singin' an' de banjos an' de cotton bolls a-bustin' . . . an' mebbe even de whaat folks up in de Big House kin shed a homely tear er two. . . ." He was almost crying; a weird tenderness had come over him in bed, as if he had indeed given birth, birth to this voice, a voice crying for attention from the depths of oppression. High in the window, the late-afternoon sky blanched as the storm lifted. In the warmth of the bed, Richard crooned to himself, and once cried out, "Missy! Missy! Doan you worreh none, ol' Tom'll see anotheh sun-up!"

But Joan was downstairs, talking firmly on the telephone.

Acts of Violence

Across the street from the Southern Poverty Law Center in Montgomery, Alabama, is an outdoor memorial to the civil rights movement. Designed by Maya Lin (the same woman who designed the Vietnam Veterans Memorial in Washington, D.C.), it is an oversized black granite rounded table engraved with fifty-three moments of the movement—from May 17, 1954 (*Brown v. Board of Education*) to April 4, 1968 (the assassination of Martin Luther King Jr.). Many of the moments are acts of violence—killings, beatings, abductions, dog attacks, bombings. Many of the killings are the work of the Ku Klux Klan; others are the work of those responsible for upholding the law, the police officers. Some are the work of anonymous "nightriders."

During the days of the civil rights movement, violence perpetrated against minorities, both random and intentional, was commonplace, and elected officials were often the ones who committed the deeds. Innocents not already intimidated by humiliating language were often beaten, castrated, raped, or killed—all to preserve the old "Southern Tradition" for those whites who feared change. Often the victims of the violence went to jail, while the people responsible for it remained free. Acts of violence were so frequent, particularly in Mississippi and Alabama, that for many people a state of terror existed. Injustice reigned.

One of the hundreds of incidents of such injustice occurred in Alabama when Jonathan Daniels, a former seminary student from Massachusetts who was doing civil rights work in the South, was gunned down by a law enforcement officer while crossing the street. Daniels had answered Martin Luther King Jr.'s call for people of faith to come to Selma to support the voting-rights marchers. After the excitement of the walk had ended, Daniels decided to stay in Alabama, working to integrate white churches and eventually participating in a demonstration in Fort Deposit against white stores that discriminated. One of a group arrested and taken to jail in Hayneville, Daniels, along with the group, was released from jail a week later without transportation back to Fort Deposit. As Daniels walked across the street with several demonstrators to purchase a soda, a man with a shotgun in the store threatened them. Instinctively, Daniels pushed a younger person out of the line of fire and took the shot himself in the stomach. He died instantly. The part-time deputy sheriff who killed him was charged with manslaughter, not murder; he testified that Daniels had pulled a knife on him. An all-white jury found him not guilty, taking less than two hours to decide the verdict.

Such violence and corresponding injustice also typifies the case of Bob Moses, Herbert Lee, and Louis Allen. Civil rights activist Bob Moses went to Mississippi in 1961 to work in voter registration. Amite County local Herbert Lee assisted Moses by driving him from house to house. Few blacks were interested in going to the courthouse to register, however, and once Moses did find a few to go with him, he was arrested and put in jail. When Moses returned a second time to the courthouse with would-be voter applicants, he was beaten. Still, Lee and Moses persevered. One morning when Lee was taking a truckload of cotton to the cotton gin, he was shot in the head by a Mississippi state representative. Another man, Louis Allen, saw what happened. He was told to testify in court, by one of the killer's accomplices, that Lee had a tire iron in his hand. Allen did that but later felt tremendous guilt in going along with the white man's lie. Allen made plans to leave the state, but the day before doing so, he was shot in the face when he got out of his car to open a gate. No one was arrested for his murder.

The Allen case mirrors some of the circumstances in "The Convert" (1963). In this story, a black man witnesses the beating and death of his minister, who enters a white-only waiting room to purchase a ticket for interstate travel. The white man who kills the minister tells the witness what he is supposed to have seen. This fictional protagonist chooses not to go along with the lie. His actions have their own set of consequences.

The next story in the section, "Where Is the Voice Coming From?" (1963), is a fictional account that closely parallels Byron De La Beckwith's June 1963 assassination of Mississippi's greatest civil rights activist, Medgar Evers. The story was published in the *New Yorker* on July 6, 1963, just a little over three weeks from the time of the event that inspired the story. The story is told from the point of view of a white racist killer.

The last four stories are related to or have their origin in voter registration. They depict a variety of disturbing occurrences that became part of the risk associated with stepping forward to change the demographics of the southern ballot. Although "Liars Don't Qualify" (1961) is free from physical violence, the degrading treatment and the verbal insults become an assault of their own kind on one black man's effort to register to vote.

In "Advancing Luna—and Ida B. Wells" (1977), a white girl is raped by a black man while on a voter-registration drive in the South. The story focuses on how rape is discussed between friends of different races, as the girl later tells her black female friend about the event. The friend must then process everything she already knows through the historical lens of what it means when a black man rapes a white woman in the 1960s South. The rape is processed and reprocessed; old stereotypes are given another chance to be dashed, and the complexity of human behavior is partially explored.

"Means and Ends" (1985) recounts the story of a local woman deeply immersed in canvassing for potential voters in 1960s Mississippi. With her actions well known to others, the woman soon finds her daughter the victim of a drive-by shooting.

In "Going to Meet the Man" (1965), one of the most disturbingly violent stories in American literature, a white officer of the law participates in the beating of a demonstrator, making him bleed from every orifice of his head. But the graphic nature of the story continues, moving toward the memory of a childhood picnic where a lynching is the chief entertainment. The excitement of that memory leads the white law officer to rape his own wife. Horrific death becomes an aphrodisiac for rough and brutal sex.

Death and loss loom large in the sometimes random, sometimes deliberate acts of violence that occurred during the years of the movement, but "death" and "loss"—the words themselves—don't begin to describe the horrific *ways* in which people came to those ends.

LERONE BENNETT JR.

The Convert

Lerone Bennett Jr. (1928–) is Mississippi born and bred. A journalist with a long and successful history with *Ebony* magazine stretching back to 1953, he is the author of a number of scholarly works on black history. "The Convert" (1963) appeared in John Henrik Clarke's *American Negro Short Stories* in 1966 and was reprinted in Clarke's *Black American Short Stories: One Hundred Years of the Best* in 1993.

A man don't know what he'll do, a man don't know what he is till he gets his back pressed up against a wall. Now you take Aaron Lott: there ain't no other way to explain the crazy thing he did. He was going along fine, preaching the gospel, saving souls, and getting along with the white folks; and then, all of a sudden, he felt wood pressing against his back. The funny thing was that nobody knew he was hurting till he preached that Red Sea sermon where he got mixed up and seemed to think Mississippi was Egypt. As chairman of the deacons board, I felt it was my duty to reason with him. I appreciated his position and told him so, but I didn't think it was right for him to push us all in a hole. The old fool—he just laughed.

"Brother Booker," he said, "the Lord—He'll take care of me."

I knew then that that man was heading for trouble. And the very next thing he did confirmed it. The white folks called the old fool downtown to bear witness that the colored folks were happy. And you know what he did: he got down there amongst all them big white folks and he said: "Things ain't gonna change here overnight, but they gonna change. It's inevitable. The Lord wants it."

Well sir, you could have bought them white folks for a penny. Aaron Lott, pastor of the Rock of Zion Baptist Church, a man white folks had said was wise and sound and sensible, had come close—too close—to saying that the Supreme Court was coming to Melina, Mississippi. The surprising thing was that the white folks didn't do nothing. There was a lot of mumbling and whispering but nothing bad happened till the terrible morning when Aaron came a-knocking at the door of my funeral home. Now things had been tightening up—you could feel it in the air—and I didn't want no part of no crazy scheme and I told him so right off. He walked on past me and sat down on the couch. He had on his preaching clothes, a shiny blue suit, a fresh starched white shirt, a black tie, and his Sunday black shoes. I remember thinking at the time that Aaron was too black to be wearing all them dark clothes. The thought tickled me and I started to smile but then I noticed something about him that didn't seem quite right. I ran my eyes over him closely. He was kinda middle-sized and he had a big clean-shaven head, a big nose, and thin lips. I stood there looking at him for a long time but I couldn't figure out what it was till I looked at his eyes: they were burning bright, like light bulbs do just before they go out. And yet he looked contented, like his mind was resting somewheres else.

"I wanna talk with you, Booker," he said, glancing sideways at my wife. "If you don't mind, Sister Brown——"

Sarah got up and went into the living quarters. Aaron didn't say nothing for a long time; he just sat there looking out the window. Then he spoke so soft I had to strain my ears to hear.

"I'm leaving for the Baptist convention," he said. He pulled out his gold watch and looked at it. "Train leaves in 'bout two hours."

"I know *that*, Aaron."

"Yeah, but what I wanted to tell you was that I ain't going Jim Crow. I'm going first class, Booker, right through the white waiting room. That's the law."[1]

A cold shiver ran through me.

"Aaron," I said, "don't you go talking crazy now."

The old fool laughed, a great big body-shaking laugh. He started talking 'bout God and Jesus and all that stuff. Now, I'm a God-fearing man myself, but I holds that God helps those who help themselves. I told him so.

---

1. Segregation in interstate travel was struck down by the Supreme Court case *Morgan v. Virginia* (1946), argued by a young Thurgood Marshall (1908–93). In the incident leading up to the case, Irene Morgan boarded a bus in Gloucester, Virginia, for Baltimore, Maryland. Although she had paid for her seat, the bus driver asked her to stand and give her seat to a white person, which she refused to do. This was the same case that the Freedom Riders were testing in 1961.

"You can't mix God up with these white folks," I said. "When you start to messing around with segregation, they'll burn you up and the Bible, too."

He looked at me like I was Satan.

"I sweated over this thing," he said. "I prayed. I got down on my knees and I asked God not to give me this cup. But He said I was the one. I heard Him, Booker, right here—he tapped his chest—in my heart."

The old fool's been having visions, I thought. I sat down and tried to figure out a way to hold him, but he got up, without saying a word, and started for the door.

"Wait!" I shouted. "I'll get my coat."

"I don't need you," he said. "I just came by to tell you so you could tell the board in case something happened."

"You wait," I shouted, and ran out of the room to get my coat.

We got in his beat-up old Ford and went by the parsonage to get his suitcase. Rachel—that was his wife—and Jonah were sitting in the living room, wringing their hands. Aaron got his bag, shook Jonah's hand, and said, "Take care of your Mamma, boy." Jonah nodded. Aaron hugged Rachel and pecked at her cheek. Rachel broke down. She throwed her arms around his neck and carried on something awful. Aaron shoved her away.

"Don't go making no fuss over it, woman. I ain't gonna be gone forever. Can't a man go to a church meeting 'thout women screaming and crying."

He tried to make light of it, but you could see he was touched by the way his lips trembled. He held his hand out to me, but I wouldn't take it. I told him off good, told him it was a sin and a shame for a man of God to be carrying on like he was, worrying his wife and everything.

"I'm coming with you," I said. "Somebody's gotta see that you don't make a fool of yourself."

He shrugged, picked up his suitcase, and started for the door. Then he stopped and turned around and looked at his wife and his boy and from the way he looked I knew that there was still a chance. He looked at the one and then at the other. For a moment there, I thought he was going to cry, but he turned, quick-like, and walked out of the door.

I ran after him and tried to talk some sense in his head. But he shook me off, turned the corner, and went on up Adams Street. I caught up with him and we walked in silence, crossing the street in front of the First Baptist Church for whites, going on around the Confederate monument where, once, they hung a boy for fooling around with white women.

"Put it off, Aaron," I begged. "Sleep on it."

He didn't say nothing.

"What you need is a vacation. I'll get the board to approve, full pay and everything."

He smiled and shifted the suitcase over to his left hand. Big drops of sweat were running down his face and spotting up his shirt. His eyes were awful, all lit up and burning.

"Aaron, Aaron, can't you hear me?"

We passed the feed store, Bill Williams' grocery store, and the movie house.

"A man's gotta think about his family, Aaron. A man ain't free. Didn't you say that once, didn't you?"

He shaded his eyes with his hand and looked into the sun. He put the suitcase on the ground and checked his watch.

"Why don't you think about Jonah?" I asked. "Answer that. Why don't you think about your own son?"

"I am," he said. "That's exactly what I'm doing, thinking about Jonah. Matter of fact, he started *me* to thinking. I ain't never mentioned it before, but the boy's been worrying me. One day we was downtown here and he asked me something that hurt. 'Daddy,' he said, 'how come you ain't a man?' I got mad, I did, and told him: 'I am a man.' He said that wasn't what he meant. 'I mean,' he said, 'how come you ain't a man where white folks concerned.' I couldn't answer him, Booker. I'll never forget it till the day I die. I couldn't answer my own son, and I been preaching forty years."

"He don't know nothing 'bout it," I said. "He's hot-headed, like my boy. He'll find out when he grows up."

"I hopes not," Aaron said, shaking his head. "I hopes not."

Some white folks passed and we shut up till they were out of hearing. Aaron, who was acting real strange, looked up in the sky and moved his lips. He came back to himself, after a little bit, and he said: "This thing of being a man, Booker, is a big thing. The Supreme Court can't make you a man. The NAACP can't do it. God Almighty can do a lot, but even He can't do it. Ain't nobody can do it but you."

He said that like he was preaching and when he got through he was all filled up with emotion and he seemed kind of ashamed—he was a man who didn't like emotion outside the church. He looked at his watch, picked up his bag, and said, "Well, let's git it over with."

We turned into Elm and the first thing I saw at the end of the Street was the train station. It was an old red building, flat like a slab. A group of white men were fooling around in front of the door. I couldn't make them out from that distance, but I could tell they weren't the kind of white folks to be fooling around with.

We walked on, passing the dry goods store, the barber shop, and the new building that was going up. Across the street from that was the sheriff's office. I looked in the window and saw Bull Sampson sitting at his desk, his feet propped up on a chair, a fat brown cigar sticking out of his mouth. A ball about the size of a sweet potato started burning in my stomach.

"Please, Aaron," I said. "Please. You can't get away with it. I know how you feel. Sometimes I feel the same way myself, but I wouldn't risk my neck to do nothing for these niggers. They won't appreciate it; they'll laugh at you."

We were almost to the station and I could make out the faces of the men sitting on the benches. One of them must have been telling a joke. He finished and the group broke out laughing.

I whispered to Aaron: "I'm through with it. I wash my hands of the whole mess."

I don't know whether he heard me or not. He turned to the right without saying a word and went on in the front door. The string-beany man who told the joke was so shocked that his cigarette fell out of his mouth.

"Y'all see that," he said. "Why, I'll——"

"Shut up," another man said. "Go git Bull."

I kept walking, fast, turned at the corner, and ran around to the colored waiting room. When I got in there, I looked through the ticket window and saw Aaron standing in front of the clerk. Aaron stood there for a minute or more, but the clerk didn't see him. And that took some not seeing. In that room, Aaron Lott stood out like a pig in a chicken coop.

There were, I'd say, about ten or fifteen people in there, but didn't none of them move. They just sat there, with their eyes glued on Aaron's back. Aaron cleared his throat. The clerk didn't look up; he got real busy with some papers. Aaron cleared his throat again and opened his mouth to speak. The screen door of the waiting room opened and clattered shut.

It got real quiet in that room, hospital quiet. It got so quiet I could hear my own heart beating. Now Aaron knew who opened that door, but he didn't bat an eyelid. He turned around real slow and faced High Sheriff Sampson, the baddest man in South Mississippi.

Mr. Sampson stood there with his legs wide open, like the men you see on television. His beefy face was blood-red and his gray eyes were rattlesnake hard. He was mad; no doubt about it. I had never seen him so mad.

"Preacher," he said, "you done gone crazy?" He was talking low-like and mean.

"Nosir," Aaron said. "Nosir, Mr. Sampson."

"What you think you doing?"

"Going to St. Louis, Mr. Sampson."

"You must done lost yo' mind, boy."

Mr. Sampson started walking towards Aaron with his hand on his gun. Twenty or thirty men pushed through the front door and fanned out over the room. Mr. Sampson stopped about two paces from Aaron and looked him up and down. That look had paralyzed hundreds of niggers; but it didn't faze Aaron none—he stood his ground,

"I'm gonna give you a chance, preacher. Git on over to the nigger side and git quick."

"I ain't bothering nobody, Mr. Sampson,"

Somebody in the crowd yelled: "Don't reason wit' the nigger, Bull. Hit 'em."

Mr. Sampson walked up to Aaron and grabbed him in the collar and throwed him up against the ticket counter. He pulled out his gun.

"Did you hear me, deacon. I said, 'Git.' "

"I'm going to St. Louis, Mr. Sampson. That's cross state lines. The court done said——"

Aaron didn't have a chance. The blow came from nowhere. Laying there on the floor with blood spurting from his mouth, Aaron looked up at Mr. Sampson and he did another crazy thing: he grinned. Bull Sampson jumped up in the air and came down on Aaron with all his two hundred pounds. It made a crunchy sound. He jumped again and the mob, maddened by the blood and heat, moved in to help him. They fell on Aaron like mad dogs. They beat him with chairs; they beat him with sticks; they beat him with guns.

Till this day, I don't know what come over me. The first thing I know I was running and then I was standing in the middle of the white waiting room. Mr. Sampson was the first to see me. He backed off, cocked his pistol, and said: "Booker, boy, you come one mo' step and I'll kill you. What's a matter with you niggers today? All y'all gone crazy?"

"Please don't kill him," I begged. "You ain't got no call to treat him like that."

"So you saw it all, did you? Well, then, Booker you musta saw the nigger preacher reach for my gun?"

"He didn't do that, Mr. Sampson," I said. "He didn't——"

Mr. Sampson put a big hairy hand on my tie and pulled me to him.

"Booker," he said sweetly. "You saw the nigger preacher reach for my gun, didn't you?"

I didn't open my mouth—I couldn't I was so scared—but I guess my eyes answered for me. Whatever Mr. Sampson saw there musta convinced him 'cause he threw me on the floor besides Aaron.

"Git this nigger out of here," he said, "and be quick about it."

Dropping to my knees, I put my hand on Aaron's chest; I didn't feel nothing. I felt his wrist; I didn't feel nothing. I got up and looked at them white folks with tears in my eyes. I looked at the women, sitting crying on the benches. I looked at the men. I looked at Mr. Sampson. I said, "He was a good man."

Mr. Sampson said, "Move the nigger."

A big sigh came out of me and I wrung my hands.

Mr. Sampson said, "Move the nigger."

He grabbed my tie and twisted it, but I didn't feel nothing. My eyes were glued to his hands; there was blood under the fingernails, and the fingers—they looked like fat little red sausages. I screamed and Mr. Sampson flung me down on the floor.

He said, *"Move the nigger."*

I picked Aaron up and fixed his body over my shoulder and carried him outside. I sent for one of my boys and we dressed him up and put him away real nice-like and Rachel and the boy came and they cried and carried on and yet, somehow, they seemed prouder of Aaron than ever before. And the colored folks—they seemed proud, too. Crazy niggers. Didn't they know? Couldn't they see? It hadn't done no good. In fact, things got worse. The Northern newspapers started kicking up a stink and Mr. Rivers, the solicitor, announced they were going to hold a hearing. All of a sudden, Booker Taliaferro Brown became the biggest man in that town. My phone rang day and night: I got threats, I got promises, and I was offered bribes. Everywhere I turned somebody was waiting to ask me: "Whatcha gonna do? Whatcha gonna say?" To tell the truth, I didn't know myself. One day I would decide one thing and the next day I would decide another.

It was Mr. Rivers and Mr. Sampson who called my attention to that. They came to my office one day and called me a shifty, no-good nigger. They said they expected me to stand by "my statement" in the train station that I saw Aaron reach for the gun. I hadn't said no such thing, but Mr. Sampson said I said it and he said he had witnesses who heard me say it. "And if you say anything else," he said, "I can't be responsible for your health. Now you know"—he put that bloody hand on my shoulder and he smiled his sweet death smile—"you *know* I wouldn't threaten you, but the boys"—he shook his head—"the boys are real worked up over this one."

It was long about then that I began to hate Aaron Lott. I'm ashamed to admit it now, but it's true: I hated him. He had lived his life; he had made his choice. Why should he live my life, too, and make me choose? It wasn't fair; it wasn't right; it wasn't Christian. What made me so mad was the fact that nothing I said would help Aaron. He was dead and it wouldn't help one whit for me to say that he didn't reach for that gun. I tried to explain that to Rachel when she came to my office, moaning and crying, the night before the hearing.

"Listen to me, woman," I said. "Listen. Aaron was a good man. He lived a good life. He did a lot of good things, but he's *dead, dead, dead*! Nothing I say will bring him back. Bull Sampson's got ten niggers who are going to swear on a stack of Bibles that they saw Aaron reach for that gun. It won't do me or you or Aaron no good for me to swear otherwise."

What did I say that for? That woman liked to had a fit. She got down on her knees and she begged me to go with Aaron.

"Go wit' him," she cried. "Booker. *Booker!* If you's a man, if you's a father, if you's a friend, go wit' Aaron."

That woman tore my heart up. I ain't never heard nobody beg like that.

"Tell the truth, Booker," she said. "That's all I'm asking. Tell the truth."

"Truth!" I said. "Hah! That's all you niggers talk about: truth. What do you know about truth? Truth is eating good and sleeping good. Truth is living, Rachel. Be loyal to the living."

Rachel backed off from me. You would have thought that I had cursed her or something. She didn't say nothing; she just stood there pressed against the door. She stood there saying nothing for so long that my nerves snapped.

"Say something," I shouted. "Say something—anything!"

She shook her head, slowly at first, and then her head started moving like it wasn't attached to her body. It went back and forth, back and forth, back and forth. I started towards her, but she jerked open the door and ran out into the night, screaming.

That did it. I ran across the room to the filing cabinet, opened the bottom drawer, and took out a dusty bottle of Scotch. I started drinking, but the more I drank the soberer I got. I guess I fell asleep 'cause I dreamed I buried Rachel and that everything went along fine until she jumped out of the casket and started screaming. I came awake with a start and knocked over the bottle. I reached for a rag and my hand stopped in midair.

"Of course," I said out loud and slammed my fist down on the Scotch-soaked papers.

I didn't see nothing.

Why didn't I think of it before?

I didn't see nothing.

Jumping up, I walked to and fro in the office. Would it work? I rehearsed it in my mind. All I could see was Aaron's back. I don't know whether he reached for the gun or not. All I know is that *for some reason* the men beat him to death.

Rehearsing the thing in my mind, I felt a great weight slip off my shoulders. I did a little jig in the middle of the floor and went upstairs to my bed, whistling. Sarah turned over and looked me up and down.

"What you happy about?"

"Can't a man be happy?" I asked.

She sniffed the air, said, "Oh," turned over, and mumbled something in her pillow. It came to me then for the first time that she was 'bout the only person in town who hadn't asked me what I was going to do. I thought about it for a little while, shrugged, and fell into bed with all my clothes on.

When I woke up the next morning, I had a terrible headache and my tongue was a piece of sandpaper. For a long while, I couldn't figure out what I was doing laying there with all my clothes on. Then it came to me: this was the big day. I put on my black silk suit, the one I wore for big funerals, and went downstairs to breakfast. I walked into the dining room without looking and bumped into Russell, the last person in the world I wanted to see. He was my only child, but he didn't act like it. He was always finding fault. He didn't like the way I talked to Negroes; he didn't like the way I talked to white folks. He didn't like this; he didn't like that. And to top it off, the young whippersnapper wanted to be an artist. Undertaking wasn't good enough for him. He wanted to paint pictures.

I sat down and grunted.

"Good morning, Papa." He said it like he meant it. He wants something, I thought, looking him over closely, noticing that his right eye was swollen.

"You been fighting again, boy?"

"Yes, Papa."

"You younguns. Education—that's what it is. Education! It's ruining you."

He didn't say nothing. He just sat there, looking down when I looked up and looking up when I looked down. This went on through the grits and the eggs and the second cup of coffee.

"Whatcha looking at?" I asked.

"Nothing, Papa."

"Whatcha thinking?"

"Nothing, Papa."

"You lying, boy. It's written all over your face."

He didn't say nothing.

I dismissed him with a wave of my hand, picked up the paper, and turned to the sports page.

"What are you going to do, Papa?"

The question caught me unawares. I know now that I was expecting it, that I wanted him to ask it; but he put it so bluntly that I was flabbergasted. I pretended I didn't understand.

"Do 'bout what, boy? Speak up!"

"About the trial, Papa."

I didn't say nothing for a long time. There wasn't much, in fact, I could say; so I got mad.

"Questions, questions, questions," I shouted. "That's all I get in this house—questions. You never have a civil word for your pa. I go out of here and work my tail off and you keep yourself shut up in that room of yours looking at them fool books and now soon as your old man gets his back against the wall you join the pack. I expected better than that of you, boy. A son ought to back his pa."

That hurt him. He picked up the coffee pot and poured himself another cup of coffee and his hand trembled. He took a sip and watched me over the rim.

"They say you are going to chicken out, Papa."

"Chicken out? What that mean?"

"They're betting you'll 'Tom.'"

I leaned back in the chair and took a sip of coffee.

"So they're betting, huh?" The idea appealed to me. "Crazy niggers—they'd bet on a funeral."

I saw pain on his face. He sighed and said: "I bet, too, Papa."

The cup fell out of my hand and broke, spilling black water over the tablecloth.

"You did what?"

"I bet you wouldn't 'Tom.'"

"You little fool." I fell out laughing and then I stopped suddenly and looked at him closely. "How much you bet?"

"One hundred dollars."

I stood up.

"You're lying," I said. "Where'd you get that kind of money?"

"From Mamma."

"Sarah!" I shouted. "Sarah! You get in here. What kind of house you running, sneaking behind my back, giving this boy money to gamble with?"

Sarah leaned against the door jamb. She was in her hot iron mood. There was no expression on her face. And her eyes were hard.

"I gave it to him, Booker," she said. "They called you an Uncle Tom. He got in a fight about it. He wanted to bet on you, Booker. *He* believes in you."

Suddenly I felt old and used up. I pulled a chair to me and sat down.

"Please," I said, waving my hand. "Please. Go away. Leave me alone. Please."

I sat there for maybe ten or fifteen minutes, thinking, praying. The phone rang. It was Mr. Withers, the president of the bank. I had put in for a loan and it had been turned down, but Mr. Withers said there'd been a mistake. "New fellow, you know," he said, clucking his tongue. He said he knew that it was my lifelong dream to build a modern funeral home and to buy a Cadillac hearse. He said he sympathized with that dream, supported it, thought the town needed it, and thought I deserved it. "The loan will go through," he said. "Drop by and see me this morning after the hearing."

When I put that phone down, it was wet with sweat. I couldn't turn that new funeral home down and Mr. Withers knew it. My father had raised me on that dream and before he died he made me swear on a Bible that I would make it good. And here it was on a platter, just for a word, a word that wouldn't hurt nobody.

I put on my hat and hurried to the courthouse. When they called my name, I walked in with my head held high. The courtroom was packed. The white folks had all the seats and the colored folks were standing in the rear. Whoever arranged the seating had set aside the first two rows for white men. They were sitting almost on top of each other, looking mean and uncomfortable in their best white shirts.

I walked up to the bench and swore on the Bible and took a seat. Mr. Rivers gave me a little smile and waited for me to get myself set.

"State your name," he said.

"Booker Taliaferro Brown." I took a quick look at the first two rows and recognized at least ten of the men who killed Aaron.

"And your age?"

"Fifty-seven."

"You're an undertaker?"

"Yessir."

"You been living in this town all your life?"

"Yessir."

"You like it here, don't you, Booker?"

Was this a threat? I looked Mr. Rivers in the face for the first time. He smiled.

I told the truth. I said, "Yessir."

"Now, calling your attention to the day of May 17th,[2] did anything unusual happen on that day?"

The question threw me. I shook my head. Then it dawned on me. He was talking about——

"Yessir," I said. "That's the day Aaron got—— 'Something in Mr. Rivers' face warned me and I pulled up—"that's the day of the trouble at the train station."

Mr. Rivers smiled. He looked like a trainer who'd just put a monkey through a new trick. You could feel the confidence and the contempt oozing out of him. I looked at his prissy little mustache and his smiling lips and I got mad. Lifting my head a little bit, I looked him full in the eyes; I held the eyes for a moment and I tried to tell the man behind the eyes that I was a man like him and that he didn't have no right to be using me and laughing about it. But he didn't get the message. The bastard—he chuckled softly, turned his back to me, and faced the audience.

"I believe you were with the preacher that day."

The water was getting deep. I scroonched down in my seat, closed the lids of my eyes, and looked dense.

"Yessir, Mr. Rivers," I drawled. "Ah was, Ah was."

"Now, Booker—" he turned around—"I believe you tried to keep the nigger preacher from getting out of line."

2. The date Aaron Lott died also happens to be the anniversary of the unanimous *Brown v. Board of Education* decision of the Supreme Court.

I hesitated. It wasn't a fair question. Finally, I said: "Yessir."

"You begged him not to go in the white side?"

"Yessir."

"And when that failed, you went over to *your* side—the *colored* side—and looked through the window?"

"Yessir."

He put his hand in his coat pocket and studied my face.

"You saw *everything*, didn't you?"

"Just about." A muscle on the inside of my thigh started tingling.

Mr. Rivers shuffled some papers he had in his hand. He seemed to be thinking real hard. I pushed myself against the back of the chair. Mr. Rivers moved close, quick, and stabbed his finger into my chest.

"Booker, did you see the nigger preacher reach for Mr. Sampson's gun?"

He backed away, smiling. I looked away from him and I felt my heart trying to tear out of my skin. I looked out over the courtroom. It was still; wasn't even a fly moving. I looked at the white folks in front and the colored folks in back and I turned the question over in my mind. While I was doing that, waiting, taking my time, I noticed, out of the corner of my eye, that the smile on Mr. Rivers' face was dying away. Suddenly, I had a terrible itch to know what that smile would turn into.

I said, "Nosir."

Mr. Rivers stumbled backwards like he had been shot. Old Judge Sloan took off his glasses and pushed his head out over the bench. The whole courtroom seemed to be leaning in to me and I saw Aaron's widow leaning back with her eyes closed and it seemed to me at that distance that her lips were moving in prayer.

Mr. Rivers was the first to recover. He put his smile back on and he acted like my answer was in the script.

"You mean," he said, "that you didn't see it. It happened so quickly that you missed it?"

I looked at the bait and I ain't gonna lie: I was tempted. He knew as well as I did what I meant, but he was gambling on my weakness. I had thrown away my funeral home, my hearse, everything I owned, and he was standing there like a magician, pulling them out of a hat, one at a time, dangling them, saying: "Looka here, looka here, don't they look pretty?" I was on top of a house and he was betting that if he gave me a ladder I would come down. He was wrong, but you can't fault him for trying. He hadn't never met no nigger who would go all the way. I looked him in the eye and went the last mile.

"Aaron didn't reach for that gun," I said. "Them people, they just fell on——"

"Hold it," he shouted. "I want to remind you that there are laws in this state against perjury. You can go to jail for five years for what you just said. Now I know you've been conferring with those NAACP fellows, but I want to remind you of the statements you made to Sheriff Sampson and me. Judge—" he dismissed me with a wave of his hand—"Judge, this *man*—" he caught himself and it was my turn to smile—"this *boy* is lying. Ten niggers have testified that they saw the preacher reach for the gun. Twenty white people saw it. You've heard their testimony. I want to withdraw this witness and I want to reserve the right to file perjury charges against him."

Judge Sloan nodded. He pushed his bottom lip over his top one.

"You can step down," he said. "I want to warn you that perjury is a very grave offense. You——"

"Judge, I didn't——"

"Nigger!" He banged his gavel. "Don't you interrupt me. Now git out of here."

Two guards pushed me outside and waved away the reporters. Billy Giles, Mr. Sampson's assistant, came out and told me Mr. Sampson wanted me out of town before sundown. "And he says you'd better get out before the Northern reporters leave. He won't be responsible for your safety after that."

I nodded and went on down the stairs and started out the door.

"Booker!"

Rachel and a whole line of Negroes were running down the stairs. I stepped outside and waited for them. Rachel ran up and throwed her arms around me. "It don't take but one, Booker," she said. "It don't take but one." Somebody else said: "They whitewashed it, they whitewashed it, but you spoiled it for 'em."

Russell came out then and stood over to the side while the others crowded around to shake my hands. Then the others sensed that he was waiting and they made a little aisle. He walked up to me kind of slow-like and he said, "Thank you, sir." That was the first time in his whole seventeen years that that boy had said "sir" to me. I cleared my throat and when I opened my eyes Sarah was standing beside me. She didn't say nothing; she just put her hand in mine and stood there. It was long about then, I guess, when I realized that I wasn't seeing so good. They say I cried, but I don't believe a word of it. It was such a hot day and the sun was shining so bright that the sweat rolling down my face blinded me. I wiped the sweat out of my eyes and some more people came up and said a lot of foolish things about me showing the white folks and following in Aaron's footsteps. I wasn't doing no such fool thing. Ol' Man Rivers just put the thing to me in a way it hadn't been put before—man to man. It was simple, really. Any man would have done it.

EUDORA WELTY

Where Is the Voice Coming From?

A lifelong resident of Jackson, Mississippi, Eudora Welty (1909–2001) was
the author of four collections of short stories, five novels, two collections of
photographs, three books of nonfiction, and a children's book. She was also
the recipient of a Pulitzer Prize for fiction and the French Légion d'Honneur.
"Where Is the Voice Coming From?" first appeared in the *New Yorker*, on July 6,
1963, a few weeks after the Medgar Evers assassination, the event that inspired
the story.

I says to my wife, "You can reach and turn it off. You don't have to set and
look at a black nigger face no longer than you want to, or listen to what
you don't want to hear. It's still a free country."

I reckon that's how I give myself the idea.

I says, I could find right exactly where in Thermopylae that nigger's
living that's asking for equal time. And without a bit of trouble to me.

And I ain't saying it might not be because that's pretty close to where
I live. The other hand, there could be reasons you might have yourself for
knowing how to get there in the dark. It's where you all go for the thing
you want when you want it the most. Ain't that right?

The Branch Bank sign tells you in lights, all night long even, what
time it is and how hot. When it was quarter to four, and 92, that was me
going by in my brother-in-law's truck. He don't deliver nothing at that
hour of the morning.

So you leave Four Corners and head west on Nathan B. Forrest
Road,[1] past the Surplus & Salvage, not much beyond the Kum Back
Drive-In and Trailer Camp, not as far as where the signs starts saying
"Live Bait," "Used Parts," "Fireworks," "Peaches," and "Sister Peebles

---

1. Nathan B. Forrest (1821–77) was a general for the Confederacy. After the Civil War ended, he was one of
the founders of the Ku Klux Klan in Pulaski, Tennessee, serving as grand wizard.

Reader and Adviser." Turn before you hit the city limits and duck back towards the I.C. tracks. And his street's been paved.

And there was his light on, waiting for me. In his garage, if you please. His car's gone. He's out planning still some other ways to do what we tell 'em they can't. I *thought* I'd beat him home. All I had to do was pick my tree and walk in close behind it.

I didn't come expecting not to wait. But it was so hot, all I did was hope and pray one or the other of us wouldn't melt before it was over.

Now, it wasn't no bargain I'd struck.

I've heard what you've heard about Goat Dykeman, in Mississippi. Sure, everybody knows about Goat Dykeman. Goat he got word to the Governor's Mansion he'd go up yonder and shoot that nigger Meredith[2] clean out of school, if he's let out of the pen to do it. Old Ross[3] turned *that* over in his mind before saying him nay, it stands to reason.

I ain't no Goat Dykeman, I ain't in no pen, and I ain't ask no Governor Barnett to give me one thing. Unless he wants to give me a pat on the back for the trouble I took this morning. But he don't have to if he don't want to. I done what I done for my own pure-D satisfaction.

As soon as I heard wheels, I knowed who was coming. That was him and bound to be him. It was the right nigger heading in a new white car up his driveway towards his garage with the light shining, but stopping before he got there, maybe not to wake 'em. That was him. I knowed it when he cut off the car lights and put his foot out and I knowed him standing dark against the light. I knowed him then like I know me now. I knowed him even by his still, listening back.

Never seen him before, never seen him since, never seen anything of his black face but his picture, never seen his face alive, any time at all, or anywheres, and didn't want to, need to, never hope to see that face and never will. As long as there was no question in my mind.

He had to be the one. He stood right still and waited against the light, his back was fixed, fixed on me like a preacher's eyeballs when he's yelling "Are you saved?" He's the one.

2. James Meredith (1933–) was the first black student at the University of Mississippi. He risked his life to enroll in the fall of 1962. A riot ensued, which left two people dead.
3. Old Ross is a reference to Governor Ross Barnett (1898–1987), who served Mississippi from 1960 to 1964. He was an outspoken segregationist and had huge support from White Citizens' Councils, organizations formed across the South to resist the mandate of *Brown v. Board of Education*.

I'd already brought up my rifle, I'd already taken my sights. And I'd already got him, because it was too late then for him or me to turn by one hair.

Something darker than him, like the wings of a bird, spread on his back and pulled him down. He climbed up once, like a man under bad claws, and like just blood could weigh a ton he walked with it on his back to better light. Didn't get no further than his door. And fell to stay.[4]

He was down. He was down, and a ton load of bricks on his back wouldn't have laid any heavier. There on his paved driveway, yes sir.

And it wasn't till the minute before, that the mockingbird had quit singing. He'd been singing up my sassafras tree. Either he was up early, or he hadn't never gone to bed, he was like me. And the mocker he'd stayed right with me, filling the air till come the crack, till I turned loose of my load. I was like him. I was on top of the world myself. For once.

I stepped to the edge of his light there, where he's laying flat. I says, "Roland? There was one way left, for me to be ahead of you and stay ahead of you, by Dad, and I just taken it. Now I'm alive and you ain't. We ain't never now, never going to be equals and you know why? One of us is dead. What about that, Roland?" I said. "Well, you seen to it, didn't you?"

I stood a minute—just to see would somebody inside come out long enough to pick him up. And there she comes, the woman.[5] I doubt she'd been to sleep. Because it seemed to me she'd been in there keeping awake all along.

It was mighty green where I skint over the yard getting back. That nigger wife of his, she wanted nice grass! I bet my wife would hate to pay her water bill. And for burning her electricity. And there's my brother-in-law's truck, still waiting with the door open. "No Riders"—that didn't mean me.

There wasn't a thing I been able to think of since would have made it to go any nicer. Except a chair to my back while I was putting in my waiting. But going home, I seen what little time it takes after all to get a thing done like you really want it. It was 4:34, and while I was looking

4. The fictional Roland Summers's death parallels that of Medgar Evers, even to the time, just after midnight on June 12, 1963. Medgar Evers (1925–63), a field secretary for the NAACP, was the leading civil rights activist in Mississippi.

5. Myrlie Evers (1933–), wife of Medgar, came to the door that night with her children when she heard the gunshot that felled her husband.

it moved to 35. And the temperature stuck where it was. All that night I guarantee you it had stood without dropping, a good 92.

My wife says, "What? Didn't the skeeters bite you?" She said, "Well, they been asking that—why somebody didn't trouble to load a rifle and get some of these agitators out of Thermopylae. Didn't the fella keep drumming it in, what a good idea? The one that writes a column ever' day?"

I says to my wife, "Find *some* way I don't get the credit."

"He says do it for Thermopylae," she says. "Don't you ever skim the paper?"

I says, "Thermopylae never done nothing for me. And I don't owe nothing to Thermopylae. Didn't do it for you. Hell, any more'n I'd do something or other for them Kennedys! I done it for my own pure-D satisfaction."

"It's going to get him right back on TV," says my wife. "You watch for the funeral."

I says, "You didn't even leave a light burning when you went to bed. So how was I supposed to even get me home or pull Buddy's truck up safe in our front yard?"

"Well, hear another good joke on you," my wife says next. "Didn't you hear the news? The N. double A. C. P. is fixing to send somebody to Thermopylae. Why couldn't you waited? You might could have got you somebody better. Listen and hear 'em say so."

I ain't but one. I reckon you have to tell *somebody*.

"Where's the gun, then?" my wife says. "What did you do with our protection?"

I says, "It was scorching! It was scorching!" I told her, "It's laying out on the ground in rank weeds, trying to cool off, that's what it's doing now."

"You dropped it," she says. "Back there."

And I told her, "Because I'm so tired of ever'thing in the world being just that hot to the touch! The keys to the truck, the doorknob, the bed-sheet, ever'thing, it's all like a stove lid. There just ain't much going that's worth holding onto it no more," I says, "when it's a hundred and two in the shade by day and by night not too much difference. I wish *you'd* laid *your* finger to that gun."

"Trust you to come off and leave it," my wife says.

"Is that how no-'count I am?" she makes me ask. "*You* want to go back and get it?"

"You're the one they'll catch. I say it's so hot that even if you get to sleep you wake up feeling like you cried all night!" says my wife. "Cheer up, here's one more joke before time to get up. Heard what *Caroline*[6] said? Caroline said, 'Daddy, I just can't wait to grow up big, so I can marry *James Meredith.*' I heard that where I work. One rich-bitch to another one, to make her cackle."

"At least I kept some dern teen-ager from North Thermopylae getting there and doing it first," I says. "Driving his own car."

On TV and in the paper, they don't know but half of it. They know who Roland Summers was without knowing who I am. His face was in front of the public before I got rid of him, and after I got rid of him there it is again—the same picture. And none of me. I ain't ever had one made. Not ever! The best that newspaper could do for me was offer a five-hundred-dollar reward for finding out who I am. For as long as they don't know who that is, whoever shot Roland is worth a good deal more right now than Roland is.

But by the time I was moving around uptown, it was hotter still. That pavement in the middle of Main Street was so hot to my feet I might've been walking the barrel of my gun. If the whole world could've just felt Main Street this morning through the soles of my shoes, maybe it would've helped some.

Then the first thing I heard 'em say was the N. double A. C. P. done it themselves, killed Roland Summers, and proved it by saying the shooting was done by a expert (I hope to tell you it was!) and at just the right hour and minute to get the whites in trouble.

You can't win.

"They'll never find him," the old man trying to sell roasted peanuts tells me to my face.

And it's so hot.

6. *Caroline* is a reference to the daughter of President John F. Kennedy. She would have been almost six years old at the time.

It looks like the town's on fire already, whichever ways you turn, ever' street you strike, because there's those trees hanging them pones of bloom like split watermelon. And a thousand cops crowding ever'where you go, half of 'em too young to start shaving, but all streaming sweat alike. I'm getting tired of 'em.

I was already tired of seeing a hundred cops getting us white people nowheres. Back at the beginning, I stood on the corner and I watched them new babyface cops loading nothing but nigger children into the paddy wagon and they come marching out of a little parade and into the paddy wagon singing. And they got in and sat down without providing a speck of trouble, and their hands held little new American flags, and all the cops could do was knock them flagsticks a-loose from their hands, and not let 'em pick 'em up, that was all, and give 'em a free ride. And children can just get 'em more flags.

Everybody: It don't get you nowhere to take nothing from nobody unless you make sure it's for keeps, for good and all, for ever and amen.

I won't be sorry to see them brickbats hail down on us for a change. Pop bottles too, they can come flying whenever they want to. Hundreds, all to smash, like Birmingham. I'm waiting on 'em to bring out them switchblade knives, like Harlem and Chicago. Watch TV long enough and you'll see it all to happen on Deacon Street in Thermopylae. What's holding it back, that's all?—Because it's *in* 'em.

I'm ready myself for that funeral.

Oh, they may find me. May catch me one day in spite of 'emselves. (But I grew up in the country.) May try to railroad me into the electric chair, and what that amounts to is something hotter than yesterday and today put together.

But I advise 'em to go careful. Ain't it about time us taxpayers starts to calling the moves? Starts to telling the teachers *and* the preachers *and* the judges of our so-called courts how far they can go?

Even the President so far, he can't walk in my house without being invited, like he's my daddy, just to say whoa. Not yet!

Once, I run away from my home. And there was a ad for me, come to be printed in our county weekly. My mother paid for it. It was from her. It says: "SON: You are not being hunted for anything but to find you." That time, I come on back home.

But people are dead now.

And it's so hot. Without it even being August yet.

Anyways, I seen him fall. I was evermore the one.

So I reach me down my old guitar off the nail in the wall. 'Cause I've got my guitar, what I've held onto from way back when, and I never dropped that, never lost or forgot it, never hocked it but to get it again, never give it away, and I set in my chair, with nobody home but me, and I start to play, and sing a-Down. And sing a-down, down, down, down. Sing a-down, down, down, down. Down.

JUNIUS EDWARDS

Liars Don't Qualify

Born in Louisiana, Junius Edwards (1929–) was educated at the University of
Oslo in Norway. "Liars Don't Qualify" first appeared in *Urbanite* in June 1961
and won first prize in the *Writer's Digest* Short Story Contest. It was reprinted
in Woodie King's *Black Short Story Anthology* (1972). The story became part of
Edwards's 1963 novel, *If We Must Die* (reprinted in 1985 by Howard University
Press). The novel adds physical violence to the story—beating, attempted
castration, and ultimately the protagonist's death.

Will Harris sat on the bench in the waiting room for another hour. His
pride was not the only thing that hurt. He wanted them to call him in and
get him registered so he could get out of there. Twice, he started to go
into the inner office and tell them, but he thought better of it. He had
counted ninety-six cigarette butts on the floor when a fat man came out
of the office and spoke to him.

"What you want, boy?"

Will Harris got to his feet.

"I came to register."

"Oh, you did, did you?"

"Yes sir."

The fat man stared at Will for a second, then turned his back to him.
As he turned his back, he said, "Come on in here."

Will went in.

It was a little office and dirty, but not so dirty as the waiting room.
There were no cigarette butts on the floor here. Instead, there was paper.
They looked like candy wrappers to Will. There were two desks jammed
in there, and a bony little man sat at one of them, his head down, his
fingers fumbling with some papers. The fat man went around the empty
desk and pulled up a chair. The bony man did not look up.

Will stood in front of the empty desk and watched the fat man sit

down behind it. The fat man swung his chair around until he faced the
little man.

"Charlie," he said.

"Yeah, Sam," Charlie said, not looking up from his work.

"Charlie. This boy here says he come to register."

"You sure? You sure that's what he said, Sam?" Still not looking up.
"You sure? You better ask him again, Sam."

"All right, Charlie. All right. I'll ask him again," the fat man said. He
looked up at Will. "Boy. What you come here for?"

"I came to register."

The fat man stared up at him. He didn't say anything. He just stared,
his lips a thin line, his eyes wide open. His left hand searched behind him
and came up with a handkerchief. He raised his left arm and mopped his
face with the handkerchief, his eyes still on Will.

The odor from under his sweat-soaked arm made Will step back. Will
held his breath until the fat man finished mopping his face. The fat man
put his handkerchief away. He pulled a desk drawer open, and then he
took his eyes off Will. He reached in the desk drawer and took out a bar
of candy. He took the wrapper off the candy and threw the wrapper on
the floor at Will's feet. He looked at Will and ate the candy.

Will stood there and tried to keep his face straight. He kept telling
himself: I'll take anything. I'll take anything to get it done.

The fat man kept his eyes on Will and finished the candy. He took
out his handkerchief and wiped his mouth. He grinned, then he put his
handkerchief away.

"Charlie." The fat man turned to the little man.

"Yeah, Sam."

"He says he come to register."

"Sam, are you sure?"

"Pretty sure, Charlie."

"Well, explain to him what it's about." The bony man still had not
looked up.

"All right, Charlie," Sam said, and looked up at Will. "Boy, when folks
come here, they intend to vote, so they register first."

"That's what I want to do," Will said.

"What's that? Say that again."

"That's what I want to do. Register and vote."

The fat man turned his head to the bony man.

"Charlie."

"Yeah, Sam."

"He says . . . Charlie, this boy says that he wants to register and vote."

The bony man looked up from his desk for the first time. He looked at Sam, then both of them looked at Will.

Will looked from one of them to the other, one to the other. It was hot, and he wanted to sit down. *Anything. I'll take anything.*

The man called Charlie turned back to his work, and Sam swung his chair around until he faced Will.

"You got a job?" he asked.

"Yes, sir."

"Boy, you know what you're doing?"

"Yes, sir."

"All right," Sam said. "All right."

Just then, Will heard the door open behind him, and someone came in. It was a man.

"How you all? How about registering."

Sam smiled. Charlie looked up and smiled.

"Take care of you right away," Sam said, and then to Will. "Boy. Wait outside."

As Will went out, he heard Sam's voice: "Take a seat, please. Take a seat. Have you fixed up in a little bit. Now, what's your name?"

"Thanks," the man said, and Will heard the scrape of a chair.

Will closed the door and went back to his bench.

Anything. Anything. Anything. I'll take it all.

Pretty soon the man came out smiling. Sam came out behind him, and he called Will and told him to come in. Will went in and stood before the desk. Sam told him he wanted to see his papers: Discharge, High School Diploma, Birth Certificate, Social Security Card, and some other papers. Will had them all. He felt good when he handed them to Sam.

"You belong to any organization?"

"No, sir."

"Pretty sure about that?"

"Yes, sir."

"You ever heard of the 15th Amendment?"[1]

"Yes, sir."

"What does that one say?"

"It's the one that says all citizens can vote."

"You like that, don't you, boy? Don't you?"

"Yes, sir. I like them all."

Sam's eyes got big. He slammed his right fist down on his desk top. "I didn't ask you that. I asked you if you liked the 15th Amendment. Now, if you can't answer my questions . . ."

"I like it," Will put in, and watched Sam catch his breath.

Sam sat there looking up at Will. He opened and closed his desk-pounding fist. His mouth hung open.

"Charlie."

"Yeah, Sam." Not looking up.

"You hear that?" looking wide-eyed at Will. "You hear that?"

"I heard it, Sam."

Will had to work to keep his face straight.

"Boy," Sam said. "You born in this town?"

"You got my birth certificate right there in front of you. Yes, sir."

"You happy here?"

"Yes, sir."

"You got nothing against the way things go around here?"

"No, sir."

"Can you read?"

"Yes, sir."

"Are you smart?"

"No, sir."

"Where did you get that suit?"

"New York."

"New York?" Sam asked, and looked over at Charlie. Charlie's head was still down. Sam looked back to Will.

"Yes, sir," said Will.

"Boy, what you doing there?"

---

1. The amendment reads: "The right of citizens of the United States to vote shall not be denied or abridged by the United States or by any state on account of race, color, or previous condition of servitude." The amendment was added to the U.S. Constitution in 1870, after the Civil War.

"I got out of the Army there."

"You believe in what them folks do in New York?"

"I don't know what you mean."

"You know what I mean. Boy, you know good and well what I mean. You know how folks carry on in New York. You believe in that?"

"No, sir," Will said, slowly.

"You pretty sure about that?"

"Yes, sir."

"What year did they make the 15th Amendment?"

" . . . 18 . . . 70," said Will.

"Name a signer of the Declaration of Independence who became a President."

" . . . John Adams."[2]

"Boy, what did you say?" Sam's eyes were wide again.

Will thought for a second. Then he said, "John Adams."

Sam's eyes got wider. He looked to Charlie and spoke to a bowed head. "Now, too much is too much." Then he turned back to Will.

He didn't say anything to Will. He narrowed his eyes first, then spoke. "Did you say *just* John Adams?"

"*Mister* John Adams," Will said, realizing his mistake.

"That's more like it," Sam smiled. "Now, why do you want to vote?"

"I want to vote because it is my duty as an American citizen to vote?"

"Hah," Sam said, real loud. "Hah," again, and pushed back from his desk and turned to the bony man.

"Charlie."

"Yeah, Sam."

"Hear that?"

"I heard, Sam."

Sam leaned back in his chair, keeping his eyes on Charlie. He locked his hands across his round stomach and sat there.

"Charlie."

"Yeah, Sam."

"Think you and Elnora be coming over tonight?"

2. John Adams (1735–1826) was the second president of the United States. He signed the Declaration of Independence as a representative from the state of Massachusetts. The only other signer who went on to become president was Thomas Jefferson (1743–1826), representing the state of Virginia.

"Don't know, Sam," said the bony man, not looking up. "You know Elnora."

"Well, you welcome if you can."

"Don't know, Sam."

"You ought to, if you can. Drop in, if you can. Come on over and we'll split a corn whisky."

The bony man looked up.

"Now, that's different, Sam."

"Thought it would be."

"Can't turn down corn if it's good."

"You know my corn."

"Sure do. I'll drag Elnora. I'll drag her by the hair if I have to."

The bony man went back to work.

Sam turned his chair around to his desk. He opened a desk drawer and took out a package of cigarettes. He tore it open and put a cigarette in his mouth. He looked up at Will, then he lit the cigarette and took a long drag, and then he blew the smoke, very slowly, up toward Will's face.

The smoke floated up toward Will's face. It came up in front of his eyes and nose and hung there, then it danced and played around his face, and disappeared.

Will didn't move, but he was glad he hadn't been asked to sit down.

"You have a car?"

"No, sir."

"Don't you have a job?"

"Yes, sir."

"You like that job?"

"Yes, sir."

"You like it, but you don't want it."

"What do you mean?" Will asked.

"Don't get smart, boy," Sam said, wide-eyed. "I'm asking the questions here. You understand that?"

"Yes, sir."

"All right. All right. Be sure you do."

"I understand it."

"You a Communist?"

"No, sir."

"What party do you want to vote for?"

"I wouldn't go by parties. I'd read about the men and vote for a man, not a party."

"Hah," Sam said, and looked over at Charlie's bowed head. "Hah," he said again, and turned back to Will.

"Boy, you pretty sure you can read?"

"Yes, sir."

"All right. All right. We'll see about that." Sam took a book out of his desk and flipped some pages. He gave the book to Will.

"Read that loud," he said.

"Yes, sir," Will said, and began: "'When in the course of human events, it becomes necessary for one people to dissolve the political bands which have connected them with another, and to assume among the powers of the earth the separate and equal station to which the Laws of Nature and of Nature's God entitle them, a decent respect to the opinions of mankind requires that they should declare the causes which impel them to the separation.'"[3]

Will cleared his throat and read on. He tried to be distinct with each syllable. He didn't need the book. He could have recited the whole thing without the book.

"'We hold these truths to be self-evident, that all men are created equal, that they . . .'"

"Wait a minute, boy," Sam said. "Wait a minute. You believe that? You believe that about 'created equal'?"

"Yes, sir," Will said, knowing that was the wrong answer.

"You really believe that?"

"Yes, sir." Will couldn't make himself say the answer Sam wanted to hear.

Sam stuck out his right hand, and Will put the book in it. Then Sam turned to the other man.

"Charlie."

"Yeah, Sam."

"Charlie, did you hear that?"

"What was it, Sam?"

3. This is the first sentence of the Declaration of Independence, which was signed on July 2 and adopted on July 4, 1776.

"This boy, here, Charlie. He says he really believes it."

"Believes what, Sam? What you talking about?"

"This boy, here . . . believes that all men are equal, like it says in The Declaration."

"Now, Sam. Now you know that's not right. You know good and well that's not right. You heard him wrong. Ask him again, Sam. Ask him again, will you?"

"I didn't hear him wrong, Charlie," said Sam, and turned to Will. "Did I, boy? Did I hear you wrong?"

"No, sir."

"I didn't hear you wrong?"

"No, sir."

Sam turned to Charlie.

"Charlie."

"Yeah, Sam."

"Charlie. You think this boy trying to be smart?"

"Sam. I think he might be. Just might be. He looks like one of them that don't know his place."

Sam narrowed his eyes.

"Boy," he said. "You know your place?"

"I don't know what you mean."

"Boy, you know good and well what I mean."

"What do you mean?"

"Boy, who's . . ." Sam leaned forward, on his desk. "Just who's asking questions, here?"

"You are, sir."

"Charlie. You think he really is trying to be smart?"

"Sam, I think you better ask him."

"Boy."

"Yes, sir."

"Boy. You trying to be smart with me?"

"No, sir."

"Sam."

"Yeah, Charlie."

"Sam. Ask him if he thinks he's good as you and me."

"Now, Charlie. Now, you heard what he said about The Declaration."

"Ask, anyway, Sam."

"All right," Sam said. "Boy. You think you good as me and Mister Charlie?"

"No, sir," Will said.

They smiled, and Charlie turned away.

Will wanted to take off his jacket. It was hot, and he felt a drop of sweat roll down his right side. He pressed his right arm against his side to wipe out the sweat. He thought he had it, but it rolled again, and he felt another drop come behind that one. He pressed his arm in again. It was no use. He gave it up.

"How many stars did the first flag have?"

" . . . Thirteen."

"What's the name of the mayor of this town?"

" . . . Mister Roger Phillip Thornedyke Jones."

"Spell Thornedyke."

" . . . Capital T-h-o-r-n-e-d-y-k-e, Thornedyke."

"How long has he been mayor?"

" . . . Seventeen years."

"Who was the biggest hero in the War Between the States?"

" . . . General Robert E. Lee."[4]

"What does that 'E' stand for?"

" . . . Edward."

"Think you pretty smart, don't you?"

"No, sir."

"Well, boy, you have been giving these answers too slow. I want them fast. Understand? Fast."

"Yes, sir."

"What's your favorite song?"

"*Dixie*,"[5] Will said, and prayed Sam would not ask him to sing it.

"Do you like your job?"

---

4. Robert Edward Lee (1807–70) could not put his love for country above his love for his native state of Virginia, so he resigned his commission and hoped he would not be called on to lead what would become the Confederate Army, but he was. In 1865, he surrendered to General Ulysses S. Grant at the courthouse in Appomattox, Virginia. He is buried, with his horse Traveller, at Washington and Lee University in Lexington, Virginia.

5. Daniel Decatur Emmett (1815–1904) wrote the song "Dixie" in 1859. The first verse is as follows: "I wish I was in the Land of Cotton / Old times there are not forgotten / Look away! Look away! Look away! / Dixie Land / In Dixie Land where I was born / Early on one frosty morning / Look away! Look away! Look away!

"Yes, sir."

"What year did Arizona come into the States?"

"1912."

"There was another state in 1912."

"New Mexico, it came in January and Arizona in February."

"You think you smart, don't you?"

"No, sir."

"Don't you think you smart? Don't you?"

"No, sir."

"Oh, yes, you do, boy."

Will said nothing.

"Boy, you make good money on your job?"

"I make enough."

"Oh. Oh, you not satisfied with it?"

"Yes, sir. I am."

"You don't act like it, boy. You know that? You don't act like it."

"What do you mean?"

"You getting smart again, boy. Just who's asking questions here?"

"You are, sir."

"That's right. That's right."

The bony man made a noise with his lips and slammed his pencil down on his desk. He looked at Will, then at Sam.

"Sam," he said. "Sam, you having trouble with that boy? Don't you let that boy give you no trouble, now, Sam. Don't you do it."

"Charlie," Sam said. "Now, Charlie, you know better than that. You know better. This boy here knows better than that, too."

"You sure about that, Sam? You sure?"

"I better be sure if this boy here knows what's good for him."

"Does he know, Sam?"

"Do you know, boy?" Sam asked Will.

"Yes, sir."

Charlie turned back to his work.

"Boy," Sam said. "You sure you're not a member of any organization?"

"Yes, sir. I'm sure."

/ Dixie Land." The chorus then follows: "Then I wish I was in Dixie / Hooray! Hooray! / In Dixie Land / I'll take my stand / To live and die in Dixie / Away! Away! Away! / Down South in Dixie."

Sam gathered up all Will's papers, and he stacked them very neatly and placed them in the center of his desk. He took the cigarette out of his mouth and put it out in the full ash tray. He picked up Will's papers and gave them to him.

"You've been in the Army. That right?"

"Yes, sir."

"You served two years. That right?"

"Yes, sir."

"You have to do six years in the Reserve. That right?"

"Yes, sir."

"You're in the Reserve now. That right?"

"Yes, sir."

"You lied to me here, today. That right?"

"No, sir."

"Boy, I said you lied to me here today. That right?"

"No, sir."

"Oh, yes, you did, boy. Oh, yes, you did. You told me you wasn't in any organization. That right?"

"Yes, sir."

"Then you lied, boy. You lied to me because you're in the Army Reserve. That right?"

"Yes, sir. I'm in the Reserve, but I didn't think you meant that. I'm just in it, and don't have to go to meetings or anything like that. I thought you meant some kind of civilian organization."

"When you said you wasn't in an organization, that was a lie. Now, wasn't it, boy?"

He had Will there. When Sam had asked him about organizations, the first thing to pop in Will's mind had been the communists, or something like them.

"Now, wasn't it a lie?"

"No, sir."

Sam narrowed his eyes.

Will went on.

"No, sir, it wasn't a lie. There's nothing wrong with the Army Reserve. Everybody has to be in it. I'm not in it because I want to be in it."

"I know there's nothing wrong with it," Sam said. "Point is, you lied to me here, today."

"I didn't lie. I just didn't understand the question," Will said.

"You understood the question, boy. You understood good and well, and you lied to me. Now, wasn't it a lie?"

"No, sir."

"Boy. You going to stand right there in front of me big as anything and tell me it wasn't a lie?" Sam almost shouted. "Now, wasn't it a lie?"

"Yes, sir," Will said, and put his papers in his jacket pocket.

"You right, it was," Sam said.

Sam pushed back from his desk.

"That's it, boy. You can't register. You don't qualify. Liars don't qualify."

"But . . ."

"That's it." Sam spat the words out and looked at Will hard for a second, and then he swung his chair around until he faced Charlie.

"Charlie."

"Yeah, Sam."

"Charlie. You want to go out to eat first today?"

Will opened the door and went out. As he walked down the stairs, he took off his jacket and his tie and opened his collar and rolled up his shirt sleeves. He stood on the courthouse steps and took a deep breath and heard a noise come from his throat as he breathed out and looked at the flag in the court yard. The flag hung from its staff, still and quiet, the way he hated to see it; but it was there, waiting, and he hoped that a little push from the right breeze would lift it and send it flying and waving and whipping from its staff, proud, the way he liked to see it.

He took out a cigarette and lit it and took a slow deep drag. He blew the smoke out. He saw the cigarette burning in his right hand, turned it between his thumb and forefinger, made a face, and let the cigarette drop to the courthouse steps.

He threw his jacket over his left shoulder and walked on down to the bus stop, swinging his arms.

ALICE WALKER

Advancing Luna—and Ida B. Wells

Born in Georgia, Alice Walker (1944–) is a poet, short-story writer, novelist,
essayist, and activist. She began publishing during the latter part of the Black
Arts movement in the 1960s. She is the recipient of both the Pulitzer Prize
and the National Book Award. During the civil rights movement, she worked
in voter-registration drives in Liberty County, Georgia, and in Mississippi.
"Advancing Luna—and Ida B. Wells" is in her 1977 collection, *You Can't Keep a
Good Woman Down.*

I met Luna the summer of 1965 in Atlanta where we both attended a political conference and rally. It was designed to give us the courage, as temporary civil rights workers, to penetrate the small hamlets farther south.
I had taken a bus from Sarah Lawrence in New York and gone back to
Georgia, my home state, to try my hand at registering voters. It had become obvious from the high spirits and sense of almost divine purpose
exhibited by black people that a revolution was going on, and I did not
intend to miss it. Especially not this summery, student-studded version
of it. And I thought it would be fun to spend some time on my own in the
South.

Luna was sitting on the back of a pickup truck, waiting for someone
to take her from Faith Baptist, where the rally was held, to whatever gracious black Negro home awaited her. I remember because someone who
assumed I would also be traveling by pickup introduced us. I remember
her face when I said, "No, no more back of pickup trucks for me. I know
Atlanta well enough, I'll walk." She assumed of course (I guess) that I did
not wish to ride beside her because she was white, and I was not curious
enough about what she might have thought to explain it to her. And yet I
was struck by her passivity, her *patience* as she sat on the truck alone and
ignored, because someone had told her to wait there quietly until it was
time to go.

This look of passively waiting for something changed very little over the years I knew her. It was only four or five years in all that I did. It seems longer, perhaps because we met at such an optimistic time in our lives. John Kennedy and Malcolm X[1] had already been assassinated, but King had not been and Bobby Kennedy had not been.[2] Then too, the lethal, bizarre elimination by death of this militant or that, exiles, flights to Cuba, shoot-outs between former Movement friends sundered forever by lies planted by the FBI, the gunning down of Mrs. Martin Luther King, Sr., as she played the Lord's Prayer on the piano in her church (was her name Alberta?),[3] were still in the happily unfathomable future.

We believed we could change America because we were young and bright and held ourselves *responsible* for changing it. We did not believe we would fail. That is what lent fervor (revivalist fervor, in fact; we would *revive* America!) to our songs, and lent sweetness to our friendships (in the beginning almost all interracial), and gave a wonderful fillip to our sex (which, too, in the beginning, was almost always interracial).

What first struck me about Luna when we later lived together was that she did not own a bra. This was curious to me, I suppose, because she also did not need one. Her chest was practically flat, her breasts like those of a child. Her face was round, and she suffered from acne. She carried with her always a tube of that "skin-colored" (if one's skin is pink or eggshell) medication designed to dry up pimples. At the oddest times—waiting for a light to change, listening to voter registration instructions, talking about her father's new girlfriend, she would apply the stuff, holding in her other hand a small brass mirror the size of her thumb, which she also carried for just this purpose.

We were assigned to work together in a small, rigidly segregated South Georgia town that the city fathers, incongruously and years ago, had named Freehold. Luna was slightly asthmatic and when overheated or nervous she breathed through her mouth. She wore her shoulder-length black hair with bangs to her eyebrows and the rest brushed behind her

---

1. John Kennedy (1917–63) was assassinated November 22, 1963, in Dallas, Texas. Malcolm X (1925–65) was assassinated February 21, 1965, in Manhattan.

2. Martin Luther King Jr. (1929–68) would be assassinated April 4, 1968, in Memphis, Tennessee. Robert Kennedy (1925–1968) would be assassinated June 5, 1968, in Los Angeles.

3. Mrs. Martin Luther King Sr. (Alberta Christine; 1903–74) would be shot by a gunman while she played the Lord's Prayer on an organ during Sunday services on June 30, 1974.

ears. Her eyes were brown and rather small. She was attractive, but just barely and with effort. Had she been the slightest bit overweight, for instance, she would have gone completely unnoticed, and would have faded into the background where, even in a revolution, fat people seem destined to go. I have a photograph of her sitting on the steps of a house in South Georgia. She is wearing tiny pearl earrings, a dark sleeveless shirt with Peter Pan collar, Bermuda shorts, and a pair of those East Indian sandals that seem to adhere to nothing but a big toe.

The summer of '65 was as hot as any other in that part of the South. There was an abundance of flies and mosquitoes. Everyone complained about the heat and the flies and the hard work, but Luna complained less than the rest of us. She walked ten miles a day with me up and down those straight Georgia highways, stopping at every house that looked black (one could always tell in 1965) and asking whether anyone needed help with learning how to vote. The simple mechanics: writing one's name, or making one's "X" in the proper column. And then, though we were required to walk, everywhere, we were empowered to offer prospective registrants a car in which they might safely ride down to the county courthouse. And later to the polling places. Luna, almost overcome by the heat, breathing through her mouth like a dog, her hair plastered with sweat to her head, kept looking straight ahead, and walking as if the walking itself was her reward.

I don't know if we accomplished much that summer. In retrospect, it seems not only minor, but irrelevant. A bunch of us, black and white, lived together. The black people who took us in were unfailingly hospitable and kind. I took them for granted in a way that now amazes me. I realize that at each and every house we visited I *assumed* hospitality, I *assumed* kindness. Luna was often startled by my "boldness." If we walked up to a secluded farmhouse and half a dozen dogs ran up barking around our heels and a large black man with a shotgun could be seen whistling to himself under a tree, she would become nervous. I, on the other hand, felt free to yell at this stranger's dogs, slap a couple of them on the nose, and call over to him about his hunting.

That month with Luna of approaching new black people every day taught me something about myself I had always suspected: I thought black people superior people. Not simply superior to white people, because even without thinking about it much, I assumed almost everyone was superior to them; but to everyone. Only white people, after all, would blow up a Sunday-school class and grin for television over their "victory," *i.e.*, the death of four small black girls.[4] Any atrocity, at any time, was expected from them. On the other hand, it never occurred to me that black people *could* treat Luna and me with anything but warmth and concern. Even their curiosity about the sudden influx into their midst of rather ignorant white and black Northerners was restrained and courteous. I was treated as a relative, Luna as a much welcomed guest.

Luna and I were taken in by a middle-aged couple and their young school-age daughter. The mother worked outside the house in a local canning factory, the father worked in the paper plant in nearby Augusta. Never did they speak of the danger they were in of losing their jobs over keeping us, and never did their small daughter show any fear that her house might be attacked by racists because we were there. Again, I did not expect this family to complain, no matter what happened to them because of us. Having understood the danger, they had assumed the risk. I did not think them particularly brave, merely typical.

I think Luna liked the smallness—only four rooms—of the house. It was in this house that she ridiculed her mother's lack of taste. Her yellow-and-mauve house in Cleveland, the eleven rooms, the heated garage, the new car every year, her father's inability to remain faithful to her mother, their divorce, the fight over the property, even more bitter than over the children. Her mother kept the house and the children. Her father kept the car and his new girlfriend, whom he wanted Luna to meet and "approve." I could hardly imagine anyone disliking her mother so much. Everything Luna hated in her she summed up in three words: "*yellow and mauve.*"

I have a second photograph of Luna and a group of us being bullied by a Georgia state trooper. This member of Georgia's finest had followed us out into the deserted countryside to lecture us on how misplaced—in the South—was our energy, when "the Lord knew" the North (where he thought all of us lived, expressing disbelief that most of us were Georgians) was just as bad. (He had a point that I recognized even then, but

---

4. Denise McNair (1951–63), Carole Robertson (1949–63), Addie Mae Collins (1949–63), and Cynthia Wesley (1949–63) died in the bombing of the Sixteenth Street Baptist Church in Birmingham on September 15, 1963.

it did not seem the point where we were.) Luna is looking up at him, her mouth slightly open as always, a somewhat dazed look on her face. I cannot detect fear on any of our faces, though we were all afraid. After all, 1965 was only a year after 1964 when three civil rights workers had been taken deep into a Mississippi forest by local officials and sadistically tortured and murdered.[5] Luna almost always carried a flat black shoulder bag. She is standing with it against her side, her thumb in the strap.

At night we slept in the same bed. We talked about our schools, lovers, girlfriends we didn't understand or missed. She dreamed, she said, of going to Goa. I dreamed of going to Africa. My dream came true earlier than hers: an offer of a grant from an unsuspected source reached me one day as I was writing poems under a tree. I left Freehold, Georgia, in the middle of summer, without regrets, and flew from New York to London, to Cairo, to Kenya, and, finally, to Uganda, where I settled among black people with the same assumptions of welcome and kindness I had taken for granted in Georgia. I was taken on rides down the Nile as a matter of course, and accepted all invitations to dinner, where the best local dishes were superbly prepared in my honor. I became, in fact, a lost relative of the people, whose ancestors had foolishly strayed, long ago, to America.

I wrote to Luna at once.

But I did not see her again for almost a year. I had graduated from college, moved into a borrowed apartment in Brooklyn Heights, and was being evicted after a month. Luna, living then in a tenement on East 9th Street, invited me to share her two-bedroom apartment. If I had seen the apartment before the day I moved in I might never have agreed to do so. Her building was between Avenues B and C and did not have a front door. Junkies, winos, and others often wandered in during the night (and occasionally during the day) to sleep underneath the stairs or to relieve themselves at the back of the first-floor hall.

Luna's apartment was on the third floor. Everything in it was painted white. The contrast between her three rooms and kitchen (with its red bathtub) and the grungy stairway was stunning. Her furniture consisted

---

5. Michael Schwerner (1939–64), Andrew Goodman (1943–64), and James Chaney (1943–64) were killed soon after they were released from jail in Philadelphia, Mississippi, on the night of June 21, 1964. Their bodies were not found until August 4.

of two large brass beds inherited from a previous tenant and stripped of paint by Luna, and a long, high-backed church pew which she had managed somehow to bring up from the South. There was a simplicity about the small apartment that I liked. I also liked the notion of extreme contrast, and I do to this day. Outside our front window was the decaying neighborhood, as ugly and ill-lit as a battleground. (And allegedly as hostile, though somehow we were never threatened with bodily harm by the Hispanics who were our neighbors, and who seemed, more than anything, *bewildered* by the darkness and filth of their surroundings.) Inside was the church pew, as straight and spare as Abe Lincoln lying down, the white walls as spotless as a monastery's, and a small, unutterably pure patch of blue sky through the window of the back bedroom. (Luna did not believe in curtains, or couldn't afford them, and so we always undressed and bathed with the lights off and the rooms lit with candles, causing rather nun-shaped shadows to be cast on the walls by the long-sleeved high-necked nightgowns we both wore to bed.)

Over a period of weeks, our relationship, always marked by mutual respect, evolved into a warm and comfortable friendship which provided a stability and comfort we both needed at that time. I had taken a job at the Welfare Department during the day, and set up my typewriter permanently in the tiny living room for work after I got home. Luna worked in a kindergarten, and in the evenings taught herself Portuguese.

It was while we lived on East 9th Street that she told me she had been raped during her summer in the South. It is hard for me, even now, to relate my feeling of horror and incredulity. This was some time before Eldridge Cleaver[6] wrote of being a rapist / revolutionary; of "practicing" on black women before moving on to white. It was also, unless I'm mistaken, before LeRoi Jones[7] (as he was then known; now of course Imamu Baraka, which has an even more presumptuous meaning than "the King") wrote his advice to young black male insurrectionaries (women were not told what to do with *their* rebelliousness): "Rape the white girls. Rape

6. Eldridge Cleaver (1935–98), one of the leaders of the Black Panthers, was a spokesman for black power. He articulated his position on race in *Soul on Ice* (1968), a collection of essays he wrote while in prison.

7. LeRoi Jones (1934–) was a powerful force in the Black Arts movement. In 1965, after adopting a black-nationalist perspective, he began to distance himself from the white culture by changing his name to Imamu Amiri Baraka, divorcing his white wife, and moving to Harlem.

their fathers." It was clear that he meant this literally and also as: to rape a white girl *is* to rape her father. It was the misogynous cruelty of this latter meaning that was habitually lost on black men (on men in general, actually), but nearly always perceived and rejected by women of whatever color.

"Details?" I asked.

She shrugged. Gave his name. A name recently in the news, though in very small print.

He was not a Movement star or anyone you would know. We had met once, briefly. I had not liked him because he was coarse and spoke of black women as "our" women. (In the early Movement, it was pleasant to think of black men wanting to own us as a group; later it became clear that owning us meant exactly *that* to them.) He was physically unattractive, I had thought, with something of the hoodlum about him: a swaggering, unnecessarily mobile walk, small eyes, rough skin, a mouthful of wandering or absent teeth. He was, ironically, among the first persons to shout the slogan everyone later attributed solely to Stokeley Carmichael—Black Power![8] Stokeley was chosen as the originator of this idea by the media, because he was physically beautiful and photogenic and articulate. Even the name—Freddie Pye—was diminutive, I thought, in an age of giants.

"What did you do?"

"Nothing that required making a noise."

"Why didn't you scream?" I felt I would have screamed my head off.

"You know why."

I did. I had seen a photograph of Emmett Till's body just after it was pulled from the river.[9] I had seen photographs of white folks standing in a circle roasting something that had talked to them in their own language before they tore out its tongue. I knew why, all right.

---

8. Stokeley Carmichael (1949–98) became chair of the Student Nonviolent Coordinating Committee (SNCC) in 1966. About this time, he also lost his faith in nonviolent tactics. In June 1966 Carmichael made his "Black Power" speech, calling on blacks to unite and build their own community. Under Carmichael's leadership of the SNCC, whites were ousted from the organization.

9. Fourteen-year-old Emmett Till (1941–55), visiting the South from Chicago, allegedly whistled at or spoke to a white woman, Carolyn Bryant, on August 24, 1955, at Bryant's Grocery and Meat Market in Money, Mississippi. In the early hours of August 28, he was abducted from his uncle's home, beaten beyond recognition, and shot. His body was thrown into the Tallahatchie River with a seventy-five-pound cotton gin fan tied to his neck with barbed wire. An unedited photograph of Till's bloated corpse, published in *Jet* magazine on September 15, 1955, became the face of racial hatred in America.

"What was he trying to prove?"

"I don't know. Do you?"

"Maybe you filled him with unendurable lust," I said.

"I don't think so," she said.

Suddenly I was embarrassed. Then angry. Very, very angry. *How dare she tell me this!* I thought.

Who knows what the black woman thinks of rape? Who has asked her? Who *cares*? Who has even properly acknowledged that *she* and not the white woman in this story is the most likely victim of rape? Whenever interracial rape is mentioned, a black woman's first thought is to protect the lives of her brothers, her father, her sons, her lover. A history of lynching has bred this reflex in her. I feel it as strongly as anyone. While writing a fictional account of such a rape in a novel, I read Ida B. Wells's autobiography[10] three times, as a means of praying to her spirit to forgive me.

My prayer, as I turned the pages, went like this: *"Please forgive me. I am a writer."* (This self-revealing statement alone often seems to me sufficient reason to require perpetual forgiveness; since the writer is guilty not only of always wanting to know—like Eve—but also of trying—again like Eve—to find out.) *"I cannot write contrary to what life reveals to me. I wish to malign no one. But I must struggle to understand at least my own tangled emotions about interracial rape. I know, Ida B. Wells, you spent your whole life protecting, and trying to protect, black men accused of raping white women, who were lynched by white mobs, or threatened with it. You know, better than I ever will, what it means for a whole people to live under the terror of lynching. Under the slander that their men, where white women are concerned, are creatures of uncontrollable sexual lust. You made it so clear that the black men accused of rape in the past were innocent victims of white criminals that I grew up believing black men literally did not rape white women. At all. Ever. Now it would appear that some of them, the very twisted, the terribly ill, do. What would you have me write about them?"*

10. Ida B. Wells-Barnett (1862–1931) was a journalist and newspaper editor who became a leader in the antilynching campaign of the 1890s. Her work in the *Red Report* (1895) effectively presented the argument that the lynching of black men was not related to the rape of white women.

Her answer was: *"Write nothing. Nothing at all. It will be used against black men and therefore against all of us. Eldridge Cleaver and LeRoi Jones don't know who they're dealing with. But you remember. You are dealing with people who brought their children to witness the murder of black human beings, falsely accused of rape. People who handed out, as trophies, black fingers and toes. Deny! Deny! Deny!"*

And yet, I have pursued it: *"Some black men themselves do not seem to know what the meaning of raping someone is. Some have admitted rape in order to denounce it, but others have accepted rape as a part of rebellion, of 'paying whitey back.' They have gloried in it."*

"They know nothing of America," she says. *"And neither, apparently, do you. No matter what you think you know, no matter what you feel about it, say nothing. And to your dying breath!"*

Which, to my mind, is virtually useless advice to give to a writer.

Freddie Pye was the kind of man I would not have looked at then, not even once. (Throughout that year I was more or less into exotica: white ethnics who knew languages were a peculiar weakness; a half-white hippie singer; also a large Chinese mathematician who was a marvelous dancer and who taught me to waltz.) There was no question of belief.

But, in retrospect, there was a momentary *suspension* of belief, a kind of *hope* that perhaps it had not really happened; that Luna had made up the rape, "as white women have been wont to do." I soon realized this was unlikely. I was the only person she had told.

She looked at me as if to say: "I'm glad *that* part of my life is over." We continued our usual routine. We saw every interminable, foreign, depressing, and poorly illuminated film ever made. We learned to eat brown rice and yogurt and to tolerate kasha and odd-tasting teas. My half-black hippie singer friend (now a well-known reggae singer who says he is from "de I-lands" and not Sheepshead Bay) was "into" tea and kasha and Chinese vegetables.

And yet the rape, the knowledge of the rape, out in the open, admitted, pondered over, was now between us. (And I began to think that perhaps—whether Luna had been raped or not—it had always been so; that her power over my life was exactly the power *her word on rape* had over the lives of black men, over *all* black men, whether they were guilty or not, and therefore over my whole people.)

Before she told me about the rape, I think we had assumed a lifelong friendship. The kind of friendship one dreams of having with a person one has known in adversity; under heat and mosquitoes and immaturity and the threat of death. We would each travel, we would write to each other from the three edges of the world.

We would continue to have an "international list" of lovers whose amorous talents or lack of talents we would continue (giggling into our dotage) to compare. Our friendship would survive everything, be truer than everything, endure even our respective marriages, children, husbands—assuming we *did*, out of desperation and boredom someday, marry, which did not seem a probability, exactly, but more in the area of an amusing idea.

But now there was a cooling off of our affection for each other. Luna was becoming mildly interested in drugs, because everyone we knew was. I was envious of the open-endedness of her life. The financial backing to it. When she left her job at the kindergarten because she was tired of working, her errant father immediately materialized. He took her to dine on scampi at an expensive restaurant, scolded her for living on East 9th Street, and looked at me as if to say: "Living in a slum of this magnitude must surely have been your idea." As a cullud, of course.

For me there was the welfare department every day, attempting to get the necessary food and shelter to people who would always live amid the dirty streets I knew I must soon leave. I was, after all, a Sarah Lawrence girl "with talent." It would be absurd to rot away in a building that had no front door.

I slept late one Sunday morning with a painter I had met at the Welfare Department. A man who looked for all the world like Gene Autry, the singing cowboy, but who painted wonderful surrealist pictures of birds and ghouls and fruit with *teeth*. The night before, three of us—me, the painter, and "an old Navy buddy" who looked like his twin and who had just arrived in town—had got high on wine and grass.

That morning the Navy buddy snored outside the bedrooms like a puppy waiting for its master. Luna got up early, made an immense racket getting breakfast, scowled at me as I emerged from my room, and left the apartment, slamming the door so hard she damaged the lock. (Luna had made it a rule to date black men almost exclusively. My insistence on dating, as she termed it, "anyone" was incomprehensible to her, since in a politically diseased society to "sleep with the enemy" was to become "infected" with the enemy's "political germs." There is more than a grain of truth in this, of course, but I was having too much fun to stare at it for long. Still, coming from Luna it was amusing, since she never took into account the risk her own black lovers ran by sleeping with "the white woman," and she had apparently been convinced that a summer of relatively innocuous political work in the South had cured her of any racial, economic, or sexual political disease.)

Luna never told me what irked her so that Sunday morning, yet I remember it as the end of our relationship. It was not, as I at first feared, that she thought my bringing the two men to the apartment was inconsiderate. The way we lived allowed us to *be* inconsiderate from time to time. Our friends were varied, vital, and often strange. Her friends especially were deeper than they should have been into drugs.

The distance between us continued to grow. She talked more of going to Goa. My guilt over my dissolute if pleasurable existence coupled with my mounting hatred of welfare work, propelled me in two directions: south and to West Africa. When the time came to choose, I discovered that *my* summer in the South had infected me with the need to return, to try to understand, and write about, the people I'd merely lived with before.

We never discussed the rape again. We never discussed, really, Freddie Pye or Luna's remaining feelings about what had happened. One night, the last month we lived together, I noticed a man's blue denim jacket thrown across the church pew. The next morning, out of Luna's bedroom walked Freddie Pye. He barely spoke to me—possibly because as a black woman I was expected to be hostile toward his presence in a white woman's bedroom. I was too surprised to exhibit hostility, however, which was only a part of what I felt, after all. He left.

Luna and I did not discuss this. It is odd, I think now, that we didn't. It was as if he was never there, as if he and Luna had not shared the bedroom that night. A month later, Luna went alone to Goa, in her solitary way. She lived on an island and slept, she wrote, on the beach. She mentioned she'd found a lover there who protected her from the local beachcombers and pests.

Several years later, she came to visit me in the South and brought a lovely piece of pottery which my daughter much later dropped and broke, but which I glued back together in such a way that the flaw improves the beauty and fragility of the design.

Afterwords, Afterwards
Second Thoughts

That is the "story." It has an "unresolved" ending. That is because Freddie Pye and Luna are still alive, as am I. However, one evening while talking to a friend, I heard myself say that I had, in fact, written *two* endings. One, which follows, I considered appropriate for such a story published in a country truly committed to justice, and the one above, which is the best I can afford to offer a society in which lynching is still reserved, at least subconsciously, as a means of racial control.

I said that if we in fact lived in a society committed to the establishment of justice for everyone ("justice" in this case encompassing equal housing, education, access to work, adequate dental care, et cetera), thereby placing Luna and Freddie Pye in their correct relationship to each other, *i.e.*, that of brother and sister, *compañeros*, then the two of them would be required to struggle together over what his rape of her had meant.

Since my friend is a black man whom I love and who loves me, we spent a considerable amount of time discussing what this particular rape meant to us. Morally wrong, we said, and not to be excused. Shameful; politically corrupt. Yet, as we thought of what might have happened to an indiscriminate number of innocent young black men in Freehold, Georgia, had Luna screamed, it became clear that more than a little of Ida B. Wells's fear of probing the rape issue was running through us, too. The implications of this fear would not let me rest, so that months and years went by with most of the story written but with me incapable, or at least unwilling, to finish or to publish it.

In thinking about it over a period of years, there occurred a number of small changes, refinements, puzzles, in angle. Would these shed a wider light on the continuing subject? I do not know. In any case, I returned to my notes, hereto appended for the use of the reader.

Luna: Ida B. Wells—Discarded Notes

Additional characteristics of Luna: At a time when many in and out of the Movement considered "nigger" and "black" synonymous, and indulged in a sincere attempt to fake Southern "hip" speech, Luna resisted. She was the kind of WASP who could not easily imitate another's ethnic style, nor could she even exaggerate her own. She was what she was. A very straight, clear-eyed, coolly observant young woman with no talent for existing outside her own skin.

Imaginary Knowledge

Luna explained the visit from Freddie Pye in this way:

"*He called that evening, said he was in town, and did I know the Movement was coming north? I replied that I did know that.*"

When could he see her? he wanted to know.

"*Never,*" *she replied.*

He had burst into tears, or something that sounded like tears, over the phone. He was stranded at wherever the evening's fund-raising event had been held. Not in the place itself, but outside, in the street. The "stars" had left, everyone had left. He was alone. He knew no one else in the city. Had found her number in the phone book. And had no money, no place to stay.

Could he, he asked, crash? He was tired, hungry, broke—and even in the South had had no job, other than the Movement, for months. Et cetera.

When he arrived, she had placed our only steak knife in the waistband of her jeans.

He had asked for a drink of water. She gave him orange juice, some cheese, and a couple of slices of bread. She had told him he might sleep on the church pew and he had lain down with his head on his rolled-up denim jacket. She had retired to her room, locked the door, and tried to sleep. She was amazed to discover herself worrying that the church pew was both too narrow and too hard.

At first he muttered, groaned, and cursed in his sleep. Then he fell off the narrow church pew. He kept rolling off. At two in the morning she unlocked her door, showed him her knife, and invited him to share her bed.

Nothing whatever happened except they talked. At first, only he talked. Not about the rape, but about his life.

"He was a small person physically, remember?" Luna asked me. (She was right. Over the years he had grown big and, yes, burly, in my imagination, and I'm sure in hers.) "That night he seemed tiny. A child. He was still fully dressed, except for the jacket and he, literally, hugged his side of the bed. I hugged mine. The whole bed, in fact, was between us. We were merely hanging to its edges."

At the fund-raiser—on Fifth Avenue and 71st Street, as it turned out—his leaders had introduced him as the unskilled, barely literate, former Southern field-worker that he was. They had pushed him at the rich people gathered there as an example of what "the system" did to "the little people" in the South. They asked him to tell about the thirty-seven times he had been jailed. The thirty-five times he had been beaten. The one time he had lost consciousness in the "hot" box. They told him not to worry about his grammar. "Which, as you may recall," said Luna, "was horrible." Even so, he had tried to censor his "ain'ts" and his "us'es." He had been painfully aware that he was on exhibit, like Frederick Douglass had been for the Abolitionists. But unlike Douglass he had no oratorical gift, no passionate language, no silver tongue. He knew the rich people and his own leaders perceived he was nothing: a broken man, unschooled, unskilled at anything. . . .

Yet he had spoken, trembling before so large a crowd of rich, white Northerners—who clearly thought their section of the country would never have the South's racial problems—begging, with the painful stories of his wretched life, for their money.

At the end, all of them—the black leaders, too—had gone. They left him watching the taillights of their cars, recalling the faces of the friends come to pick them up: the women dressed in African print that shone, with elaborately arranged hair, their jewelry sparkling, their perfume exotic. They were so beautiful, yet so strange. He could not imagine that one of them could comprehend his life. He did not ask for a ride, because of that, but also because he had no place to go. Then he had remembered Luna.

Soon Luna would be required to talk. She would mention her con-

*fusion over whether, in a black community surrounded by whites with a
history of lynching blacks, she had a right to scream as Freddie Pye was
raping her. For her, this was the crux of the matter.*

And so they would continue talking through the night.

This is another ending, created from whole cloth. If I believed Luna's
story about the rape, and I did (had she told anyone else I might have
dismissed it), then this reconstruction of what might have happened is
as probable an accounting as any is liable to be. Two people have now
become "characters."

I have forced them to talk until they reached the stumbling block
of the rape, *which they must remove themselves*, before proceeding to a
place from which it will be possible to insist on a society in which Luna's
word alone on rape can never be used to intimidate an entire people,
and in which an innocent black man's protestation of innocence of rape
is unprejudicially heard. Until such a society is created, relationships of
affection between black men and white women will always be poisoned—
from within as from without—by historical fear and the threat of violence,
and solidarity among black and white women is only rarely likely to exist.

Postscript: Havana, Cuba, November 1976

I am in Havana with a group of other black American artists. We have
spent the morning apart from our Cuban hosts bringing each other up to
date on the kind of work (there are no apolitical artists among us) we are
doing in the United States. I have read "Luna."

High above the beautiful city of Havana I sit in the Havana Libre
pavilion with the muralist / photographer in our group. He is in his mid-
thirties, a handsome, brown, erect individual whom I have known casually
for a number of years. During the sixties he designed and painted street
murals for both SNCC[11] and the Black Panthers,[12] and in an earlier discussion with Cuban artists he showed impatience with their explanation
of why we had seen no murals covering some of the city's rather dingy

11. The Student Nonviolent Coordinating Committee (SNCC) formed in the spring of 1960 to organize student activists participating in the sit-in movement.
12. The Black Panther Party was a militant black political group founded in 1966 to end white political dominance.

walls: Cuba, they had said, unlike Mexico, has no mural tradition. "But the point of a revolution," insisted Our Muralist, "is to make new traditions!" And he had pressed his argument with such passion for the *usefulness*, for revolutionary communication, of his craft, that the Cubans were both exasperated and impressed. They drove us around the city for a tour of their huge billboards, all advancing socialist thought and the heroism of men like Lenin, Camilo, and Che Guevara, and said, "These, *these* are our 'murals'!"

While we ate lunch, I asked Our Muralist what he'd thought of "Luna." Especially the appended section.

"Not much," was his reply. "Your view of human weakness is too biblical," he said. "You are unable to conceive of the man without conscience. The man who cares nothing about the state of his soul because he's long since sold it. In short," he said, "you do not understand that some people are simply evil, a disease on the lives of other people, and that to remove the disease altogether is preferable to trying to interpret, contain, or forgive it. Your 'Freddie Pye,'" and he laughed, "was probably raping white women on the instructions of his government."

Oh ho, I thought. Because, of course, for a second, during which I stalled my verbal reply, this comment made both very little and very much sense.

"I *am* sometimes naive and sentimental," I offered. I am sometimes both, though frequently by design. Admission in this way is tactical, a stimulant to conversation.

"And shocked at what I've said," he said, and laughed again. "Even though," he continued, "you know by now that blacks could be hired to blow up other blacks, and could be hired *by someone* to shoot down Brother Malcolm, and hired *by someone* to provide a diagram of Fred Hampton's bedroom so the pigs could shoot him easily while he slept,[13] you find it hard to believe a black man could be hired *by someone* to rape white women. But think a minute, and you will see why it is the perfect disruptive act. Enough blacks raping or accused of raping enough white women and any political movement that cuts across racial lines is doomed.

"Larger forces are at work than your story would indicate," he contin-

---

13. On the morning of December 4, 1969, Chicago police stormed Fred Hampton's apartment and shot him in the head. Hampton (1948–69) was a charismatic leader of the Chicago chapter of the Black Panther Party.

ued. "You're still thinking of lust and rage, moving slowly into aggression and purely racial hatred. But you should be considering money—which the rapist would get, probably from your very own tax dollars, in fact—and a maintaining of the status quo; which, those hiring the rapist would achieve. I know all this," he said, "because when I was broke and hungry and selling my blood to buy the food and the paint that allowed me to work, I was offered such 'other work.'"

"But you did not take it."

He frowned. "There you go again. How do you know I didn't take it? It paid, and I was starving."

"You didn't take it," I repeated.

"No," he said. "A black and white 'team' made the offer. I had enough energy left to threaten to throw them out of the room."

"But even if Freddie Pye *had been* hired *by someone* to rape Luna, that still would not explain his second visit."

"Probably nothing will explain that," said Our Muralist. "But assuming Freddie Pye was paid to disrupt—by raping a white woman—the black struggle in the South, he may have wised up enough later to comprehend the significance of Luna's decision not to scream."

"So you are saying he *did have* a conscience?" I asked.

"Maybe," he said, but his look clearly implied I would never understand anything about evil, power, or corrupted human beings in the modern world.

But of course he is wrong.

ROSELLEN BROWN

Means and Ends

Rosellen Brown (1939–) is an essayist, poet, and novelist. The recipient of many
literary awards, among them a Guggenheim, the Bunting Institute Fellowship,
and a National Endowment for the Arts grant, she has taught at the University of
Houston and the School of the Art Institute of Chicago. During the civil rights
movement she was on the faculty of Tougaloo College in Mississippi. Her work
has been included in *The Best American Short Stories*, the O. Henry Award
anthology, and the *Pushcart Prize* anthology. "Means and Ends" first appeared
in the journal *Chelsea* in 1985 and was reprinted in *A Rosellen Brown Reader:
Selected Poetry and Prose* (1992).

This is Mrs. Winston's daughter. What is her name? Hattie, Hennie,
Hettie?

She faces the narrow world head-on, like someone posing for a por-
trait angrily, trying to shame the photographer by shaming herself. Here,
she likes herself at the greatest possible disadvantage: she is eleven, maybe ten, all bust, all waist, all hips. Already her blouses part between buttons, her lap is rumpled with fault lines. She has a wrinkled neck, like a
grandfather turtle's, made for drawing in. Sometimes she strokes it with
disgust as if it were a foreign limb.

When she was a baby Hattie-Hennie-Hettie seemed to put out her
right hand and catch every sickness that blew by, seemed to stuff her
mouth with it the way some children eat dirt. She would swallow it down
and the next day there would come hives or scarlet fever, blisters or the
asthma that made her roll her round eyes back in her head as if she were a
slot machine. Oh Luvester, Mrs. Winston would say to her silent husband,
all my beautiful babies and then her. She didn't care about the beauty
much—not the actual facts of feature and proportion, she herself was all
nursing woman's bust and sitting woman's butt and dark, dark as polished
black walnut. It was a question of spirit, high or low. This girl seemed

born defeated and Mrs. Winston couldn't say why. Last babies ought to have high blood and a carefree nature, all those others to love her and carry her around, do the work, and she beloved sitting in the dirt making sand babies and nobody minded. Maybe, she told Luvester, I was wore out inside when she come on and she couldn't find a good rich place to grip on to. Maybe she was just born hungry. They would have taken a good look at her thumb if they'd suspected, to see if she'd been wearing it down the whole nine months.

There had been a lot of Winstons growing up tight in the house—we a pack of Winstons, they liked to say, only ain't none of us white or filter tip. There were six or seven children and a premature set of grandchildren and then Mrs. Winston was one of the famous providers of sustenance, physical and psychological, to everyone from sweet mama's girls to the Movement desperadoes who lived in Yazoo City, camped there, perched or passed on through. This is the 60s we're talking about; early 60s. She was one of those women, still called Negro and never did mind, who wanted to give a son or a daughter to Freedom the way Catholic families hope for a nun or a priest to dedicate, even if that means they are lost to daily affection. Even a child in jail for the right reasons would do.

Now they were down to Hattie-Hettie-Hennie who slept, or these days could not sleep, in the back room with Cliantha and her baby. Cliantha was fourteen and had no visible figure yet—she was long and flat and rudder-footed—but apparently someone had wanted her even without visibly enticing parts, someone had known what to do. Absent from sixth or seventh grade, she had spent all her time getting her baby boy and then noisily delivering it, shouting for Mama like a five-year-old with her hand caught in a door, and now having it around to keep her younger sister awake. (Or so the sister claimed, as if insuring her discomfort might be sufficient motivation for months of Cliantha's morning sickness and assorted asymmetrical miseries from toothache to ankle bloat. "Think I gave up my belly button just for you?" Cliantha would say into her sister's face. "Don't strike me so unlikely," the younger one would answer, scowling, her lips pulled out toward a smile.) But she liked the baby, called Willie, in spite of its mother. It wanted to be held against her pillows of bosom and Cliantha let it be so she could get some time cut free from him.

One time Hattie-Hettie-Hennie even seemed to run off with the baby. It looked like she had kidnapped him (with no diapers, as far as Cliantha could see, and only the bottle he had lying beside him for his morning sleep.) Jack Cuff, neighbor, had been driving his pickup to Jackson to price a new transmission and, seeing Hattie-Hettie-Hennie coming down the steps on her way to school, had asked if she'd keep him company; he'd had to sell his radio to pay a bill and keep the sheriff from his door.

It happened that Jack Cuff was one of the few people in Yazoo City that she managed to like: an old man working on his third family and waiting for his third set of teeth, two things you could apparently do with no loss to either, since they each took a different kind of concentration. Something about him always seemed to be patient and contented, waiting for whatever might happen. Her mother made everything happen and her father's teeth stayed clenched to resist them, but Jack Cuff was more like an amiable old dog, color of a beagle, who might be bigger than you but had no plans to overpower you. She said "Sure I'll come"—the fact that this was a school day made it the best idea she'd heard in a month—and just as she was going down to his truck she said "Can I bring Willie? He never been nowhere."

"Sure, bring Willie," Jack Cuff said. "He don't take no room, and if things get too quiet we can always make him sing."

So she appropriated the baby in his diaper and his short-sleeved undershirt, both of them pinned together for some reason with tabs—to keep his stomach in, she supposed, though what would be the matter with a baby with his stomach out? He wasn't any barrel-shaped ten-year-old.

And they went down the highway. As they approached the city they passed the motels and the shopping centers and Willie slept on her knees against the bolster of her chest so quietly he didn't seem to be there at all; he cried from hunger all the way back. Hattie-Hettie-Hennie hoped, without giving it much head-on thought, that Cliantha had come looking for her baby and figured they were only out for the longest walk ever. Another part of her hoped her sister had fainted flat-out with terror, maybe even hit her head on some furniture, and called the police. She personally was convinced that she loved the baby more than its mother, who yielded to an alarming temptation to get out of its sight every chance she got. (She was still going down to see its father and they had plans that didn't include a reminder of what could always happen again, what might even be happening already.) She couldn't wait to have her own Willie, although she wished she could fix it so she wouldn't have to touch anybody to get it.

"All you want is attention!" Cliantha shouted when her sister got out of Jack Cuff's truck and handed her son back to her, sopping and starving. "Just like to make trouble, get everybody worked up!"

"I'm not worked up," Hattie-Hettie-Hennie said. "That's you you're talking about. I baby-sitted your baby and this is my thanks. You was just hoping I run off with him for good and now I can see you're sorry I brought him back."

Cliantha clutched her howling baby against where her breast should be and tried out various styles of revenge in her mind. But she couldn't think of a single thing her sister loved too much to have broken, or wanted too much to be kept from it. For a split second, until the baby's yiping distracted her, Cliantha saw her little sister with a nearly restraining sympathy: cheeks like a groundhog, shape of a groundhog, plus that waddle, all alone at the bottom end of the family, and look, having to take Willie, stinking Willie, for a friend. No boy would ever walk her into the dark and start a Willie in her. Stay with Mama forever, that was what her sister was going to do.

The other Winston children had failed their mother too, one after another like leaves detaching themselves from a tree, falling in a desultory pile, and blowing away. They all left Mississippi behind. Every one had a double name—Lotha Lu and Danda Marie, Torrence Tee, Luvester Junior called Lutie, Cliantha Joy, Hattie-Hettie-Hennie Ann, and Johnnie G. who was on the wrong side of the law in Sarasota. Each did a zealous job of keeping in touch with their mother, sending the bad news on down. They also sent their children and then took them back without much warning and wrenched her heart each time she lost one. She was right to think they'd have been remarkable freedom-fighters because they all seemed unshakeably bent on assertion. But freedom, or the organized fight for it, had come too late and all of them, the three boys and the two departed girls, seemed to be embroiled in seamy enterprises and doomed love affairs far from home, each more desperate than the next, when voter registration came to convert their mother.

Mr. Luvester Winston was neither pro it nor con it: he was strong-armed from his work, which was loading and unloading the big colored wagons down at the gin, and silent about most other things, a born-steady man where steadiness was an amazing grace. When he drank he only got more silent, which could be irritating but—praise the Lord! said Mrs. Winston and looked at heaven with smart shining eyes—not about to be dangerous.

Mrs. Henrietta Winston was a serious woman and she never took scared. Up in church, up at meetings, her knees forgot how to bend to get her in her seat again. She got three fireballs through her window for thanks, firebombs that somehow failed. They rolled skidding across her living room linoleum and then probably they sank back in sparks because of the way she scowled at them, like dust devils. "Luvester!" she shouted. "Come douse some water over here on these." There had been a sound like a car door slamming out front but no lights, no sound of feet coming closer. Cowards threw them like a paper boy tossing the *Evening Bulletin* in the general direction of the house.

She went on every march after that; she took a clipboard and knocked on doors and used herself as the model of a brand-new voter who wasn't born thinking on Freedom. (Don't need schooling or money or friends in high places, just the itch to be a first-class citizen.) She spoke whatever language she had to and passed no judgments on the fearful.

How bout a bulletproof vest? some of her neighbors asked her. Better get you one of them, size double X and a half.

You gon die anyway, why not go out like a hero, she liked to say cheerfully. Either way the Lord be waiting on you with wide-open arms. Then she would lean forward—this got to be a polished performance with nuances cut to fit the listener—and whisper some vile gossip about the town government, the justice of peace at his games, the council at its pleasure. People struck from the commodity food lists, women sterilized when they were still under, families sent north, banished like criminals with barely any time to pack. Some true, some not so true, but all of it, from her point of view, moral. Every abomination was true in essence; what hadn't happened simply hadn't been thought of yet, or dared. Ends and means was a new phrase to her and it made a lot of sense because we all know already everyone lives like that: ends are what you want to and means are what you got to. Men, children, employers—everybody plays means and ends every day, you learn it the way you learn about money: there's giving, taking, waiting, and saving up. A kind of life and death economy. The means is now and the end comes later.

So she was famous in Yazoo City and Mrs. Winston, energy unflagging, was truly happy. Probably it was the first time in her life every part of her was occupied, more than one at a time, not just the cooking or the nursing, the gardening or the loving side. She was good at tactics, going a long day without sitting down or eating anything to speak of, remembering names, convincing the preacher, healing rifts.

She was taken to Washington once to see the Poverty People and when the Big Cheese (the only thing she ever called him, unless it was to mispronounce his name deliberately) took off into his hindmost office to wait for her and her contingent to leave, and told his receptionist to say he wasn't in, she was sick to her stomach. Did he not want to make them less poor because he might lose his job if that worked too well? Why not if it didn't work at all? Their arrival in the moneyed class didn't feel to her like an immediate problem. She sat down in a swivel chair outside his office door and told the pale secretaries she would wait. To keep busy she studied the bunch of them: they all had red nails sprouting from their fingertips like roses. They looked impatient and panicked at the same time. Even Luvester had more guts than that. If somebody came to his door to settle something, he never would take off out the back window. She was tired of having the power to scare people but not to change them. That was the power of weakness without shame, it made your enemies nervous but it wouldn't butter your parsnips or keep your toes warm into January.

But this is what happened near the end of summer and how it changed some things, if not others. They were all sitting on the little porch of their house just as the sun was dropping down, draining off the light. Hattie-Hettie-Hennie was up top on a cane chair and Cliantha sat on a step with the baby in her lap. She was sitting a little longer than she ought to, putting off changing him well past the point of common decency, even all in the family. Luvester Winston was there with his mind somewhere else and Mrs. Winston was telling a story on Mrs. Verney Tuttle, the voting registrar who had more trouble reading the written word than any three sharecroppers come in to fail their test. She sat in her office and listened to her radio dialed to the Daily Ministry of Souls that was sponsored by a major feed company that talked about making cattle healthy for God and man. If there had been someone there to take their picture this would have made a good one to remember, they looked gathered together for some purpose beyond the passing of time: it looked like it might be a family reunion. Everybody was benefitting these days from Mrs. Winston's mood of absorbed energy. There was less of it to spend forcing the girls to make up their quarrels or Luvester, slouched, to take an interest. No grandchildren as far as she knew were set to arrive (and then, inevitably, leave and rip another layer off her skin).

Suddenly there came a flash, exactly as if that photograph had been taken by an old-fashioned camera with its explosion of phosphorus that parted the dark for a split second. Everybody's voice seemed to rise in a great "Aah!" of bewilderment and surprise and one of the chairs went down with a crack of its own, but no one knew what had happened. They all turned and shouted "What? What?" and the baby, startled by the commotion, set up the only cry that sounded indisputably angry. A car took off in dust that obliterated every detail, only the tip of its roof visible like a piece of something solid hurtling up out of a smoky fire.

It was then that they saw the younger sister, Hattie-Hettie-Hennie, running around in a circle down on the ground in front of the porch where her chair lay with its legs up like an overturned animal too clumsy to right itself. She was making a strange small noise in her throat, a gull's or a pigeon's, and holding her hands to her eyes. Even in the dark, which had thickened, it was easy to see something black washing over her fisted hands and raining on the ground where she scuffled it under. Square and solid as a woman in a ritual dance she traced the same steps around and around, bobbing her head. When Mrs. Winston caught her they collided with a damp resounding smack. She held her daughter's strong shoulders as if the girl were going to break and run off into the evening. She might have been.

Luvester couldn't start his car, whose battery was suspect, and no one had a working phone, so Mrs. Winston raced down the street trying to hold her daughter up by clutching her under her far arm. They zigzagged across littered lots until someone she knew finally picked them up as they rounded a corner still a mile from the fluorescent-lit grounds of the County Hospital.

The hurrying didn't help because, of course, the eye was already gone, splintered along with a bit of bone and a handful of flesh into shards, like a smashed glass. There were twelve pellets in the eye socket alone. The girl, silent, blamed no one but her mother. Mrs. Winston, who could get a distance back from herself, was contemptuous, among other things. It was like the time of the bomb—why were these boys such cowards? I dare go sit with my family out on the porch right there for anybody to see who don't mind driving down such a raggedy street and they come sniffing around at night and their hand quiver so much they can't barely get their aim.

Who say they didn't take good aim? protested Mrs. Winston's detractors, who had always thought she was asking for what she got if it was bad enough. Everybody know you make a dent in someone like her by shooting one across instead and getting a dear one. She don't matter for herself, she got a hide like a hippo. And if they get the baby right in the diaper, better still. They probably gunning for Willie.

Maybe so. But who they got was Hattie-Hettie-Hennie, who was identified for the news people (with their notebooks and their microphones and even their panel truck full of shiny heavy equipment, cameras that young white boys hoisted on their T-shirt shoulders) as Henrietta Winston, Jr. It galled the County Hospital to have these crews of insolent young media people prowling around; it further irritated them that there was a pile of mail for this child and flowers arriving as fast as the florist truck could get into reverse and come back again. To look at the return addresses it was clear that this was nationwide sympathy coming in. It was easier to love this child from far away, the admissions nurse (deliverer of the daily mail) was heard to say: she's round and she's sour and she's the exact color of mop water. And now to make her perfect, she's missing an eye and going to have to get it plugged.

But Henrietta, Jr., was making a turn around, even while she lay in bed with her face in gauze, like a caterpillar wrapped in a chrysalis. They poked a microphone under her nose and wondered if she had given any thought to Freedom since she had given an eye up for it. (Nobody had asked, of course, but she guessed she had, if that was the answer they wanted.) Did Henrietta, Sr., tell Henrietta, Jr., about her plans for opposition and disruption? (She supposed she did, they were all one family, even she who was the last of them.)

These answers seemed to please everyone who heard them. Her law-yer—she had one now, though it wasn't clear they were going to find any-one to prosecute for the shooting—clipped an article out of the New York *Times* and glued it to red cardboard so that she could prop it up on her dresser. She memorized it hungrily with her one eye. It was about heinous acts and cowardly spite and was called And A Little Child Shall Judge Them. Although they didn't call her name, she was certainly the child so biblically and respectfully referred to in two sizes of print. Cliantha and all her school friends were made to read it. She hoped they envied her.

Mrs. Winston was very gentle with her for a while, not so much from guilt as from pity: she did not like pain and she didn't think you should have to pay for being right and doing right. But she told her daughter she was a means now, and that was where the pain and sorrow tended to puddle up. When they got closer to the end, which she was helping them toward, she would see what the purpose had been; right now it was still a long way out of sight.

Some of the sourness cleared off her face when Henrietta, Jr., dis-covered how much of the world she couldn't see even from Jackson, and how strange it was that a lot of people who weren't even related could love her for her loss. She didn't miss her eye much—people overdid the sympathy on that but she wasn't about to say so. There was a fund for her College Education and another for Hospital Expenses, which would include a black patch now and later a brand-new eye: she thought she might try a different color. Cliantha gagged but Henrietta, Jr., said Why not? More people ought to get into the line of fire, she thought (but kept it to herself) as long as they're left with one of everything. It was better than selling off your radio and having to listen to the road.

JAMES BALDWIN

Going to Meet the Man

Born in Harlem, James Baldwin (1924–87) was a prolific writer of essays, short
stories, novels, and plays—one of the latter inspired by the lynching of Emmett
Till, *Blues for Mister Charlie* (1964). He lived in Paris and Istanbul to separate
himself from the racism in America, but he returned in 1957 to become involved
in the civil rights movement. "Going to Meet the Man" is the title story of his
1965 collection.

"What's the matter?" she asked.

"I don't know," he said, trying to laugh, "I guess I'm tired."

"You've been working too hard," she said. "I keep telling you."

"Well, goddammit, woman," he said, "it's not my fault!" He tried
again; he wretchedly failed again. Then he just lay there, silent, angry,
and helpless. Excitement filled him like a toothache, but it refused to
enter his flesh. He stroked her breast. This was his wife. He could not ask
her to do just a little thing for him, just to help him out, just for a little
while, the way he could ask a nigger girl to do it. He lay there, and he
sighed. The image of a black girl caused a distant excitement in him, like
a far-away light; but, again, the excitement was more like pain; instead of
forcing him to act, it made action impossible.

"Go to sleep," she said, gently, "you got a hard day tomorrow."

"Yeah," he said, and rolled over on his side, facing her, one hand still
on one breast. "Goddamn the niggers. The black stinking coons. You'd
think they'd learn. Wouldn't you think they'd learn? I mean, *wouldn't*
you."

"They going to be out there tomorrow," she said, and took his hand
away, "get some sleep."

He lay there, one hand between his legs, staring at the frail sanctuary
of his wife. A faint light came from the shutters; the moon was full. Two
dogs, far away, were barking at each other, back and forth, insistently, as

though they were agreeing to make an appointment. He heard a car coming north on the road and he half sat up, his hand reaching for his holster, which was on a chair near the bed, on top of his pants. The lights hit the shutters and seemed to travel across the room and then went out. The sound of the car slipped away, he heard it hit gravel, then heard it no more. Some liver-lipped students, probably, heading back to that college—but coming from where? His watch said it was two in the morning. They could be coming from anywhere, from out of state most likely, and they would be at the court-house tomorrow. The niggers were getting ready. Well, they would be ready, too.

He moaned. He wanted to let whatever was in him out; but it wouldn't come out. Goddamn! he said aloud, and turned again, on his side, away from Grace, staring at the shutters. He was a big, healthy man and he had never had any trouble sleeping. And he wasn't old enough yet to have any trouble getting it up—he was only forty-two. And he was a good man, a God-fearing man, he had tried to do his duty all his life, and he had been a deputy sheriff for several years. Nothing had ever bothered him before, certainly not getting it up. Sometimes, sure, like any other man, he knew that he wanted a little more spice than Grace could give him and he would drive over yonder and pick up a black piece or arrest her, it came to the same thing, but he couldn't do that now, no more. There was no telling what might happen once your ass was in the air. And they were low enough to kill a man then, too, every one of them, or the girl herself might do it, right while she was making believe you made her feel so good. The niggers. What had the good Lord Almighty had in mind when he made the niggers? Well. They were pretty good at that, all right. Damn. Damn. Goddamn.

This wasn't helping him to sleep. He turned again, toward Grace again, and moved close to her warm body. He felt something he had never felt before. He felt that he would like to hold her, hold her, hold her, and be buried in her like a child and never have to get up in the morning again and go downtown to face those faces, good Christ, they were ugly! and never have to enter that jail house again and smell that smell and hear that singing; never again feel that filthy, kinky, greasy hair under his hand, never again watch those black breasts leap against the leaping cattle prod, never hear those moans again or watch that blood run down or the fat lips split or the sealed eyes struggle open. They were animals, they were no better than animals, what could be done with people like that? Here they had been in a civilized country for years and they still lived like animals. Their houses were dark, with oil cloth or cardboard in the windows, the smell was enough to make you puke your guts out, and there they sat, a whole tribe, pumping out kids, it looked like, every damn five minutes, and laughing and talking and playing music like they didn't have a care in the world, and he reckoned they didn't, neither, and coming to the door, into the sunlight, just standing there, just looking foolish, not thinking of anything but just getting back to what they were doing, saying, Yes suh, Mr. Jesse. I surely will, Mr. Jesse. Fine weather, Mr. Jesse. Why, I thank you, Mr. Jesse. He had worked for a mail-order house for a while and it had been his job to collect the payments for the stuff they bought. They were too dumb to know that they were being cheated blind, but that was no skin off his ass—he was just supposed to do his job. They would be late—they didn't have the sense to put money aside; but it was easy to scare them, and he never really had any trouble. Hell, they all liked him, the kids used to smile when he came to the door. He gave them candy, sometimes, or chewing gum, and rubbed their rough bullet heads—maybe the candy should have been poisoned. Those kids were grown now. He had had trouble with one of them today.

"There was this nigger today," he said; and stopped; his voice sounded peculiar. He touched Grace. "You awake?" he asked. She mumbled something, impatiently, she was probably telling him to go to sleep. It was all right. He knew that he was not alone.

"What a funny time," he said, "to be thinking about a thing like that— you listening?" She mumbled something again. He rolled over on his back. "This nigger's one of the ringleaders. We had trouble with him before. We must have had him out there at the work farm three or four times. Well, Big Jim C.[1] and some of the boys really had to whip that nigger's ass today." He looked over at Grace; he could not tell whether she was listening or not; and he was afraid to ask again. "They had this line you know, to register"—he laughed, but she did not—"and they wouldn't stay

1. Sheriff James G. Clark of Selma, Dallas County, Alabama, had a reputation for beating up the county's black citizens. He was especially aggressive during the voter-registration drives in the spring of 1965. Only 1 to 2 percent of blacks old enough to vote were registered.

where Big Jim C. wanted them, no, they had to start blocking traffic all around the court-house so couldn't nothing or nobody get through, and Big Jim C. told them to disperse and they wouldn't move, they just kept up that singing, and Big Jim C. figured that the others would move if this nigger would move, him being the ring-leader, but he wouldn't move and he wouldn't let the others move, so they had to beat him and a couple of the others and they threw them in the wagon—but *I* didn't see this nigger till I got to the jail. They were still singing and I was supposed to make them stop. Well, I couldn't make them stop for me but I knew he could make them stop. He was lying on the ground jerking and moaning, they had threw him in a cell by himself, and blood was coming out his ears from where Big Jim C. and his boys had whipped him. Wouldn't you think they'd learn? I put the prod to him and he jerked some more and he kind of screamed—but he didn't have much voice left. 'You make them stop that singing,' I said to him, 'you hear me? You make them stop that singing.' He acted like he didn't hear me and I put it to him again, under his arms, and he just rolled around on the floor and blood started coming from his mouth. He'd pissed his pants already." He paused. His mouth felt dry and his throat was as rough as sandpaper; as he talked, he began to hurt all over with that peculiar excitement which refused to be released. "You all are going to stop your singing, I said to him, and you are going to stop coming down to the court-house and disrupting traffic and molesting the people and keeping us from our duties and keeping doctors from getting to sick white women and getting all them Northerners in this town to give our town a bad name—!" As he said this, he kept prodding the boy, sweat pouring from beneath the helmet he had not yet taken off. The boy rolled around in his own dirt and water and blood and tried to scream again as the prod hit his testicles, but the scream did not come out, only a kind of rattle and a moan. He stopped. He was not supposed to kill the nigger. The cell was filled with a terrible odor. The boy was still. "You hear me?" he called. "You had enough?" The singing went on. "You had enough?" His foot leapt out, he had not known it was going to, and caught the boy flush on the jaw. *Jesus*, he thought, *this ain't no nigger, this is a goddamn bull*, and he screamed again, "You had enough? You going to make them stop that singing now?"

But the boy was out. And now he was shaking worse than the boy had been shaking. He was glad no one could see him. At the same time, he felt very close to a very peculiar, particular joy; something deep in him and deep in his memory was stirred, but whatever was in his memory eluded him. He took off his helmet. He walked to the cell door.

"White man," said the boy, from the floor, behind him.

He stopped. For some reason, he grabbed his privates.

"You remember Old Julia?"

The boy said, from the floor, with his mouth full of blood, and one eye, barely open, glaring like the eye of a cat in the dark, "My grandmother's name was Mrs. Julia Blossom. *Mrs.* Julia Blossom. You going to call our women by their right names yet.—And those kids ain't going to stop singing. We going to keep on singing until every one of you miserable white mothers go stark raving out of your minds." Then he closed the one eye; he spat blood; his head fell back against the floor.

He looked down at the boy, whom he had been seeing, off and on, for more than a year, and suddenly remembered him: Old Julia had been one of his mail-order customers, a nice old woman. He had not seen her for years, he supposed that she must be dead.

He had walked into the yard, the boy had been sitting in a swing. He had smiled at the boy, and asked, "Old Julia home?"

The boy looked at him for a long time before he answered. "Don't no Old Julia live here."

"This is her house. I know her. She's lived here for years."

The boy shook his head. "You might know a Old Julia someplace else, white man. But don't nobody by that name live here."

He watched the boy; the boy watched him. The boy certainly wasn't more than ten. *White man*. He didn't have time to be fooling around with some crazy kid. He yelled, "Hey! Old Julia!"

But only silence answered him. The expression on the boy's face did not change. The sun beat down on them both, still and silent; he had the feeling that he had been caught up in a nightmare, a nightmare dreamed by a child; perhaps one of the nightmares he himself had dreamed as a child. It had that feeling—everything familiar, without undergoing any other change, had been subtly and hideously displaced: the trees, the sun, the patches of grass in the yard, the leaning porch and the weary porch steps and the card-board in the windows and the black hole of the door which looked like the entrance to a cave, and the eyes of the pickaninny, all, all, were charged with malevolence. *White man*. He looked at the boy. "She's gone out?"

The boy said nothing.

"Well," he said, "tell her I passed by and I'll pass by next week." He started to go; he stopped. "You want some chewing gum?"

The boy got down from the swing and started for the house. He said, "I don't want nothing you got, white man." He walked into the house and closed the door behind him.

Now the boy looked as though he were dead. Jesse wanted to go over to him and pick him up and pistol whip him until the boy's head burst open like a melon. He began to tremble with what he believed was rage, sweat, both cold and hot, raced down his body, the singing filled him as though it were a weird, uncontrollable, monstrous howling rumbling up from the depths of his own belly, he felt an icy fear rise in him and raise him up, and he shouted, he howled, "You lucky we *pump* some white blood into you every once in a while—your women! Here's what I got for all the black bitches in the world—!" Then he was, abruptly, almost too weak to stand; to his bewilderment, his horror, beneath his own fingers, he felt himself violently stiffen—with no warning at all; he dropped his hands and he stared at the boy and he left the cell.

"All that singing they do," he said. "All that singing." He could not remember the first time he had heard it; he had been hearing it all his life. It was the sound with which he was most familiar—though it was also the sound of which he had been least conscious—and it had always contained an obscure comfort. They were singing to God. They were singing for mercy and they hoped to go to heaven, and he had even sometimes felt, when looking into the eyes of some of the old women, a few of the very old men, that they were singing for mercy for his soul, too. Of course he had never thought of their heaven or of what God was, or could be, for them; God was the same for everyone, he supposed, and heaven was where good people went—he supposed. He had never thought much about what it meant to be a good person. He tried to be a good person and treat everybody right: it wasn't his fault if the niggers had taken it into their heads to fight against God and go against the rules laid down in the Bible for everyone to read! Any preacher would tell you that. He was only doing his duty: protecting white people from the niggers and the niggers from themselves. And there were still lots of good niggers around—he had to remember that; they weren't all like that boy this afternoon; and the good niggers must be mighty sad to see what was happening to their people. They would thank him when this was over. In that way they had, the best of them, not quite looking him in the eye, in a low voice, with a little smile: We surely thanks you, Mr. Jesse. From the bottom of our hearts, we thanks you. He smiled. They hadn't all gone crazy. This trouble would pass.—He knew that the young people had changed some of the words to the songs. He had scarcely listened to the words before and he did not listen to them now; but he knew that the words were different; he could hear that much. He did not know if the faces were different, he had never, before this trouble began, watched them as they sang, but he certainly did not like what he saw now. They hated him, and this hatred was blacker than their hearts, blacker than their skins, redder than their blood, and harder, by far, than his club. Each day, each night, he felt worn out, aching, with their smell in his nostrils and filling his lungs, as though he were drowning—drowning in niggers; and it was all to be done again when he awoke. It would never end. It would never end. Perhaps this was what the singing had meant all along. They had not been singing black folks into heaven, they had been singing white folks into hell.

Everyone felt this black suspicion in many ways, but no one knew how to express it. Men much older than he, who had been responsible for law and order much longer than he, were now much quieter than they had been, and the tone of their jokes, in a way that he could not quite put his finger on, had changed. These men were his models, they had been friends to his father, and they had taught him what it meant to be a man. He looked to them for courage now. It wasn't that he didn't know that what he was doing was right—he knew that, nobody had to tell him that; it was only that he missed the ease of former years. But they didn't have much time to hang out with each other these days. They tended to stay close to their families every free minute because nobody knew what might happen next. Explosions rocked the night of their tranquil town. Each time each man wondered silently if perhaps this time the dynamite had not fallen into the wrong hands. They thought that they knew where all the guns were; but they could not possibly know every move that was made in that secret place where the darkies lived. From time to time it was suggested that they form a posse and search the home of every nigger, but they hadn't done it yet. For one thing, this might have brought the bastards from the North down on their backs; for another, although the niggers were scattered throughout the town—down in the hollow near the railroad tracks, way west near the mills, up on the hill, the well-off ones, and some out near the college—nothing seemed to happen in one part of town without the niggers immediately knowing it in the other. This meant that they could not take them by surprise. They rarely mentioned it, but they *knew* that some of the niggers had guns. It stood to reason, as they said, since, after all, some of them had been in the Army. There were niggers in the Army right now and God knows they wouldn't have had any trouble stealing this half-assed government blind—the whole world was doing it, look at the European countries and all those countries in Africa. They made jokes about it—bitter jokes; and they cursed the government in Washington, which had betrayed them; but they had not yet formed a posse. Now, if their town had been laid out like some towns in the North, where all the niggers lived together in one locality, they could have gone down and set fire to the houses and brought about peace that way. If the niggers had all lived in one place, they could have kept the fire in one place. But the way this town was laid out, the fire could hardly be con-trolled. It would spread all over town—and the niggers would probably be helping it to spread. Still, from time to time, they spoke of doing it, anyway; so that now there was a real fear among them that somebody might go crazy and light the match.

They rarely mentioned anything not directly related to the war that they were fighting, but this had failed to establish between them the un-spoken communication of soldiers during a war. Each man, in the thrilling silence which sped outward from their exchanges, their laughter, and their anecdotes, seemed wrestling, in various degrees of darkness, with a secret which he could not articulate to himself, and which, however directly it related to the war, related yet more surely to his privacy and his past. They could no longer be sure, after all, that they had all done the same things. They had never dreamed that their privacy could contain any element of terror, could threaten, that is, to reveal itself, to the scrutiny of a judgment day, while remaining unreadable and inaccessible to themselves; nor had they dreamed that the past, while certainly refusing to be forgotten, could yet so stubbornly refuse to be remembered. They felt themselves mysteriously set at naught, as no longer entering into the real concerns of other people—while here they were, out-numbered, fighting to save the civilized world. They had thought that people would care— people didn't care; not enough, anyway, to help them. It would have been a help, really, or at least a relief, even to have been forced to surrender. Thus they had lost, probably forever, their old and easy connection with each other. They were forced to depend on each other more and, at the same time, to trust each other less. Who could tell when one of them might not betray them all, for money, or for the ease of confession? But no one dared imagine what there might be to confess. They were soldiers fighting a war, but their relationship to each other was that of accomplices in a crime. They all had to keep their mouths shut.

I stepped in the river at Jordan.

Out of the darkness of the room, out of nowhere, the line came flying up at him, with the melody and the beat. He turned wordlessly toward his sleeping wife. *I stepped in the river at Jordan.* Where had he heard that song?

"Grace," he whispered. "You awake?"

She did not answer. If she was awake, she wanted him to sleep. Her breathing was slow and easy, her body slowly rose and fell.

I stepped in the river at Jordan.
The water came to my knees.

He began to sweat. He felt an overwhelming fear, which yet contained a curious and dreadful pleasure.

I stepped in the river at Jordan.
The water came to my waist.

It had been night, as it was now, he was in the car between his mother and his father, sleepy, his head in his mother's lap, sleepy, and yet full of excitement. The singing came from far away, across the dark fields. There were no lights anywhere. They had said good-bye to all the others and turned off on this dark dirt road. They were almost home.

I stepped in the river at Jordan,
The water came over my head,

I looked way over to the other side,
He was making up my dying bed!

"I guess they singing for him," his father said, seeming very weary and subdued now. "Even when they're sad, they sound like they just about to go and tear off a piece." He yawned and leaned across the boy and slapped his wife lightly on the shoulder, allowing his hand to rest there for a moment. "Don't they?"

"Don't talk that way," she said.

"Well, that's what we going to do," he said, "you can make up your mind to that." He started whistling. "You see? When I begin to feel it, I gets kind of musical, too."

Oh, Lord! Come on and ease my troubling mind!

He had a black friend, his age, eight, who lived nearby. His name was Otis. They wrestled together in the dirt. Now the thought of Otis made him sick. He began to shiver. His mother put her arm around him.

"He's tired," she said.

"We'll be home soon," said his father. He began to whistle again.

"We didn't see Otis this morning," Jesse said. He did not know why he said this. His voice, in the darkness of the car, sounded small and accusing.

"You haven't seen Otis for a couple of mornings," his mother said.

That was true. But he was only concerned about *this* morning.

"No," said his father, "I reckon Otis's folks was afraid to let him show himself this morning."

"But Otis didn't do nothing!" Now his voice sounded questioning.

"Otis *can't* do nothing," said his father, "he's too little." The car lights picked up their wooden house, which now solemnly approached them, the lights falling around it like yellow dust. Their dog, chained to a tree, began to bark.

"We just want to make sure Otis *don't* do nothing," said his father, and stopped the car. He looked down at Jesse. "And you tell him what your Daddy said, you hear?"

"Yes sir," he said.

His father switched off the lights. The dog moaned and pranced, but they ignored him and went inside. He could not sleep. He lay awake, hearing the night sounds, the dog yawning and moaning outside, the sawing of the crickets, the cry of the owl, dogs barking far away, then no sounds at all, just the heavy, endless buzzing of the night. The darkness pressed on his eyelids like a scratchy blanket. He turned, he turned again. He wanted to call his mother, but he knew his father would not like this. He was terribly afraid. Then he heard his father's voice in the other room, low, with a joke in it; but this did not help him, it frightened him more, he knew what was going to happen. He put his head under the blanket, then pushed his head out again, for fear, staring at the dark window. He heard his mother's moan, his father's sigh; he gritted his teeth. Then their bed began to rock. His father's breathing seemed to fill the world.

That morning, before the sun had gathered all its strength, men and women, some flushed and some pale with excitement, came with news. Jesse's father seemed to know what the news was before the first jalopy stopped in the yard, and he ran out, crying, "They got him, then? They got him?"

The first jalopy held eight people, three men and two women and three children. The children were sitting on the laps of the grown-ups. Jesse knew two of them, the two boys; they shyly and uncomfortably greeted each other. He did not know the girl.

"Yes, they got him," said one of the women, the older one, who wore a wide hat and a fancy, faded blue dress. "They found him early this morning."

"How far had he got?" Jesse's father asked.

"He hadn't got no further than Harkness," one of the men said. "Look like he got lost up there in all them trees—or maybe he just got so scared he couldn't move." They all laughed.

"Yes, and you know it's near a graveyard, too," said the younger woman, and they laughed again.

"Is that where they got him now?" asked Jesse's father.

By this time there were three cars piled behind the first one, with everyone looking excited and shining, and Jesse noticed that they were carrying food. It was like a Fourth of July picnic.

"Yeah, that's where he is," said one of the men, "declare, Jesse, you going to keep us here all day long, answering your damn fool questions. Come on, we ain't got no time to waste."

"Don't bother putting up no food," cried a woman from one of the other cars, "we got enough. Just come on."

"Why, thank you," said Jesse's father, "we be right along, then."

"I better get a sweater for the boy," said his mother, "in case it turns cold."

Jesse watched his mother's thin legs cross the yard. He knew that she also wanted to comb her hair a little and maybe put on a better dress, the dress she wore to church. His father guessed this, too, for he yelled behind her, "Now don't you go trying to turn yourself into no movie star. You just come on." But he laughed as he said this, and winked at the men; his wife was younger and prettier than most of the other women. He clapped Jesse on the head and started pulling him toward the car. "You all go on," he said, "I'll be right behind you. Jesse, you go tie up that there dog while I get this car started."

The cars sputtered and coughed and shook; the caravan began to move; bright dust filled the air. As soon as he was tied up, the dog began to bark. Jesse's mother came out of the house, carrying a jacket for his father and a sweater for Jesse. She had put a ribbon in her hair and had an old shawl around her shoulders.

"Put these in the car, son," she said, and handed everything to him. She bent down and stroked the dog, looked to see if there was water in his bowl, then went back up the three porch steps and closed the door.

"Come on," said his father, "ain't nothing in there for nobody to steal." He was sitting in the car, which trembled and belched. The last car of the caravan had disappeared but the sound of singing floated behind them.

Jesse got into the car, sitting close to his father, loving the smell of the car, and the trembling, and the bright day, and the sense of going on a great and unexpected journey. His mother got in and closed the door and the car began to move. Not until then did he ask, "Where are we going? Are we going on a picnic?"

He had a feeling that he knew where they were going, but he was not sure.

"That's right," his father said, "we're going on a picnic. You won't ever forget *this* picnic—!"

"Are we," he asked, after a moment, "going to see the bad nigger—the one that knocked down old Miss Standish?"

"Well, I reckon," said his mother, "that we *might* see him."

He started to ask, *Will a lot of niggers be there? Will Otis be there?*— but he did not ask his question, to which, in a strange and uncomfortable way, he already knew the answer. Their friends, in the other cars, stretched up the road as far as he could see; other cars had joined them; there were cars behind them. They were singing. The sun seemed suddenly very hot, and he was at once very happy and a little afraid. He did not quite understand what was happening, and he did not know what to ask—he had no one to ask. He had grown accustomed, for the solution of such mysteries, to go to Otis. He felt that Otis knew everything. But he could not ask Otis about this. Anyway, he had not seen Otis for two days; he had not seen a black face anywhere for more than two days; and he now realized, as they began chugging up the long hill which eventually led to Harkness, that there were no black faces on the road this morning, no black people anywhere. From the houses in which they lived, all along the road, no smoke curled, no life stirred—maybe one or two chickens were to be seen, that was all. There was no one at the windows, no one in the yard, no one sitting on the porches, and the doors were closed. He had come this road many a time and seen women washing in the yard (there were no clothes on the clotheslines) men working in the fields, children playing in the dust; black men passed them on the road other mornings, other days, on foot, or in wagons, sometimes in cars, tipping their hats, smiling, joking, their teeth a solid white against their skin, their eyes as warm as the sun, the blackness of their skin like dull fire against the white of the blue or the grey of their torn clothes. They passed the nigger church—dead-white, desolate, locked up; and the graveyard, where no one knelt or walked, and he saw no flowers. He wanted to ask, *Where are they? Where are they all?* But he did not dare. As the hill grew steeper, the sun grew colder. He looked at his mother and his father. They looked straight ahead, seeming to be listening to the singing which echoed and echoed in this graveyard silence. They were strangers to him now. They were looking at something he could not see. His father's lips had a strange, cruel curve, he wet his lips from time to time, and swallowed. He was terribly aware of his father's tongue, it was as though he had never seen it before. And his father's body suddenly seemed immense, bigger than a mountain. His eyes, which were grey-green, looked yellow in the sunlight; or at least there was a light in them which he had never seen before. His mother patted her hair and adjusted the ribbon, leaning forward to look into the car mirror. "You look all right," said his father, and laughed.

"When that nigger looks at you, he's going to swear he throwed his life away for nothing. Wouldn't be surprised if he don't come back to haunt you." And he laughed again.

The singing now slowly began to cease; and he realized that they were nearing their destination. They had reached a straight, narrow, pebbly road, with trees on either side. The sunlight filtered down on them from a great height, as though they were under-water; and the branches of the trees scraped against the cars with a tearing sound. To the right of them, and beneath them, invisible now, lay the town; and to the left, miles of trees which led to the high mountain range which his ancestors had crossed in order to settle in this valley. Now, all was silent, except for the bumping of the tires against the rocky road, the sputtering of motors, and the sound of a crying child. And they seemed to move more slowly. They were beginning to climb again. He watched the cars ahead as they toiled patiently upward, disappearing into the sunlight of the clearing. Presently, he felt their vehicle also rise, heard his father's changed breathing, the sunlight hit his face, the trees moved away from them, and they were there. As their car crossed the clearing, he looked around. There seemed to be millions, there were certainly hundreds of people in the clearing, staring toward something he could not see. There was a fire. He could not see the flames, but he smelled the smoke. Then they were on the other side of the clearing, among the trees again. His father drove off the road and parked the car behind a great many other cars. He looked down at Jesse.

"You all right?" he asked.

"Yes sir," he said.

"Well, come on, then," his father said. He reached over and opened the door on his mother's side. His mother stepped out first. They followed her into the clearing. At first he was aware only of confusion, of his mother and father greeting and being greeted, himself being handled, hugged, and patted, and told how much he had grown. The wind blew the smoke from the fire across the clearing into his eyes and nose. He could not see over the backs of the people in front of him. The sounds of laughing and cursing and wrath—and something else—rolled in waves from the front of the mob to the back. Those in front expressed their delight at what they saw, and this delight rolled backward, wave upon wave, across the clearing, more acrid than the smoke. His father reached down suddenly and sat Jesse on his shoulders.

Now he saw the fire—of twigs and boxes, piled high; flames made pale orange and yellow and thin as a veil under the steadier light of the sun; grey-blue smoke rolled upward and poured over their heads. Beyond the shifting curtain of fire and smoke, he made out first only a length of gleaming chain, attached to a great limb of the tree; then he saw that this chain bound two black hands together at the wrist, dirty yellow palm facing dirty yellow palm. The smoke poured up; the hands dropped out of sight; a cry went up from the crowd. Then the hands slowly came into view again, pulled upward by the chain. This time he saw the kinky, sweating, bloody head—he had never before seen a head with so much hair on it, hair so black and so tangled that it seemed like another jungle. The head was hanging. He saw the forehead, flat and high, with a kind of arrow of hair in the center, like he had, like his father had; they called it a widow's peak; and the mangled eye brows, the wide nose, the closed eyes, and the glinting eye lashes and the hanging lips, all streaming with blood and sweat. His hands were straight above his head. All his weight pulled downward from his hands; and he was a big man, a bigger man than his father, and black as an African jungle Cat, and naked. Jesse pulled upward; his father's hands held him firmly by the ankles. He wanted to say something, he did not know what, but nothing he said could have been heard, for now the crowd roared again as a man stepped forward and put more wood on the fire. The flames leapt up. He thought he heard the hanging man scream, but he was not sure. Sweat was pouring from the hair in his armpits, poured down his sides, over his chest, into his navel and his groin. He was lowered again; he was raised again. Now Jesse knew that he heard him scream. The head went back, the mouth wide open, blood bubbling from the mouth; the veins of the neck jumped out; Jesse clung to his father's neck in terror as the cry rolled over the crowd. The cry of all the people rose to answer the dying man's cry. He wanted death to come quickly. They wanted to make death wait: and it was they who held death, now, on a leash which they lengthened little by little. *What did he do?* Jesse wondered. *What did the man do? What did he do?*—but he could not ask his father. He was seated on his father's shoulders, but his father was far away. There were two older men, friends of his father's, raising and lowering the chain; everyone, indiscriminately, seemed to be responsible for the fire. There was no hair left on the nigger's privates, and the eyes, now, were wide open, as white as the eyes of a clown or a doll. The smoke now carried a terrible odor across the clearing, the odor of something burning which was both sweet and rotten.

He turned his head a little and saw the field of faces. He watched his mother's face. Her eyes were very bright, her mouth was open: she was more beautiful than he had ever seen her, and more strange. He began to feel a joy he had never felt before. He watched the hanging, gleaming body, the most beautiful and terrible object he had ever seen till then. One of his father's friends reached up and in his hands he held a knife: and Jesse wished that he had been that man. It was a long, bright knife and the sun seemed to catch it, to play with it, to caress it—it was brighter than the fire. And a wave of laughter swept the crowd. Jesse felt his father's hands on his ankles slip and tighten. The man with the knife walked toward the crowd, smiling slightly; as though this were a signal, silence fell; he heard his mother cough. Then the man with the knife walked up to the hanging body. He turned and smiled again. Now there was a silence all over the field. The hanging head looked up. It seemed fully conscious now, as though the fire had burned out terror and pain. The man with the knife took the nigger's privates in his hand, one hand, still smiling, as though he were weighing them. In the cradle of the one white hand, the nigger's privates seemed as remote as meat being weighed in the scales; but seemed heavier, too, much heavier, and Jesse felt his scrotum tighten; and huge, huge, much bigger than his father's, flaccid, hairless, the largest thing he had ever seen till then, and the blackest. The white hand stretched them, cradled them, caressed them. Then the dying man's eyes looked straight into Jesse's eyes—it could not have been as long as a second, but it seemed longer than a year. Then Jesse screamed, and the crowd screamed as the knife flashed, first up, then down, cutting the dreadful thing away, and the blood came roaring down. Then the crowd rushed forward, tearing at the body with their hands, with knives, with rocks, with stones, howling and cursing. Jesse's head, of its own weight, fell downward toward his father's head. Someone stepped forward and drenched the body with kerosene. Where the man had been, a great sheet of flame appeared. Jesse's father lowered him to the ground.

"Well, I told you," said his father, "you wasn't never going to forget *this* picnic." His father's face was full of sweat, his eyes were very peaceful. At that moment Jesse loved his father more than he had ever loved him. He felt that his father had carried him through a mighty test, had revealed to him a great secret which would be the key to his life forever.

"I reckon," he said. "I reckon."

Jesse's father took him by the hand and, with his mother a little behind them, talking and laughing with the other women, they walked through the crowd, across the clearing. The black body was on the ground, the chain which had held it was being rolled up by one of his father's friends. Whatever the fire had left undone, the hands and the knives and the stones of the people had accomplished. The head was caved in, one eye was torn out, one ear was hanging. But one had to look carefully to realize this, for it was, now, merely, a black charred object on the black, charred ground. He lay spread-eagled with what had been a wound between what had been his legs,

"They going to leave him here, then?" Jesse whispered.

"Yeah," said his father, "they'll come and get him by and by. I reckon we better get over there and get some of that food before it's all gone."

"I reckon," he muttered now to himself, "I reckon." Grace stirred and touched him on the thigh: the moonlight covered her like glory. Something bubbled up in him, his nature again returned to him. He thought of the boy in the cell; he thought of the man in the fire; he thought of the knife and grabbed himself and stroked himself and a terrible sound, something between a high laugh and a howl, came out of him and dragged his sleeping wife up on one elbow. She stared at him in a moonlight which had now grown cold as ice. He thought of the morning and grabbed her, laughing and crying, crying and laughing, and he whispered, as he stroked her, as he took her, "Come on, sugar, I'm going to do you like a nigger, just like a nigger, come on, sugar, and love me just like you'd love a nigger." He thought of the morning as he labored and she moaned, thought of morning as he labored harder than he ever had before, and before his labors had ended, he heard the first cock crow and the dogs begin to bark, and the sound of tires on the gravel road.

Retrospective

Although initiatives for civil rights continue to appear on our national agenda, the most active days of the civil rights movement ended forty years ago. During the main decade of the movement, recent advancements in technology made it possible to reveal to the world the troubles of minority life in the South. In particular, the August 1963 march on Washington, Freedom Summer in 1964 Mississippi, and the 1965 activities in Selma demonstrated the usefulness of grassroots-level direct action to college students and people of faith all over America, as laws were changed in response. After thirty thousand people gathered in Montgomery in the spring of 1965, however, the civil rights movement took a turn. The Student Nonviolent Coordinating Committee became less welcoming to whites. Some black initiatives—for example, the Black Panther Party—became more militant. Martin Luther King Jr. and the Southern Christian Leadership Conference turned their attention to the poverty of many black citizens living in Mississippi. If life were to change for people living well below the poverty line, often with no indoor plumbing, the government would need to supply funds, and such monetary programs produced different kinds of challenges for the national leadership than the movement for civil rights.

Civil rights volunteers, who came to the South in the days of frenzied activity, were motivated by idealism. They knew that a single individual's presence could make a difference in integrating a lunch counter, changing hiring practices in local downtown stores, canvassing for potential voters, or teaching young black children in Freedom Schools. Around such things, young people of the country could rally.

Time spent by affluent white students in the Mississippi Delta on the back roads in the homes of black citizens was a brand new life experience for both races. Interracial activity often led to interracial lovemaking and, in some cases, interracial marriages. A new day was dawning, a new way of thinking about life's possibilities. Then Martin Luther King Jr. was shot, and riots spread rapidly across the country. Once his voice was stopped, the movement grew quiet.

Since those days, there has been time for reflection, as the last three stories in this collection demonstrate. In each of these stories, a character looks back on his or her past actions or inactions during the era. In "Flora Devine" (1995), an aging would-be activist is haunted by her failure to become involved; taking action now against a Confederate flag suggests that it may not be too late to right old wrongs. "Paying My Dues" (1996), set mostly in 1960 Virginia, spotlights a moment in the movement when white men learned they could be part of something bigger than themselves. In the story, the narrator recounts being sent to Lynchburg, Virginia, along with two friends, during the period of the sit-ins, to support a picket line at Woolworth's. Eventually, a black lawyer uses a white volunteer in a hoax on a southern courtroom. The anthology ends with "To My Young Husband" (2000), wherein the first-person narrator relives days spent in Mississippi decades ago, trying to figure out what happened and why and how it all came to an end.

As these stories make clear, we have a compelling need to review our days, to think about those periods of life that took everything we had and to which we were willing to give all that we had. It makes sense that we cannot shake such times easily.

Flora Devine

Born in Charlottesville, Virginia, Anthony Grooms (1955–) is a poet, short-story writer, playwright, and novelist. A recipient of several Fulbrights, he is a professor of English at Kennesaw State University near Atlanta, Georgia. "Flora Devine" is in his 1995 collection, *Trouble No More*, winner of the Lillian Smith Award.

During the perilous days of segregation, the Crossed Bars was a rowdy, blue-collar lounge frequented by aging WSB radio stars and Ku Klux Klansmen. The radio stars, people like Fiddlin' Tom Benson and Peewee White, hung around the front of the long bar that ran right down the middle of the large square room. The bar was a rectangle with a narrow island in the middle which held all the liquor and glasses. In the back, away from the windows, the Klansmen met. No one bothered them, unless summoned. In the front were pictures of country-and-western singers, both the local WSB performers and famous ones from around the country. In the back, barely lit, hung a Confederate flag.

But new times had come, and little was left of the Crossed Bars clientele. The only ruckus the old men who now populated the bar caused was an occasional beef over a game score or a pinch to the rear of one of the women. The women knew how to handle rough play. It was the kind of place where a woman did not wear a dress.

Flora Devine wore a dress. Joe, the bartender, looked up when she came in. He did not take his eyes off her for a moment, but not because of her color. Black girls, usually prostitutes, came in all the time and caused no trouble. And not because she was pretty. Though neatly dressed, she was middle-aged, and had a plain, worried face. He stared because she seemed strange to him. Sad. Sad eyes. Sad mouth. A sad stooped, slow walk. Even her hair, held by bobby pins, seemed to lie as if someone shaken by grief had styled it. She made him nervous.

"Can I help you, ma'am?" Joe said. He was in his late twenties, a business college graduate. "Ma'am, can I help you?"

Flora came to the bar, across from Joe, and said nothing. She stared past him into the dimly lit back of the room where the flag hung. She stared so hard that Joe looked over his shoulder to see what she was staring at. He cast a bemused look at Smith, a regular, and turned back to the frail, watery-eyed woman. "What will you have, ma'am?"

"What's this place known for?" Flora asked. She placed her satchel on a barstool and continued to look around. She had been wandering for two days, looking for a fight. Now she knew she was at the right place. It had an old smell to it, something other than the smell of stale beer and burger grease. It was something ghostly and deadly. Something she had run from all her life until now: she smelled death. It smelled like sweat. Like dust. Like old wood. It made her bones ache. It frightened her.

"She's one of them crazies, Joe," Smith said. "You'd just as soon scoot her on out the door before she causes some trouble."

"She's OK," Joe answered, but was still examining Flora. "She looks harmless. She can sit unless she causes trouble."

"Hell, I'd kick 'er, Joe. I wouldn't give her a chance to put a knife in my back. You heard about that loony down on Ponce de Leon last week? Had an attack and stuck a couple of people with a' ice pick. Nearly killed one of 'em."

"She's OK, Smith," Joe said.

Flora blushed when she realized the men were talking about her. She had been studying the Confederate flag which hung so that its crossbars made a vertical X, like a standing man. "The old rascal," she had been thinking. "Old Mr. Man, old Mr. Dixie himself." She had had plenty of trouble over the years, and in some way, Mr. Dixie had always been there.

Her earliest memory of the crossed-bar symbol was seeing it flying on a flagpole at the black elementary school. It was in the mid-fifties, and the state had just changed its Bonnie Blue, the colonial flag, to one that incorporated the Confederate symbol. She asked her teacher why the flag had been changed. The teacher crossed her arms and snorted. "It's a reminder so that you will never forget."

"A reminder of what?"

"What you already know, or will learn soon enough." The teacher had walked away, but her words bothered Flora. A few days later she asked again. The teacher laughed and patted her on the head. "Misery. Misery, my sweet child. Nothing but misery." She laughed again, a high, hollow sound. "You'll get used to it."

From that time Flora saw the crossed bars everywhere, not only on flagpoles but in other places, too. It flew on aerials from pickup trucks. It was plastered on billboards. On television men waved it at the cameras. Every time she saw it, she thought about the teacher. "Misery. Nothing but misery." The teacher had been laughing when she had said it, but even in her laughter there had been sadness.

After she finished high school, Flora attended an all-black college. The college, located in a quiet town, was isolated from the civil rights protests in the cities. To Flora, the movement seemed to unfold at a distance, as though it were an event in a foreign country. She learned about Goodman, Schwerner and Chaney from television.[1] She read about Malcolm X in newspapers.[2] When SNCC or SCLC recruiters came to her campus,[3] she listened and agreed with them and sometimes gave money to the cause, but only once was she tempted to commit to activism.

The day of Martin Luther King's funeral, some of the professors organized a march. A group of about fifty planned to march once around the campus and then across the railroad tracks into downtown.[4] They would stop at the courthouse steps and say a prayer for Dr. King. The march around the campus was successful, but when the group reached the campus gates, it was met by the sheriff's deputies who ordered them back to their dormitories. Flora was at the back of the group and couldn't hear the exchange between the march leaders and the deputies. A cry went up from the crowd, and those at the front turned and began to flee. Flora

1. Andrew Goodman (1943–64), Michael Schwerner (1939–64), and James Chaney (1943–64) were civil rights workers who were killed in June 1964, in Philadelphia, Mississippi. Their bodies were found in August, after a massive FBI hunt. Goodman, a Freedom Summer volunteer, had been in the state twenty-four hours. Schwerner, one of the organizers, had been there for six months. Chaney, a black native Mississippian, was on the Freedom Summer staff.

2. Malcolm X (1925–65) was assassinated in Manhattan in February 1965. The militancy espoused in his speeches provided an alternative to Martin Luther King Jr.'s position of nonviolence.

3. The Student Nonviolent Coordinating Committee and the Southern Christian Leadership Conference were two organizations through which one could become involved in civil rights activities.

4. Impromptu marches from campus to the downtown courthouse were popular protests at historically black colleges throughout the South in April 1968.

saw one of her professors holding his head and another being helped toward the infirmary. The march was dispersed so suddenly she didn't panic; rather, it seemed to her that she was dreaming. People moved in one direction, then another, like corralled cattle. She caught a glimpse of a flag, whether state or Confederate she couldn't tell, and for the first time she understood what her teacher had meant about misery.

Few people were in the barroom: a black man slumped on his stool to Flora's left; a couple sat in a nearby booth; a waitress, smoking and drinking, shuffled between the tables and the back end of the bar. In the corner, against the wall where the flag hung, sat a solitary man. Flora could not see his face. She only saw his cigarette brighten when he inhaled. Country music played on the jukebox.

"I . . . I'll . . . have a beer," Flora said to the bartender, who was just turning away.

"Ma'am?"

"A beer, please."

"You know it'll cost you a dollar and a quarter."

Flora stared stonily. She made a show of taking a twenty-dollar bill out of her purse and flattening it on the countertop. "You don't have anything for twenty, do you?"

"No, ma'am," Joe said, "I just thought . . ."

"You just thought 'cause I'm black . . ."

"No, ma'am!" Joe held out his hands to her. "I didn't think that at all. Honest."

"Crossed Bars." Flora tossed her head. "Crossed Bars. You think I don't know what that means?"

"Ma'am?"

"Steppin' Fetchit over there may not know." Flora nodded toward the old black man. "But I know."

"Ma'am," Joe said, "we don't allow that kind of talk in here. Tyroll is a valued customer of ours. We don't go for that kind of name-calling in here."

"What do you go for then?"

"Kick 'er, Joe," Smith said.

Joe considered for a moment. "Ma'am. What kind of beer do you want? We got Schlitz and we got Old Milwaukee."

"That figures," Flora said. "And I wanted me a Colt 45."

"You'll have to go somewhere else to get it."

"I'll have a . . . ," Flora paused to exaggerate her indecisiveness, and then ordered. "The Crossed Bars," she said, emphasizing "crossed." "Do you know why it's called the Crossed Bars?"

"If you've got a problem with it, you can go somewhere else."

"I *do* have a problem with it." Flora tasted the beer, just wetting her lips on the foamy head.

Joe went to the other end of the bar and wiped the counter. Smith shook his head and talked to himself. "Was a time you could come in here—go into anyplace up Ponce de Leon—the Blue Light, MacHenry's, Sam and Dick's—anyplace on Ponce, on North, and things were just nice and peaceful. No foolishness whatsoever. The colored, they had their own over on Dekalb and on Hunter. Nobody bothered nobody. We just had it peaceful."

"Cut the baloney," Joe snapped at him. "You know it wasn't so peaceful. Just a bunch of Cabbagetown hillbillies cutting each other up. And the other side wasn't any better. Isn't that right, Tyroll?"

The old man, half asleep, raised his head from his chest. "Uhh?"

"I said . . . Never mind."

"Tell me something," Flora called to Joe. "If things are so different now, how come you still flying the old stars and bars? How come you still got them pinned up high so everybody can see? And how come you don't change the name of this place?"

Joe came back to confront Flora. "Say what you want. It's not what you think. Look, you're black . . ."

Flora made a mockery by looking at her hands.

"You know what I mean! You have a heritage. Well, so do I. And that's part of my heritage. Can't I display my own heritage?"

"That's telling her," Smith said.

Flora smiled and sipped her beer. She felt strong and much happier now than when she had come in. "Listen. That old banner you white folks are so proud of . . . you know what that means to me? While you calling the name of Robert E. Lee and Jeff Davis, I see nothing but slaves. You know that? It's *my damn heritage, too*. That's why I'm going to go up there and tear it down and *stamp* on it."

"I ain't owned a slave in a long time," Smith said to the couple in the booth, but the two paid no attention.

"What is your problem? What do you want? Nobody in here's done a damn thing to you," Joe said to Flora.

"It's what you stand for." She was enjoying the argument. "It's your system—that flag—the Crossed Bars. You haven't changed a bit. Now, the law has made some changes, but it's places like this that's got to change."

The young man laughed. "Come on, ma'am. We aren't prejudice'. Hell, I believe in justice and freedom for all, just like you do."

The solitary man crossed the room and went toward the door. He was lean and young and looked unhappy. As he reached for the door he studied Flora. Flora could feel him looking at her, but she did not look back. She was afraid; he made her bones ache.

"You come back," Joe called to the man.

The man said nothing and pushed through the door.

The waitress came up to the bar. "That jerk didn't leave me a cent."

"Run out and ask him," Joe said.

"The hell if I am," the waitress turned away. "He was a weird one. I tell ya."

"You get *all* types." Smith rolled his eyes at Flora.

"Don't you roll those bug eyes at me. You don't know who I am. You don't remember me, do you?"

"Me?" Smith said.

"Not you." Flora sneered. "You wouldn't." She pointed to Joe. "Aww, but . . . you're probably too young. You have heard of Rosa Parks?" Tyroll lifted his head and stared at Flora. "What about Martin Luther King?"

"You mean Martin Luther Coon." Smith laughed.

"Shut up, Smith," Joe said. "Martin Luther King was a great American hero."

"Where did you learn that?" Flora tilted her head at Joe.

"At school. Hell, everybody knows that."

"What do you know about Martin Luther King?" Flora shook her head and sipped.

"I know as much as you." Joe threw the dish towel into the sink. "Just because I'm white doesn't mean I can't appreciate what black people have been through. I have black friends, you know."

Flora let her voice sound flat to emphasize her incredulity. "I'm sure you do. Steppin' Fetchit and who else? Young folks like you who haven't lived through anything yet. I lived through it, you see. So when I say Martin was a good man, I know what I'm talking about. I'm not just mouthing something I read."

"Are you trying to tell me you knew Martin Luther King?"

Flora held the glass to her lips and closed her eyes. She was feeling less happy now. Misery was creeping up on her. She was going to lie, and she didn't want to. On the other hand, she couldn't face the truth just then. She put down the glass and faced Joe. "More than just knew him. I used to march all over Georgia, all over the South."

"You knew him? For real? You helped him? What's your name?"

"Flora Devine."

At the end of a long pause Joe let out a guffaw. "No, ma'am. I'm sorry. I never heard of you."

Two years after the aborted march, she moved to Atlanta, and for the first and only time she visited the King grave site. That was as close as she ever got to Martin Luther King. Looking at the crypt with its "Free At Last" message, she shivered and drew close to her husband and baby. Her husband put his arm around her to comfort her. "No," she said, "it's not that." Then she knew she would have a hard time explaining. It was not grief she was feeling but a deeper regret. Remorse. "I should have done something for the movement. Joined SNCC, or marched, or something."

Her husband, a man ten years her senior, laughed. "You'll do well enough just to do well. Raise baby Priscilla and keep food on the table." His smile encouraged her. "There's more than one way to help the movement." She took the baby from her husband's arms and hugged her. She would dedicate this child to Martin Luther King. She would do the best she could to realize in her child the dream King spoke about.

For the next ten years, life went as she expected. She was one of the first black teachers to integrate the public schools. The position seemed an honor. She felt she was helping King's dream come true. But in just a few years after integration, all the white students had moved away. Even though her school remained a good school in a good neighborhood, it became as segregated as before the law had changed. Like the schools of her childhood, the crossed bars flew over this school, too.

Her husband, a Meharry-trained dentist,[5] never established a strong practice. He made the mistake of locating his office in the main shopping mall. Since blacks were deserting the old black business districts in droves to shop in the white-owned mall, he thought the mall location would be perfect for attracting both black and white clientele. However, neither blacks nor whites who came to the mall were looking for a black doctor. Flora argued with her husband that he should move his office to a black neighborhood. The issue became a point of pride for Dr. Devine, and he stayed at the mall until the practice went bankrupt. Unfortunately for Flora, her husband associated his business failure with his marriage and left her for a new life in California. The divorce intensified the gnawing guilt she had about having been complacent in an inequitable country, but worse, she felt powerless, too.

Smith called to Tyroll, "You ever hear of 'er?"

Tyroll studied her. His yellowed eyes struggled to focus.

"He don't know you from Eve," Smith said.

Flora took a long drink from the beer and waited for the alcohol to make her feel warm. The effect was slow to come, and when it did, it was not warmth but a slow spinning sensation. Her breath became shallow, and she began to examine her chapped hands. They seemed to belong to a stranger. Smith's laughter was a backdrop to the dense confusion of noises in her own head. What was she trying to prove, wandering around the city looking for a Confederate flag to tear down? Why was she drawn to this place when the flags were everywhere? Dixie this and Dixie that. On bumper stickers. In the newspaper. On T-shirts. Everywhere she turned was a reminder. She thought about her daughter.

"Have you ever had a day . . . ," she mumbled.

"Ma'am?" Joe called to her. "Are you all right?"

"Have you ever had a day when it felt like the earth wasn't moving?

---

5. Meharry Medical College, open since 1876, is located in Nashville, Tennessee. Today it is the largest private comprehensive historically black institution for the training of health-care professionals.

You wake up, and the sunlight is not streaming through the window; it's just a bright gray light from an overcast sky. You don't hear birds in the trees. No sound. Not even traffic. Outside everything is so still you think everything must be dead. So you just lie. You lie like you're dead. Whether you lie for minutes or for hours, you don't know. The light doesn't change; there is no sound. Things are so quiet, so still, you think that you have to move. You have to make some noise. So you get up and go to the window. You see that the sky is blue, and you think, 'What a fool, I have been lying up in bed all this time on such a blue day.' But the blue is deeper than sky blue. It's even deeper than the blue-black of storm clouds. There are no clouds, just this deep, flat blue. You look higher in the sky, and you see why. It's not the sky you're looking at. It's a giant flag, and the blue background of one bar. Across the sky, like two high rainbows, are a crisscross of stars." Flora's voice trailed off and there was silence for a moment.

"I told you she was a loon," Smith said.

Tyroll asked Joe for another drink, but Joe ignored him. "Ma'am, can I call someone for you? You got family?"

"Family?" Flora's hands trembled as she pressed her hair against her skull and smoothed her clothes. "I had a daughter. Her name was Priscilla. She was fifteen."

"*Was* fifteen? I'm sorry," Joe said. He had learned in these situations not to ask questions but just to let the customers talk. They would tell as much as they wanted to. He waited a moment for Flora to continue, and when she didn't he asked, "What happened to Priscilla?"

Flora looked directly at Joe. She smiled. Her voice was soft and musical. "She was killed."

Joe leaned toward her. Now she seemed so fragile to him, not at all the argumentative woman of a few minutes ago. He swallowed hard. "How was she killed?"

Flora looked past Joe. "That flag. That flag killed her. That's why I'm going to stamp on it."

"Bullshit!" Smith said. "You can't blame everything on us. We don't do everything that's wrong with the world."

"As sure as I'm breathing, that flag killed her."

"Kick 'er, Joe. Boot 'er right out the door."

"I used to march all over the South. Used to sit in at lunch counters."

"You ain't did nothing. Kick 'er, Joe."

"You don't know her, do you Tyroll?" Joe asked.

Tyroll wiped his face with his palm.

"He don't know you. Never heard of you. You just another one of these crazies come in from Milledgeville.[6] Crazy as a loon in June. Kick 'er out, Joe."

Flora felt Tyroll studying her. She threw back her head, trying to appear confident, but she could not look at him. She looked at the flag, then glanced across the room to the couple in the booth who were locked in embrace.

"Flora Devine." She tossed her name out carelessly, not thinking to aim it at Tyroll. "Flora Devine. I marched in Selma." She thought to berate Tyroll. What did he know? He was just a drunk. "I marched in Selma."[7]

"You marched to the toilet," Smith said. "To the goddamn toilet 'n' back."

Tyroll cleared his throat. "I reckon I know her," he said slowly. "I reckon I do."

"Who is she then?" Smith pressed.

"I seen her on the TV."

"Who is she then?"

Tyroll looked uneasy. "She who she say she is." He ran his palm over his face and let his head slump.

"Flora Devine." She lifted her head. "Thank you, sir." She turned to Joe and Smith. "You see who I am."

"I'm sorry, ma'am," Joe said.

"Shit!" Smith said.

"Be respectable," Joe warned him.

"Yes," Flora said. "You all should be respectable and take down that flag. Change the name of this place."

---

6. Milledgeville, Georgia, is the home of Central State Hospital, Georgia's largest facility for persons with mental illnesses.

7. Thousands of people came from all over the country to participate in some aspect of the fifty-mile walk from Selma to Montgomery. At the destination point, the state capitol, there were about thirty thousand people present. Because the concluding rally was so large, it was easy to say one had been there, even if one had not.

"I can't do that," Joe said. "I'm not the owner, and besides, the customers like it."

"I'm a customer," Flora said. Her energy was waning. "He's a customer." She pointed to Tyroll.

"I'm a customer, too," Smith said.

Her nerve was going. The sadness was beginning to creep up on her. "Here." She shoved the twenty at Joe. "Take my money."

"Oh, no, ma'am. It's on the house."

"Don't insult me. I can pay."

Joe took the money and went to get the change.

Flora was standing, steadying herself against the bar. She moved a step toward Smith and stopped. He was drinking a Schlitz from the can. His face was haggard and grizzly with white stubs of beard. "Now take my friend, Tyroll, over there," he said, his roan teeth showing. "Tyroll 'n' me been knowing each other since we were boys—'n' we always got along. You just got to know where you are wanted."

Flora stepped the other way toward Tyroll. His chin was slumped on his chest. He looked asleep, but his hand rubbed the bald spot on his head. Taking her hand from the counter only long enough to get around Tyroll, Flora unsteadily walked toward the flag. The X, the bars, were taller than a man. It was a Confederate soldier or one of Bull Connor's policemen with raised billy club.[8] The rest of the barroom was a blur as she tunneled down the length of the counter toward the flag.

"Wouldn't do that if I were you, ma'am," Joe said.

She heard him but reached out for the flag and twisted the corner of it into her fist. The fabric was old and soft and her fingers easily punched through it.

"Don't do that!" Joe shouted. "I told you I'm not the owner."

Flora increased the tension on the flag, pulling it away from the wall. A rip began on one side about halfway up the X. "I'm gone get that man in there.[9] You see him? I'm gone cut him in half before he gets to me."

8. Theophilus Eugene "Bull" Connor (1897–1973) was the commissioner of Public Safety for Birmingham, Alabama, in the spring of 1963. Under his authority and armed with billy clubs, police arrested and jailed about twenty-five hundred children and adults.

9. From 1956 to 2001, over half of Georgia's state flag was a Confederate flag, crossed blue bars, containing thirteen white stars, over a red field. On the left side of the flag, in a vertical blue strip, was the seal of the state of Georgia. Within the seal, standing under an archway, was a very small soldier.

After the divorce, she and Priscilla moved into an apartment complex located along a busy highway. The children who lived in the complex often took a shortcut across the highway in order to get to school.

One day when Flora came home from teaching, a policeman stopped her outside the apartment door. "Are you Mrs. Devine?" he asked. He was sandy-haired and baby-faced, too young to be a policeman, she thought. "I'm sorry to inform you," he said. "There has been an accident. It was bound to happen. It could have happened to anyone."

Flora remained calm. She kept thinking about what a lovely day it was. How the big, white clouds were rolling across the sky. She went to the morgue to identify Priscilla's jewelry. They wouldn't let her see the body. The truck driver who had hit Priscilla was waiting outside the morgue. He was a stout, grizzled white man. He had been crying. He took Flora's hand. "I swear, I didn't see her. I didn't see her," he said. Flora accepted his apology. She walked in a circle. "Can I take you home?" he asked. She declined. He sat her on a bench outside the morgue.

"Is that the truck?" she asked. It was a semi. On the grill was painted a Confederate flag.

"Crazy bitch," Smith shouted. "Do that 'n' I'm fixin' to kick yo' black ass out of here myself." Flora pulled again. Dust flew up and the rip made its way to the waist of the X but did not cut it.

Joe had come through the gate in the counter. He walked slowly with both palms out. "Ma'am, I don't want to call the police. I can appreciate what you want, but there's nothing I can do about it. What's past is past. We have got to think about the future."

"I just want to get that man!"

"This is not the way to do it. This will only cause trouble."

"Ain' no trouble for me." Flora jerked. A long ripping sound knifed the room. Except for Tyroll, the customers were looking at Flora and the flag, but no one, not even Smith, moved.

The night was moonless and a fog had settled along Ponce de Leon Avenue. Flora only vaguely knew where she was. She lived in Westend and she needed to find a bus stop. She walked through two boarded-up blocks, and in the third, near a pawnshop, she saw the bus stop next to a telephone pole. She steadied herself against the pole. About her, in the fog, the streetlights glowed in eerie yellow spheres. A car passed. She closed her eyes. She heard nothing.

Suddenly an arm was around her neck. She could not scream. She was dragged into the darkness of a back alley. Her heels drummed across the asphalt. She clawed at the forearms, digging her fingertips into the sinew. Her ears were ringing. Her head was swelling from lack of breath. She flailed. She tasted the sweaty, hairy forearm. Her heels made music on the pavement. She was dropped on her back. She gasped. The air rushed in, hurting her throat.

She could not see the man, but she knew he stood over her. Suddenly his face glowed in the flare of a match as he lit a cigarette. She struggled to stand, but the man pushed her down and sat on her knees. He put the blade of a hunting knife to her throat.

"Do you know who I am?" he whispered. "Do you know who I am?" She did not answer. "Do you know who I am?" Ashes from the cigarette fell on her chest and burned her. The knife punctured the skin under her neck. "Answer me," he pleaded. "Do you know who I am?"

"Yes. You're Mr. Dixie."

He took the blade from her throat and held it arm's length above his head. "I'm Mr. Death," he said. "Just Death to you."

She heard the first thud as the blade struck her chest, and she heard the dozen that followed, but they seemed to become fainter and fainter as if coming from a greater and greater distance. After awhile, the man went away.

Quiet followed, but she was not afraid. Then there were lights and voices. She heard someone ask, "Who is she? Do you know who she is?"

"Flora Devine," she thought. "Flora Devine."

VAL COLEMAN

Paying My Dues

Val Coleman (1930–) is the author of ten plays and a book of short stories. He
was the director of public information for twenty-two years at the New York City
Housing Authority. During the civil rights movement, he was a press secretary
for CORE. He has also taught at Columbia University. "Paying My Dues" is in
his 1996 collection, *Beverly and Marigold*.

It was like this: Three white guys, two of them drunk, were riding around
New York City in a 1950 Dodge in the fall of 1960. Happily, the driver
was sober, and the two drunks were in the backseat barking orders as
they studied a large road map of the city.

I barked first, "This is big! Twenty-six Woolworth stores and we got
fifteen covered. George!" I leaned over and tapped the driver, "head for
Forty-second and First. That's an NAACP picket line and they probably
won't show up."

"To hell with the NAACP," slobbered Jack Barney, my buddy in the
backseat who had a pint of Red Label in the vest pocket of his corduroy
jacket. "I have," he announced, "decided on the anthem! New lyrics to
'Onward Christian Soldiers'!"

There was a two-beat pause before George stomped on the brakes.
Jack and I pitched forward.

I cracked my head seriously on the driver's seat, and Jack dived all
the way over the front passenger seat and landed upside down looking *up*
at George, all pink and puckish and very drunk.

" 'Onward Christian Soldiers'?" said George Goldstein malevolently,
" 'Onward *Christian* Soldiers'!"

"I forgot," said upside-down Jack to rightside-up George, "a lot of the
Christian Soldiers will be Jewish."

This silly tableau in the middle of Manhattan traffic was all my sister's fault. About a year before, I had called her from my desk at United
Artists, where I had been stored in the publicity department by my ex-in-

laws. Sissy (she'll never forgive me for using her childhood nickname in this story) was already a big-shot doctor in Washington, D.C., and I was getting a reputation in the family as a loser and a drunk who was circling my destiny over a back booth of Jim Downey's saloon on Eighth Ave.

On the phone I told my sister that I hated the movie business and wanted to do something useful with my life. She suggested that I call Marvin Rich[1] at the National Office of CORE down on Park Row right across from City Hall.

You see, Sissy had paid her civil rights dues in the fifties as a leader of the Washington and Baltimore chapters of a tiny organization named the Congress of Racial Equality. CORE was eighteen years old in 1960, founded by James Farmer[2] in Chicago in 1942 when he and some friends had sat down to eat at Jack Spratt's, a segregated restaurant. Farmer had made the intellectual link between the nonviolence of Mahatma Gandhi and the struggle for Negro freedom. CORE had bumped along for those eighteen years with a scattering of chapters on the East Coast, and although they had organized some brave and spirited protests, nobody much noticed or cared, with the notable exception of the prescient Eleanor Roosevelt.

I called Marvin, and he was delighted to recruit an uptown publicity type. For years, CORE people had been quietly getting their heads cracked open, sitting-in in segregated restaurants, and Marvin, like crafty old Gandhi himself, knew the value of some serious New York ink.

Marvin even made me a member of the National Action Council of CORE. Since they met during the daytime, I was able to attend meetings sober and actually make some constructive suggestions.

Sissy was right; it was fast becoming a heady, exciting period in America, and I had, through a combination of boredom and luck, landed in the right place at the right time.

What we now call the movement really busted loose in February of 1960 when a group of black divinity students[3] sat down at a segregated Woolworth five-and-dime lunch counter in Greensboro, North Carolina.

---

1. At the time in which the story takes place, Marvin Rich served as the community relations director for the National CORE, the second highest executive position in CORE.
2. James Farmer (1920–99), working with George Houser (1916–) and Berniece Fisher, established CORE in 1942 in Chicago. CORE pioneered nonviolent direct action, especially sit-ins and freedom rides.
3. In real life, the four young men credited with starting the sit-in phase of the movement on February 1, 1960, were not divinity students; they were undergraduates at North Carolina A & T University.

They were promptly arrested and thrown in jail.[4] CORE got the word in New York and immediately sent one of our best field organizers, Gordon Carey, down to Greensboro to conduct workshops in nonviolence and try to spread the protest around the South to other Woolworth lunch counters. Woolworth was a godsend, a very visible national chain that was everybody's next-door neighbor, an American fixture that turned pocket change into pennywhistles and even had a scandalous heiress romping around the world marrying everybody in sight.

The Woolworth lunch counter sit-ins spread all over. Gordon had been busy.

Up in New York City we called for a national boycott of Woolworth stores everywhere in the nation. Marvin Rich, the steady hand on CORE's tiller, then made a mistake. He asked me to help organize the Woolworth picketing.

I immediately recruited my two smartest drinking buddies, Jack Barney and George Goldstein, and we bought a map of the five boroughs, a cork bulletin board, and some colored pushpins. We figured out where the Woolworth stores were and got on the phone, calling every organization we could think of to join us on picket lines throughout the city.

It must've been time. Everybody we called said yes.

And that was why three smart-assed white boys were running around New York City in a 1950 Dodge convinced we were God's gift to a fledgling civil rights movement that breathlessly awaited our decision on such matters as where to demonstrate, what to wear, and what to sing.

" 'The Battle Hymn of the Republic'!" squealed Jack. "New lyrics!"

"You're gonna improve on 'trampling out the vintage where the grapes of wrath are stored'?" asked George.

"And we oughta wear suits," I added. "Everybody wears a black suit with a black tie. Long black picket lines against the horizon," I saw the future, "with umbrellas!"

"Umbrellas!" shouted Jack, "that's our symbol! Great black umbrellas everywhere! Even on the stationery!"

"Not bad," agreed George. "I like the umbrellas, but the suits are out."

"What's wrong with the suits?" I asked.

4. In real life, the students were not arrested and did not go to jail.

"Too expensive," said George sternly, "and too hot in the South."

"Right," I said. "Forget the suits."

Despite the sophomoric, patronizing dialogue, it was, in the end, some serious business. After all, Jack Barney, George Goldstein, and, yes, even I, Beverly Reynolds, were there, in the early years of this nation's first healing since Reconstruction. We may have been fast-talkin' pompous little wiseguys from New York, but we *were there*, taking our turn in the American lists, trying to fix things that had been broken for five hundred years.

We had always been great talkers and had closed a lot of bars pontificating about the lot of our Negro brothers, but this time we were actually doing something about it. It was just too goddamn good to be true. We simply didn't know what to do with our good luck, so we drank whiskey, composed slogans, and walked in circles. Don't misunderstand me. We were little more than bit players, extras . . . but that was a good deal more than most folks.

As I look back, I can see that our principal problem was that we didn't know much about the people we had set out to save. Being black in America in 1960 was to have an ancestry of insult, a great accumulation of small and large grievances, a five-hundred-year pile of torn promises with the Emancipation Proclamation lying somewhere in the middle.

For example, when CORE's senior black field secretary, Sam Briscoe, got home from the Second World War, he started taking his neighbors down to the courthouse in Sumter, South Carolina, to register to vote. He figured he'd earned it. They goddamn near lynched him.

So the three guys in the Dodge were something of an absurdity, a made-in-America absurdity. But it was a new beginning, and new beginnings required new tactics and all sorts of lunatics.

As we turned the corner at First Avenue and Forty-second Street, Jack Barney, author of "The Battle Hymn of the Republic" plan, suddenly said, "Everybody shut up and listen."

I was wrong. The NAACP picket line was enormous, running the entire length of the long red Woolworth sign. But the marchers were absolutely still, surrounding a tall young man with a big old twelve-string guitar. He had a cranky, aching voice that could break your heart. He was singing an old song on a new stage.

It was Pete Seeger,[5] and for the first time in our lives we heard "We Shall Overcome."

Somewhere through here, the three musketeers got our first lesson in humility when we met Bill Smoke. Attorney Smoke was a careless, noisy, wise, and funny black lawyer who liked himself so much that he was honestly astonished that racial discrimination existed at all.

Bill popped into the civil rights family without so much as a nod and immediately saw himself as man of policy who would reorganize the movement, parse the future, and generally straighten out this clutch of white boys who had fallen into what was to be, in Bill's words, America's "redemption." He went to work on George, Jack, and me with a lot of such talk, and we were quickly and properly riddled with guilt. We actually moved our regular saloon from Louie's on Sheridan Square to Gar's Bar on Park Row to accommodate our new drinking partner who held forth with blood-soaked African-American history and ways to whack the common law into line.

If we were the musketeers, Bill was the king of France.

One thing about Bill Smoke, you didn't make jokes about his last name. To this day, I don't know if it was his real name, but Bill played it like a virtuoso, lying in wait for you to say something racial like "Smoky" so he could strafe you with something like, "You peckerwood son of a bitch! You wanna say 'nigger' say 'nigger'! You Irish cracker! Be a man! Spit it out!"

After which I would pick up my pieces and leave the room.

By now it was getting to be the early winter of 1960 and, as you know, New York City doesn't work in the winter. Elevators panic, the subway ices up, and people generally lose touch with one another separated by fat coats and knit caps that cover your face.

The Woolworth picket lines dwindled as it got colder, and the three musketeers and the king of France zipped around town in the old Dodge trying to find ways to keep the things happening. We got the phone num-

5. Recipient of the Kennedy Center Honors Award and the National Medal of Arts, Pete Seeger (1919–) was a leader in the revival of interest in folk music in mid-twentieth-century America. His version of an old spiritual, "We Shall Overcome," became the anthem for the civil rights movement.

ber of David Susskind,[6] the father of the television talk show, and convinced him that a two-hour debate on civil rights was long overdue. The problem was that we couldn't find anybody to argue with us until Ralph Kilpatrick agreed to join the panel. In the end, he gave as good as he got from this covey of amateurs who had just been flushed out of Gar's Bar.

And there were terrible and wounding days to come. Over the next five years more than thirty civil rights workers would be killed and literally hundreds battered and beaten in the struggle. Hundreds of thousands of days would be spent in the prisons and county jails of the South, and grand and eloquent men like James Farmer would emerge from years of waiting to capture the day.

Even the booze diminished for a while. I remember a particularly sober and touching evening when the four of us visited the playwright Lorraine Hansberry,[7] who was profoundly ill and talked to us from her bed. I don't remember everything she said, but her eyes burned through me when she talked of what she called the "unspeakable" history of the black American, and she asked each of us to embrace her briefly as she gave us her blessing and our fiercest challenge. She died untimely on the threshold.

We were much too busy to notice Christmas, but I distinctly remember carols coming out of Gar's jukebox when somebody rushed in and told us that Marvin Rich wanted to see Bill and me upstairs. The messenger added cryptically, "You're going south."

You see, the civil rights movement had not yet achieved its "Selma celebrity,"[8] so Marvin was short of troops and reduced to sending bozos like me on missions to the South. We were chasing butterflies and one had landed on the Woolworth lunch counter in Lynchburg, Virginia. (Before I forget, Lynchburg was allegedly named after John Lynch, whose last name became a verb because his brother Charles loved to string up the

6. David Susskind (1920–87) was a longtime television talk show host during the middle years of the twentieth century. Although he had a reputation for being confrontational and arrogant, several presidents agreed to be on his show.

7. Lorraine Hansberry (1930–65), award-winning playwright of *A Raisin in the Sun*, was a civil rights activist. She died from cancer at the age of thirty-five.

8. Those who walked from Selma to Montgomery to protest the need for voting-rights legislation in 1965 achieved a bit of fame, especially if they were involved in "Bloody Sunday," on March 7, 1965, when state troopers attacked the marchers with clubs and tear gas.

neighbors. More recently, Jerry Falwell[9] tastefully chose Lynchburg as the home of his ministry.)

Anyway, an almost saintly, disciplined group of black Baptist students had asked to be served at the Woolworth in Lynchburg, and the whole lot of them had been roughed up and tossed in jail. Their first court appearance was in two days and Marvin had made arrangements for Bill Smoke to be their lawyer. We had a policy that nobody traveled alone, so I was chosen to make the trip with Bill.

Now understand what we're talking about here. We're talking about a zany, certifiable black attorney and a permanently hung-over white wimp being sent into battle armed with only the moral brass of Mahatma Gandhi and what the Irish call a terrible thirst.

We took the train to Washington, D.C., that evening, rented a car, and headed west into Virginia in the middle of a moonless night.

I drove. After all. Bill was the king of France, and the king of France has a chauffeur, right?

I like to tell this story in four parts.

Our first stop was for gas, a rookie civil rights worker mistake for not topping off the tank in Washington. The gas station was a small stain of fluorescent light in the Virginia backwoods, and as we got closer I saw a lot of very tough-looking white guys in bib overalls squeezing beer cans and sitting on the hoods of two pickup trucks. The trucks had shotgun racks in the back windows.

Bill said, "Pull in," and like a lemming, I obeyed.

We both got out and Bill got a skull-faced young man to fill the tank. Now remember, this was 1960, and the sight of a black man and a white man, traveling together, dressed in city clothes, raised the local temperature ever so much. The white guys jumped down off the trucks and were headed slowly in our direction when Bill decided to raise the ante.

He kissed me.

That's right, a big, wet kiss right on the mouth.

The rednecks went crazy.

Somebody screamed "get 'em!" and a bent beer can bounced off my

---

9. Pastor of Lynchburg's Thomas Road Baptist Church with over twenty thousand members, founder of the Moral Majority and Liberty University, Jerry Falwell (1933–) is one of the country's most vocal conservative evangelical ministers.

elbow as we jumped in the car and took off. The nozzle of the gas hose yanked out and we thundered down the two-lane cement highway trailing a stream of fuel. The chase was on as both pickup trucks pulled onto the road and roared after us. I floored the accelerator and prayed that we had rented a Maserati. For about five minutes it was like a bad movie, but we slowly pulled away from the pickup trucks, and eventually they gave up.

During this entire episode Bill was laughing so hard that I got confused and instead of yelling obscenities at him, I began to wonder if this was some sort of formal hazing ritual that I was supposed to go through as a civil rights newcomer in the South. I had no idea that the simple truth was that I was, for the moment, hanging out with a madman.

That's one.

Bill stole a gas cap in the next town. Thanks a lot, Bill.

We dawdled the next fifty miles or so and arrived in Hopewell, Virginia, where another demonstration had taken place, to file some papers when the courthouse opened at nine A.M. They were important papers, various motions, appropriate and even sometimes crucial in civil rights cases. As we rode into Hopewell, I noticed that Bill was erasing the names, dates, and signatures on the papers, and as soon as we came to a stop, he lettered in new names and dates and re-signed them with a different name.

I said, "Is that legal? Don't we have to be very careful down here? Don't they throw away the key for the slightest little thing?"

Bill Smoke smiled wearily and said, "These peckerwoods can't read."

Not reassured, I drove on to Lynchburg, and we pulled up in front of the Woolworth at about ten o'clock.

It was a thrilling, stirring scene. Maybe fifty young black men and women, dressed in blue and black college uniforms, were walking a slow circle in front of the store. Their absolute, disciplined silence at the center of a howling, livid mob of white Lynchburg citizens was magnificent. I saw for the first time what we had been talking about up in New York. There was a lucid, abiding strength in that picket line that would surely overcome any resistance that the South, with all its brutal history, could muster.

Bill and I joined the line. We grabbed cardboard placards and started circling. The crowd enclosing the picket line could easily spot an outsider, particularly a white one, and someone immediately spat on me and screamed, "Nigger lover!"

We went round and round, the temper of the crowd rising with each circuit. I saw Bill whispering to the student leaders. He walked over to me and said, "I'll be right back."

With that, everyone on our side disappeared. *Disappeared!* The students melted away, Bill melted away, and I was left alone in the middle of a mob. I looked down at the forlorn sign that had been looped around my neck, saying something heroic like FREEDOM NOW, and the crowd began to close in. I remember one particularly ugly, skinny old man who had his hand in his pocket as if he were fingering a knife or a gun. I was going to be goddamned if I was going to run, but I gotta tell you I was heart-attack scared. It lasted maybe five minutes, but I was sure an hour had passed before I heard the screech of a car and I cut through the mob to the curb to see my pal Bill roar up in our car, throw open the passenger door, and yell, "Jump in, hero!"

That's two.

By this time I was an emotional wreck. I had been up all night, kissed, deserted, and nearly killed, but William Smoke, Esquire, was having the time of his life. As we sped away down Main Street, he slapped me on the back and pronounced, "Well done!"

All I could do was sputter.

Now the reason we were in Lynchburg in the first place was to represent twenty-two young divinity students who had been jailed the week before and were due in court that morning. We drove directly to the courthouse and when we got inside, Bill put on his "serious advocate" look and asked me to sit next to him at the defense table. I was so disoriented by everything that I just sat down, suspecting nothing.

The twenty-two student defendants filed in respectfully and sat in two rows to our left. We were instructed to rise, and the judge came in, a wizened old specter who was probably the great-grandson of the city's namesake.

The judge banged his gavel, and Bill rose solemnly.

"Your honor," he said.

"Boy?" the judge answered.

"Your honor," Bill continued unperturbed, "I would like to introduce my distinguished colleague, the Honorable Beverly Reynolds, the assistant attorney general of the sovereign State of New York."

And he wasn't even smiling.

Here I was, in Lynchburg, Virginia, inside a heavily guarded courtroom, impersonating both a lawyer and a public official. If the judge had any idea I really was a quickly aging press agent, he probably would have hung me at sunrise.

But he didn't. He simply grumbled something about "Goddamn Yankees" and proceeded with the hearing. About a half hour later, with the hearing over and the kids sent back to jail for trying to eat lunch in a five-and-ten-cents store, we got the hell out of there. I was having severe breathing distress.

As soon as we were out of earshot of the courtroom, I started screaming, "What the hell was that? Attorney goddamn general of what?!"

That's three.

Bill suggested we have a drink. Finally we agreed on something. Finally it was over. Little did I know.

We headed for a bar in the black section of town. It was the first story of a three-story frame house, and it sported an aluminum sign announcing "Bernie's."

Bill said, "You go on in while I park the car."

I was very thirsty when I stepped through the front door. I was home. I was safe.

But then the whole place, including the jukebox, came to a sudden, deathly stop.

Apparently no white man had entered that saloon since 1873. I saw about thirty very angry black men, fists clenched, ready to do me in. Just as the bartender was reaching for his baseball bat, Bill came in behind me and held up both hands for silence.

"This," said William Sonofabitch Smoke, "is Beverly Reynolds, the brave young white boy from New York City who walked the picket line alone this morning!"

A rousing cheer went up and I was lifted and seated on the bar itself and supplied with liquor and congratulations late on into the night.

It was one hell of a party. It turned out that every secretary and janitor, every black worker on Main Street across from Woolworth, had watched me walk the picket line that morning, and I was, as Bill had announced, something of a local hero for a day.

That is four.

We slept it off in somebody's house that night. As an old veteran of the southern wars, I flew out the next morning back to New York City to lord it over Jack and George.

Bill headed west and south, chasing the butterfly of freedom.

I never saw him again.

ALICE WALKER

To My Young Husband

Born in Georgia, Alice Walker (1944–) is a poet, short-story writer, novelist, essayist, and activist. She began publishing during the latter part of the Black Arts movement in the 1960s. She is the recipient of both the Pulitzer Prize and the National Book Award. During the civil rights movement, she lived in Mississippi with her new husband. "To My Young Husband," from her 2000 collection, *The Way Forward Is with a Broken Heart*, is autobiographical.

Memoir of a Marriage

Beloved,

A few days ago I went to see the little house on R. Street where we were so happy. Before traveling back to Mississippi I had not thought much about it. It seemed so far away, almost in another dimension. Whenever I did remember the house it was vibrant, filled with warmth and light, even though, as you know, a lot of my time there was served in rage, in anger, in hopelessness and despair. Days when the white white walls, cool against the brutal summer heat, were more bars than walls.

You do not talk to me now, a fate I could not have imagined twenty years ago. It is true we say the usual greetings, when we have to, over the phone: How are you? Have you heard from Our Child? But beyond that, really nothing. Nothing of the secrets, memories, good and bad, that we shared. Nothing of the laughter that used to creep up on us as we ate together late at night at the kitchen table—perhaps after one of your poker games— and then wash over us in a cackling wave. You were always helpless before anything that struck you as funny, and I reveled in the ease with which, urging each other on, sometimes in our own voices, more often in a welter of black and white Southern and Brooklyn and Yiddish accents— which always felt as if our grandparents were joking with each other— we'd crumple over our plates laughing, as tears came to our eyes. After tallying up your winnings—you usually did win—and taking a shower—as I chatted with you through the glass—you'd crawl wearily into bed. We'd roll toward each other's outstretched arms, still chuckling, and sleep the sleep of the deeply amused.

I went back with the woman I love now. She had never been South, never been to Mississippi, though her grandparents are buried in one of the towns you used to sue racists in. We took the Natchez Trace from Memphis, stopping several times at points of interest along the way. Halfway to Jackson we stopped at what appeared to be a large vacant house, with a dogtrot that intrigued us from the road. But when we walked inside two women were quietly quilting. One of them was bent over a large wooden frame that covered most of the floor, like the one my mother used to have; the other sat in a rocking chair stitching together one of the most beautiful crazy quilts I've ever seen. It reminded me of the quilt I made while we were married, the one made of scraps from my African dresses. The huge dresses, kaftans really, that I sewed myself and wore when I was pregnant with Our Child.

The house on R. Street looked so small I did not recognize it at first. It was nearly dark by the time we found it, and sitting in a curve as it does it always seemed to be seeking anonymity. The tree we planted when Our Child was born and which I expected to tower over me, as Our Child now does, is not there; one reason I did not recognize the house. When I couldn't decide whether the house I was staring at was the one we used to laugh so much in, I went next door and asked for the Belts. Mrs. Belt (Did I ever know her name and call her by it? Was it perhaps Mildred?) opened the door. She recognized me immediately. I told her I was looking for our house. She said: That's it. She was surrounded by grandchildren. The little girl we knew, riding her tricycle about the yard, has made her a grandmother many times over. Her hair is pressed and waved, and is completely gray. She has aged. Though I know I have also, this shocks me. Mr. Belt soon comes to the door. He is graying as well, and has shaved his head. He is stocky and assertive. Self-satisfied. He insists on hugging me, which, because we've never hugged before, feels strange. He offers to walk me next door, and does.

Its gate is the only thing left of the wooden fence we put up. The sweet gum tree that dominated the backyard and turned to red and gold in autumn is dying. It is little more than a trunk. The yard itself, which I've thought of all these years as big, is tiny. I remember our dogs: Myshkin, the fickle beloved, stolen, leaving us to search and search and weep and weep; and Andrew, the German shepherd with the soulful eyes and tender heart, whose big teeth frightened me after Our Child was born.

The carport is miniscule. I wonder if you remember the steaks we used to grill there in summer, because the house was too hot for cooking, and the chilled Lambrusco we bought by the case to drink each night with dinner.

The woman who lives there now, whose first act on buying the house was to rip out my writing desk, either isn't home or refuses to open the door. Not the same door we had, with its three panes at the top covered with plastic "stained glass." No, an even tackier, more flimsy door, with the number 1443 affixed to its bottom in black vinyl and gold adhesive.

I am disappointed because I do want to see inside, and I want my lover to see it too. I want to show her the living room, where our red couches sat. The moon lamp. The low table made from a wooden door on which I kept flowers, leaves, Georgia field straw, in a gray crockery vase. The walls on which hung our Levy's bread poster: The little black boy and "You Don't Have to Be Jewish to Love Levy's." The white-and-black SNCC (Student Non-violent Coordinating Committee) poster of the large woman holding the small child, and the red-and-white one with the old man holding the hand of a small girl that helped me write about the bond between grandfather and granddaughter that is at the heart of my first novel. There by the kitchen door was the very funny Ernst lithograph, a somber Charles White drawing across from it.

In Tupelo where I lectured I saw an old friend who remembered the house better than I did. She remembered the smallness of the kitchen (which I'd never thought of as small) and how the round "captain's table" we bought was wedged in a corner. She recalled the polished brown wood. Even the daisy-dotted placemats. The big yellow, brown-eyed daisy stuck to the brown refrigerator door.

I wanted to see the nondescript bathroom. If I looked into the mirror would I see the serious face I had then? The deeply sun-browned skin?

The bushy hair? The grief that steadily undermined the gains in levity, after each of the assassinations of little known and unsung heroes; after the assassination of Dr. King?

I wanted to see Our Child's room. From the porch I could see her yellow shutters, unchanged since we left. Yellow, to let her know right away that life can be cheerful and bright. I wanted to see our room. Its giant bed occupying most of the floor, in frank admission that bed was important to us and that whenever possible, especially after air-conditioning, that is where we stayed. Not making love only, but making a universe. Sleeping, eating, reading and writing books, listening to music, cuddling, talking on the phone, watching Mary Tyler Moore,[1] playing with Our Child. Our rifle a silent sentry in the corner.

The old friend whom I saw in Tupelo still lives in Jackson. When we met two decades ago she had just come home from a college in the North where she taught literature. She'd decided to come back to Jackson, now that opportunities were opening up, thanks to you and so many others who gave some of their lives and sometimes all of their life, for this to happen. She hoped to marry her childhood sweetheart, raise a family, study law. Now she tells me she hates law. That it stifles her creativity and cuts her off from community and the life of the young. I tell her what I have recently heard of you. That, according to Our Child, you are now writing plays, and that this makes you happy. That you left civil rights law, at which you were brilliant, and are now quite successful in the corporate world. Though the writing of the plays makes me wonder if perhaps you too have found something missing in your chosen profession?

She remembers us, she says, as two of the happiest, most in love people she'd ever seen. It didn't seem possible that we would ever part.

It is only days later, when I am back in California, that I realize she herself played a role in our drifting apart. This summer she has promised to come visit me, up in the country in Mendocino—where everyone my age has a secret, sorrowful past of loving and suffering during the Sixties time of war—and I will tell her what it was.

1. Mary Tyler Moore (1936–) appeared on the *The Dick Van Dyke Show* from 1961 to 1966. On the television sitcom she was Laurie Petrie, the stay-at-home wife of the star, Dick Van Dyke (1925–), who was Rob Petrie, a television-comedy writer.

Maybe you remember her? Her name is F. It was she who placed a certain novel by a forgotten black woman novelist into my hands.[2] I fell in love with both the novel and the novelist, who had died in obscurity while I was still reading the long-dead white writers, mostly male, pushed on everyone entering junior high. F.'s gift changed my life. I became obsessed, crazed with devotion. Passionate. All of this, especially the passion and devotion, I wanted to share with you.

You and I had always shared literature. Do you remember how, on our very first night alone together, in a motel room in Greenwood, Mississippi, we read the Bible to each other? And how we felt a special affinity with the poet who wrote "The Song of Solomon?" We'd barely met, and shared the room more out of fear than desire. It was a motel and an area that had not been "cleared." Desegregated. We'd been spotted by hostile whites earlier in the day in the dining room. The next day, after our sleepless night, they would attempt to chase us out of town, perhaps run us off the road, but local black men courageously intervened.

Over the years we shared Shakespeare, Dostoyevsky, Tolstoy. Orwell. Langston Hughes. Sean O'Faolain. Ellison. But you would not read the thin paperback novel by this black woman I loved. It was as if you drew a line, in this curious territory. I will love you completely, you seemed to say, except for this. But sharing this book with you seemed everything.

I wonder if you've read it, even now.

Our Child was conceived. Grew up. Went to a large Eastern university. Read the book. She found it there on the required reading list, where I and others labored for a decade to make sure it would be. She tells me now she read it before she even left home, when she was in her early teens. She says I presented it to her with a quiet intensity, and with a special look in my eyes. She says we used to read passages from it while we cooked dinner for each other, and that she used to join me as I laughed and sometimes cried.

What can one say at this late date, my young husband? Except what was surely surmised at the beginning of time. Life is a mystery. Also, love

2. The novel she is referring to is likely *Their Eyes Were Watching God*, by Zora Neale Hurston (1891–1960). Walker was a leading figure in the rediscovery and promotion of Hurston's work. She is also responsible for finding Hurston's grave site and ordering a tombstone.

does not accept barriers of any kind. Not even that of Time itself. So that in the small house that seemed so large during the years of happiness we gave each other, I remain

Yours,
Tatala

Begging

Did I ever tell you about the woman who used to come begging at our door? I wonder if you met her? She was thin, somber, brown. Neatly dressed. About thirty-five, I would guess. Her head was always covered, and now when I think of her I feel there was something ascetic, religious, about her. She would suddenly appear, every three weeks or so, and she would ask if I had "a few pennies" to spare. I always gave her more, of course. But she would not accept dollars, only pennies and, reluctantly, it seemed, "silver money." Each time she came I invited her in; she never accepted. You remember how hot it was in summer: I would offer her a glass of water; she always refused. I never saw her coming. I watched from the window as she left. I think she stopped at the Belts' next door, but I am not sure.

Who was she? She was the only beggar I ever encountered in Mississippi, where family kinship networks were so strong. Over the years this woman's unrelenting begging—but with such stoic restraint!—has plagued me with questions. For I realize now that each time I opened the door, smiled at her and attempted to make her welcome, while I searched the house for coins, she regarded me with a coolness that I can only admit now was really hostility. Why? Also, no matter how hot the day, this neatly dressed beggar was never sweaty when she appeared at the door. Did she park an air-conditioned car just out of sight of our house? Was she, in fact, an agent of some sort, sent to keep an eye on us?

I could not bear to think of this then. I was home alone most of the time. Then, after the birth of Our Child, I was home with a small child. But now I realize, especially after visiting our old house, how odd it was to have a regular, well-dressed beggar appear at the door, obviously not that interested in money, and resentful of my kindness. I wonder now if seeing her there on my porch, begging—she held out one hand limply, carelessly, as she looked her hostile look—aroused my guilt at having a house, a husband who loved me, a child. Or was I always afraid that she was really me, or as I might become someday, out on the street, begging, with nothing but my—hopefully—clean rags of clothes.

This was at the same time that I was discovering the ancestors who'd died unsung and impoverished. I was uniquely placed to see how far the end could be from beginning and even middle. The writer I cared so much about, for instance, had died really poor. And yet, now that I am older, less easily frightened by images of poverty, now that I know poverty can also contain richness—deep friendship, for instance, or a faithful, devoted love—I wonder more than ever about the inner life of those who have been up and now are down. There is always the outsider's look at an impoverished life: it seems pitiful, a waste, a shame. Yet seen from within the poverty, perhaps a different reality might be sketched. A reality of lessons learned the hard, hard way that lessons *are* learned. Perhaps to finally know one or two true things about life makes up for the lumpy bed and chilly solitude.

And so I wonder now, if I asked you, if you would remember this woman? If, on my journeys away from home, she rang our bell and you answered the door? And what your take of her situation was. Did she accept only pennies and "silver money" from you? Did she refuse dollars? Refuse water. Refuse to temper her hostility.

Sometimes, in my wooden house in Mendocino, with its yellow pine, barnlike slanted roof, I think of her dignity, if she *was* a beggar. I think of her going from brick house to brick house, in our suburban neighborhood. Behind each door a striving black middle-class family. Men and women who would rarely own more than their own houses and cars in their lifetimes, and know this as success. Women who would feel fear, to think of this woman out on the street—a phenomenon associated entirely with big city or Northern living; men who would speculate, feel embarrassed and surely—one or two of them—prurient. Was this why she never smiled?

Her look, her manner, everything said very clearly: I will never work again. I prefer to beg. If, in fact, she was a beggar, and not an agent sent by the Klan, the White Citizens Council[3] or other white supremacy groups of Mississippi. I used to wonder who slipped "The Eyes of the Klan Are Upon You" cards in our mailbox, which was on the front porch. Could this have been her task? And if so, how had she been recruited? To whom was she, or her children—I always felt she had children—a hostage?

There is a bitterness that does not dissolve when I think of black women begging. I feel their rage, and it is mine too. I am here and you are there, we say to the well fed. Why are we both not on the side of plenty? That is what I want to know, as I look into the eyes of someone who has given everything, if only symbolically, and is left with nothing. And the black woman begging does not let me get away with giving more than is asked. Once, in New York City when it still shamed me deeply to see a black woman beg—not that it still doesn't, but my emotions have been battered into a more bearable numbness—there was a woman on the corner who reminded me of the stiff-necked beggar who came to our door. She too asked for coins, for "silver money" only. In my shame and do-goodyness I offered a twenty-dollar bill. She chased me down the block to give it back. Grim, unsoftening. In fact, clearly disgusted with me.

There has been no response to my letter, which Our Child dutifully delivered. And one is not required. You are someone else now; someone I do not know. It is as if the young man I knew is dead, and you have colonized his early life. I know you sometimes speak of that time in Mississippi among people who loved you, so far away from Brooklyn and the tiny, contentious house from which you fled; but you must realize that the person you speak of is not you. But perhaps this is too bitter. Perhaps it is better to speak of the sadness one feels as the result of directly experiencing any sort of waste, whether in material or human terms. I miss you. We were good people. And together we were good. Allies and friends. Too good to have those years stolen from us, even by our grief.

3. In the summer of 1954, after the passage of *Brown v. Board of Education*, White Citizens' Councils began appearing in the Mississippi Delta. The organizations soon spread across the South, advocating resistance to *Brown*.

Finding Langston

How were we to know Langston[4] would die so shortly after we refused him a ride with us? I remember introducing you to him as if he were my father. I was so proud. He was so seemingly at home in any world. The huge Central Park West apartment we were in, for instance, with its windows overlooking the Natural History Museum. How young we were! Sometimes, thinking of our youth, the image that sums it up is the back of your neck, just after you'd "taken a haircut" and your brown shiny hair was shaved close to the back of your head and abruptly, bluntly, terminated, leaving your neck extremely vulnerable and pale. For some reason, I was moved by this; it always made me think of you as someone who would, and did indeed, stick his neck out. Langston liked you from the start.

I was too shy to notice anyone else, or even to hazard a thought about the politics of the gathering. Writers and poets and agents and editors, I know now. Some famous, some not. But what was fame to me? It seemed too far away even to contemplate. It was winter, I was, as always, longing for a father. How odd life is: Now, one of my brothers is very ill. He tells me, when I visit him in the hospital, that the father I always wanted was the one he actually had. He remembers my father organizing in our community to build the first consolidated school for blacks in the county, which was burned to the ground by whites. Then starting again, humbly, asking a local white man—who might indeed have been one of those who torched the first school—to let the community rent an old falling-down shed of his, until a second school could be built. He tells me my father traveled to other counties looking for teachers, because our county was so poor and black people kept in such ignorance there were no teachers to be chosen among us. It was my father who found the woman who would become my first-grade teacher. My brother's words are both fire and balm to my heart. Now, in my fifth decade, I know what it is to be deeply exhausted from the struggle to "uplift" the race. To see the tender faces of our children turned stupid with disappointment and the ravages of poverty and disgrace. To think of the labor of Sisyphus to get his boulder to the top of

---

4. Langston Hughes (1902–67) was one of the leading figures of the Harlem Renaissance. A prolific writer of poetry, plays, short stores, and novels, he was also a friend of and collaborator with Zora Neale Hurston.

the hill as the only fit symbol for our struggle. I am thankful that, when I went North to college, one of my teachers introduced me to the work of Camus. Sisyphus, he said, transcends the humiliation of his endless task because he just keeps pushing the boulder up the hill, knowing it will fall down again, but pushing it anyway, and forever.

We had the little red bug then, and you were teaching me to drive it, at two or three o'clock in the morning, when there was less traffic on the streets of New York. I loved those early morning hours: Sometimes we would go swimming. We'd have the university's pool all to ourselves, in the middle of the night, and you taught me the breaststroke (so graceful!) and the sidestroke; and sometimes after swimming we'd go out in your car.

Langston left the gathering, of which he was star, and came down with us, and saw us head toward the bug. What he didn't know was that the backseat was filled with a large wicker basket we'd bought, our first piece of furniture, and a painting of turtles that proclaimed "We are more alike than different." Perhaps we should have thrown them out on the street, to make room for him. He was that precious, though we did not fully appreciate that then. He said, Are you going uptown? Hopefully. We said, with a regretful shrug, No, we are going downtown. We did not say there was no space for him. We watched, grimacing—for he had made us laugh, and more than that, feel comfortable—in the high-rise apartment filled with all white people, looking out over Central Park and the Museum of Natural History. He began walking toward the subway. And I shivered, for it suddenly seemed very cold. And he seemed the father I sort of knew. He'd given everything, been history, entertainment and example throughout the evening, telling wonderful stories of his adventures, as his eyes twinkled and the ashes from his cigarette—which rarely left his mouth—drifted down to dust his tie. Now he was tired and needing a ride, as my father might have, and I was going off into a life so different from his, I thought, that he could not even warn me about it, except cynically. As he, Langston, did later, after we were married, when he wrote to me and said: You married your subsidy.

It would be years before I learned of the elderly white woman who'd subsidized his early work, and what a "primitive Negro" she tried to make of him, and of how he became sick from loving and wanting to please her, and needing to grow and be himself.[5] When I read about this, how his health only returned after the last of the money she'd given him was gone, I wanted to return to that cold evening we had spent listening to his funny stories and drag him into a corner and force him to really talk to me.

Too late! Is anything more painful than realizing you did not know the right questions to ask at the only time on earth you would have the opportunity? There were other subsidizers in Langston's life. Mainly white men who supported and understood him. One of them built him a little cottage near his own house in California. Langston would live there peacefully for months on end. Did you remind Langston of these men? And did our relationship remind him of relationships he had known? And was he saying I did not love you? Or that love was only part of it?

We were invited to his funeral, and we went. We were husband and wife. It was a party. Like him, it turned us back on ourselves, while being superbly—with its lively music and energetic poetry reading—entertaining. At this "celebration" and for years afterward I thought of his words, especially as you, unfailingly generous, supported me, supported my work. Read it, critiqued it, praised it, ran off multiple copies of it on the big Xerox machine in your law office. Sat in the audience wherever I read it with the biggest glow of all on your face. I had never experienced such faith before.

And now, thinking of the two of us sitting evening after evening reading Langston's stories and his autobiography to each other, as we mourned his passing and as Mississippi howled all around us, I hope this was the faith, the "subsidy" of spirit and work, that Langston had also, in his own handsome youth.

Burned Bridges

Last night a friend and I were on our way to see a movie, in her small, far from new car. A helmeted policeman on a motorcycle pulled her over. "What did I do?" she asked. He did not respond to her question: "Is this

---

5. Charlotte Osgood Mason (1854–1946) was the white patron of Langston Hughes and Zora Neale Hurston, among others, during the high days of the Harlem Renaissance, the decade of the 1920s.

your car?" he gruffly questioned her. She is a middle-aged black woman, portly, bespeckled and in dreadlocks. For fifteen minutes he grilled her about whose car she was driving and whether it was stolen. I sat in the car, leaning out the window. I had such a feeling of déjà vu. Should I get out of the car and stand beside her? Or should I remain in my seat? Even though this was San Francisco in the Nineties and not Greenwood, Mississippi,[6] in the Sixties, I found myself suddenly grappling with a dilemma I thought we had put to rest twenty-five years ago. What is the proper behavior during confrontations with obviously disrespectful, hostile police? If I got out of the car and questioned what was happening and was ordered to get back inside, and refused, what were likely to be the consequences? How could they be dealt with nonviolently, when he was the only one of us armed?

My friend's face was tense with suffering as she rummaged through a rather messy glove compartment for proof of ownership of her car. Having called in her information and verified ownership, he explained why he thought her vehicle might have been stolen: a sticker on her license plate seemed haphazardly placed.

Throughout their exchange the policeman, white, solidly built, with cold eyes and a graying mustache, showed no sign of human feeling.

"And why would I have stolen this battered little car," my friend said, when we were finally free to go. "And not a new BMW or a Mercedes-Benz?"

On we went to see *The Bridges of Madison County*. A wonderful movie that reminded me of you, of us, the summer we met in Jackson, Mississippi. When I think of that summer I think of how perfectly my hair was straightened, and how neatly shaped. I think of the tiny, sexy dresses I wore. Dresses that bared my shoulders and rose above my knees. Dresses that said "Africa" in a seductive whisper, not like the dresses I would later

6. Greenwood, Mississippi, was the home of Byron De La Beckwith (1921–2001), the killer of Medgar Evers (1925–63). Just a few miles north of Greenwood is the hamlet of Money, Mississippi, where Emmett Till (1941–55) was abducted from his great uncle's home and lynched. In the 1960s, Greenwood was not a welcoming place for blacks.

wear, that I made myself, from yards of vibrant fabric that made me feel like a member of a distant tribe. I shaved legs and underarms in those days, and was silky smooth all over. I had barely enough money to exist, but I did not care. Being in the South, in Mississippi, was what mattered. Not missing what was happening there. And almost immediately, we met.

It was like a dream, really. And also karmic. I was one of those who complained bitterly about white people having the nerve to be in "our" movement. And yet of course I noticed you immediately, as a man. Your warm congenial manner in the cafe next to the law office on Farrish Street, as you shared lunch with your colleagues. Your laughter and flushed face above a crisp, cool blue shirt. Later you would tell me you noticed me too. I would have been in the company of Larry (not his real name), the lawyer for whom you worked, and whose errands you were required to run. He had picked me up at the airport, and remained near, "showing me around." An arrogant, rich Yalie in his thirties whose father owned a chain of hardware stores, Larry drove a blue Mercedes convertible as if he were lord of the world, and would later squire me about in it; as if this were something Mississippi saw every day: a handsome, suavely dressed white man and a fashionably dressed young black woman who was actually perplexed to wind up, briefly, in his bed.

But there was no feeling, with Larry. Besides, he was engaged, I had thought, to the black woman who partly inspired me to come to Mississippi in the first place. Which made his seduction of me all the more puzzling. Not to mention my sleepwalker's response. I don't even remember having sex with him. I remember only a moment of standing next to a motel bed on which he lay waiting for me, and that I was wearing peach-colored bikini panties and a low-cut bra. He pretended an enthusiasm for what would come next that I felt sure he didn't feel. I did the same. I was embarrassed to be part of whatever game he was playing with the woman who loved him. And yet, in those days, sex was casual and often meaningless, simply because that's what it meant to be a person of those times. I understand now that it was she, so distant, cool, cut off from me as a woman, I was trying somehow to reach. Much later I would wonder if my behavior annoyed or hurt her. If so, she never let on, but continued her firm, unequivocal advocacy of the rights of black people and of children, and later married a good man and raised a family. It was she whom I loved and admired, and wanted to be with. Not in a sexual way; at the time it was only men who set me sexually abuzz, but simply to talk, to ground, to move forward together as sisters. Because of my stupidity with this man who called you at odd hours to go to the cleaners and pick up his shirts, or to go to the corner and pick up cigarettes, I lost any chance of that possibility.

He was annoyed that you and I chose each other. Not because of anything he felt for me, but because you were an underling. A law student, yes, but also his servant, his gofer. Though you smiled, I could feel your humiliation, to be forced to do the trivial tasks Larry dreamed up for you: go to the pharmacy, the deli, the car wash. Make sure they don't scratch the paint or get grease on the leather top.

After weeping our way through the ending of *Madison County* my friend said: "What this story proves is that love will find you." And for us, that is what love did. And it had a sense of humor.

Because of the heat, ice cream was very big in Mississippi. We were always eating it. Do you remember? I came up the steep stairs to your air-conditioned offices—neatly renovated suites in an otherwise dilapidated building—wearing my littlest slipping and sliding dress, my slightest sandals, carrying a huge chocolate ice cream cone. You sat smiling at me from your desk beneath a window that framed your whole body in sunlight. Your hair was glowing. Your brown eyes filled with warmth. You loved, just loved, chocolate, you said. Especially ice cream. I offered the cone to you, after taking a huge lick. You accepted it happily and licked rapturously, as if it were the best ice cream you'd ever had. It was a highly erotic moment, an eroticism heightened by the fact that just by licking the same ice cream cone a huge portion of the Old South that had kept my soul and my free expression of eroticism chained was forced to fall. That was it, for me. The moment we bonded, the moment we fell in love. I felt the wonder, the oddness, the rightness, the sureness of it. My body, without moving from my side of the desk, seemed to lean into yours. And yours, though you kept your seat, met mine.

Everyone could see what had happened. It was as if we'd fallen into a separate space that contained just the two of us, even when we were apart. Larry thought up more and more errands for you to run, even coming to your apartment in the evening to tell you what they were, as if he forgot he had a phone. I listened to him instruct you from behind the closed door of your bedroom, thinking of the journey we made together to arrive there. Of riding out to the Ross Barnett Reservoir with you and Carolyn (not her real name), the blond secretary from your office, who clearly had designs on you, and who sat in the backseat with you and playfully put her foot in your lap. You and I were in one world, ours, she was in another. And when the police appeared, I was comforted to realize you and I remained in one world, the two of them in another. For of course the cop thought you and the white woman were a couple, albeit a couple of troublemakers from out of state. I was just a young colored girl tagging along. Carolyn played into this, snuggling up to you and trying to impress both the policeman and me that she was the queen of our car. But you had not touched her foot. And now you did not return her cooing attentions. Your whole soul was wrapped around my feelings, as I sat with the ice-cold dread Southern cops always inspired, telling me without words to have no fear.

And that is what you would tell me for years to come. That you were there, with me. That your chosen role in life was to love and to protect me. That I was safe. It was music I had never heard.

The other evening I got to see the new civil rights lawyer everybody's been talking about. They don't talk about him just because he's a civil rights lawyer. They talk about him because he's got a black wife. And she's pregnant.

I think maybe I'm one of the first people to know this. They keep to themselves a lot, and you hardly ever see her. But I was in Estelle's Place; and way late, must have been around eleven o'clock, here come this cute white guy, with brown curly hair and a cute, courteous smile. And went right to the counter like he was a regular, and he ordered chitlins. Yes, he did.

And you know how black people are. Estelle acted like it was the most natural thing in the world, but when she came back to the back where my cousin Josie is one of the cooks, they all just fell out laughing. She said: He's Jewish, you know. Like that explained everything. But it was funny enough to the rest of us without throwing that part in. I mean, how many white men do any of us see slamming into a chitlin joint in the middle of the night. He don't eat them himself, of course, said Estelle. But his wife's pregnant, and it's chitlins that she has a craving for. And she nearly split her sides, laughing.

I stood near the door, where there's glass, and got a real good look at him. What struck me about him, to tell the truth, is that he looked happy. In fact, he was probably the happiest-looking person I've ever seen. You could just sort of feel it rolling off of him. And when he'd paid for the plate of chitlins, all nicely wrapped up and everything, he kind of waved at us back in the kitchen—where I didn't think he could even see us—and left. And we felt like maybe we wasn't such dogs, after all, for loving our collard greens, chitlins and hog maws, and our cole slaw and potato salad.

Passion

There is a languor I associate with being in love, and having satisfying sex. A dreamy look in the eye, a looseness in the joints. A dazed expression, even in the face of danger. And danger that summer was everywhere. Violence, everywhere. Pain and suffering, everywhere. Heroism too, everywhere. Knowing this, we stayed in bed a lot, doing our part to make it all real at the most basic level: making love to each other, we worshiped the miracle of what was possible.

The first time, though, was awkward. And why not? We made love in Carolyn's apartment, where I stayed, sleeping on a fold-up cot in her small living room. I think it was bad because she was in her room asleep. Or was she? It is hard now to imagine that we were so desperate that we might have done this. Invaded her space in this way. Our only excuse, perhaps, is that in such a violent, racially polarized city we had nowhere else to go. Going with you to your room so shortly after meeting would have felt brazen, presumptuous. You also had a roommate. I was shocked by the intense heat of your body, by the profusion of hair on your chest, your wide shoulders and gentle hands. Even though the sex was off, our breathing together was not, and it was the perfect harmony of our breaths that I fell asleep, after you left, thinking about.

It wasn't long before we were trying to explain to each other what it was we did. You were taking depositions from dispossessed sharecroppers who'd opposed their bosses and been thrown off the land. I was doing freelance movement work, but really I was writing a novel that required a closer look at the South. You read the writing I had done so far, in a notebook I carried with me everywhere, and became my champion, instantly. Your work, defending and empowering black people who might have been my parents, my family, endeared you to me, effortlessly. We were a couple: black and white to the people who saw us pass by on the street, but already Sweetheart and Darling to ourselves.

It really did seem at times as if our love made us bulletproof, or perhaps invisible. When we walked down the street together the bullets that were the glances of the racist onlookers seemed turned back and sent hurtling off into outer space. The days passed in a blur of hard work, constant awareness of violence, and unutterable tenderness between ourselves. At the end of the long afternoons listening to the sorrows of your clients, we crept close to the cranky air conditioner in your room—just by the bed—and read poetry to each other. Yeats, Walt Whitman, cummings. We spent the humid evenings learning to give pleasure to each other. Soon, our shaky start in Carolyn's living room was forgotten. One day we made love during a rousing afternoon thunderstorm. Torrents of rain cascaded down the streets; the air was blue with it. Lightning streaked our bodies with silver. Nature supports what *is*, we felt, as our bodies moved passionately together. We were a part of it, no questions asked. When I left for New York, you promised to join me, later, at the end of summer. Your last year of law school was coming up; I was going back to the cheap, cockroach-infested apartment and typewriter-on-the-kitchen-table life of the beginning writer.

Handling It

I think I am handling it all very well. Preparing to see you again, to actually engage in meaningful talk, after so many years. Our Child has arranged for us to meet with her and her therapist in a brownstone in Upper Manhattan. Because it is the beginning of summer and already quite warm, I am wearing a long, thin cotton dress and a light jacket. Something about the dress feels strange, and I do not realize what it is until I get out of the taxi at the therapist's door. I have put it on backward. You have arrived early and are sitting in the therapist's reception room. We say hello, and embrace briefly. I duck into the toilet and swiftly rearrange my dress. When I come out you and Our Child and the therapist are seated, chatting.

For years Our Child has been the only visible, public evidence of our years together. She sits tall and poised. Twenty-five, and used to making her own way in the world. Her only obstacle, she feels, is a certain ignorance about who her parents really are. I ask that the seating be rearranged so that you are seated between us. You are compliant, and as you move across me to take your seat I look at you. You are heavier, your hair is thinning. I sense both weariness and wariness. I believe this is the first time you've set foot in a psychiatrist's office. Your brown eyes smile, and I can now see that it is your eyes that smile in situations like this—that you feel threatened by but are determined to endure—not you. I sense an unsmiling you carefully concealed behind your face. The same unsmiling you who smiled when the racists called you "Jew lawyer," and reminded you they'd already lynched two "outside agitator Jews from New York" shortly before you arrived to work in Mississippi. In your stylish, rumpled suit and sensible tie, you look like the successful corporate lawyer and devoted nuclear family head in Westchester County that you now are.

It is difficult to believe we were once married to each other. Or that when we were, you would occasionally play poker all night, sleep much of the day, and get to the office just as most offices were closing, at five o'clock. Or that, routinely, you would go to work around noon and stay at the office until late at night. Sometimes I would visit you there, and we'd have a picnic on your desk around midnight. And work together, snuggle and kiss well into morning. Like Our Child, who inherited this trait from you, so that getting her out of bed before noon is a chore, you are a night person. Or you were a night person. Apparently now you are not. You get up, according to Our Child, at the crack of dawn, catch a train and come into Manhattan at an hour you and I would have been still cuddled up together in bed, oblivious of the time. I remember how shocked I was, when she told me this. You, shaved and dressed, on a moving train, headed for New York City, before ten in the morning? Maybe even before nine? My heart ached for you.

The therapist wants to know what it is we want from the two-hour session Our Child has arranged for. I wonder this myself. In my case, it is some kind of closure. My mind flashes on the last brief conversation we had after receiving verification of our divorce. We'd left the federal building in which severance had occurred—whether in Brooklyn or Manhattan, I no longer recalled—and stood, after ten years of marriage, suddenly free, legally, of each other. And, because we were now legally free of each other, I was feeling very close. The humor with which I was able to see so much of our life together, suddenly returned. I smiled at you, gave a sigh of relief and said: "Well, that's over. Let's go somewhere and have a cup of tea." But your face reflected none of my lightheartedness. You were morose. "No thank you," you said. "I have to get back to the office." It was a response emblematic of our problem. My face fell. However, still determined to prove to myself at least that divorce need not mean the end of simple civility, I stuck out my hand. You reluctantly, it seemed to me, took it. We shook hands woodenly, like a couple of strangers, and you turned and disappeared down the street. And I must have said, to the emotions crowding around my chest: Get away from me.

Our Child is speaking. What she wants, she says, is to better understand something that has always puzzled her. She has been the go-between all these years. Eighteen, or so. What she has noticed about each of us when we speak of the other is a kind of wistfulness. We seem to her bemused, often. Puzzled, frequently. Not quite sure ourselves what happened to us. The moment she describes us in this way, I see that it is the truth, and I feel an enormous wave of pity for us, her parents. What did happen to us? It seems now a question well worth considering.

You are sitting, still smiling, your legs crossed. The therapist is looking from you to me. What did happen? she asks. You are silent, waiting, as if you'd also like to know. Two hours will go quickly, I know. I decide to take the plunge.

I tell her about our courtship and early marriage. The sense we both had of finding, and bonding with, a miraculously compatible mate. The long years of trying to accommodate ourselves to a violent, and often boring, environment. The isolation. The racism. The sexism. The slow breakdown of my spirit after I'd finished this novel or that, this story or that, this poem or that, and looked about and found little to amuse, divert or sustain me. Of your retreat into the secluded quiet of your office, night after night. The loneliness. The old conflict resurfacing between loyalty to "other" and loyalty to myself.

It was the same struggle I'd faced with my mother, I said. I always under-stood her work was important. She had to be away from home in order for there to *be* a home. It was her earnings that meant food, clothes, a tooth-brush. A roof over our heads. I dared not complain. And yet I missed her with every fiber of my being. I died each day she was away. Yet I could say nothing. It was the same in my marriage. Each day my husband went out, often in danger, to slay the dragons of racism and ignorance that prolif-erated in Mississippi. Many, many people depended on him. More than I did, I sometimes thought. How could I say I also needed him?

The therapist is a middle-aged refugee from Latvia. She has a thoughtful face and a faint accent. The language of her body says: This is a space in which it is safe to express. Her large Irish wolfhound lies in front of the tiled fireplace, asleep. What a difference such a person, such an ear, would have made in our lives all those years ago, I think. And flash on the five-mile bike ride that had taken me for several weeks to the office of Dr. Hickerson, who casually prescribed Valium, and sent me numbly careening on my way. She did not care enough to suggest per-haps we were simply trying to do too much. That we were throwing our young lives against a system that had crushed lovers and idealists for centuries.

I sigh, into the quiet room. I think, I say, that Mississippi, living inter-racially, attempting to raise a child, attempting to have a normal life, wore us out. I think we were exhausted. In our tiredness we turned away from each other. Next to me on the couch, I feel you relax. Perhaps you antic-ipated blame.

But how can I blame you for being human? For wearing out. For running on empty eventually. Just as I did. Now you begin to talk. You mention how, in the final days in Mississippi, you became afraid to leave me alone in the house. That one day you locked the door behind you and I ac-cused you of locking me in. That was the day, you say, you knew we had to leave. I don't remember this particular day, but I certainly do recall the feeling of being incarcerated. Solitary confinement might be ideal for certain forms of mental creativity, but it is horrible for someone who craves a social world, whose spirit yearns for the refreshment of compan-ionship. Between "projects," my books, there were days that contained only a scream into the silence. I combated this by teaching at two of the local black colleges, for practically no money. I planted trees and flowers. I learned to shop in a way that took hours rather than minutes. I joined an exercise club, to which my slim, bored neighbor Phyllis and I went each week. I quilted, I began making a rug. I actually did needlepoint. I talked to my mother on the phone.

Our Child does not remember any of the happiness that surrounded her arrival in our house. And yet, it is this happiness for which she yearns. It is the security of two doting parents, adoringly attentive, adoringly present, that is the quality of comfort she misses. She has become angry at us over the years because no matter what she has tried, this quality of being completely loved by both of us, together, has remained beyond her reach. I feel sad for her. I see the little girl running to the door at the sound of her father's car, a huge brown and black Toronado that was always, because of its incongruous stylishness, comical for a civil rights lawyer. I see her father fly out from around the car, running to meet her wet and openhearted kisses, her widespread, chubby arms. I see him down on one knee, lifting her against his chest, his wide face transparent with love. I see myself standing, smiling, in the doorway. In his eagerness to embrace and kiss me as well, his thin lips are already stuck out. He is the only white person in the neighborhood at this hour of the day, but even if I think of this it is with amusement. The three of us collide in the doorway, laughing to think we have outwitted racism and racist laws one more time and lived to love another day.

On such an upbeat day I would have worked well, whether at typewriter, quilting or flower planting. Our Child and I would have played. She would have napped. I would have shopped, driven out for a walk around the reservoir, taught. But most important, you would have come home in time for dinner, and would perhaps spend the evening at home, not, as was often the case, in the office, where one or another case of a black family being terrorized by whites would have called you, immediately after dinner, and compelled you to work on it through the night.

I have a question to ask you. I look at the therapist to see if it is okay. She nods. Why do you work so much? You look surprised by the question. I don't know, you say. I've always done it. I know this is true. I remember how, when we met, you were still selling life insurance—a lucrative job finagled from a friend of the family, by your mother—which you'd done for years, even though you were a law student and so young. You also taught swimming at the law school and took care of the pool. In fact, you were poor. You owned two pairs of slacks, one blue and one yellow, and the shiny hazel-colored suit in which you were married. You owned two ties and half a dozen shirts. Two pairs of shoes. I too could pack everything I owned, including my typewriter, in a couple of suitcases. When we finally moved in together, in your room overlooking Washington Square Park, there was an absence of clutter simply because our possessions were so few. A bedspread doubled as a tablecloth, a folding table doubled as a desk. Your single bed seemed fine and comfortable for the two of us. We shared a bathroom with your suitemate.

I wanted to scream at you, as I'd wanted to scream at my mother: Come back! Don't go to work! I miss you! I am in danger while you are gone! But now it is too late to scream this, even though I finally understand this is exactly what I should have screamed. We were divorced seventeen years ago. I cannot stop the tears, however, and they roll down my cheeks, just as they did after you closed the door to our house, those lonely mornings so many years ago. I take tissues from the box at my left. Glancing down as I wipe my face, I see your well-shod foot. The cuffs of your designer slacks. We have both done phenomenally well, materially. It strikes me suddenly as astonishing. Because it was never something we set out to do. Today I own large, beautiful houses, overcompensation for the shacks in which I was raised; and when I travel, my hotel suite is nearly as large as our old house. You have a powerful New York law practice, and the best of whatever Westchester County has to offer. There is a rumor that you play golf. I confess that I can't quite imagine this. Both of us have been hard workers all our lives, and yet much of what we have today—at least speaking for myself—seems to have fallen into our laps. Or do all poor people who become successful in America feel like this?

What is this road on which there is so much beauty and so much pain? So much love and so much suffering? Such surprise. How can it be that we have lost each other all these years? That even though it took my mother thirteen years to die, you never sent her a card. It would have been easier for me to believe you murdered someone than that this could happen. Was it because, on meeting you, she hurt your feelings by identifying you with the only label her fundamentalist Christian upbringing gave her for Jews: Christ-killer. Or that she said, even though she knew better, because I had told her you were only twenty-two, that you seemed like an old man. Once again I look down at your stylish Italian leather shoes. Even your feet have changed, I think, recalling the black "space" shoes you used to wear because your Pisces feet (fish feet) were so tender and often sore. You appeared to roll a bit as you walked, in an attempt to alleviate the discomfort; perhaps this is what struck her as odd, as old. An old man's walk. But it was like her, in any case, to be critical of whomever I brought home. Except for Porter, the young man I fell in love with when I was six and became intimate with when I was sixteen. This was her son-in-law, the one she chose, the one she wanted, though he and I separated as friends when I was eighteen. She never said about him, as she did about every other boy or man: He has a homely face, you will soon tire of it; his feet are slightly splayed, his wrists are too thin, he will be bald before he's thirty. I was dismayed, of course, that she could not really see you. That my father could not. My whole family could not. To them, you were for many years merely a white male blur wearing clothing. No matter how gentle you appeared, you struck an ancient terror in their hearts. To them, all white people had a vampire quality, they were seen as people who devour, who suck dry. They waited for this to happen to me. And there was the awful history of black women and white men.

Our Child is curious about her birth, though I have told her about it many times. She turns to you and says: I understand you were away somewhere when Mama went into labor. You tell her the story of being in court, when the word came. Of arguing a school desegregation case before the Fifth Circuit Court of Appeals in New Orleans. Of being told by one of the judges that having planted the seed, you didn't have to be present for the harvest. But that you hadn't listened, but hastened home, to accompany me to the hospital. And that, while I was still in the hospital, your mother also came, and set up camp in our house. At last accepting that there was another woman in your life. But there was no one but you to visit me in the hospital—or am I forgetting someone? Perhaps our friend Barbara, perhaps the secretaries from your office? In any case, I only remember you. Your pale, stricken face and fear at the sight of blood. Your apparent helplessness. My attention so focused on the pain that seemed about to drown me, that I could not offer anything except muffled silence. For my gynecologist I had chosen the only woman doctor—it was rumored she was lesbian—in the hospital. Her bedside manner turned out to be chilly and abrupt. She waited until the last possible moment to relieve me of pain—at the precise moment I felt the pain might be turning into its opposite, a completion for which my body has never ceased to yearn. Her hands had not an ounce of gentleness. Her episiotomy unnecessarily savage. No one could believe we were there together, married, to have our neither black nor white child. We were a major offense. And yet, the side of this experience that I have consciously remembered all these years is the look in Our Child's eyes when she emerged into our world: a long, searching look at you, then an equally inquiring glance at me. It shocked us; it felt so much like an old acquaintance reentering a room we happened to be in. And I remember the red roses, dozens of them, behind which your beaming face, later in my room, appeared. The black nurses delighted in the discomfiture of the white ones, who could not, as the black ones could not, fathom such behavior. Most white fathers of black children in the South never even saw the mothers pregnant, not to mention actually saw the child after birth. The white nurses were soon captivated by your charm and good looks, casting you in the role of a contemporary Rhett Butler, but of course bemoaning the fact that you had chosen the wrong Scarlett. We were the nightmare their mothers had feared, the hidden delight generations of their fathers enjoyed. We were what they had been taught was an impossibility, as unlikely as a two-headed calf: a happy interracial couple, married (and they knew this was still illegal in their state), having a child, whom we obviously cherished, together.

Did you ever wonder how we must have appeared to our mothers? I have often wondered this. Once, in the days following the birth of Our Child—for she would not speak of sex or childbirth before I had a child—my mother broke a self-imposed taboo to speak to me of rape. Or rather, of how she had avoided rape. I have a feeling now that she was the kind of woman who would have said a woman could not be raped: though her own light-colored face belied this, surely. People who are routinely violated over centuries make curious denials. But I would speak to her of rape, as I spoke to her of everything that mattered. And she told me the following story: That one day she and her sisters and brothers were walking down a deserted road, and white men began to make advances toward and then to chase the girls. Her brothers ran away, leaving the girls to fight or run as best they could. She understood their behavior, of course, but there was sadness in her telling of it. If they had tried to protect their sisters they would have been murdered without a thought. Luckily, she and her sisters were strong and fast; they simply outran their would-be rapists.

Do you remember how I used to suddenly develop passions? I am still that way. In Mississippi I began to crave arrowheads. It came upon me as suddenly as the desire, years before, to write poetry. I hungered for the sight of them. I ached for the feel of them in my hand. Now I think this was perhaps another beginning of the endless understanding of who

I really am. In childhood I must have longed for pebbles, for certain tree leaves, for the sight of the river. For the taste of earth. I remember that I placed an ad in the paper, and that there was a response. I began to collect arrowheads. A few wondrously whole, many broken or chipped. All precious to me. I even collected the stone from a tomahawk. I collected arrowheads for years, and then began the slow, deeply satisfying ritual of passing them on. And yet, since then I've never been without. On the kitchen table where I am writing this there is a small wooden bowl from Africa that holds a remnant of what was once a large collection. Our Child has never known her mother without arrowheads, without Native American jewelry, without photographs of Native Americans everywhere one could be placed. Craft and art and eyes steadied me, as I tottered on the journey toward my tri-racial self. Everything that was historically repressed in me has hungered to be expressed, to be recognized, to be known. And these three spirits—African, Native American, European— I knew I was bringing to you. In the early days I wrote you a poem about this. And now I wonder if these three spirits were fighting, some of the time I was so depressed. That the Native American and European, no less than the African, desired liberation. Exposure to the light. My sister, who looks more Cherokee than me, and more European, tells me the Cherokee great-grandmother from whom we descend was herself mad. She was part African. What did that mean in a tribe that kept slaves and were as colorist, no doubt, as the white settlers who drove them from their homes? I do feel I have had to wrestle with our great-grandmother's spirit and bring it to peace. Which I believe I have done. So that now when I participate in Indian ceremonies I do not feel strange, or a stranger, but exactly who I am, an African-AmerIndian woman with a Native American in her soul. And that I have brought us home.

Collecting the arrowheads from white people who'd found them on their land caused me to think a lot about how empty of Indians Mississippi was. I felt I was walking through a land thick with two- and three-hundred-year-old sorrows, thick with ghosts. Indians are always in my novels because they're always on my mind. Without their presence the landscape of America seems lonely, speechless. No matter how long we live here, I feel Americans will never know anything about it. In any case, it has been destroyed now beyond knowing.

Last night Harold and I took the kids and we went shopping at that big new supermarket out on Stribling Road. It is a wonderful place. Really huge, and with everything anybody could imagine to want or buy. From grits to lawn chairs. And the best part is that it stays open all night.

So we got our two carts, me and Harold pushing one, the kids pushing the other, and we started down the aisles. Harold makes a real good salary, and he lets us buy anything we want. We bought a gallon of ice cream, after we'd bought all the daily kind of foodstuff.

It was really funny, though, because ordinarily in Mississippi you never see interracial couples. Never. Though you see mixed-race children as much as you ever did. Mama says that's not true; she said that, to let her grandmother tell it, it was during slavery that you saw more mixed-race children. Those were the ones by the masters that they had off the slave women. They would keep them or sell them, as they saw fit. Then during Reconstruction there were a lot of them because of all the white and black folks who worked together and fell in love, or in lust, or whatever. Anyhow, that's kind of like now, I guess. But what that means is that here in Jackson, if you want to see interracial couples, the place to do it is at midnight at this all-night supermarket.

Folks stare at us so much in the daytime, you start to feel like your skin is crawling. But at midnight there's nobody much at the supermarket. Just the silly clerks, and they're too sleepy to be as mean as they've been brought up to be.

We saw Ruby and Josh, and Ruby's four kids. Josh always looks so outnumbered. Their own baby, Crissy, has light hair, but she's as brown as her mom. And we saw Jerry and Tara; and I think she was drunk. She was wheeling that cart like it was Big Wheels. And then we saw the Lawyer and the Writer. Which is how Harold refers to them. I think he's jealous, myself. He didn't finish law school, and he claims women shouldn't write about themselves.

I asked him Why not? and he said that white male writers, like Faulkner and Hawthorne and Mark Twain, never wrote about themselves, and that they were masters at it. And I asked him whether this didn't come out of a tradition of being a writer but needing to keep quiet about the slaving and gunrunning and Indian killing in your family tree. In other words, I said, if white men wrote truthfully about themselves, how could they continue to fool the rest of us?

Sometimes I make him so mad.

The Lawyer and the Writer had their little chubby baby in their cart. And they were talking to her just like she was as grown as they were. No baby talk at all, and she's still crawling. Do you want us to buy some eggs? they were asking her as we passed them. She said something back, like "goop," and they thought that was yes, so they put some eggs next to her.

I think the Writer suspects Harold doesn't care for her. She always speaks real warmly to me; but she leaves her husband the job of saying anything much to Harold. I even think she knows he talks about her. Because one time we ran into them at the picture show—also in the middle of the night—and this was just about the first time we met them, I think. Harold and the Lawyer were making small talk, looking just like two ordinary white men, anywhere. And then when me and the Writer walked back over to them—we'd been to the rest room—Harold turned around to her and said: I hear you're a writer. Kind of smirking, the way he can do. Kind of sniffy. What kind of writer are you? And she looked him up and down and said, real firmly: A shameless one.

The Lawyer couldn't help it. He loved his wife so much, anyhow. But when she said that, he just bust out laughing. His face turned as red as a beet. It is so funny to me that white people turn red like that. You can see all their blood. And she didn't crack a smile, just turned on her boot heel and stalked off to the show. And after the show they were all hugged up on the way home, and the Lawyer was just kissing on her and she was kissing him back and everything about them said: Fuck Mississippi, this is good stuff.

The Ruin

Our Child is trying to figure out where she fit in during those years. Where was she, for instance, when we moved from Mississippi and bought "the ruin" in Brooklyn.

But here I shall do something I did often when we lived together: veer off into another world. A world of musing, of speculation, of merged fact and fiction. The world of lives glimpsed, but glimpsed to the bone; the world in which one passing word might become a written life.

Do you remember Harold and Dianne? He was blond, from Idaho. She was a local black woman with children. I used to wonder why we were not closer to them; I envied them their raucous and colorful and child-battered household. And I remember that you always commented on the fact that Dianne was "so humorless" and you wondered what Harold "saw in her." One day you said he'd told you: Her secret apparently was her expertise at oral sex. I had not warmed to Harold; now I knew why. Although it was Harold who one day said something I've thought about all these years: To stay alive to yourself, you must keep doing the thing that gets you kicked out. He had laughed, saying this. Every choice I make in life, he said, to my Republican family, is more abhorrent than the last. They'd almost committed suicide after meeting Dianne.

I could imagine him up there in Idaho, on the family ranch, six thousand acres wide, his eye pressed against the aperture of the television screen, lusting after the possibility of growing a wider internal, spiritual self that seemed, at the time, to be offered by black and white confrontation in the South. As far as he knew, there were no black people in Idaho, and, curiously, it was his love of the cattle his family raised, his empathy as they were loaded onto boxcars and shipped to a market back east, that made him think the blacks he saw being beaten up on television might be people too.

He was one of the white men who supplied me with arrowheads. It was from his ranch that the tomahawk came. He definitely thought no Indians still lived in Idaho. I think of him whenever I give readings there, and Indians, some of them friends of mine, claim front-row seats.

Harold and Dianne are both dead now.

At a reading in Oxford, a shy son and daughter came up to me. I was busy hugging on Ned Bing, the indomitable white pastor whose house was firebombed and whose face was badly battered by members of the Klan. It had been years since we'd seen each other. He has no idea how much I love his face; and I didn't tell him, as I should have, as we stood surrounded by half the town. However I did manage to kiss him just where they'd laid open his jaw, and I pulled on the big, bright pink ear that was stitched back on halfheartedly at the racist hospital, and that managed, out of sheer love, to hang on. And then I stepped back, and there they were, the grown children of Harold and Dianne. Black children, because she'd had them by someone else, some black high school sweetheart, long before Harold arrived. Big brown eyes, dimpled smiles, skin like warm silk. Hair in dreads.

We are the children of Harold and Dianne, they said in unison. Clearly a line rehearsed, since they'd anticipated being shy in front of me. Goddess, I thought, who are they talking about. And please ma'am, I pleaded with Her, let me soon remember. They were that impressive. I wanted to be worthy of them. My face, you always said, was completely readable. It must have been so then, as I rummaged through my Mississippi memory bank, because they laughed. Bust out laughing, in fact. And I saw Dianne's lips, her rarely glimpsed dimple—and realized she'd almost never smiled—and what her hair would have looked like if she'd ceased to straighten it, and just let it grow. I even saw, especially in the boy, some of Harold's supercilious cockiness. The way, in Mississippi, he seemed arrogant even just standing on a corner. He was a hard white man for blacks to cotton to, so to speak. Ah, I said, seeing now what he might have looked like as a black man, and opened my arms.

They flowed into me, both of them, in an embrace that seemed to last forever. They flopped and draped, one to a shoulder, about my body, which met them as if it were a tree. Not a stiff tree, but one that just bends to the ground when there's a wind. A weeping willow. Do you ever wonder, old lover of mine, where so much love comes from? I wonder this often, because no matter how distressing the world is, wherever I am, there never seems to be a shortage of love. Is this true, as well, for you? We hugged for so long, in fact, that Reverend Bing returned, and gathered the three of us close to him.

Maybe the love is there because of shared suffering? Maybe it rises up wherever we perceive that another human has survived. As human. In any case, the three of us left the throng that had filled the reading venue and went next door to a cafe that specialized in fried oysters and grits. The food was bad when we lived in Mississippi. Remember? We used to drive all the way to New Orleans, a four-hour trip, just to eat decent food once a month. But here, in the town of Oxford, a bicycle ride from Rowan Oak, Faulkner's old plantation house, the food is exquisite, and I stuffed myself with oysters, while thinking of my father, whose taste buds I seem to have inherited, and who adored oysters, raw, stewed or fried.

Ernesto and Rosa ate heartily. I would not have guessed tragedy was such a part of their life if they had not hugged me so deeply, as if my body were a kind of raft.

You are one of the few people who knew our parents, said Rosa, after explaining that both she and Ernesto were completing degrees at the university.

We lost them, you know. Said Ernesto.

No, I said. I don't know.

Reverend Bing looked at me quizzically. I shrugged. I have dropped out of so much of the world that I am aware I miss news I should have heard. Did you know of their deaths? Did you read about it in the paper? Did someone tell you? I pushed away the remains of my lavishly buttered grits.

Nowadays, when everywhere you look there is so much tragedy, so much sadness, whenever I am about to hear more of it, I scrutinize the person or persons who are about to speak. I am looking to see if they are still beautiful, regardless of the tale they are about to tell. And if they are still beautiful, before they say anything, I tell them that they are. This is because Greatness of Beauty is how I see God. God being the common name given by many people to that which is undeniably unsurpassable, obvious and true.

You could not be more beautiful, I said to them. And this is so.

Did you know that Dianne wanted to be a writer? I had no idea.

But that was the first thing Rosa told me. Ernesto chimed in to say that Harold had not permitted her to publish anything. Blinking a bit nervously he said Dianne had spoken admiringly of my work, but that Harold had ridiculed it. He thought, said Rosa, that because you wrote about your own life, that you were shameless. He was terrified to think our mother would write about herself.

And now we know why, said Ernesto.

Yeah, said Rosa, throwing her napkin over her plate.

You have always pestered me to tell you where I was the night before I moved in with you.

This first line from Dianne's diary conjured up her face for me. It is a funny line, no? A great opening statement for the novel she might have written, had Harold let her.

How did I end up living with a white man from Idaho? The first time I saw you I hated your guts. I thought all blond people were stupid and that white skin looked diseased. We were taught that white people smell funny. Like wet dogs. But thank the Lord you didn't have blue eyes, those hard glass eyes that might as well be playing marbles, and never show emotion and never even show fear. And you were busy trying to teach people how to vote and being impatient because, in their fear of you as a white man, they had a hard time hearing anything you had to say. If you'd cursed them and called them dumb niggers they would have heard you perfectly. But you were so polite, even while impatient, and called them Sir and Ma'am, and you just about shocked them out of their clothes.

What was kissing you like, the first time? I remember feeling fear, because I was thinking Good Lord, where are this man's lips? What must have happened to them? I mean long ago, maybe when the earth's climate or something changed. I have kissed a lot of men in my life, and they all had lips, sometimes more than enough lips to tell you the truth. But kissing you I felt my mouth just kind of spreading all over your face looking for lips to match up to mine. I was seriously worried that I was blocking your nose. But you just kept going ummm, ummm, ummm, and pretty soon I quit worrying about it.

Who would have thought? That very morning my daddy had reminded me that white men are lower than snakes. But he wasn't too high off the ground his own self. And the black men who fathered my children didn't exactly fly among the clouds. Still, it was with a black man, the father of one of my children, that I spent the last night of my life as a pure black woman. He was out on bail, or maybe he'd run away from the jail, black men often did; and he'd come to see me and the children and one thing led to another. He was the one my mama always liked; you know how mothers sometimes be. And she came by, just as nice, and took all the children over to her house. And Daniel and me just fell in the bed together and hugged each other a long time and just started crying. And he asked me if it was true that I was going out with a white man, and I said yes. And he asked me if I thought he and I could ever get together again, even though he was set to go to prison for twenty-something years, and I said I didn't think so. And then he asked me if he could spend the night. And I said no. But then we cried so much we tired ourselves out and went to sleep. And then around midnight we woke up, and just started to make love. And we made love over and over for the next six or seven hours, until the children came back and he had to leave.

The next night I moved in with you. And I wouldn't make love with you because I could still smell Daniel in my body. And the next night I said I had my period. And when we finally did make love, I felt like I had just given up.

Every time you got mad with me about something, you always yelled that I didn't really love you. I think it upset you that all my children were so dark. But you felt like this because until you were twenty-seven years old the thought of a black person's life never entered your head. It was news to you that us poor black folks down in Mississippi had even survived. You thought we were just like the Indians you said no longer existed in Idaho. Sometimes, even when you were looking me straight in my face, I could see you were still surprised. I used to think I should gain a lot of weight and put on a head rag to make you feel more at home.

I knew you were jealous of black men. And envious at the same time. You'd heard things about black men, growing up. Sexual things, that made you feel inferior. And after you saw a picture of Daniel in the newspaper, after he'd escaped from prison and was thought to be hiding out in New York City, you were evil for weeks. I was happy he'd got away. Every day of my life it hurt me to think of him in a cage. But you never understood about prison in the South. That prisons were just the modern version of the plantation. That if someone like Daniel stole something because he was hungry, he shouldn't be forced to work cotton for the rest of his life.

I feel somehow embarrassed, reading Dianne's diary. I protested when Ernesto and Rosa (after Ernesto Che Guevara and Rosa Parks, of course) sent it to me. At first, I wouldn't even open it; I was almost afraid. Afraid of what? Of seeing the writing self, my own, that might not have become. After all, there we all were, in Mississippi, at the same time, encountering the same violence, racism, sweltering heat. Only you supported me in the work I chose to do in the world. Harold did not support Dianne; though he was, apparently, a good father to her children. Whenever I think of Ernesto I actually see Harold; the way he used to stand, legs spread, his arms folded across his chest, his glasses pushed up on his head, glinting in the sun atop his turbulent blond hair.

No, no, she wanted you to read what she was writing, even while she was writing it and you lived a few miles away! She was desperate for someone to share her writing with. This is what the children tell me. Rosa is herself thinking of writing a novel, just because Dianne never could. Ernesto thinks perhaps he will be a journalist for television.

I sat in bed with the diary after it arrived. It is not like my journals, which are sequential, systematic, by years. It is not even finished, and is haphazard. Dianne's thoughts are jotted down raw, just as they came to her; with no attempt to mold them into anything other than what she actually felt at the time. A diary like this, with so many blank pages, seems to reflect a life permeated with gaps, an existence full of holes. But perhaps that is what happens when one's experience is so intensely different from anything dreamed of as a child that there seems literally to be no words for it. For living with a white man, and having him be, somehow, in brutal Mississippi, an exemplary father to her black children, must have seemed to Dianne stranger than any childhood fantasy she might have had.

I used to feel that way, myself. Though what I've come to realize about myself is that I honestly like living on the edge, wherever it is; that is where I feel most alive and most free. And so I cherished the strangeness of us; and sometimes as we sat down to eat breakfast together, I looked at you across the table and thought you might as well have been a leopard lying waiting for prey on the limb of a tree. Strange, maybe dangerous, but so exciting and beautiful!

But back to "the ruin."

Your mother did not understand the concept of "brownstoning." Buying a dilapidated row house in the wilds of Brooklyn and transforming it into a comfortable and spacious home. Why we thought she'd get it, and give us a favorable report on the house we'd chosen by photograph sent to us by a Brooklyn realtor, I know not. The exquisitely remodeled, light-filled triplex, three doors from Prospect Park, in the very best part of Park Slope, she told us was in a slum. What did we know? Essentially, what did I know? Sleepwalking through the heat of our last Jackson, Mississippi, summer, subsisting on bicycle rides and Valium, I knew only what I read in the few books on brownstoning I'd managed to buy on trips to New York.

Your mother was born and raised in Brooklyn, as you were. I thought her opinion held water, until, months later, I saw with my own eyes the house she'd encouraged us not to buy. The most perfect house in Brooklyn.

Instead, with time running out for us in Mississippi, and New York once again calling, we found ourselves with one week in which to house-shop. And chose a beautiful but literal ruin, on a calm, out of the way street in Brooklyn, that it would take a year to get completely clean, and nearly three to renovate.

Our blood went into that house. And the last shred of the love that had so characterized our life. The plumbing alone cost every cent you received from the sale of your share of your law firm. Every word I wrote was transformed into lighting fixtures, doorknobs and paint. We were not wise enough to know not to try to live in this foolishness. We did not know we should have done something else. At times like this, I felt our isolation most keenly. That we lacked parents or friends who would say: Look how tired you both are. It's obvious. Sell the law firm, yes, but take the money and go to Negril for six months. Write from a resort in the Rocky Mountains, if write you must, and save the money to live on the Upper West Side in New York, in a part of town already renovated. Enough, already! You don't have to keep challenging and "improving" the world by avoiding yourselves! For we did learn to avoid ourselves, avoid each other. Our pitiful attempt to avoid our failure, avoid our pain.

The night before we decided to buy the ruin we'd stayed at your mother's house. She had magnanimously given us her bed. But as I sat on the edge of the bed, after putting Our Child to sleep next door, in your old room, she came in, and warned me not to put anything on her dresser because whatever I put there—hairbrush or whatever—might scratch the finish. And I knew I could not sleep in her bed. And so I went, lucky for us we'd been given the keys until we made up our minds, straight to "the ruin." And slept alone on the floor, during what turned out to be my first night in the new house.

We were so far apart by then I would not have wanted you to come with me. Still, I missed your nearness, in the strange, gloomy house, in which only a few lights on the first floor, and a couple on the fourth floor, worked. It was a house with eight fireplaces! Were we hoping for warmth and coziness, or what?

But it was not to be. Not for the two of us, who, in the enormous house, passed each other like ships in the night. You went each day to a law office in midtown Manhattan, far away from the clients in Mississippi whose slow, drawling comments and stories you loved, and who sometimes paid you with fried chicken and watermelons. I could see your deep unhappiness to be back in the city you'd so eagerly left. Seeking to ignore my own disorientation, I learned everything there was to know about fireplace tile and floor varnish and grout. Twice a week I went into the city to work for a women's magazine. I had anxiety attacks of such severity I thought I would, one day, simply fail to arrive at my destination. For several years, I often felt as though I were floating through the streets of Brooklyn and New York. And that you were somewhere out there, too, but I felt little connection to you.

But Our Child seemed happy. She had friends her own age up and down our street. She loved her school and her teachers. She had a babysitter across from us who was from the Islands and taught her to make wonderful simple food, like *arroz con pollo*, her favorite dish. This I say now, to her, in her therapist's office, as she sits, pensively, all five feet six of her, leaning slightly forward, and, I am sad to note, silently weeping. How odd it feels to realize she could not have known, although perhaps she did, being so sensitive, the pain and sorrow that was so heavy in our hearts. That perhaps we were not dragging around the house in her child's mind, as we were dragging around it in our own.

And now, beloved, it seems to me that our major fault, all these years, is that we never took the time before, any of us, to properly grieve what we lost. What *we*, as a perky little human family in a frighteningly unloving culture and country, lost, when our small dream of an indomitable love ended. And this is in addition to the fact that we also failed to properly mourn the deaths by assassination and terrorism of so many people in public life whom we admired and loved, because to do so would have simply overwhelmed us. We would have given up and died. Maybe the beginning of our end as a couple was the day when we learned Martin had been killed and I promptly miscarried. How will anyone ever understand how much we loved him?

Even today I can barely bring myself to listen to his voice. At times I force myself to do so. And sure enough, after thinking that my heart will break one more unendurable time, he resolutely pulls me through the pain. He left us on such a high note of fearlessness and hope. Maybe he lied to us, though. Maybe there is no "promised land" for us. Just look at this poor country, like the orphan of the Universe. But even this fails to frighten me anymore. I believe only the moment we are in is promised, and that it, whatever it is, should always be "the future" we want.

And that is why I am thinking of you, and reminding you of a moment in which we, unlikely us, shared a vision and a reality of love, that need not be completely lost. If North America survives, it will not look like or be like it is today. One day there will be, created out of all of us lovers, an American race—remember how Jean Toomer,[7] whom we sometimes read to each other, in Mississippi, was already talking about this American race, even in the Thirties? We will simply not let the writers of history claim we did not exist. Why should the killers of the world be "the future" and not us?

---

7. Jean Toomer (1894–1967) refused to be labeled either black or white, believing that he alone possessed the right to identify himself as he decided. Today he is most remembered for his book *Cane*.

BRIEF CHRONOLOGY
OF THE CIVIL RIGHTS MOVEMENT

May 17, 1954	Passage of *Brown v. Board of Education of Topeka*
July 11, 1954	First meeting of White Citizens' Council
August 1955	Abduction and death of Emmett Till, Money, Mississippi
December 1955	Start of Montgomery bus boycott
December 1956	End of Montgomery bus boycott
January 1957	Founding of Southern Christian Leadership Conference (SCLC)
September 1957	Integration of Central High School, Little Rock, Arkansas
February 1, 1960	First sit-in in Greensboro, North Carolina
April 1960	Founding of Student Nonviolent Coordinating Committee (SNCC)
May 1961	Freedom Rides begin in Washington, D.C.
Fall 1962	Integration of University of Mississippi
Spring 1963	Project Confrontation in Birmingham; King's "Letter from a Birmingham Jail"
June 11, 1963	President Kennedy's first major civil rights address
June 12, 1963	Assassination of Medgar Evers, Jackson, Mississippi
August 28, 1963	March on Washington, D.C.
September 15, 1963	Bombing of Sixteenth Street Baptist Church—four girls die
November 22, 1963	Assassination of President John Kennedy
Summer 1964	Freedom Summer in Mississippi
June 21, 1964	Deaths of Michael Schwerner, Andrew Goodman, James Chaney, Philadelphia, Mississippi

July 2, 1964	Civil Rights Act signed
August 4, 1964	Bodies of Schwerner, Goodman, and Chaney found
August 1964	Mississippi Freedom Democratic Party (MFDP) at Democratic National Convention, Atlantic City, New Jersey
December 10, 1964	Martin Luther King Jr. wins Nobel Peace Prize
February 21, 1965	Assassination of Malcolm X, Manhattan, New York
March 7, 1965	"Bloody Sunday," Selma, Alabama
March 21–25, 1965	March from Selma to Montgomery for voting rights
August 6, 1965	Voting Rights Act signed
April 4, 1968	Assassination of Martin Luther King Jr., Memphis, Tennessee

CREDITS

James W. Thompson, "See What Tomorrow Brings": © 2006 James W. Thompson. First published in the *Transatlantic Review* 29 (summer 1968). Reprinted by permission of the author.

R. V. Cassill, "The First Day of School": Reprinted by permission of Kay Cassill, from R. V. Cassill's *The Happy Marriage and Other Stories* (Purdue University Studies, 1966). Originally appeared in the *Northwest Review* (fall 1958).

Diane Oliver, "Neighbors": First published in the *Sewanee Review* 74, no. 2 (spring 1966). Copyright 1966 by the University of the South.

Joan Williams, "Spring Is Now": Reprinted by permission of Harold Ober Associates Incorporated. First published in *Virginia Quarterly Review*. Copyright © 1968 by Joan Williams.

Joanne Leedom-Ackerman, "The Beginning of Violence": Reprinted by permission of the author, from Leedom-Ackerman's *No Marble Angels* (Montrose, Ala.: Texas Center for Writers Press, 1985).

Lee Martin, "The Welcome Table": Reprinted by permission of Sarabande Books, Inc., from Martin's *The Least You Need to Know* (Louisville, Ky.: Sarabande, 1996).

Anthony Grooms, "Food That Pleases, Food to Take Home": Reprinted by permission of the author / Kennesaw State University Press, from Grooms's *Trouble No More* (Palo Alto, Ca.: La Questa Press, 1995; Kennesaw, Ga.: Kennesaw State University Press, 2006).

Mike Thelwell, "Direct Action": Reprinted by permission of Ekwueme Michael Thelwell, from *The African American West: A Century of*

Welty. "Where Is the Voice Coming From?" originally appeared in the *New Yorker*, July 6, 1963.

Junius Edwards, "Liars Don't Qualify": Originally appeared in *Urbanite 1*, no. 4 (June 1961) and was reprinted in *Black Short Story Anthology*, edited by Woodie King (New York: Columbia University Press, 1972), and as part of Edwards's novel *If We Must Die* (Garden City: Double-day, 1963; Washington, D.C.: Howard University Press, 1985).

Alice Walker, "Advancing Luna—and Ida B. Wells": From *You Can't Keep a Good Woman Down*, copyright © 1977 by Alice Walker, reprinted by permission of Harcourt, Inc.

Rosellen Brown, "Means and Ends": © Rosellen Brown. First appeared in *Chelsea* 44 (1985); reprinted in *A Rosellen Brown Reader* by Rosellen Brown (Hanover, N.H.: Middlebury College Press, 1992). Reprinted by permission of the author.

James Baldwin, "Going to Meet the Man": Collected in *Going to Meet the Man*, © 1965 by James Baldwin. Copyright renewed. Published by Vintage Books. Used by arrangement with the James Baldwin Estate.

Anthony Grooms, "Flora Devine": Reprinted by permission of the author / Kennesaw State University Press, from Grooms's *Trouble No More* (Palo Alto, Ca.: La Questa Press, 1995; Kennesaw, Ga.: Kennesaw State University Press, 2006).

Val Coleman, "Paying My Dues": From *Beverly and Marigold*, by Val Coleman, copyright © 1996 by the author and reprinted by permission of St. Martin's Press, LLC.

Alice Walker, "To My Young Husband": From *The Way Forward Is with a Broken Heart*, by Alice Walker, copyright © 2000 by Alice Walker. Used by permission of Random House, Inc.